Duckinwilla Days Books 1-3

Coming Home
Secrets and Surprises
Wishes and Whispers

ANNIE SEATON

Heartwarming and compelling tales of love, self-discovery, and second chances in the heart of rural Australia.

Annie Seaton

Coming Home

ANNIE SEATON

Duckinwilla Days: Book 1

Heartwarming and compelling tales of love, self-discovery, and second chances in the heart of rural Australia.

Duckinwilla Days 1-3

Annie Seaton

The Johnson family

Grandmère and Papa: Margot and Robert Johnson

The parents: Hugo and Ellen Johnson

The Johnson siblings:

Charlotte Johnson - Book 1 - *Coming Home*

Julien Johnson - Book 2 - *Secrets and Surprises*

Oliver Johnson - Book 3 - *Wishes and Whispers*

Guy Johnson - Book 4 - *New Beginnings*

Amelia Johnson - Book 5 - *Chasing Dreams*

Lisette Johnson - Book 6 - *Together at Last*

Duckinwilla Days 1-3

Chapter 1

Brisbane

The staffroom at Helen's Creek High smelled of chocolate and rang with farewells. Charlotte Johnson stared at the massive cake Rose was carrying through the doorway, its candles flickering like the warning signals in her mind. Another goodbye, another step further from home.

'Bushfire warning?' She forced a laugh, gesturing at the blazing candles.

'It's not that big.' Rose's brown eyes sparkled with mischief as she navigated between desks. 'Mandy, grab this before I recreate the Great Brisbane Cake Disaster of 2023.'

The familiar banter wrapped around Charlotte like the comfort "blanky" she'd had when she was a toddler. For two years, this Brisbane staffroom had been her refuge—the place where she'd rebuilt herself after fleeing Duckinwilla Creek. The thought of her hometown sent that familiar ache through her chest, one she'd learned to ignore.

'Last day,' Mandy announced, rescuing the cake from Rose's precarious grip. 'Last chance to change your mind about France.'

Charlotte's smile turned wistful. 'I know. I've had a fabulous two years working here with you guys. They never told me at uni that I'd laugh most of the day when I joined an English staffroom at a school.'

'It's not like that everywhere.' Rose shook her head. 'Mind you, I've worked in some pretty tough schools over the past ten years.'

Mandy nodded. 'Me too. My first appointment was a nightmare. The playground at Breakwater High was like a war zone during most breaks. You've had a gentle introduction, Charlotte.'

'I know, I've been very lucky. And I'm really going to miss you both. Who am I going to go to for advice now?'

Rose put a hand to her chest and pretended to swoon. 'Some gorgeous Frenchman, of course!'

Charlotte grinned at her. 'One can only hope.'

The trio of language teachers had forged a strong friendship since Charlotte arrived at Helen's Creek High School in Brisbane two years ago. At first, Charlotte lacked confidence and was slow to respond, but Mandy and Rose were persistent. Their bond had seen them through both fun and challenging times, including the sudden passing of their head teacher at the end of Charlotte's first year.

The cake found its way to the centre of the table, chocolate ganache glistening in the fluorescent light. Around her, colleagues gathered, their chatter filling the room with warmth. She'd miss this, miss them. Miss belonging somewhere that didn't hurt.

'Come on, Charlotte. The candles are going to burn down if you don't hurry up.'

'I'm not expected to blow that fire out, am I?' Charlotte joked.

'Well, it's not going to go out by itself, and if you don't hurry up, it's going to burn down to that yummy chocolate ganache,' Mandy replied.

Cake always drew a crowd in the shared English and Language Department staffroom. Regret fluttered through her briefly, and she wondered if she was crazy to leave this school and head overseas to an unknown teaching environment. The staff here—and the majority of the students—were fabulous to work with. She pushed away the thought. Going to France had been a dream that Grandmère had fostered since Charlotte was a little girl.

Fifteen minutes later, empty paper plates littered the table. The remnants of the cake sat at an uneven angle, crumbs scattered over the bench.

'Mrs Barber makes the best cakes ever, doesn't she?' Mandy said, brushing the crumbs from the front of her dress.

'You can always depend on Mrs Barber,' Rose agreed. 'Mandy, you've got a chocolate moustache.'

Mandy raced to the small mirror near the door. She looked at her reflection and then pulled a face at Rose. 'I have not!'

Rose chuckled. 'You're so easy to wind up, Mandy.'

'So, heading off to the airport tomorrow, Charlie?' Rose asked.

'No,' she replied slowly. 'I've got some family stuff to do first. I don't fly out till the first week in January.'

'Gosh, it'll be cold in France then—middle of their winter! Crazy woman, leaving our beautiful summer,' Mandy teased.

'Listen, if you're not going for another three weeks, you might have time to come and join us up in the islands,' Rose suggested.

Charlotte shook her head. 'No, family duty calls.'

'You've never told us where you grew up.' Mandy's voice cut through her thoughts. 'Come on, Charlie. Last day—spill some secrets.'

Charlotte hesitated, then made a face. 'You wouldn't have heard of it.'

'Try us,' Rose said, a determined gleam in her eye.

'Yeah, come on—you've never told us where you grew up or went to school.'

'I'll bet you ten bucks you've never heard of it.' Charlotte grinned. She was going to miss this banter.

'You're on.' Rose folded her arms and waited.

'Little place south of Bundaberg. Sugarcane country.' The words tasted of childhood summers and broken promises. 'Duckinwilla Creek.'

Rose and Mandy exchanged glances, and Rose shook her head. 'I guess I owe you ten bucks.'

'I've never heard of it either,' Mandy said.

'I have.'

Charlotte's heart stumbled. Greg Barrett, their head of department, stood in the doorway, his presence filling the room the way it always did. She'd been fighting her attraction to him for months, telling herself it didn't matter—she was leaving anyway.

'My parents' farm's just over at Dunmora,' he continued, and Charlotte's world tilted slightly.

'Over the hills from us,' she managed, memories flooding back—summer storms rolling in across those same hills, the heavy sweetness of burnt cane on the wind, the way the creek water turned gold at sunset.

'Haven't been back lately?' His question was gentle, but Charlotte heard the curiosity beneath it.

'Five years.' She forced the words past the tightness in her throat. 'Not since before uni.'

'You've never told us you grew up on a farm, Charlotte,' Mandy said.

'Your last day at school, and we're learning more about you than we have in the last two years,' Rose added.

'It never came up in conversation.'

'Like you said, it's a small town,' Greg said. 'But it's become quite gentrified and touristy lately. The last time I was up there, I couldn't get over the change. Apparently, after COVID, the local chamber of commerce reinvigorated the town. Have you seen all the painted cows and sculptures that are through the town now, Charlotte? It's become quite arty.'

Charlotte shook her head. 'I really don't know, Greg. I haven't been out there for a long time.' Changing the subject, Charlotte turned to Greg. 'Where are you headed for the holidays?'

His slow smile made her pulse skip.

'Funny thing—France. My sister lives there.'

'What a coincidence.' Rose's voice dripped with innocence that fooled no one. 'Near Lyon, Greg?'

Heat crept up Charlotte's neck as Greg nodded.

'We'll have to meet for coffee,' he said, and something in his voice made her look up, catching his gaze.

'Oh . . . well . . . um, yes, that would be nice.'

Heat rushed into her face as she stumbled over her words. She swallowed the regret that rose. Development of this attraction was something she couldn't afford to consider. Not now, not when she was finally escaping. Not when home was calling her back first, in the form of Grandmère's letter burning a hole in her bag.

Come home, ma petite. *It's time to face the past.*

Charlotte pushed away the little flare of attraction that was becoming way too frequent lately. Greg was a fine-looking man and had led the department well. She'd never heard him say a cross word or anything negative. He'd made a difference to the culture in the staffroom.

She didn't miss the knowing look that Mandy and Rose exchanged.

Chapter 2

Duckinwilla Creek

Julien Johnson's attention was not on the town like it usually was as he drove down the main street of Duckinwilla Creek towards his grandparents' house. In his role as president of the Chamber of Commerce, he usually kept a close eye on the main street. Their new home sat on top of the rise, looking over the small township to the east and the valley to the west. The house that had been his grandparents' home when he had been a child was now sitting empty, and no matter how often the family encouraged them to sell it, Grandmère refused to part with it.

'Our Charlotte loves that house, and one day she will live there.' No matter that she'd lived in Duckinwilla Creek since she'd fallen in love with an Aussie boy and followed him to Australia in her twenties, Grandmère's accent was pronounced. 'And don't you look at me like that, Lisette,' she chastised her granddaughter. 'You will all get your fair share when our time comes.'

'I wasn't going to say anything, Grandmère.'

Julien had kept silent, too. Lisette had been in a foul mood ever since Mum had announced that Charlotte was coming home and they would be holding a farewell function for her.

Lisette had been vocal. 'That's ridiculous. We haven't seen her for five years, now she's coming home for a day or two, and you're giving her a party? I didn't even get a party for my twenty-first.' She flounced out of the living room before anyone could reply.

The setting sun painted Duckinwilla Creek's main street in

shades of amber and gold as he passed their store, but Julien barely noticed. The pretty picture of the refurbished buildings bathed in the golden light failed to settle him. The stores, the bright flower baskets and the inviting aroma filling the street from the bakery in the family's store failed to lift his mood. All the sight of the General Store did this evening was bring back the tensions simmering between his siblings.

He was looking forward to Charlotte's return, but he was worried about the reception she'd get from the rest of the family. Even Mum and Dad hadn't seemed pleased to hear their eldest daughter was coming home, and that made him sad. On top of his other worries, Julien had to deal with this one.

Their dad, Hugo, was Grandmère and Papa's only son, but he and their mum, Ellen, had produced a brood of six children. Theirs had been a happy family unit until five years ago. There had been much change since the money had been stolen from the store. Dad had gone to work the farm with Oliver and Guy when the long-term manager had retired. To his surprise, Dad had asked Julien to take over the store, and he'd enjoyed every day he'd worked there and was proud of the changes he'd made.

Bloody Lisette. This situation was all her fault, and she was the one who harped on about it and bad-mouthed Charlotte every chance she got. No wonder Charlotte had stayed away for so long.

As he parked his ute at the end of the narrow laneway leading to the unique French provincial house on the side of the hill, Julien tried to shake off his bad mood. The new place was always referred to as Grandmère's house, despite Papa living there too. Grandmère cherished her role as the matriarch of the family, and he just hoped she could keep everyone in order tonight. Charlotte was arriving tomorrow, so he had no doubt what the summons to dinner was about.

Walking along the cobblestoned pathway leading to the house, he took a deep breath, trying to steady his nerves. The residence that Papa had built for his wife when he'd retired stood as a striking anomaly amidst the sugar cane farms with their old weatherboard Queenslanders; its symmetrical stone facades and tall, arched windows exuded old-world French charm. The lavender bushes lining the path released their fragrance, a subtle nod to the French heritage Grandmère cherished. As he approached the entrance, the ornate chandeliers inside cast a warm glow through the arched windows, illuminating the rich tapestries that adorned the walls. There was no doubt that Grandmère certainly had an eye for colour and design.

With a final, steadying breath, Julien opened the double cedar doors and stepped into Grandmère's *salon*. He knew the family meeting would be tense, with issues rehashed as they always were when the family got together.

Grandmère was trying to ease the way for Charlotte's return, but knowing his family, there would be raised voices tonight as everyone tried to give their opinion. But always positive, Julien held onto a sliver of hope that Charlotte's return might start to heal the rift that had fractured the family for more than five years.

'Julien! You are late.' His grandmother's voice hinted at her displeasure.

'Sorry, everyone. I was late closing the store. A busy afternoon.'

Truth be told, he'd dawdled. Any minute now, Lisette would start up about Charlotte again, and he was tired of being the referee. He hurried across the room where his grandparents, parents, two brothers and two of his three sisters sat at the dining room table. After kissing Grandmère's cheek and squeezing Papa's shoulder, he took his place beside Dad and smiled at Mum, who sat on the other side of the table with the girls. Guy and Oliver were talking quietly—no doubt about the cane harvest, as that was their main focus these days since Dad had handed the farm over to his sons. Lisette, wearing her perpetual scowl, and Amelia, sneaking glances at her phone. Only one empty chair, the one that had been vacant for five years.

Amelia looked up and caught Julien's eye, and he frowned at her. There would be enough discussion tonight without a rant about mobile phones.

'Put it away,' he mouthed.

She nodded and leaned down, putting it away.

Grandmère stood and tapped a silver spoon on the side of a crystal wine glass. Her dark eyes gleamed with steely resolve as she addressed the family.

'Now that Julien is *finally* here, we shall talk about the next two weeks. Charlotte's return is imminent, and I expect *each* of you to treat her with the respect she deserves. Every one of you. She is family, and our family bond is unbreakable. The time for resolution is long overdue.'

Dad's jaw tightened, his weathered hands clenching the edge of the table. '*Maman*, it's not that simple. Charlotte's actions created the situation, and she left us all to deal with the fallout.'

'Created the situation?' Julien couldn't help himself. 'Or is it that we all chose to believe one side of the story?' He had defended Charlotte's actions on countless occasions, but everyone wanted to judge her and not the hard-done-by Lisette. If it weren't for the store, he and Emily would leave town, too.

Couldn't they see how unfair they were being? Charlotte

had been hurt, but everyone had listened to Lisette.

'Here we go again.' Lisette's voice dripped with disdain. 'Saint Charlotte can do no wrong.'

'That's enough.' Papa's voice cut through the brewing argument. Despite marrying his French love, he was as direct as any farmer in the valley. 'Our granddaughter, your daughter, your sister will be here tomorrow. And you'll all be kind to her. Got that?'.

Mum's voice wavered; her frustration was evident. 'Charlotte was the one who chose to leave Duckinwilla Creek.'

'And left her family,' Lisette chimed in. 'With all respect, Grandmère, this farewell party you're planning is stupid.'

Uh-oh. No one called Grandmère stupid and got away with it.

Grandmere's gaze settled on Lisette. Everyone waited.

She straightened her posture and folded her hands elegantly on her lap before responding.

'Lisette,' she began, her tone measured. 'I appreciate honesty when it is tempered with thoughtfulness. However, to dismiss the planned farewell—a gesture of respect for your sister—as "stupid" displays a lack of discernment. Such words, my dear, should be chosen with greater care if you wish them to carry the weight of wisdom rather than a lack of thought.'

Julien kept his voice calm when Lisette jumped to her feet. 'Sit down, Lisette, and get over the attitude. And if you think about it, whatever happened, Charlotte would have left home anyway to go to uni. It was the attitude here that's kept her away for so long. And this attitude has hung around for far too long.'

Lisette, her dark eyes flashing with indignation, sat down and glared at her brother. 'Attitude? You expect me to welcome her back with open arms after what she did? She acted like she was better than us, and now we're supposed to forget and forgive all that?'

The silence that followed was heavy, with five years of hurt and misunderstanding. Through the windows, Julien could see the cane fronds waving in the gathering dusk. Somewhere out there was the childhood they'd all shared before secrets and accusations had torn them apart.

Oliver, his youngest brother, leaned forward, his expression serious. 'Lisette, maybe it's time to move on. You've let this blow up out of all proportion. You're obsessed with making Charlotte the baddie in this, and she's not even been here to defend herself.'

'*She* was in the wrong,' Lisette said.

Guy shook his head. 'Oliver's right. Charlotte is coming home, and I, for one, think she's very brave to be doing that. I mean, how many of you have talked to her in the last few months? She always sends us birthday cards, and those of us who call her know how lonely she's been.'

'Pffft,' Lisette spluttered.

Amelia glared at her sister. 'I remember how much happier we all were before she left. I miss that. I miss us being a family. A happy family. Look at us now. All arguing, and she's not even here. She's had little to do with us over the past five years, and she's never said a cross word to any of us when she's called, has she, Mum? Charlotte is mature enough to have moved on.'

'And are you saying that I'm not?' Lisette's voice was shrill.

'If the cap fits,' Guy muttered.

'Mum!' Lisette turned to her mother for support, and Ellen went to speak.

'Enough!' Grandmère's gaze swept over her family. 'We cannot change the past, but we can choose how we move forward. Charlotte's return is a chance to mend what has been broken. I ask you all to consider what kind of family we wish to be. Attitude is a good word, Julien. I would ask you to think deeply about yours, Lisette.'

Lisette's face flushed with anger, her hands trembling. 'This is unbelievable. You're all so quick to welcome her back and forget how she made us feel. Well, I won't be a part of this charade.'

Dad sighed deeply, rubbing his temples. 'This is exactly what I was afraid of with her coming home. As hard as it sounds, Charlotte would have been better off not coming home before she went to France.'

Julien placed a reassuring hand on his father's shoulder. 'No, Dad. It's going to be hard, but we owe it to Charlotte.'

His mother dabbed at her eyes with a handkerchief. 'It's gone too far, and it's gone on too long. She has caused the damage.'

'We all have our flaws.' Grandmère's voice was gentle yet firm. 'We must be willing to listen, to forgive *each other* despite them.' Her glare settled on Lisette.

'You realise that she's only going to France to get in your good books, Grandmère.' Lisette returned the glare as Mrs Hyslop appeared with the first course, the familiar scent of garlic a counterpoint to the tension around the table. Julien watched his family—his mother's trembling hands on her cup, his father's distant gaze, Amelia's hopeful eyes.

The once-heated discussion gradually gave way to a fragile peace; everyone was lost in their own thoughts, worrying about Charlotte's return and wondering what tomorrow would bring.

Julien broke the silence as coffee was served, his voice steady. 'So, do we all agree? Charlotte's return is a chance to put the past away once and for all?'

His parents put their heads down and focused on their coffee. He gave them the benefit of the doubt. Maybe they thought he hadn't included them in the question.

Oliver nodded. 'Yes, we'll be here for Charlotte.' He turned to Lisette with his eyebrows raised, but she put her head down and ignored him.

Guy gave Julien a thumbs-up.

Amelia looked up, her eyes filled with a mixture of hope and apprehension. 'I want to know my big sister. I don't want her to go to France and never come home again.'

Her words hung in the air. Outside, a magpie called its evening song, and somewhere in the distance, a dog barked. Just another night in Duckinwilla Creek, except nothing about tomorrow would be ordinary.

Charlotte was coming home, and none of them were ready for what that meant.

Chapter 3

Maison de Rêve

The crunch of gravel under Charlotte's feet seemed too loud in the evening stillness. She eased her car door shut, heart thudding as she faced her grandparents' old home. *Maison de Rêve*—house of dreams. The name felt like poetry, dreams and memories tangled together.

She was pretty sure no one lived here now but was prepared to be surprised. Communication in the Johnson family had been fragmented since the big blow-up the weekend before she left home five years ago.

Maison de Rêve stood proud against the darkening sky, its weathered facade telling stories of fifty years of Johnson family life. Papa had built this, their first home, with his own hands when Grandmère followed him home from her tiny French village, trading Beaune's vineyards for Queensland's cane fields. She had loved listening to Grandmère's stories of spending her childhood in the small village. Margot had never dreamed of leaving her village, nestled in the heart of the *Côte d'Or* vineyards, until a handsome Aussie came to work on the vines, and she fell in love with him.

Charlotte walked to the edge of the lawn, drinking in the vista below. Someone was keeping the grounds neat—the grass clipped short, the garden beds weeded—though there weren't as many flowers as when Grandmère had tended them. Charlotte had inherited Grandmère's love of gardening. For a short while, before she'd started her teaching degree, she'd toyed with the idea of studying horticulture. She closed her eyes and took a deep breath, inhaled the sweet fragrance of lavender, and pushed away the uncertainty about returning to her hometown.

Charlotte turned and walked across the gravel towards the front door, pushing away the nerves that were making her legs feel shaky. She reached into the cavity behind the weathered frog sculpture and nodded as her fingers closed around the big brass key.

Focus on the good memories—the days when her grandparents lived in *Maison de Rêve. When everyone was happy.*

Walking to the door, she hesitated. She still wasn't ready for this, for the memories she knew would rush in and overwhelm her. But she had come to say goodbye—not just to *Maison de Rêve*, or the town, but to the life she had once had here. The life she'd foolishly believed to be her future. It was time to move on once and for all. She'd foolishly thought that five years away would have restored her strength, but no, the nerves skittering in her stomach proved her wrong.

The door creaked open, and the musty smell of disuse greeted her. Dust motes danced in the last rays of sunlight streaming through the picture window, settling on surfaces that had once gleamed with Grandmère's careful attention. She closed her eyes, remembering the happy days she'd spent here in her childhood. Curled up with Grandmère on the window seat, learning French when she was still at primary school, playing chase with Papa around the sofa as he pretended to be a bear, happy family dinners around the massive timber dining room table that had obviously been moved to the new house. Charlotte hadn't seen their new house on the other side of town yet, but Grandmère had told her all about it in her weekly calls. She had been the one constant connection to home.

Charlotte dropped her bag by the door and crossed to the window seat. She ran her fingers over the sill, leaving trails in the dust with her fingertips.

Duckinwilla Creek Valley stretched out below, patchwork fields gilded by sunset. How many times had she sat here with Grandmère, learning French verbs and family stories? How many times had she watched Papa chase her siblings around the massive timber dining table that now lived in their new house?

Charlotte stood at the window until darkness crept across the valley and the town's lights began to twinkle like earthbound stars. Her reflection in the glass stared back at her, pale and tired. Teaching French at the high school in Brisbane had kept her busy, given her new friends and a new life, but she still hadn't regained the trust she'd lost here. Coming back to Duckinwilla Creek was like reopening an old wound, but she knew she had to do it—shedding that layer of family before stepping into a new chapter of her life.

An exciting new chapter. One that she would seize with both hands.

She opened the sliding door to let in the crisp evening air and locked the screen door. As darkness crept across the valley, she stood at the window again, gazing into the darkness. She wasn't sure how she felt. Strange was one word that came to mind.

The old house was familiar, but coming here after those years away felt different. Memories of growing up in Duckinwilla Creek flooded her mind: her mother's laughter, her brothers' teasing, her sisters' whispered secrets late at night. The French names her father had insisted on—Julien, Oliver, Guy, Lisette, and Amelia—were a constant reminder of their heritage. Grandmère had brought a piece of France with her when she had married Papa in the nineteen sixties and passed it on to Dad. The whole time, one question echoed in her mind: *What am I doing here? I should have gone straight to France.*

Her family didn't want her, so why had she jumped to Grandmère's summons?

For now, she'd push her worry aside. There would be time to deal with the family drama later. Tonight, she would let the quiet of the hills lull her to sleep.

With a determined sigh, Charlotte headed out to the car to bring in her overnight bag and then made her way upstairs to the room she had always slept in when Grandmère and Papa had lived here.

Upstairs, her old room waited exactly as she'd left it five years ago. Clean sheets on the bed—Grandmère's touch, she knew—and the same goose-down mattress that had cradled her through final exam study sessions. Back then, this room had been her sanctuary from the chaos of five siblings at home. It was almost as if it had been kept ready for her now despite the rest of the house being dusty.

A huge yawn overtook her, and she looked at the bed, which beckoned. She had a quick wash in the adjacent powder room, wiped her face with the flannel in her toiletries bag, slipped on her pyjamas, and climbed into the soft bed. As she slipped between crisp sheets, the sweet scent of lavender drifted in across the balcony and through the open door. The fragrance was one thing that always reminded her of home, and when she could find a bunch of lavender in Brisbane, Charlotte would buy it and place it on her desk at school.

She stared into the darkness, remembering the girl who'd dreamed of France in this very bed. She'd loved growing up at Duckinwilla Creek and loved her family with a fierceness that made her estrangement so difficult to bear.

One incident. That's all it had taken to shatter their harmony. As always, Charlotte knew she was overthinking, and she tried to breathe deeply, trying to compose herself. Overthinking the family situation was making her feel sick to her stomach, and she was stressed about seeing all of them tomorrow, even Grandmère, who had been her staunch supporter. The knowledge that her parents hadn't believed in her still cut deep.

Now Lyon beckoned with its six-month teaching contract, offering escape or opportunity—she wasn't sure which.

Spending time here with Grandmère had given her an interest in all things French; she had made French history a major in her degree, and her dream had always been to go to France to teach, and now that was about to happen. She lay back in bed and closed her eyes as the darkness cocooned her.

But as sleep pulled her under, carried on waves of lavender-scented air, Charlotte wondered: *where was home now?*'

Chapter 4

Maison de Rêve

Charlotte woke as the first fingers of dawn filtered through the open cedar doors. For a moment, the years fell away and she was eighteen again, full of dreams and certainty. She opened her eyes and stretched, feeling calm and rested; she would not let that heavy ache return to her chest. And she would not worry about the reception from her family.

If they didn't want to resolve the ongoing situation—a ridiculous situation for which she took no blame—she would go to France, make a go of it, and maybe she would stay there for a lot longer.

If she didn't like it there, she'd find another school somewhere closer to home, not necessarily in Queensland. Perhaps she needed to see more of Australia.

Charlotte climbed out of bed and walked up the hallway to the bathroom. There was nothing in there; perhaps Grandmère hadn't prepared the room for her after all. She walked down the hall and opened the linen cupboard, but it was empty. She had all her toiletries in her bag but hadn't thought to pack a towel. She grabbed her soap and shampoo from her bag, took a quick shower, and washed her hair. At least she had a hairdryer. By the time she stood in front of the mirror drying her hair, she had no need for a towel, and she walked out onto the small balcony to let the sun dry her skin, goosebumps rising on her bare flesh. She took a deep breath of the clean, fresh valley air.

I love this place.

The morning air held a hint of December chill as she stood, letting the sun warm her skin. Below, Duckinwilla Creek was starting to stir.

The sky was cloudless, and the heat wouldn't take long to build as the sun rose higher. She walked back into the room and made the bed before she turned to her bag and pulled out the dress she was going to wear to meet her family.

Once she pulled the bright yellow dress dotted with large red poppies over her head, Charlotte walked back into the bathroom and looked in the mirror. All she needed now was a bit of makeup, and she would look like the totally confident and happy woman she intended to present to her family. She reached for her brush and brushed her hair, then twisted it into a loose chignon before she found the red lipstick that matched the poppies in her dress. With one last satisfied look in the mirror—she looked very different from the eighteen-year-old who had left here—she nodded, turned, and went back to her bag to put everything away.

For a moment, she stood there, wondering whether to take the bag with her or to stay here again tonight. The only thing she'd need to bring back would be a towel. She shook her head. No, that was the coward's way out. If things got nasty, she would stay at Grandmère and Papa's new house; there would always be a welcome there.

She picked up her bag, headed downstairs, and locked the door behind her before she went to her car.

##

Duckinwilla Creek

The gravel crunched beneath the tyres as her small Audi navigated the winding road leading into town. A cloud of red-brown dust billowed behind her, settling stubbornly on the sleek black paint. She smiled to herself, imagining Julien's expression when he saw her car. He'd always dreamed of travelling, escaping the work of the family sugarcane farm, yet his loyalty to Dad had kept him tethered to Duckinwilla Creek.

Charlotte slowed as she passed the family farm where she had spent her childhood. The sign above the gate, *La Rêverie*, Dad's acknowledgment of his mother's French heritage, stood framed by lush greenery. The sugarcane fields swayed gently in the morning breeze, their bright green stalks vibrant against the windbreak of she-oaks.

In the distance, she spotted a truck parked by the machinery shed. The rhythmic sound of the harvester drifted faintly across the fields as it sliced through the tall stalks, reducing them to manageable lengths. Behind the harvester, a train engine waited on narrow tracks, its wagons lined with wire cages ready to transport the cane to the local mill.

She glanced around, half-expecting to see Julien directing operations from his usual spot by the shed, but there was no sign of him. Her three brothers—Julien, Oliver and Guy—had worked the farm since Papa retired just before Charlotte left home. Mum and Dad ran the family store in town.

Charlotte took a deep breath. She'd go there to see them; the store would be open by now. At least no one could make a scene in front of customers.

Shaking off the thought, she continued along the road toward town. She would see the rest of the family before she left—maybe. For now, she wanted to reconnect with Duckinwilla Creek on her own terms.

The landscape gradually shifted as she neared the outskirts of the small town. The dirt road gave way to asphalt, and the rolling hills opened into a charming main street. Her heart lifted as she took in the transformation. Greg had been right—there were big changes.

Five years ago, Duckinwilla Creek's shops had looked like relics of the last century—faded signs, peeling paint, and an air of quiet resignation. Now, the town seemed to hum with life. She widened her eyes, unable to believe the number of shoppers in the street, even this early in the day. Each side of the road was lined with parked cars.

As Charlotte cruised down the familiar main street, nostalgia washed over her. The small cluster of businesses had been painted and refurbished but still retained their charm and quirky character. If anything, the charm had been enhanced.

She slowed as she passed Lucy-Lou's Hairdressing Salon, a cheerful shop front painted in soft pastel hues of pink and lavender. The scalloped awning added a touch of whimsy, and the bold, looping sign with 'Lucy-Lou's' scrawled in gold glitter paint sparkled in the sunlight. Inside, she caught a glimpse of Lucy-Lou herself, a petite woman with a bright red beehive, chatting animatedly as she trimmed a client's hair. Lucy-Lou was known for her retro style and infectious laughter that often spilled out onto the street.

Just next door, Jerry's Barber Shop stood in contrast, with a newly polished wooden exterior and red-and-white striped pole.

The windows were filled with posters of classic cars and old rock bands, and the interior had always had an unmistakable masculine vibe, with dark leather chairs and a faint scent of cedar. Jerry, with his neatly trimmed grey moustache and suspenders, was busy chatting with a customer while wielding a pair of scissors. Charlotte had sat here in the school holidays when Papa had his hair cut.

Lucy-Lou and Jerry were a delightfully odd pair—married for decades but adamant about keeping their businesses and homes separate.

Further along, Charlotte passed the milk bar, a retro-looking shop with checkerboard tiles. She wondered if Con still ran it. When she was growing up, he'd run his milk bar through the day and played guitar in the local bowling club at night. The milk bar where she'd spent countless afternoons sharing hot chips and secrets with friends bore a fresh coat of paint but still had its fading Coca-Cola sign. It had been a favourite stop after coming home on the long bus ride from high school in Maryborough. Then she'd had a part-time job there the last two summers she was home.

She smiled, remembering the bus trips—how she'd tried to sit quietly and read, only to be drawn into the hijinks of her friends. Marley's sarcastic quips, Sabina's contagious laugh, and Jenny's endless curiosity about everything they passed along the way had made those journeys unforgettable.

Now, Marley was a high-flying lawyer in Perth. Sabina was pursuing her passion in an Adelaide art gallery, and Jenny had found her calling at a wildlife park in the Northern Territory. They'd all taken different paths, yet Charlotte knew their connection hadn't faded. Once she settled in France, she would email them, sharing the news that she, too, had finally achieved her dream. The thought made her happy, and she promised herself she wouldn't let too much time pass before she reached out to them.

Mr Elliott's butcher shop, once a tired brick building, now boasted a vintage-inspired façade with cream-coloured paint and a neat striped awning. A blackboard sign leaned against the wall, listing daily specials in elegant chalk script.

Next door, Mrs Boyd's haberdashery charmed with its display of colourful wares. Pots of silk flowers flanked the entrance, and hand-knitted jumpers in soft pastels swayed gently on a rack outside. Her eyes widened; if she was seeing correctly, there were fresh tulips for sale in jugs on a table near the step.

Further along, where there had once been a bakery, a small dress boutique filled the building. The bakery had once been the busiest shop in the street, and she was surprised it had closed.

Even the Duckinwilla Hotel had undergone a transformation. Its weathered exterior was now a vision of French provincial charm, complete with shuttered windows and climbing vines. There was a new car park at the side, a clear sign that the pub was thriving.

Charlotte slowed, her eyes widening as she took it all in. Duckinwilla Creek had changed—and for the better. Perhaps Grandmère had had a say in the refurbishment; there was definitely a French feel to the town. Guilt niggled at Charlotte as she realised how long she'd stayed away. Five years was a long time to hold a grudge.

But it was the family store that stopped her heart. Gone was the cluttered, dimly lit shop of her father's era. The old store with the tables and chairs outside in their mishmash of timber laminated tops, with some timber, but mostly plastic chairs, the store that she'd loved.

She knew it had annoyed Grandmère, but Dad had had no thought of creating an ambience that was enticing to customers. He saw the store as a grocery and hardware store and had fought against the installation of the coffee shop at the front. Grandmère had won that argument. The interior had been dark and cluttered, but in its own way, it had held a timeless charm. There were few old stores like that left in the country these days.

In place of the family store stood an elegant establishment with The General Store spelled out in gold letters on a sleek black sign. It looked classy. The shopfront was a delightful hodgepodge of French-inspired charm, with crates of fresh produce arranged under the awning. Strings of garlic and onions hung from the rafters, and a penny-farthing bicycle leaned against the wall. Black wrought iron tables and chairs sat on the side of the two steps that led up into the interior of the store, and another half-dozen tables scattered along the footpath were covered with brightly coloured tablecloths. Baskets of colourful flowers hung from the awning over the footpath, and a jug of flowers sat on each table.

This was what Greg had been talking about. A flutter of warmth filled her as she imagined him walking into her family store.

Charlotte shook her head as she stared at the new exterior. Grandmère had told her nothing of the refurbishment of the main street. Three of those tables had customers seated there even at this early hour. The enticing smell of freshly brewed coffee and baked goods drifted across to Charlotte and made her nose twitch.

Things had certainly changed. She walked up the steps and pushed open one of the double doors, and the bell tinkled above the door as it always had.

Her surprise deepened as she looked around; it was as though she was in a different place: bright lights, shiny cabinets, a new coffee machine, and aisles filled with crates of potatoes and onions gave it a welcoming and modern feel.

The store was now open and spacious, with a counter along the wall where the plumbing bits used to be. Her eyes tracked along to the side wall, where an upmarket delicatessen counter now filled the space. It was as though she had stepped into a French patisserie; it reminded her of the trendy delicatessens in Brisbane.

Even though it was only just after nine, the shop was full, and three women served behind the two counters and another one at the main cash register at the back of the store. That had always been there—well, the old register had been there, but now it was modernised with a white Square EFTPOS screen on a stand, sitting next to a jug of colourful flowers. Apart from that, there was nothing on the counter.

The counter was usually a mess of Dad's creation; it had been covered with receipts and dockets and invoice books, and half the time, a cup of cold instant coffee usually sat beside the register. Memories filtered down as Charlotte looked around. Dad had always refused to drink the brewed coffee from the machine.

Was he here?

She shook her head, unable to believe what she was seeing. There was no sign of him, and she wondered where he was. And, more to the point, how he'd ever agreed to these changes. The staff working seemed to be efficient, and the customers looked satisfied with their purchases. She didn't recognise a single person in the whole store.

She took a step further into the store and smiled when she

saw Julien, who had stayed in touch regularly over the last five years, standing at the back of the store talking to Rowena Billings. She'd never been friends with Rowena even though they'd been in the same year at high school. She decided to wait until they finished their conversation, but her attention focused on them as Rowena's voice rose, and Julien took a step back. He held one hand up and shook his head.

'Obviously an unhappy customer,' she thought, as Rowena's whining voice drew attention, and heads began to turn.

'I'm not going to let this go, Julien,' she said loudly.

Charlotte could see the concern on her brother's face, and she decided to intervene.

She hurried past the stands of colourful tropical fruit and the hanging bunches of herbs and stepped around to the corner where bags of pasta lined the shelves.

'Julien,' she said quietly. The first time, he didn't hear her, so she took a step closer. 'Julien,' she repeated.

This time, his head lifted, and a strange expression crossed his face: discomfort, embarrassment, and then joy.

'Charlotte!' He stepped forward with both his hands outstretched, his voice a mix of happiness and surprise. 'When did you get here? You must've left Brisbane very early. We weren't expecting you until the afternoon.'

'I got here last night,' she said, turning to be polite to Rowena, who was watching them with a scowl.

'Hello, Rowena.'

Rowena gave out a sound that was a cross between a grunt and a brief greeting, and Julien ignored her as he took both of Charlotte's hands. 'Come into the office with me, and we'll catch up.'

'Don't you ignore me, Julien! This will be going further. I'll be back later,' Rowena said, anger filling her voice.

Julien shrugged and led Charlotte to the office.

For a moment, Charlotte worried that Rowena was going to make a scene, and she glanced back at her. She was standing there with a malicious look on her face, staring after them.

'An unhappy customer?' Charlotte asked.

'Yes,' her brother said briefly, but he looked frazzled.

Julien opened the door to Dad's office, and again Charlotte was taken aback by the clear room—a desk, a phone, a filing cabinet, and a whiteboard filled with instructions: order coffee, cancel the last order, fix the roster.

She shook her head silently and then looked at her brother.

'Bit different to working on the farm, hey Charlie?'

'It certainly is,' she said. 'What happened?'

'Dad's decided to become a farmer these days. Cane's been getting a good price, and Oliver and Guy are still working on the farm. They do most of the heavy work, so when I came back from Sydney, he asked me whether I'd take over the store. And I did. You know how much I hated working on the farm.'

'You never mentioned you were in Sydney,' she said.

'I went down for a couple of years. I did a traineeship there at one of the top bakeries in the city.'

'So, all the time we were talking on the phone and by email, you weren't even at home. That explains why you didn't say much about the family. I thought it was because you thought I wouldn't want to hear anything.'

'I knew you had your demons to get over, sweetie, so I just wanted you to know that I'd always be here for you.'

'You didn't even tell me you had left and come home again,' she said.

'Well, there was no point when you didn't know that I'd gone in the first place.'

'Or that you had been studying!'

'I'm a qualified pastry chef now.' He looked sheepish and proud.

'How long have you been looking after the store?'

'About eighteen months,' he said. 'When Dad pulled the pin to go and work on the farm, I closed the shop for a week and had a massive clean-out. The community was up in arms because they had to travel to Maryborough for their groceries. I had a mate from Sydney who came up and did all the shop-fitting for me.'

'It's incredible. You're in charge of the store! I mean, Mum and Dad used to run this by themselves, and now you've got what? How many staff?'

'Eight different girls who come in and work, and one guy who does the alcohol side of things.'

'And what do you do? Everything?' she asked, raising her eyebrows.

'I bake. And I supervise,' Julien said simply. 'That was the only reason I went to Sydney. To learn the trade.'

'You're amazing, Julien Johnson, I can't believe what you've done.'

'We open longer hours too. At night now, we open from five till seven on Friday, Saturday, and Sunday. We're licensed now, and we serve pizza. The response has been amazing. People come out here from Maryborough just for the pizzas.'

Charlotte gestured outside. 'The store looks amazing, and I love the new name: The General Store. Great sign. Did you do all of that, or did you have help?'

Julien's face brightened. 'Emily looks after the accounts and orders.'

'Emily?'

'You'll meet her while you're home. She came back from Sydney with me. I moved out of home, and we've renovated the flat above the store. We live there.'

'Gosh, you're a dark horse. You've never mentioned you had a partner. I'll look forward to meeting her.'

Her brother pulled a face. 'I'm thinking about whether to invite her to this dinner Grandmère's having. Maybe, maybe not.'

'Dinner? What dinner?' Charlotte rolled her eyes.

'Sorry, I thought you would have heard by now.'

'No, if Grandmère had mentioned a family dinner, I probably wouldn't have come home. And she would have known that, the shrewd old bird. When is it?'

'Tonight. I guess it can't hurt for Emily to see our family, warts and all, when we're together. So far, she's only met the family in bits and pieces. But the good news is that she and Grandmère have really hit it off.'

'Well, I'll come and meet Emily tonight here because I'm not going to any family dinner. I'll stay one night, and that's it. I can put up with being at home for one night.'

Julien went to speak and then stopped.

Charlotte's suspicions flared. 'What? What else is there?'

'Nothing. If you're leaving town, you don't need to know. Anyway, enough about me,' he said. 'Tell me how you're feeling about being back here.'

'Honestly? You haven't picked up on that yet?' she asked.

'Yep, honestly.'

'Okay, I'm scared shitless. And I'm angry at myself for feeling that way because none of this stupid carry-on was my fault.'

'You look very composed and fresh. Love the dress.' He looked at her thoughtfully for a long moment before he spoke. 'Can I make you a coffee?'

'Yes, please.'

'Have you had breakfast?'

'No, I haven't.'

'Okay, I'll get Jenny to plate you a croissant. Do you want to sit out the front? I've got a couple of things to organise for the day, and then I'll come out and join you.'

'Sounds good. Sweet croissant too, please, not savoury.'

'You don't need to tell me that; I know your sweet tooth. Go and wait outside.' He reached out and put his arms around her. 'It's great to have you home, Charlie, even if it's only for a short while.'

Warmth flooded her, followed by regret for the loss of closeness the family once had.

After a moment, Charlotte stepped back, blinking back the tears that had formed as her brother had held her. 'It's good to see you, too.'

She was aware that Julien was watching her as she walked through the store and went outside. There was no sign of the woman who had been talking to him before. She stepped outside, looked around, and headed for a vacant table past the barrels of polished, rosy apples and bright red tomatoes.

No sign of her out here either; she was curious about what had been going on. Julien had looked upset, but it was none of her business. She also sensed that he was holding back on something she should know, and that unsettled her. Her decision had been made; she'd see Mum and Dad at the farm, then go and visit Grandmère and Papa. Then she'd decide how long she was going to stay. Julien's welcome had been warm and genuine.

As she settled at the table and leaned back to look around, her phone buzzed on the table next to her. A horrid feeling crawled through her stomach again as she noticed that it was her mother calling. She hadn't spoken to her for several months.

For a moment, Charlotte considered ignoring the call and waiting until she headed home after she'd had her coffee; she was in no rush, and their house was only three streets away.

Pulling a face, she pressed the answer button and sighed. 'Hi, Mum.' Charlotte forced brightness into her voice.

'Charlotte, where are you?' her mother said.

'I'm on my way,' she said.

'How far out are you?'

'An hour or so.' There was no need to tell her that she had stayed the night or that she was at the store. Mum would get upset that she hadn't come straight home first.

'So, you'll be here in an hour?'

'Yes, about that,' Charlotte said.

'We're home.'

'Okay. I'll see you soon.'

'Charlotte, hang on, wait. I've got a room ready for you at the farm. We're having dinner at Grandmère's new place tonight; everyone's coming to see you.'

Dread settled in Charlotte's stomach like a brick. 'At Grandmère's?'

'Yes, the farm's not good enough, apparently. Your father's mother has always thought she was better than I am.'

Charlotte closed her eyes. *Can I just turn around and leave now?*

'There's no need to have a dinner. I can just catch up with everyone when I'm here.'

'And how long will that be for?'

'I'm not sure yet.'

'No, I know you won't do that. Julien and your grandmother will be the only ones you talk to.'

For a moment, Charlotte wondered if Julien had called Mum, and she shook her head; he wouldn't have done that.

'We'll talk about it when I get there.'

'*No*, we're having dinner tonight. It's all organised.'

The dread in Charlotte's stomach deepened; it was just so typical of her mother. Everything was always so negative, and Lisette had inherited that trait. Charlotte, Julien, Oliver, Guy, and Amelia always looked on the positive side.

Poor Dad; no wonder he'd spent most of his time either buried in the store or now apparently out at the farm. The last thing he would want would be for Mum to be out there with him, criticising everything he did.

'Okay, Mum, I'll be out there in a while. I'll see you then, and yes, all right, I will be at dinner tonight.' She disconnected before her mother could say anything more.

Why did I come home?

She needed a very strong coffee. Maybe even a shot of brandy in it.

No, she didn't need Dutch courage. She'd dig deep and get through this.

Annie Seaton

Chapter 5

Duckinwilla Creek

Charlotte slipped her phone into her handbag, switching it to silent with movements that had become a habit whenever her mother called. The morning sun warmed the wrought iron table as she tried to ground herself in the present moment. One day in Duckinwilla Creek. She could manage that.

The main street hummed with unfamiliar life—tourists with cameras and shopping bags, voices carrying the accent of the city. It was like watching a play being performed on a familiar stage with an entirely new cast.

Julien appeared with a massive latte and what looked like heaven on a plate—a croissant spilling with custard and fresh fruit. The sight of it momentarily pushed away the knot in her stomach.

'Oh, yum,' she said. 'Just what I need to cheer me up.'

'You need cheering up, do you?'

'No, just a figure of speech,' she said quickly. 'I'm fine, Jules.' The lie came easily after five years of practice. 'I just can't get over the change in town.'

'Wait till you see the locals—what's left of them anyway.' He grinned. 'They only come out at dawn or dusk these days, like shy wildlife. Some reckon the tourism's got out of hand.'

'But surely it's good for business?'

'It is.' Something flickered across his face. 'Though not everyone's happy about the changes. Grandmère and I aren't exactly winning popularity contests.'

Ah. That explained the French provincial touches. Charlotte gestured at the wrought iron furniture and hanging baskets. 'Her design?'

'Got it in one.' He squeezed her hand. 'Anyway, the girls are busy inside. I'll have to go and help for a while. I'll see you tonight at Grandmère and Papa's.'

'Apparently everyone's been summoned.'

'Don't worry, Charlie. What you imagine is always worse than reality. We've got your back.'

'We?'

'Most of us.' The careful choice of words spoke volumes. 'And Grandmère, of course.'

Most, but not all. Not their parents, clearly. And definitely not Lisette. As Julien went back into the store, her thoughts were sad.

Most of her siblings, and no mention of Mum or Dad. Lisette was the one she was dreading seeing because she didn't know whether she could keep her thoughts to herself. If she said what she was thinking, it could destroy her relationship with the family forever.

Before Charlotte could dwell on that thought, a familiar voice cut through the morning bustle.

'Charlotte?'

She turned, and her heart did a complicated little dance. Greg Barrett stood there, looking decidedly un-head-teacher-like in jeans and a faded T-shirt that showed off arms more suited to farm work than staff meetings.

'May I sit?' Greg Barrett said.

She nodded, hoping the heat creeping up her neck wasn't visible. 'What on earth are you doing here?'

'Visiting family.' His smile reached his eyes, crinkling the corners in a way she'd always found distracting during staff meetings.

'Well, wow, it's good to see you.'

'It'll be good to have a chat as normal people,' he said. 'It's hard being a head teacher. I shouldn't say that, but it's true. You can't really socialise with staff when you're in charge, so you're better off keeping a professional distance. But I can chat with you now because you're not on staff anymore.'

Charlotte smiled. 'Yes, I thought it might be hard being in charge. They're a nice group of people, but there are definitely some strong opinions in the staff room.'

'And we'll leave it at that,' Greg said. 'School holidays and you're not going back—when did you arrive?'

'Last night.' She pulled a face. 'For the obligatory family catch-up before I head overseas. What about you? I thought you were going to Dunmora.'

'Oh, I'll get there,' he said with a shrug. 'I took a few detours sightseeing.'

'You don't sound like you're in a hurry to get home.'

'It's always difficult going back home when you don't meet family expectations.'

'Tell me about it.' The words slipped out before she could catch them. 'So you're off to France for a holiday?' she said, still unable to believe Greg was here.

'I am. When I drove away from school the other day, I took all of my things with me. Can I be honest with you? Promise you won't say anything to the others?'

'I won't. You can trust me.'

'I'm thinking about not going back to the school,' he admitted. 'I've spoken to the principal, and he's keeping the job open for me for two weeks while I decide.'

'That really surprises me, Greg. You always seemed happy

there.'

'It's a job,' he said with a shrug. 'It pays the bills. Teaching wasn't really a calling for me.'

'But you've done so well—you're a head teacher at your age!'

'I'm not that young,' he chuckled. 'It's given me flexibility to travel, but now I need to figure out if I want to keep going for another year.'

'So, when do you leave for France?'

'In a week. I thought I'd spend a week with the olds first.'

'Me too,' she said. 'I'm here for at least one night. Maybe more. Family's always—interesting.'

'Sounds like we both have stories to tell.' His eyes met hers. 'Save them for that coffee in France?'

'Or you could join me now?' The invitation surprised her even as she made it. 'My brother makes a mean coffee.'

His eyes crinkled at the corners as he looked at her. 'I'd love to. I'll go and order now. Thanks, Charlotte.' Greg's grin widened as he stood and disappeared inside. Charlotte reached for her fork and cut the croissant into three pieces. She couldn't resist. She brought a creamy, light piece to her mouth and closed her eyes.

Superb.

Duckinwilla Creek did have some redeeming qualities.

While she waited for Greg, she turned her attention to the growing crowds on the main street, still fascinated by the changes in the town and the number of unfamiliar faces.

Until she noticed the young woman standing at the edge of the footpath.

Charlotte rolled her eyes, but her stomach clenched, and her breathing quickened.

Duckinwilla Days 1-3

Chapter 6

Duckinwilla Main Street

'Home to show us how well you've done, are you?' Her sister, Lisette, stood there glaring at her.

For a moment, the dread in Charlotte's stomach was physical, sitting there like a hard ball. She swallowed, terrified that she was going to bring up the croissant she had just eaten.

Then common sense prevailed. If Lisette wanted a confrontation, this wasn't the right place for it. Besides, Greg would be back outside any moment, and she didn't want him to see what trouble she'd apparently caused in the family.

Charlotte kept her voice even. 'Hello, Lisette. How are you? Not happy, I see.'

'What do you care? I never want to speak to you again.'

'You're the one who started this conversation.' She forced a smile to her face.

'Why are you back here?'

'To see my family.'

'Well, I don't want to see you. None of them realise what you're like.' Lisette's face was red, and her mouth was pursed.

'You know what?' Charlotte said softly, aware of the curious looks from the people at the table beside her. 'I let what you did worry me for a long time, but now I've realised that, in the scheme of life with tragedies and sadness, what happened doesn't matter. I've forgiven you,' Charlotte said.

Lisette's face went bright red. '*You've* forgiven me? How dare you say that!'

More heads began to turn at the nearby tables. Charlotte

lifted her napkin and dabbed at her mouth to keep her composure.

'This isn't the place to have this conversation,' she said calmly. 'Perhaps we can continue it tonight. Shall we meet a little earlier? Before we go to Grandmère's?'

'No. I don't even know if I'm going. If you're going to be there, I don't want to be. I couldn't eat anything, so there's no point.'

Charlotte shrugged. 'Suit yourself. But, as I said, I'm not having this conversation here. You've always liked the attention. Remember I always said you should go into acting? Still a drama queen, I see.'

Lisette glared at her, then turned and strode away. She disappeared around the pub corner.

By the time Greg came back out, Charlotte had calmed down and smiled at him when he sat down. She looked up as Julien placed a coffee and another croissant in front of Greg.

'I didn't realise you were with Charlotte.'

'Julien. This is my friend, Greg. We worked at the same school together in Brisbane, and it's a pure coincidence that we happen to be here at the same time. We just bumped into each other.'

'A cosy coincidence.' Julien winked at her, and the heat flew up her neck again.

'Julien, don't you start.'

'I won't, Charlie. You know I'm only teasing you. Hi, Greg. Good to meet you.'

Greg smiled at him. 'Ditto. Love the store, and this croissant looks amazing.'

'It is,' Charlotte said. 'It's certainly cheered me up.'

Julien flashed her an enigmatic look. 'Lisette? I saw her

walking away when I brought the coffee out to the table near the door.'

Charlotte nodded.

Her brother shook his head as he headed back to the door. 'I'll get you another one.'

'I like Charlie. Suits you.'

'Julien has always called me that. To the rest of the family, I'm Charlotte.'

'You need cheering up?' Greg asked.

'No, all good,' she said. 'I'm fine, but thanks, Greg.' Charlotte reached for her coffee, but it spilled into the saucer as her hand shook.

Quickly, Greg grabbed a napkin from the middle of the table and dabbed at the spill. 'You didn't burn yourself, did you?'

Charlotte shook her head. 'No, sorry. I'm fine, just clumsy.'

'Are you okay?'

'Yeah, I'm okay. Just my thoughts were elsewhere.'

'I hope they're happy thoughts.'

'I wish,' Charlotte said.

'Now,' he said, 'tell me your travel itinerary. You'll be starting pretty early in January, I guess, with the school year?'

'Actually, no. I have a couple of weeks to travel because the person I'm replacing is going on maternity leave. She'll work for the first two weeks, then stay the third week to show me the ropes. I'll take over around early February.'

'Sounds good.'

'Yeah, and I figured being in France would give me a real opportunity to immerse myself in the language. What about you? Where are you going?'

'Well, I decided not to start in Paris. I'm flying into the *Côte d'Azur*, hiring a car, and making my way through the countryside. My sister lives in a little village near Avignon. Beaune.'

'Really? That's where my grandmother came from,' she said.

'So, you'll visit there, I guess?'

'For sure. Like you, I'm flying to Nice. I figured I'd explore the south of France before heading to Lyon. But, unlike you, I'm not driving. I'm bad enough on Australian roads, let alone driving on the wrong side at those speeds.'

'How will you get around?'

'I'll bus and train it. My schedule is pretty flexible.'

'Once I get the car, I'm free. We should exchange numbers, and if you're stuck over there, please don't hesitate to call. I could take you sightseeing.'

'That's very kind of you, Greg.'

'It'd be nice to have company before I meet up with my sister. Give it some thought.'

'I will.'

It was hard to reconcile this friendly, cheerful man with the head teacher, who had kept to himself, only speaking to staff during meetings.

Maybe he was unhappy, and no one noticed.

Greg interrupted her thoughts. 'We all tend to get caught up in our own world, don't we?'

'Yes, even at school,' she agreed.

'And families,' he said. 'But I'm going to do my duty, try to get back in Dad's will.' He chuckled. 'Dad always joked about me being in there in pencil. Don't get me wrong; I do love my parents.'

Charlotte smiled. It was nice to hear a man say that.

'But they can make it very hard at times. I never measured

up.'

'What do they do?'

'They live on a cane farm, but Dad has a manager who looks after the day-to-day operations. Dad's a lawyer, and his office is in Maryborough. He expected me to follow him into law.'

'But you wanted to teach,' she said.

'Yes, I thought I did. But after eight years of it, I think Dad might've been right. Maybe I should have done law.'

'Well, you've got a logical mind. I appreciated your logic as head teacher—your instructions and programs were clear and easy to follow.'

'Teaching didn't give me what I expected,' he admitted.

They shared a look of understanding.

'I think part of it was I'd loved school so much as a student, and I wanted to be a part of that, but it's very different when you're teaching children or teenagers, I suppose, and dealing with staff—many of whom don't want to be there either. It wasn't a very pleasant place to be, and the expectations of the department now, with outcomes and data, make the role of the executive very difficult.'

'You never had any aspirations to go higher?'

'Hell no. I think my biggest aspiration these days is to get out of there.'

'I guess you've answered your own question, then—that you had two weeks to make up your mind?'

Greg shrugged and nodded. 'I think I have.'

'You'll be missed.'

'So will you.'

'I guess we're a pair,' she said, looking searchingly. 'Looking for our place in life and what we really want to do.' She looked past him and said half to herself, 'and where we want to do it.'

'Without family expectations,' he said.

The conversation between Charlotte and Greg was animated as they discovered they had more in common than coming from the local area.

'You know, we've wasted the last two years,' she said. 'We could've known about each other earlier.' She glanced at her watch. 'I'm going to have to be rude and go soon, though. My parents are expecting me out at the farm around eleven.'

She pushed her plate in front of her and placed her cup and saucer on it. Greg did the same, nodding, but there was not a crumb left on either plate. 'I can't believe I ate two of those croissants.'

'They were only small. I'm going to buy some to take home,' Greg said.

He's a good chef, isn't he?'

'Julien, your brother—he is a chef?'

'Yes. A pastry chef. He's been working in Sydney for a couple of years, apparently, and he came home to take over the family store. I don't know all the details, but I guess I'll find them out tonight at dinner.'

'I can see you're not looking forward to that,' Greg said.

'I'm certainly not.'

He stood, came around, and held her chair as she stood. She smiled at his lovely manners.

'Thank you,' she said.

'It's been fabulous to catch up. Do you still have the same number you had at school, or is that your work mobile?'

'No, same number,' she said.

'Would you mind if I gave you a call in the next week or so? Maybe we could spend a day together, go for a drive, or have a picnic?'

'Escape from your family?' she said with a grin.

'Respite from yours?' he replied.

'Yes, that would be lovely,' she said. 'I'm not sure how long I'll stay, but if things get too bad, I'll just pack up and go back to Brisbane.'

'Maybe a bit of different company in the middle of your visit will make it easier.'

'I'll look forward to it,' she said.

'You know what?' he said. 'So will I.'

'Greg, please call me.'

'I promise. I'll text you when I go back to the car, and if you need rescuing earlier, give me a call.'

The morning sun warmed Charlotte's face as she watched Greg walk away, a spring in his step she'd never seen during their school days. Something had shifted between them over coffee and croissants—the strict head teacher replaced by a man questioning his own path just as much as she was questioning hers.

'Give me a call if you need rescuing,' he'd said, and she knew he meant it.

She might take him up on that sooner than expected, especially after Lisette's performance. Her sister's bitter words still echoed: "None of them realise what you're like." The accusation carried five years of festering resentment.

Chapter 7

The family farm

As Charlotte strolled back to her car, she let the town's transformation distract her from darker thoughts. The town had a lively feel now, and she enjoyed the buzz of tourists and cheerful chatter. She wasn't in a rush to get to the farm; her mother would be busy in the kitchen, and her father would be out in the cane fields with her brothers. It was easier to avoid one-on-one conversations with her mother, who would dive straight into the heavy stuff. If Lisette's behaviour was anything to go by, nothing had changed. If she left tomorrow, she'd have to ring Greg and tell him she was going back to Brisbane. She didn't want him to think she was giving him the flick.

The new dress boutique caught her eye—designer labels that would have been unthinkable in the old Duckinwilla Creek Charlotte browsed through racks of clothing, pulling out a white jumper and holding it against herself in the mirror. Out of the corner of her eye, she noticed a woman watching her; it was Rowena Billings.

'That's a pretty dress,' Charlotte said, gesturing to Rowena's selection.

'Yes, I need some maternity dresses.' Rowena's tone was carefully neutral, but something in her expression made Charlotte's instincts prickle.

'Congratulations,' she managed, but as she moved left, snippets of a hushed conversation reached her ears.

'He wouldn't talk to me,' Rowena bitterly.

Another voice that sounded suspiciously like Lisette's answered. 'That's awful. What are you going to do?'

Charlotte's stomach clenched. What new drama was

brewing in Duckinwilla Creek?

The drive to the farm was pleasant. Charlotte opened a Spotify calm music selection on her phone, and Bluetoothed it to the car's audio system. She repeated an affirmation she kept pinned to her fridge in Brisbane. By the time she reached the dirt road leading to the farmhouse, her nerves had settled.

A little.

The family farm stretched out before her as Charlotte pulled up to the shed, work utes lined up like sentries by the creek. The smell of roasting meat drifted from the house, along with memories she wasn't ready to face.

After reapplying her lipstick and smoothing her hair, she made her way to the house. She hesitated at the front door, debating whether to knock or just walk in. Five years had turned her into a stranger in her childhood home. Instead, she circled to the back, where her mother would see her from the kitchen window.

The garden had gone wild, flowering shrubs tangled with long grass. Her mother had always kept it neat when they were kids, worried about snakes. But there were no small children here now. So much had changed, and she knew so little about her siblings' lives.

'You there, Mum?'

The house was quiet, but she spotted her parents by the shed, heads close in conversation. For a moment, she watched them— her father greyer she remembered, her mother's shoulders stiff with tension.

'Hey, Mum, Dad!'

They jumped apart like guilty teenagers. Her father managed a smile as Charlotte hugged him, feeling him stiffen before relaxing slightly. Her mother's greeting was frost-edged.

'It's been a long time, Charlotte.'

'Five years,' her father muttered, raising an eyebrow.

'Please don't start.' Charlotte fought to keep her voice steady. 'I want this to be a pleasant visit.'

'Not much chance of that,' her mother muttered under her breath.

Charlotte swallowed the lump forming in her throat. 'Well, I'm determined to enjoy seeing everyone,' she said brightly.

Even if they don't make it easy.

'Put the kettle on, love. There's no point starting an argument,' Dad said, running a hand through his hair.

Dad squeezed her hand as they walked to the house, the gesture worth more than words. Charlotte stared at him as Mum headed up the back steps. Dad had lost weight.

'Are you well, Dad?' she asked as he walked beside her.

'I'm okay. It's been a big harvesting season. It's good to see you home, Charlotte.'

She blinked back tears as Dad held the screen door open for her.

Inside, her mother's ramrod-straight back at the sink spoke volumes. It wouldn't take much more for her just to get in the car and go. She fought the tears that were threatening. How did her life come to this?

And why did I come home?

Swallowing hard, she put a chirpy note into her voice. 'I was really surprised when I drove through town. It's really nice, and I was even more surprised when I went to the store and saw how different it looked. And then I found Julien there.'

'Is that where you've been?' Mum said.

'Yes, I had a quick cup of coffee there, and I met a friend who happened to be in town. That's what delayed me.'

'Fair enough.' Her mother accepted her excuse. 'Grab the cups for me, would you please, Charlotte? If you remember where they are?'

Charlotte forced a smile to her face. 'I do remember where they are. I'm surprised you came to work on the farm, Dad. I thought the boys were going to do it.'

'Guy and Oliver do the heavy stuff. Your father had a bit of a health scare last year, and the stress of running the store for the last two years was too much for him.'

'A health scare? No one told me.'

'Would you have been interested?' Mum said.

'Mum, don't be unfair. Of course I would've been interested.' Charlotte swallowed again and folded her arms. 'Look, can we just move past all of this anger? I'm home. It's lovely to see you, and I'd like to have a happy time here with you all before I head to France. Is that too much to ask?' To her dismay, her voice broke on the last words.

Dad reached for her hand again, and this time, she was unable to catch that single tear that spilled down her cheek.

'Of course we can. Now tell us about what you've been doing at the school in Brisbane.' He pulled out a chair for her to sit on. 'Have you been teaching French?'

'I have, and doing that has really helped me with the language, I think. Grandmère is going to be very pleased, although there's nothing like being immersed in the language of the country. I'm looking forward to going to France and learning some more.'

'Do you like being a teacher?' Mum's contribution to the conversation was made in a slightly disapproving tone.

'I do, and I enjoyed working with the girls in the language department. It was a very good school.'

'Then why are you leaving?'

'I want to experience new things. Spend some time in France, see some of Europe.'

'Duckinwilla Creek is enough for the rest of our kids,' Mum said.

'Julien went to Sydney. He told me he did his pastry chef training there.'

'He did. He's very good,' Mum said. 'But he came home and—'

Dad interrupted, 'And as much as I hate to say it, he has done a great job at the store. I could never have got myself organised to do that.'

Mum smiled for the first time. 'And Emily is a lovely young woman. Did you meet her?'

'No, I'm looking forward to it. I believe Julien is thinking about bringing her to dinner tonight.'

'I hope so. I'll give her a call and make sure she comes. Is that alright with you, Charlotte?' Every word niggled.

'Of course it is. Tell me about the others. Julien said Oliver and Guy are working on the farm. I saw a few utes when I drove past the shed earlier.' She stumbled over her words as she realised what she had said.

'Earlier?' Mum looked at her. 'What were you doing out this way earlier? Why didn't you stop?'

'I just went for a bit of a drive. I went to town.'

'It's a strange way to come in from Brisbane.'

Charlotte laughed it off. There was no way that her mother was going to find out she'd spent the night at *Maison de Rêve*. 'I just wanted to see the district again. It's very beautiful. It looks like you've had a lot of rain, have you, Dad?'

'Yes, it's been a good season, and the cattle are going well too.'

Charlotte swallowed. 'And what about the girls? What are Lisette and Amelia up to?'

'Have you not been talking to them recently?'

'I saw Lisette briefly in town, but we didn't talk.' *Civilly, anyway.* 'I know Amelia was enrolling in the preschool course after school. Has she finished it?'

Mum's chest puffed out with pride. 'Not only has she finished it, but she got a job for next year at the kindergarten in town.'

'Oh, that's wonderful. I can imagine her doing that.'

'She's doing very well,' Dad said.

'And Lisette?'

'She works part-time in the bistro at the pub,' Mum said, lifting her chin. 'We couldn't afford to send her to uni.'

There was a sting in her words, but Charlotte didn't remind her mother that she had put herself through university. Nothing was stopping Lisette from doing the same.

And now for the elephant in the room, Charlotte thought. She took a deep breath and tried to speak calmly.

'And Brett?'

Her mother's expression held disbelief that Charlotte had raised him. 'I'm sure she'll tell you tonight.'

Charlotte didn't miss the glance her parents exchanged. 'So, what time tonight?' she asked.

'Are you going over to your grandmother's this afternoon, or do you want to get ready here?'

'I'll go after I finish my cup of tea.' The cup of tea that Mum still hadn't made. 'In fact, don't worry about one for me. I'll head over there now and see if I can help.'

'Your grandmother will be holding court in the kitchen,

giving poor Mrs Hyslop a hard time.'

'It will be good to see everyone,' Charlotte said, ignoring the barb directed at Grandmère.

She was just about out of conversation, and that made her so sad. Five years since she had been home, and the conversation with her parents felt shallow.

No questions about her life, whether she'd met anyone, whether she was happy. She felt abandoned; she shouldn't have come home.

That feeling of abandonment had given her some issues over the first couple of years she'd been away. Her counsellor had explained that was why she felt disconnected, as though she couldn't belong anywhere. It had even taken six months before she'd succumbed to Rosie and Mandy's friendship overtures at Helen's Creek High School.

Her father must have picked up her sadness. 'Stay and have a cuppa, love. You've only just got here.'

Mum went over to fill the teapot. 'Do you want a biscuit, or did Julien feed you at the store?'

'A biscuit would be nice, thank you.' At least if she were chewing, she wouldn't have to talk. Charlotte could feel herself spiralling down, not the depression that had led her to see the counsellor in her first year at university, and he'd told her she was suffering from depression. The feeling that was bubbling up into her throat was exactly the way she'd felt that year.

Coming home was a huge mistake. She should have stayed in Brisbane and got on that plane to France and forgotten about her family.

When Mum's back was turned, Dad reached over and took her hand again. He squeezed it gently and looked at her, shaking his head slightly.

Charlotte could have sworn his eyes were brimming with tears.

Chapter 8

Her grandparents' house

The sugarcane fields blurred past Charlotte's window, their waving mauve flower fronds a backdrop she'd once loved but now barely registered. Tears pricked at her eyes as she drove away from her parents' farm, the morning's stilted conversation replaying in her mind. The vibrant greens and the golden sun cast a warm glow over the land, but she felt none of its warmth.

Her heart closed as the conversation—or lack thereof—with her parents stayed with her; why did everyone hate her so much? Was she so unworthy? She had tried so hard to be a good child and a good daughter. As she navigated the winding road, memories of happier times, interspersed with moments of tension, filled her thoughts.

When she finally arrived at Grandmère and Papa's new house, she barely had time to catch her breath before stepping out of the car.

As she approached the entrance, Charlotte caught sight of Papa through the window. It felt like walking into a haven, a sanctuary that promised acceptance. Her distress lifted slightly; she could always rely on her grandparents.

The door swung open, and Papa stood there, his face lighting up with joy. 'Charlotte, my dear!' he called, his arms wide open. Before she could even think, she felt herself enveloped in a warm embrace. The smell of his cologne, coupled with a hint of lavender from the garden, wrapped around her like a comforting blanket. At that moment, all her worries began to subside.

'Papa,' she whispered, the word barely escaping her lips

through the lump in her throat.

He stepped back slightly, his hands still resting on her shoulders as he studied her face. 'You're here now, *ma chérie*,' he said softly, his voice soothing. 'Come inside.'

As he ushered her in, Charlotte could barely focus on her surroundings. The foyer faded into the background as her emotions threatened to overwhelm her. She felt her knees weaken, and before she could centre herself, she collapsed into his embrace again, tears spilling down her cheeks.

'Oh, my sweet girl, what's wrong?' Papa murmured; his voice was filled with concern. The genuine love in his eyes brought more tears.

Charlotte, barely able to speak, clung to him. The pain, the isolation, and the struggles she had faced over five years bubbled to the surface. Held in the warmth of her grandfather's embrace, she slowly calmed.

She wiped her eyes. 'I'm sorry, Papa. It was just so lovely to see you that I couldn't hold my tears back. I know how welcome I am here.' She gestured around. 'I adore your new house.'

'I guess your welcome at the farm wasn't very warm?' Grandmère stood in the doorway watching them. She held out her hand and led Charlotte to the couch. 'It is wonderful to see you, my sweet Charlotte. It's been too long. We have been guilty of neglecting you, too.'

Charlotte knew that Grandmère would not criticise Mum directly, but they had never had a close relationship. On the other hand, Mum took every opportunity to criticise Grandmère; she had never been happy with the time Charlotte had spent there. Lisette had quickly become Mum's favourite daughter, and even though it had made her sad, Charlotte had accepted the way things were. She often wondered what Lisette had said to her parents for them to be so distant when she moved to Brisbane.

Charlotte shook her head as she sat on the plush couch adorned with floral patterns; Grandmère looked at her with a softness that belied her backbone of steel. 'My dear, we've missed you immensely,' she began, her voice gentle yet unwavering. 'Where are you staying? At the farm? You are most welcome to stay here if you would like some space.'

'I stayed at *Maison de Rêve* last night. I hope that was all right?'

'Of course it was.' Grandmère sat forward and looked at her intently.

Charlotte took a deep breath, the warmth of their welcome clashing with the coldness of her mother's. 'I just . . . I need to go back to Brisbane sooner. I can't stay here and fix the past. I thought I could. It's just too hard when I don't know what I'm supposed to have done.'

Papa leaned forward, his expression earnest. 'But Charlotte, we want you to stay. We all do. Tonight's dinner is a chance to confront what has happened finally. You can't run away from that.'

'What's done is done,' Charlotte murmured, shaking her head. 'There's no point in bringing it all up again. I don't want to relive it. I don't think I'm strong enough.'

'Of course you are, dear,' Grandmère interjected, her voice holding a firm but loving tone. 'It's time for the truth to come out. It is what I want for you. And Papa does, too. That way, you can go off to France and let all the sad memories go. Wait until I see your father. He will get a piece of my mind.'

'Dad was good.' A lump formed in her throat. 'You don't understand . . .' she began, her voice faltering.

'We do,' Papa said softly. 'We've witnessed the behaviour since you left.'

'Perhaps it was foolish to flee as you did,' Grandmère said. 'There have been so many stories; I don't think anyone knows the truth anymore. Some of our family has turned against you without knowing the truth.'

'What do you mean? What happened?' Charlotte asked, her heart racing.

Grandmère exchanged a glance with Papa, a silent understanding passing between them before she spoke. 'We found out from a neighbour about Lisette and Brett. Your grandfather had a conversation with them when they were out one day in town, unbeknownst to you. It was clear they'd been seeing each other behind your back for quite a while.'

'For how long?' Charlotte asked.

'A few months,' Grandmère said

'But Lisette would have only been fifteen then.'

Papa intervened. 'I spoke to your father about Lisette being underage, but I was told in no uncertain terms to mind my own business.'

'We tried to tell your parents that it had happened behind your back—' Grandmère hesitated—'but Lisette had already poisoned their minds against you.'

Charlotte's chest tightened. 'What do you mean poisoned?'

'Your sister has a way with words, my dear,' Papa explained gently. 'Your grandmother won't say it, but I will, so please forgive me. Your sister has a lot of your mother's traits.'

Charlotte frowned. 'I know she's always been the favourite.'

Papa reached out and took her hand. 'She painted you as the villain, saying you were cruel to Brett, that you thought you were better than him. Your mother believed her, and the lies got bigger with each retelling of Lisette's interpretation of what happened.'

'You know Lisette can be very, shall we say, persuasive.'

Charlotte's chest tightened as the pieces fell into place. Her little sister's talent for twisting truth, their mother's eagerness to believe the worst of her eldest daughter. The web of lies that had driven her from home five years ago.

'That is a polite way of describing what she does.' Charlotte pulled a face. 'I think she's stirring up trouble for Julien now.'

'She is very much like Papa's mother; God rest her soul. She focuses on the negatives, and the truth gets distorted in any way that can make her look better. It is the only way she can feel good about herself. It is quite sad.' Grandmère reached over and took Charlotte's hands. 'But you, darling girl, are strong. You have completed your studies, you have worked in a good school, and now you have the wonderful opportunity to live in France. If I were younger, I would come with you!'

Charlotte felt something unfurl in her chest—not quite hope, but maybe its cousin. 'I still don't want to face everyone tonight.'

'You must. The truth will be told, and you can go overseas without the burden you have been carrying since you left here.'

Charlotte closed her eyes, remembering that day—seeing Brett kiss Lisette, the fight that followed, the way her world had shattered. 'I didn't think anyone would believe me. I was just so hurt. But why did they side with her? I thought they knew me, knew who I was. And I thought I knew my sister.'

'They didn't see everything,' Grandmère said, her eyes glistening with empathy. 'You became a scapegoat for Lisette's actions, and it wasn't fair to you. Sometimes the truth gets buried under lies and clever manipulation.'

'So, you knew?' Charlotte asked, a mix of disbelief and

gratitude filling her heart.

'We knew,' Papa affirmed. 'But we were helpless against Lisette's influence. She spun that delicate web, and your parents became entrapped in it—just like you were. Oliver, Guy and Amelia stayed out of it.'

'And Julien?'

'He always believed in you.'

Something sparked in Charlotte's chest—not quite anger, not quite determination, but maybe both. 'Why should I face them again?'

'Because you deserve to reclaim your place in this family.' Grandmère's voice was fierce with love. 'Tonight's dinner will be the first step in healing. If you stay, you can finally express how you truly feel. It won't be easy, but it's necessary.'

Charlotte closed her eyes, feeling the warmth and love radiating from her grandparents. Something flickered in her chest—strength.

I can do this. Maybe it was time to stop running.

'Will you stay here tonight?' Papa asked gently.

'Would you mind terribly if I went back to *Maison de Rêve*, ?'

'Wherever you feel comfortable, *ma chérie*. As long as you come to dinner.'

Charlotte thought for a long minute, and then she smiled at her grandparents. 'Okay,' she said softly, 'I'll stay for dinner. I owe it to myself to face them—and to confront Lisette. But . . . could I bring a guest?'

She smiled at the surprise on their faces. It actually mirrored the surprise that she was feeling at the random decision to invite Greg to dinner. Grandmère's eyebrows rose with elegant surprise. 'A guest?'

'Someone I worked with in Brisbane.' Heat crept up Charlotte's neck. 'He's actually from around here—Greg Barrett. His family has the cane farm at Dunmora.'

'Ah, the Barretts.' Papa nodded approvingly. 'Good people.'

'He's visiting his family too,' Charlotte added quickly. 'We bumped into each other at the store this morning.'

A knowing smile played at the corners of Grandmère's mouth. 'The head teacher you mentioned in your calls? The one who was always so . . . professional?'

Charlotte felt her cheeks warm. Trust Grandmère to remember every detail she'd let slip over the years. 'He's different outside of school. More relaxed.'

'I'm sure he is.' Grandmère's eyes sparkled. 'And of course he's welcome. The more witnesses to tonight's truth-telling, the better.'

'I haven't asked him yet,' Charlotte cautioned. 'He might not want to get involved in family drama.'

'*Ma chérie*,' Grandmère said softly, 'a man who follows you from Brisbane to Duckinwilla Creek—even by coincidence— might be willing to face more than you think.'

Charlotte's heart did a little skip. She pulled out her phone, and Greg's number was already appearing on the screen. Sometimes, the scariest decisions were the ones that felt most right.

Chapter 9

Dunmora

Contentment hummed through Greg as he drove toward Dunmora, the memory of Charlotte's smile warming him more than the Queensland sun. She'd looked different from the quiet teacher he knew—radiant in her yellow dress, red lipstick highlighting a smile that reached her eyes. He caught himself grinning as he turned up the radio, singing along without a care in the world.

He'd detoured to Duckinwilla Creek hoping to run into Charlotte, though he'd never admit it. Now, with the promise of dinner ahead, even the dreaded homecoming felt lighter.

The Barrett family home stood silent when he arrived, its familiar rooms feeling oddly distant. Memories echoed off the walls—childhood laughter, heated discussions about his future, the weight of expectations he'd spent years trying to escape. Greg sank onto the couch, pulling out his phone for distraction.

He decided he'd call Charlotte earlier than midweek. The thought of spending time with her in France cheered him up, too, and he pushed aside the unease about meeting his parents—a summons he wasn't particularly looking forward to. At least he'd have some time with Mum before his father got home from the office.

Greg sat on the couch in his parents' living room, glancing around the familiar space that felt oddly distant as he waited for them to return. Memories echoed off the walls—childhood laughter, heated discussions about his future, the weight of expectations he'd spent years trying to escape. Greg sank onto the couch, pulling out his phone for distraction. The small screen lit up, revealing Charlotte's name, and he quickly pressed the call button.

'Hey, Charlotte,' he said, trying to sound upbeat, aware of how much he wanted to ease whatever tension she was under.

'Hi, Greg. How are you?' she replied, attempting to sound cheerful, but he could hear the underlying strain.

'So-so. No one was home,' he admitted, disappointment creeping into his tone. 'I let myself in, but I feel like a stranger in my family home.'

The warmth in her voice made him smile. 'I completely understand. It's been complicated here, too. I'm really glad you called. I was about to phone you myself.'

'For a chat?' He tried not to sound too hopeful.

'Actually' she hesitated, 'would you consider being my support person at a family dinner tonight? It's complicated, but having you there would mean a lot.'

Greg's pulse quickened. 'I'd be honoured to be your support person.'

Her laugh came through the line, warm and genuine. 'It's weird asking you, but I could really use the backup.'

'You know,' he said softly, surprising himself with his honesty, 'I've been thinking about you since I left the store.'

Her breath caught. 'That's really . . . nice. Unexpected, but nice.'

'And I am free. My parents have plans. I called Mum to see where they were. They're on their way home now,' he answered, excitement sparking at the possibility of making plans with Charlotte.

'It's strange to think about having you there, but it might

help me keep my head above water.'

'So, it's a date then? I'll bring a bottle of something nice,' he suggested, confidence rising.

'Sounds good.'

'Are you staying there?' he asked, curious about her plans.

'No, I'm back at *Maison de Rêve*, ,' she answered.

'Can I pick you up?' he offered, eager to make things easier for her.

She gave him directions to the house, and as he wrote them down, a flutter of excitement started to dance in his stomach. This felt like more than just a simple dinner; it was a step closer to the connection he'd been hoping for since they'd crossed paths.

Greg's parents arrived home about half an hour before he planned to leave to pick Charlotte up. The welcome was warmer than he had expected. Dad was particularly chatty, and Mum held him close.

'I'm so sorry we have to go out tonight,' she said. 'It's a function we can't get out of. I'm on the committee.'

'It's okay, Mum. As it turns out, I'm going out too.'

'Excellent. Tell me more about it shortly. Your father and I have to go and get ready. We'll have a quick sherry with you before we leave.'

Greg was ready to leave and was sitting in the living room when his father walked out wearing a tuxedo.

'You look very swish tonight, Dad.'

'Yes, your mother has organised some fancy do for Rotary. I've got to look the part. I'd rather stay home and watch the cricket, though.'

Greg smiled.

'Where are you going, son?' His father crossed to the bar

and held up a decanter of whisky.

'Just a small one, thanks,' he said. 'A friend of mine has asked me to go to her family's house for dinner tonight over at Duckinwilla Creek.'

'I didn't realise you knew anyone over there.'

'It's actually someone I've been working with for the past couple of years.'

His father's eyebrows rose. 'A romance? Is that why you've come back home?'

'No, no, it's the first social occasion I've spent with Charlotte—her family owns a cane farm over in the valley.'

'What's her last name?'

'Johnson.'

'I think I know her dad; he goes to the cane farmer meetings. Hugo Johnson?'

'I'm not sure; I haven't met him. I've met her brother, Julien.'

'Yes, that's the family. Julien used to come to the meetings with him, but I believe he's working at their store in town now.'

'Yes, that's right. Nice bloke.'

'They're a decent family; they've been in the district for many years.'

His father sat down and looked at the floor, and Greg sensed there was something on his mind.

'Is there something wrong, Dad?'

'Yes. I've been tough on you the last few years, and I'm sorry. You made your choice of teaching, and you've done very well in the short time that you've been doing it. I just want you to know I'm proud of you, mate.'

Greg's eyes widened. This was totally out of character for his usually quiet father.

'Thank you, Dad. I really appreciate that. You don't know how much it means to me. But you know, I've been thinking, you may have been right.'

'Right? In what way?'

'I'll tell you now. I'm putting in my notice at Helen's Creek High. I'm thinking about going back to uni.'

'Can you afford to do that without working?'

'Yes, I've saved over the last few years, and I think it's time to make a change.'

'And what will you be studying?'

Greg sat back and watched his father as he answered. 'What would you say if I said law?'

His father sat up straight and stared back at him. 'Law? I didn't think you were interested in it.'

'I think I had to find my own way to come to it myself. If you're happy to have me working with you in a couple of years, I'd be happy to be part of the firm.'

His father stood up and walked over, grasping his shoulder. 'You don't know how happy you've made me, Greg. Don't get me wrong; you made your own choice, and it was difficult, but I've come to accept it. Even so, I have to accept you're a grown man and that it's your life. But, mate, you've made my day.'

They both turned to the door as Greg's mother walked in.

'What's going on here?' she said, her eyebrows raised. She wore a gold sheath dress; a small evening bag in the same fabric hung from her arm on a gold chain.

'You look lovely, Mum.'

'Thank you, Greg. It's not often I get complimented on my appearance.' She smiled at her husband.

'You know you always look nice, love.' He glanced across at Greg, his eyebrows raised.

'Yes, Dad. You can tell her.'

'Tell me what? You're not going to France anymore?'

'Yes, I am, but I'm going back to university next year. I'm going to study law.'

His mother's smile was as wide as his father's, and Greg knew he had made the right decision. In his heart, he knew that was the career path he wanted to take.

'Anyway, it's time I left. How long till you go?'

'We're going now; no time for your sherry, Madeleine,' Dad said. 'Drive safe, son; that road back from Duckinwilla can be pretty bad at night. Watch out for the roos.'

'I will, Dad. It's good to be home.' He shook his father's hand and kissed his mother, anticipation building as he headed out to the car.

Greg grinned as he slid behind the wheel. He was going home in more ways than one—to the career he'd been avoiding, to the family he'd been distant from, and maybe, just maybe, towards something unexpected with a woman in a yellow dress who made him want to sing along with the radio.

Duckinwilla Days 1-3

Chapter 10

Her grandparent's house

Charlotte sat on the edge of her bed in Grandmère's house, her heart still racing from the conversation with her grandparents earlier. The room was filled with the perpetual scent of lavender wafting in from the garden outside, but anxiety roiled in her stomach. Just as she was about to clear her mind and call Greg, her phone rang.

She smiled the whole time she was talking to him, and when she disconnected, she hurried down the hall to find Grandmère in the kitchen, her back turned as she arranged a bouquet of fresh flowers.

'Grandmère,' Charlotte called, stepping into the room. 'We do have an extra guest for dinner tonight.'

'Oh? And who may that be?' Grandmère's smile was curious.

'Greg,' Charlotte replied, her cheeks warming. 'He's going to come to support me. Is that alright?'

Grandmère raised an eyebrow, her expression a mix of amusement and intrigue. 'Do you think that will make Lisette behave, or is jealousy your motive?'

'Neither,' Charlotte said quickly. 'I genuinely enjoy Greg's company. I just thought—it might help ease the tension. Having someone not family beside me.'

'Very well, my dear,' Grandmère said, her voice laced with wisdom. 'It sounds like a delightful plan. It's good to have someone else there for you. Now, you look tired. I'll take you up to the guest room and run you a deep bubble bath. I want you to relax.'

'That sounds lovely, but would you mind if I go back to *Maison de Rêve*, ?'

'Of course not, *ma chérie*. Let me pack you a few things to take with you.'

'I'll be back here in an hour and a half, Grandmère.'

'Yes, but I want you to look your absolute best tonight.'

##

Charlotte was soon back at *Maison de Rêve*, She opened one of the two bags Grandmère had handed her as she left: two fluffy towels, face washers, a hand towel, a bath mat, and some French bubble bath. She looked at the deep bath in the small bathroom and then at the bottle of bubble bath that Grandmère had packed, and she smiled. She put in the plug and turned the taps on full as she reached the bottom of the bag. There was a small bottle of champagne in there, along with a wineglass, and her smile grew; Grandmère was an absolute gem.

Since she had spent time with her grandparents, Charlotte was much calmer. She knew whatever happened, she would give it her best, and if her mother wanted to stay alienated, that was her choice. She had done nothing wrong, and tonight—in public, in front of the family—she would state that fact. After dinner, she intended to step outside and try to talk to Lisette. If her sister wouldn't listen, so be it.

Excitement bubbled away as she unfolded the towels and put them in the bathroom. She loved this house, and if things had been different, she would have considered moving in. She would insist on paying rent because she didn't want to give her siblings any idea that she was getting unfair benefits from their grandparents.

How sad was it to have to worry about that?

One thing that did worry her was how unwell Dad looked, and that was another reason to try to make peace. She'd have a talk with Mum, too, and see what was going on.

Charlotte's excitement grew as she took one last look in the mirror. All of the nervousness she'd held about having dinner with the family had dissipated, and she was very much looking forward to having Greg beside her tonight. The fact that he had accepted her invitation and agreed to accompany her to dinner— despite the potential awkwardness—made her heart swell with happiness.

She knew, after working with him for a year, that he was a good person. He had always been kind to the staff, even when making policy decisions that could be unpopular. All in all, he was a very nice man, and the attraction that had been growing all year was starting to blossom. Now that they weren't working together, she wouldn't fight that attraction.

The thought that Greg would be travelling to France at the same time as she was made her happy. She wondered how long he was going to stay there, especially since he had decided not to go back to school.

The crunch of tyres on the gravel driveway outside had her hurrying to the window. She smiled as she looked at the car in the driveway; Greg had good taste in cars. She hadn't known that he drove an Audi, too. She smoothed down the emerald green silk dress she was wearing and reached up to check that her hair was still smooth. She had put in the effort with her makeup, shadowing her eyes in dark green and wearing pale lipstick tonight. The emerald green complemented her auburn hair and fair skin, and she knew she looked good. She needed to look good for her confidence, and she felt that all would be well.

Charlotte hurried down the stairs and across the foyer, opening the door before Greg could knock. 'Come in,' she said, 'and please excuse the state of the house. It hasn't been lived in for a year or two.'

'It's a beautiful house,' he said, looking around. 'It might be old, but it has great bones.'

Charlotte smiled. 'That's what Papa used to say. He built it when they first moved here. I think it would've been in the 1970s.'

'It's beautiful. How come you're staying here?' he asked. 'Is the family situation that bad?'

'No, I just needed some space. I stayed here last night, too.'

He stood back and took her hands. 'You look absolutely stunning, Charlotte. I hope you don't mind me saying that.'

'That's lovely, thank you.'

'That's the second time I've complimented a woman on her appearance this evening. My mum and dad are going to Maryborough for dinner, and Mum looked pretty good, too.'

'I'm sure she appreciated you saying it.'

'She did. Things have been good at home this afternoon.' He nodded as he let her hands go. 'I told Dad what my plans were for next year, and I don't think I'll hear any complaints from the family for quite a while.'

'You've made your plans?'

'I have. I'll tell you about it later. Let's get moving so we can get this dinner over and done with.'

Chapter 11

Her grandparent's house

Greg turned the Audi into the cul-de-sac that Charlotte pointed out to him as they headed back towards Duckinwilla Creek. It was an upscale estate with lots of houses on sizeable lots that he hadn't realised were around here. She pointed up the hill. 'Grandmère and Papa's house is at the top, at the end of the cul-de-sac. Just turn into the drive. There's a circular driveway and a little parking area on the left-hand side. I'm sure there'll be a few cars there already, so just . . .' she pointed. 'That's right, this one parked next to the white ute—that's Julien's. I'm pleased he's here already. A little bit more moral support.'

'Are you nervous?' he asked.

'No, I'm feeling good. And thank you, Greg,' she reached out for his hand as he turned off the Audi. 'I really appreciate your support. It was a big ask and probably a bit out there.'

'No, Charlotte, I really enjoy your company, and I hope our friendship can grow.' His eyes held hers, and she knew there was something on his side as well. Warmth filtered through her body as he held her gaze.

'Are you ready to go in?'

'Yep, let's do this.'

'Wait there,' he said as she sat in the passenger seat; then he walked around and opened her door. He glanced over at the house, opened the door and held out his hand to her. Charlotte took it and climbed gracefully out of the car, clutching her small bag. The emerald silk felt good against her skin; the silk rustled softly as she walked beside Greg. He stopped and put his hand on her elbow. 'Do you think anyone will be watching from inside?'

'Quite possibly. It depends if Lisette is there or not. I'm not sure what she drives.'

'In that case, we'll put on a show.' He leaned forward and brushed his lips across hers. 'Thank you for inviting me tonight.'

As he pulled back, there was a sparkle in her eyes that made his heart race.

He took her hand, and they walked across the paved circular driveway and past the fountain in the centre. As they reached the front door, it opened, and Charlotte's grandparents ushered them in.

Their welcome was warm, and as Greg was introduced to the rest of the family, her grandmother worked hard to put everyone at ease. Greg was struck by the way Margot engaged with everyone. Her gentle laughter rang out like music, and it was clear how much the family respected their grandmother.

Even Charlotte's sister, Lisette. Her eyes narrowed when they were introduced, but she had been polite.

Conversation over drinks was lively, and Greg could see Charlotte relaxing, although her glance darted towards her parents a few times. They sat quietly and didn't speak much.

When she spoke about teaching French, her passion lit up her eyes. 'It's been hard work, but I've really enjoyed the last two years,' she said, her voice animated.

Greg chuckled softly in agreement. 'She's a very good teacher too! I've seen her in action, and she makes learning fun and engaging,' he said, eager to support her.

After half an hour, Margot summoned them to the large dining room table.

Greg settled into his seat beside Charlotte at the long table in her grandmother's elegantly decorated dining room. The soft golden light from the chandeliers cast a warm glow, creating a cosy atmosphere that felt welcoming. Nerves had kicked in when they walked into a full living room, but he had soon been put at his ease, and having Charlotte by his side eased his tension. She looked beautiful, her smile brightening the room as she introduced him to her grandparents, her parents, and the rest of her family.

As Charlotte sat beside him, the warm ambience of the room contrasted with the tension that was still there. The food was superb. The woman who had cooked the meal had outdone herself: hors d'oeuvres, soup, then Beef Wellington with baked vegetables, and now she had just brought out a huge Bombe Alaska.

Greg smiled when Charlotte sat back, placing her hands on her stomach. 'Oh, my goodness, I don't think I can eat any more.'

'You need fattening up, girl,' her father said. 'You're way too thin. You've been working too hard.'

He looked at Greg with a measured expression, and Greg knew Charlotte would be answering some questions later on.

***

Charlotte sat beside Greg at the table. The conversations around the table were loud, but Lisette remained subdued. Charlotte noticed her sister's eyes flicking to Greg and then back to her, and every time Charlotte caught her eye, Lisette looked down, a hint of anxiety crossing her face.

Emily was delightful, sitting on Charlotte's left, with Julien on her other side. Julien had made a good choice. She and Emily chatted away so enthusiastically that eventually, Grandmère interrupted, saying, 'May we have a conversation with you two girls as well?' She smiled, her eyes twinkling with warmth.

'Oh, I'm sorry, Margot,' Emily replied. 'It's just that Charlotte and I are getting to know each other.'

'I hope she's not telling you my childhood secrets,' Julien chimed in playfully.

'You'd be surprised,' Charlotte quipped back at him.

Charlotte noticed the interest that Dad was showing in Greg. He had been a fabulous companion, and she was pleased she'd asked him to come. She would tell Dad that Greg was a friend if he asked.

If he cared.

There was no point in delving into any relationship details— not that there was anything to tell—especially since she was heading off to France soon.

The dessert was eaten, and a cheese platter was brought out, accompanied by two pots of coffee. Grandmère cleared her throat, drawing everyone's attention. The soft conversation ceased, and everyone waited with anticipation.

'Family,' Grandmère began, her dignified presence filling the space, 'I have an announcement to make. This Saturday night, we are having a community function at the hall to farewell Charlotte before she heads to France.'

Charlotte's eyes widened, and she put a hand to her chest. A farewell gathering? She had expected a few quiet goodbyes, but the thought of the whole community gathering for her overwhelmed her.

'That's so lovely, Grandmère,' she exclaimed. 'I appreciate everyone's support, but please, no function.'

'Nonsense, *ma chèrie*,' Grandmère replied, her gaze steady. 'You have always been a part of this community, and they want to celebrate your new journey. It's an opportunity for everyone to show their love and support, just as you've always done for them.'

Before Charlotte could respond, she caught movement from the corner of her eye. Lisette had straightened in her chair, her expression shifting as the implications of Grandmère's words sank in.

'What do you mean, farewell? It's not like she's going to some distant place,' Lisette said sharply, her voice dripping with disdain. 'You're acting as if she's some sort of hero, and now everyone needs to come and say goodbye. It's absolutely ridiculous!'

Charlotte's cheeks burned at Lisette's harsh tone, the familiar knot of tension tightening in her stomach. 'Lisette, it's just—'

'Just? Just what? You think this is all about you, don't you?' Lisette snapped, eyes flashing with irritation. 'You're leaving us again, just like before. Why should the whole town make a fuss over it? It's embarrassing. It's always about you.'

'They're not making a fuss over just me,' Charlotte said quietly.

Lisette scoffed. 'Not making a fuss? They're throwing a party? You don't think the entire town knows what you did? They're just curious to see how this whole charade plays out!'

'Lisette, please,' Julien interjected gently, trying to diffuse the situation. 'This is a family dinner for Charlotte, not a platform to air grievances. And we have a guest.'

Charlotte straightened as tension crackled in the air.

'Grandmère, may we be excused for a moment?' Charlotte asked.

'Of course, my dear,' her grandmother replied, her eyes full of concern.

Charlotte glanced across the table at her sister, who was sitting up from Julien on the other side, between Oliver and Guy. 'Right, Lisette, would you come outside with me, please?' Determination flowed through her, and her tone meant business. 'A chat that's long overdue.'

Lisette's eyes widened, and she looked scared.

Grandmère looked at Lisette and said, 'Go, my child.'

Charlotte stood up. Greg reached for her hand and squeezed it, his reassuring touch giving her the strength she needed.

There was a small balcony adjacent to the dining room, and Charlotte opened the sliding doors and walked out. Lisette followed her, her arms folded and her glare holding malice. The balcony doors closed behind them with a soft click, leaving Charlotte and Lisette alone under the star-filled Queensland sky. Below, the lights of Duckinwilla Creek twinkled like fallen stars, the town seemingly peaceful from this distance.

'What's with you and the guy from Dunmora?' Lisette came on the attack right away.

'Greg and I are friends,' Charlotte said firmly. 'We worked together in Brisbane.'

'What do you want to talk about?'

'I think we need to clear the air. I don't want to go to France feeling like I have for the past few years. We need to address this situation between us. I want to do it tonight so the family can see we're *both* making an effort. I'm sure you haven't been happy either. So tell me, why do you hate me so much?'

'I don't hate you. I just hate what you did.'

'What did I do? It was you who stole my boyfriend.'

'It wasn't that. Brett did the wrong thing by coming on to me while he was still with you,' Lisette said begrudgingly. 'I know that.'

'He did. And you were only fifteen. You were underage. He could have been charged.'

'Nothing happened.' Lisette looked away, but Charlotte knew that sly look her sister got when she was lying. She'd seen it many times when they were growing up.

'Really?'

'Well, maybe, but don't you dare tell Mum and Dad. You want to know why I really hate you?' Lisette's voice trembled. 'Because you left. You just ran away and left me to deal with everything.'

'Left you to deal with what, Lisette? With the lies that you and Brett obviously told about me? Lies that I don't even know, so I can't defend myself.'

'You don't understand. You never understood.' Lisette wrapped her arms around herself. 'Brett was working at the store that summer, remember? He told me things—about the missing money, about how you were helping him cook the books because you thought the family wasn't sophisticated enough for you.'

'What!' Charlotte's chest tightened. 'And you believed him? Your own sister?'

'I was only fifteen! And you were always so . . . perfect. Grandmère's favourite, Dad's pride and joy, the one who was going to university, the one who was going to escape this town.' Bitterness edged Lisette's words. 'Brett said you were planning to take the money and run away to France anyway. He made it sound like I was protecting the family by backing up his story.'

'The missing money that nearly destroyed the store? That gave Dad his first heart turn? Julien told me about that, but I never had any idea that I had been blamed. *You* told them I was responsible for that? You let them believe that?' Charlotte put a hand to her chest, trying to take air into her lungs.

'Brett showed me the altered books with your signature. He said if I didn't back him up, Dad would lose everything.' Tears spilled down Lisette's cheeks. 'I was so scared, Charlotte. And then when everything exploded, and Dad collapsed . . . it was easier to keep lying than admit what we'd done.'

'It's all lies. I knew nothing about any money. I signed nothing! What about Mum? How could she believe the worst of me? She's my mother; she knew me inside and out, and yet you managed to make her believe that?'

Lisette's laugh was hollow. 'Because you're everything she fears, Charlie. You're Grandmère's granddaughter through and through—sophisticated, ambitious, French. Mum's always felt like an outsider in this family, and you . . . you remind her of everything she's not.'

The truth of it hit Charlotte like a physical blow. All these years, she'd thought it was just about Brett, about teenage jealousy. But the roots went so much deeper. She'd left town because she thought everyone had blamed *her* for dumping Brett. No wonder she could never understand the depth of the rift. All this time, her parents thought she was a thief. She would bet that they hadn't told Grandmère.

'Brett took over ten thousand dollars,' Charlotte said quietly. 'Dad nearly lost the store. His heart has never been the same.'

'And you've let them blame me for five years.'

'I was trapped! The longer it went on, the harder it was to tell the truth. And Brett threatened to tell everyone about what happened between us if I ever spoke up. He said I encouraged him, and he would be the one to go to jail because I was only fifteen. And I didn't want Dad to know that he—you know what.'

'That he had sex with an underage girl?' Charlotte's

stomach lurched. 'You were fifteen, Lisette. Whatever happened, he took advantage of you.'

'I know that now.' Lisette's voice broke. 'I see him sometimes in Maryborough. He's got a new scam going with some other business. And every time I see him, I remember what I helped him do to you, to our family.'

'Does anyone else know the truth?'

'Julien suspected. That's why he was happy to take over the store—to figure out exactly what happened. He's the one who eventually caught Brett's pattern, but you were long gone, and the damage was done.'

'And he didn't tell Dad?'

'He was worried about Dad having another heart attack because you'd been blamed. It was all water under the bridge by then, and Dad recovered. We didn't want to risk his health.'

'So I was the fall guy,' Charlotte said bitterly.

'You had everything, Charlotte. Grandmère and Papa paid for you to go to university, you were living in the city, and you had a great job. And now you're going to France.'

'Everything? I paid my own way. I had no family,' Charlotte said quietly, knowing she was going to have to find the strength to forgive Lisette, but she could understand why her sister had believed Brett's lies at first. 'And Brett was never charged.' Understanding dawned. 'I wondered why Julien gave up his dream of being a chef. To protect Dad from it happening again.'

'Julien's been trying to fix everything I broke.' Tears spilled down Lisette's cheeks. 'And now Rowena—she's threatening to tell everyone about Brett and me unless Julien—'

'Unless Julien what?'

'It doesn't matter. That's not relevant to this. It's not a part of it.' Lisette looked away.

Charlotte stepped forward, taking her sister's hands. 'Then help me fix it. Tell Mum and Dad the truth—all of it. Let me help you make this right.'

'Mum will never forgive me.'

'Maybe not right away. But this secret is poisoning our family, Lisette. Look what it did to Dad's health, and to Julien, and to you.'

And to me.

For a long moment, only the chirp of crickets broke the silence. Then Lisette squared her shoulders. 'Okay,' she whispered. 'Okay. But will you help me tell them?'

Charlotte squeezed her hands. 'That's what big sisters are for. But not now. We'll tell everyone we've made up, and we'll see Mum and Dad privately tomorrow.

'Okay.' Lisette stopped and put her hand on Charlotte's arm. 'It's so good to have you home.

The truth was finally going to come out. She was still in shock. As they turned back toward the dining room, Charlotte caught Greg's eye through the window. His steady gaze gave her strength. Whatever came next, she wasn't alone anymore.

'We should go back in. Mum will be stressing,' Lisette said with a shaky smile.

'And Grandmère.'

Together, they walked back into the dining room, where a curious silence met them. She sat straight and spoke firmly. 'Right everyone, Lisette and I have had a chat, and we've sorted our differences.'

Grandmère smiled. '*Bien fait, les filles.*'

Papa stood. 'Well done, girls!'

Charlotte looked at her parents; her mother looked away, but Dad smiled at her. He was looking better tonight, although his skin had a blotchy pallor, and she noticed that he hadn't eaten much. She'd follow that up tomorrow when she and Lisette went over to talk to them.

Greg reached for her hand and squeezed it, this time not letting go; Charlotte's happiness almost bubbled over, warming her from the inside out.

She glanced at Julien; he was staring out of the window, looking as though his thoughts were miles away. Maybe he needed to have a chat with Lisette as well.

Chapter 12

Maison de Rêve

Greg pulled up outside the front door at *Maison de Rêve*.

'Thank you, Greg. You'll never know how grateful I am to you for taking me tonight.'

'It turned into a good night after all of your worry,' he replied, a warm smile spreading across his face.

'It did, and I finally got things sorted with Lisette. I just need to see Mum and Dad tomorrow and talk to them. I'm worried about them, and I need to get things sorted there before I can focus on France.' She would tell Greg what had ensued after Mum and Dad had found out the truth.

'Don't forget you've got your big farewell function on Saturday night. Your grandmother invited me too. Is that okay with you?'

'Of course it is! And you know what? I'm excited about it now. I think there might be some surprises in store for me. Julien hinted at some special guests that I'm going to be pleased to see, but he wouldn't tell me who they were.'

'It sounds like it's going to be a good night.'

As Greg opened the car door for her, a massive clap of thunder boomed overhead, followed by a bright flash of lightning.

'Oh wow, look at those clouds boiling over the mountain,' she said. 'Quick, come inside with me. I'll make a coffee before you head back.'

Greg followed her into the kitchen at the back of the house as she began searching the cupboards for a coffee maker. The kitchen was bare, but the essentials were still there. Charlotte opened the small bag that Grandma had given her as they left after dinner and smiled. Inside were some coffee granules, long-life milk, sugar, and a small box of chocolates. 'I'm certainly well looked after,' she said.

They stood together at the kitchen window as the coffee brewed, watching the sheets of torrential rain sweep across the back garden, the sound almost drowning out conversation.

'This is flood rain,' he said, his brow furrowing with concern. 'In fact, perhaps I should go now because there are a couple of creeks I have to cross on the other side of the mountain to get home.'

Charlotte frowned. 'It doesn't sound safe. It's very late.' She bit her lip and hesitated, torn between the anxiety of his safety and the desire to keep him close. 'Perhaps you could stay the night,' she suggested, holding up her hands in a gesture of innocence. 'I mean, just stay the night in the spare room. I'm not making a move on you,' she added with a mischievous grin.

The coffee machine clicked off, but before she could move towards it, Greg's arms wrapped around her waist, pulling her against him.

Greg gave her a knowing smile. 'I wouldn't mind if you were making a move,' he whispered, his voice low and filled with intent. The words hung between them, and before Charlotte could respond, he moved closer.

His hand gently cupped her face, tilting her chin up. The space between them vanished, and their lips met in a kiss—soft at first, tender, and then, it deepened, yet still filled with sweetness. The kiss was a promise, a quiet agreement shared between them without a single word spoken.

When they finally parted, their foreheads rested against one another. Neither spoke for a moment, but the need to be close—to be together—went without saying.

Charlotte's pulse raced, and with a smile that bordered on teasing, she whispered, 'There's only one bed made up.'

Greg chuckled softly, his fingers brushing through her hair. 'What a shame,' he said, his voice a whisper against her lips. 'And the water for the coffee's gone cold, too. What will we do?'

He kissed her again, this time with more urgency, his arms holding her against him. Charlotte was caught between happiness and desire; she knew exactly what they would do. As she led Greg upstairs, his hand holding hers tightly, there was no sound apart from their breathing.

All the while, she smiled to herself. The coffee, after all, could wait.

The next morning, Charlotte awoke to soft dawn light filtering through the curtains, the sounds of the storm replaced by the gentle chirping of birds outside. She turned to find Greg beside her, a peaceful expression on his face as he slept. Her eyes roved over his features—his dark lashes resting against his tanned skin, the faint stubble on his jaw adding a rugged edge to his otherwise serene face. She couldn't help but trace the line of his lips as an ache of longing stirred deep within her. In that warm moment, contentment and a glimpse of the future filled her. She knew it wasn't too soon—everything about them felt right. She put her head next to his and closed her eyes as happiness filled her. She could face anything today; even the talk with Mum and Dad.

The morning light filled the room, casting a warm glow over everything when she woke the second time. She stirred awake, the soft goose-down mattress cradling her like a cloud. As her eyes fluttered open, she looked up to find Greg lying beside her, propped up on one elbow, a playful grin spreading across his face.

'Good morning, sleepyhead,' he said, his voice low and smooth as honey.

'Good morning,' she murmured, still slightly dazed.

He tilted his head, looking at her with a combination of affection and mischief. 'You know, I've been meaning to tell you something.'

Charlotte blinked, her heart racing at the prospect of his confession. 'What's that?'

Greg shifted closer, resting his head on his hand while gazing earnestly into her eyes. 'I've been fighting this attraction to you for the past year. It was like trying to hold back a tidal wave, and it took a lot of doing. Maybe I should have given in back then.'

Her breath caught in her throat. 'You too?' she confessed, a soft smile breaking on her lips. 'I never wanted to acknowledge it either. I thought it was just me being foolish or impulsive. I mean, falling for the boss?'

'Foolish? Hardly. I mean, look at us,' he chuckled softly. 'It took us this long to get here. The universe has a funny way of pushing us together, don't you think?'

Charlotte nodded, her heart swelling with both excitement and trepidation. 'It's kind of coincidental. You coming to France?'

Greg's expression grew serious, a hint of sincerity lining his features. 'To be honest, I only planned the trip to France because I knew you'd be over there. I was hoping to see you—maybe run into you at a café or something. I knew what school you were going to because I wrote the reference.'

Charlotte's breath caught again, a rush of warmth flooding her cheeks. 'Really? You would have come looking for me?'

'Absolutely,' he replied earnestly. 'I want to spend more time with you, Charlotte, wherever that might lead.'

'Well, a picnic sounds good,' she said with a teasing smile. 'What's the plan for today?'

Greg chuckled, the sound rich and warm. 'I have to head back to my parents' house this morning. But I'd love to take you out for a picnic later—if that's okay with you.'

Charlotte nodded. 'That sounds perfect! I'll be ready for a break from the whirlwind of family drama. Things should be a bit easier since Lisette and I sorted everything out last night.' She shifted, propping herself up on her elbow to face him better. 'So, what are your plans after France?'

Greg's expression changed, his voice becoming more thoughtful. 'Well, I'm planning to go back to university and study law.'

Charlotte felt a pang of bittersweet sadness. 'That's amazing! But—it makes me sad to think about how I'll be in France for six months, and you'll be back here in Australia.'

Greg reached out, gently tucking a loose strand of hair behind her ear. 'Life has its twists and turns, but I believe we can make this work. You never know what could happen in six months.'

Later, they sat on the balcony, enjoying a coffee together as they looked out over the lush valley of Duckinwilla Creek. The view of the rolling hills and trees was breathtaking, and Charlotte's contentment grew as she sipped her coffee.

'This is perfect. I feel like I've woken up from five years of sleep,' she said softly, savouring the moment. The crisp air filled her lungs as she took in the beauty around her. 'Woken up by the kiss of a prince.'

'As long as it wasn't a frog,' Greg replied, a happy grin on his face as he watched her. 'I feel so lucky to be here with you already. It's fast-forwarded all my expectations.'

'Meant to be.' Charlotte looked at him, returning his happy smile as he put his hand on hers.

Chapter 13

Sunlight streamed through the windows as Charlotte hummed softly.

Her phone buzzed: Lisette. **At the farm. Mum's in the kitchen. You coming?**

Charlotte took a deep breath. **On my way.**

Greg appeared in the doorway, hair damp from the shower. 'Ready?'

'As I'll ever be.' She reached for him, drawing strength from his solid presence. 'Thank you for staying.'

'Wild horses couldn't have dragged me away.' He kissed her softly. 'Want me to come with you?'

'No, this needs to be just family. But—' She smiled up at him. 'Picnic lunch?'

'Try and stop me.'

The drive to the farm was too short. Charlotte's hands tightened on the steering wheel as she pulled up beside Lisette's car. Her sister waited on the back steps, pale but determined.

'You look different,' Lisette said quietly.

Heat crept up Charlotte's neck. 'Good different?'

'Happy different.' A ghost of a smile touched Lisette's lips. 'Greg's good for you.'

They found their mother in the kitchen, aggressively kneading bread dough. Ellen's shoulders stiffened as they entered, but she didn't turn around.

'Mum?' Lisette's voice shook. 'We need to talk to you.'

'Your father's resting,' Ellen said sharply. 'He didn't sleep well. He's worried about you being here, Charlotte.'

'This can't wait, Mum.' Charlotte said gently. 'It's about the money. About what really happened five years ago.'

Ellen's hands stilled in the dough. 'I don't want to hear it.'

'You need to.' Lisette stepped forward. 'Because it wasn't Charlotte. It was Brett. He stole the money, and I—I helped him cover it up.'

The colour drained from Ellen's face. She gripped the counter, leaving floury handprints. 'What are you saying?'

'He manipulated me, Mum. I was fifteen and stupid and jealous, and he showed me how to alter the books to make it look like Charlotte's fault. And then when Dad had his heart turn—' Lisette's voice broke.

'All this time?' Ellen's whisper was harsh. 'You let us blame Charlotte all this time?'

'I was scared,' Lisette sobbed. 'Brett threatened to tell everyone about—about what happened between us. And then Dad got sick, and I couldn't—'

'Couldn't what?' Hugo stood there, one hand pressed to his chest, his face grey.

'Dad!' Charlotte rushed to him. 'You should be resting.'

'I heard.' His voice was thin, strained. 'I heard everything.'

'Hugo, please,' Ellen started forward, but he waved her off.

'My own daughters.' He swayed slightly, and Charlotte slipped an arm around him. 'One betrayed by a man I trusted in my store. The other too young to know better. And I blamed the wrong one.'

'Daddy, please sit down.' Lisette grabbed a kitchen chair. 'Your colour's not good.'

He sank into it, still clutching his chest. Ellen hovered, her face a mask of worry and confusion. 'Should I call the doctor?'

'No.' Hugo reached for Charlotte's hand. 'I need to say this. I'm sorry, love. I should have trusted you. Should have looked harder for the truth.'

'It doesn't matter now,' Charlotte said quietly, but he shook his head.

'It matters. Letting you go, believing the worst . . . that's on me. Your mother and I, we—'

'We were wrong,' Ellen finished quietly. She opened a bottle and passed a tablet to Hugo. He put it under his tongue and closed his eyes. She still wouldn't quite meet Charlotte's gaze, but something had shifted in her stance. 'About so many things.'

Hugo's grip on Charlotte's hand tightened, but as the medication took effect, his colour slowly improved. After a few minutes, he opened his eyes, looking steadier.

'Dad?' Charlotte studied his face with concern. 'You're not well, are you?'

'I've got an appointment with a specialist in Brisbane next week,' he admitted. 'Your mother's been fussing over me something fierce.'

'With good reason,' Ellen said, her voice softening as she touched his shoulder. 'You need to take better care of yourself.'

Hugo looked between his daughters, then opened his arms. 'Come here, both of you.'

Charlotte and Lisette moved into their father's embrace, and for a moment, they were children again, safe in his strong arms. Through her tears, Charlotte caught her mother's eye and saw something there—not quite forgiveness yet, but perhaps the beginning of understanding.

'My girls,' Hugo murmured, holding them close. 'No more secrets, hey? This family's had enough of those.'

Charlotte nodded against his shoulder, breathing in the familiar scent of him, thankful that the truth hadn't cost them more than it had. There would be time to heal, to rebuild.

Time to be a family again.

Annie Seaton

Chapter 14

The soft burble of the creek mingled with the laughter of birds flitting among the trees, creating a serene backdrop for the afternoon picnic. Sunlight filtered through the leaves, dappling the ground with playful patterns and warming Charlotte and Greg as they lounged on a checkered picnic rug. Surrounded by lush greenery and the sweet scent of wildflowers, the creek sparkled nearby, inviting them to dip their toes in its gentle flow.

Charlotte lay back, a soft sigh escaping her lips as she traced circles in the river sand with her finger. With a smile, she turned to Greg, who was propped up on one elbow, casually tossing bits of grass into the water.

'Are you looking forward to Saturday night?' he asked, his voice punctuating the tranquil atmosphere.

'I am,' Charlotte admitted, but there was a hint of hesitation in her tone. 'Still, I can't shake the feeling that the gossip mill is going to be in full swing. People just don't understand what it was like for me. They want to label everything as right or wrong when life isn't that simple.'

Greg raised an eyebrow, considering her words. 'Sure, it might have felt monumental for you, but to the community, it was just a broken relationship. They didn't know what Lisette did. You were young and headed off to university. I doubt it was the scandal you're imagining.'

Charlotte nodded slowly, her brow furrowing in thought. 'I get that now, but back then, it consumed me. Leaving was a whirlwind; I had no idea how messed up everything would get. If I had, I'd still be here.'

'And we wouldn't have met.'

'We wouldn't.' Charlotte bit her lip, her uncertainty reemerging. 'Part of me feels like I've moved on, yet another part feels so unresolved. Did I make a mistake in leaving so suddenly? Did I give up too easily?'

'Your past does not define you, Charlotte,' Greg reassured her, gently brushing a stray hair from her face. 'Whatever happens, just make sure it's right for you. Enjoy your farewell.'

His words brought a faint smile to her lips as gratitude filled her. 'You're right.'

Greg laughed softly, coaxing her spirits higher. 'Maybe this is their way of trying to say sorry. You know how gossip works in small towns—there's a new story every day. I'm sure everyone who's coming will be there to wish you the best.'

Feeling lighter than she had in days, Charlotte joined in his laughter. 'You are a wise man. This picnic is lovely, and spending this time with you has helped more than I can say.'

'Julien can certainly cook.' Her brother had put a picnic basket together for them.

Seeing Charlotte relax was a joy for Greg, and he smiled as the soft sounds of nature surrounded them.

'I can't believe how quickly everything is sorting itself out,' she continued, her excitement blooming. 'And with us flying to France together—what a twist!'

Greg's grin broadened. 'It's like the universe has been nudging us towards this moment. The thought of exploring those quaint streets with you feels like a dream.'

Charlotte laughed lightly, her eyes sparkling with joy. 'I never expected all of this to happen. Grandmère and Papa were shocked when Lisette went to see them and told them the truth. She went there before she went to Mum and Dad's this morning.'

'You are very special to your grandparents. They trusted you.'

'They are special to me too. Even Mum seems to be coming around, although slowly. Maybe she's finally realising that I'm not the same girl who left home.'

'She must be worried about your dad.'

'Yes, I'll be pleased when he goes to see the specialist. I can't get anything out of either of them. I think Grandmère knows something, but she won't say either. She sounded worried when she called me. I asked her, but she closed down.'

'Maybe your mum just needs time to adjust. She'll see how happy you are, and it will all fall into place.'

'I do love your optimism, Greg.' Charlotte beamed at him, her heart lighter. 'It feels wonderful. You've lifted a weight from my shoulders. I can almost see a brighter future ahead for us.'

'I haven't done anything.' He held her eyes with his. 'Apart from falling in love with you.'

His words hung between them like a promise, and the world around them faded into a gentle blur as Greg leaned in, and Charlotte met him halfway, their lips brushing softly in a tender kiss. It was gentle and unhurried, a sweet declaration of a future.

Chapter 15

Duckinwilla Creek Community Hall

Over the next few days, Greg and Charlotte spent most of their time together. Every second night, he stayed at *Maison de Rêve* with her, and their relationship deepened in ways neither of them had anticipated. Warmth filled her whenever she was near him, a sense of belonging she'd been missing since she left home.

Greg had changed his flights so that they would be flying to France together. They planned to have a holiday before Charlotte had to start work at the school, and the thought filled her with excitement. The prospect of exploring new places with him felt like a dream come true.

The week flew by, and soon it was Saturday night. Days spent with Greg had been wonderful, and he looked happier now that he and his father had sorted out their differences. Greg shared with her that he had submitted all of his university applications and was excited to tell Charlotte that when he returned from his holiday, he would be starting a few hours a week at his father's office in Maryborough.

'I can do a lot of the degree remotely. I'll just have to go down to Brisbane a few times a year,' he explained.

Charlotte reached up and cupped his cheek, her heart swelling with pride. 'You look so much happier and relaxed. I think you've made the right decision.'

'I'll miss you, Charlotte,' he said, his expression turning sombre.

'I'll miss you too,' she replied, her voice soft. 'You know, in some ways, I wish I wasn't going. Now that I'm home, I feel as though I should stay longer. But I've got the contract; I have to go.'

'You'll enjoy every minute of it, and we'll have some time together there first before I come home.'

A mixture of excitement and regret filled Charlotte as the day of the farewell approached. She couldn't believe how many were coming; Julien and the girls had catered for finger food and drinks for over a hundred friends and community—it seemed everyone she hadn't seen in years was coming. Even two of her old school teachers from Maryborough had been invited, and she wondered whether the family had gone a bit over the top. But when Grandmère organised something, it had to be the best.

'Are you nearly ready, Charlotte? I thought you wanted to be there before everyone arrived,' Greg called out from downstairs. They were getting ready at *Maison de Rêve*. When Charlotte had decided to stay there, Grandmère had organised a maintenance man and a cleaner to come and tidy up, despite Charlotte's protests that she'd only be there for two weeks.

'I do. I just can't decide what to wear,' she shouted back, standing in her underwear as she stared at the four dresses that had remained untouched since she'd arrived. 'Come and help me choose, Greg.'

His footsteps thudded up the stairs, and she smiled as he appeared in the doorway. 'I really don't know what to wear. You pick.'

He surveyed the four dresses hanging by the window. 'Okay, eeny, meeny, miney, mo,' he said playfully.

'No, don't pick like that! You tell me which one looks the best, okay?'

'I like the yellow one,' he said, his eyes lighting up. 'It's nice and fresh, and it makes you look sunny and happy. And it goes with the colour of your hair. How's that?' He looked proud of himself.

'The yellow one it is!' she exclaimed, quickly reaching over to pull it over her underwear.

'That's a shame,' he teased.

'What's that? It's not good,' she said with a frown.

'No, you covered up that pretty underwear! I was enjoying looking at it.'

She reached over and tapped his shoulder. 'Enough of that—we have to go to town.'

***

Greg stood with Charlotte's younger brothers, Oliver and Guy, watching her as she walked around the room. She'd smiled more tonight than he had ever seen her smile; the shadows had gone from beneath her eyes. She looked genuinely happy and content. He nodded approvingly when he saw her hug Lisette. Amelia, her younger sister, trailed behind like a loyal shadow. Oliver nudged Greg lightly and whispered, 'There's a bit of hero worship there; Amelia adores Charlotte.'

'Not hard to do,' Greg said with a soft chuckle. 'She's adorable.'

'So, what's the go with you two?' Oliver asked, curiosity in his tone.

'If I'm not overstepping the line, I think very highly of your sister,' Greg replied earnestly. 'I intend to spend a lot more time with her.'

'Even with her going away?'

'She'll be back,' Greg assured them.

Julien and Emily walked over to join them.

'You two are doing a fabulous job at the store,' Greg said.

108

'We've enjoyed your coffee and croissants a few times this week. I took some home to my parents, and I think they're making a special trip over next week to check out the General Store. The picnic you packed for Charlotte and me to take out to the national park the other day was superb.'

From across the room, Charlotte caught Greg's eye, and he smiled back as Charlotte pointed to her empty glass. He nodded.

'Drink, guys?' Greg asked. 'I'm heading over to the bar to grab another tonic water for Charlotte.'

'I'll have a white wine, thank you, Greg.' Emily linked her arm through Julien's.

'A beer for me,' Julien added.

'I'll come with you, and I'll take Charlotte's drink over if you like,' Emily said. 'I need to catch up with her; I haven't talked to her much tonight.'

'She's having a great time,' Greg said. 'She hasn't stopped smiling.'

'I think that has a lot to do with you,' Emily said with a grin. 'Although it has been a relief for her to get all that family stuff sorted. I don't think she'll stay away as long next time.'

It took a while for Greg to be served because of the crowd waiting for drinks. As he waited, he was struck by how many people lived in Duckinwilla Creek. It had turned into a fabulous night, filled with laughter and joyful reunions. Charlotte's Grandmère sat in her chair, holding court, and he was sure she had spoken to everyone who had come through the hall that night.

The big surprise for Charlotte had been the arrival of one of her best friends who'd travelled from the Northern Territory. When she'd walked in, Charlotte's scream filled the room, startling everyone. Greg turned, thinking something had gone wrong, but instead, he saw Charlotte hugging a tall woman with long black hair.

'Jenny!' she exclaimed. 'Oh my God, Jenny!'

When he was served, Greg handed the tonic water to Emily. 'I'll go back to Julien with the rest of the drinks while you go and find Charlotte.'

He juggled the tray, and as he crossed the hall, he noticed a woman he hadn't seen before standing with Julien. He hesitated to join them; their conversation seemed intense and serious.

But then Julien's face lost colour as he watched, and Greg's concern deepened. He glanced at their exchange, unsure of what was going on. Just then, the woman's voice rose above the crowd, and people near them turned to look. Lisette hurried over to them and spoke to the woman, but she shook her hand off her arm.

'You think you can just walk away from this, Julien?' the woman accused, her tone fierce.

'What are you talking about?' Julien stared at her. 'If it's about the store, this isn't the time to talk about it.'

'I'll have this conversation whenever I like. You have to stop avoiding me,' the woman shot back.

Greg stepped in, taking the woman's arm gently but firmly. 'Perhaps it's not the time to have this conversation,' he said, trying to defuse the rising tension.

As he looked up, he spotted Emily walking back to them, her forehead set in a frown.

'It's your child, Julien Johnson and you're going to do something about it!' the woman shouted, her accusation hanging in the air like a thunderclap. Greg watched, his heart sinking, as Emily's hand shot to her mouth. Turning swiftly, she hurried out of the room, leaving a shocked silence in her wake.

Chapter 16

Duckinwilla Creek Community Hall

Charlotte glanced at her father, who stood beside the table with colourful decorations and loaded with plates of food, as she hurried across to Julien. She'd noticed Dad's pallor, too; he must have heard the confrontation between Julien and Rowena. The tension in the room still crackled from the words that everyone had overheard.

Rowena's words rang in her ears, and she could see Julien's distress.

The warm atmosphere was filled with laughter and chat from those who hadn't heard the conversation. Mum was bustling about, arranging snacks on the buffet table in the midst of several loud conversations around the table. Rowena's loud words hadn't reached that far. When she checked that Julien was okay, she'd see if Dad wanted to go outside for some quiet and fresh air.

Before she could walk over to Julien, their father clutched his chest suddenly, his hand shaking violently, causing a splash of punch to spill onto the tablecloth. A pained expression crossed his face, and he gasped for air, his eyes wide with fear as he staggered back and knocked a chair over.

'Dad!' Charlotte screamed, her voice cutting through the conversations. Everything slowed as she dashed toward him, desperate and frantic. Mum froze mid-motion, the colour draining from her face as she reached for the edge of the table for support.

Oliver and Guy leapt up from their seats, eyes wide with

disbelief and horror as their father toppled backward, his body contorted in a way that sent shivers down Charlotte's spine. The cheerful atmosphere of the hall stilled, replaced by a harsh silence punctuated only by the sudden, shallow gasps of her father, each breath a frantic attempt to draw air.

The world spun around Charlotte, her heart pounding furiously as she watched Greg run across to Dad. He shoved chairs aside, creating space around her father, who was now lying motionless on the floor.

'Call triple zero!' Greg barked, dropping to his knees beside him, his face set with determination. His urgency snapped everyone into action, with Guy fumbling for his phone, fingers trembling as he dialled for help.

Greg began CPR, his hands pressing down rhythmically on Dad's chest. Charlotte looked around and saw the shock on Grandmère's face as her son lay fighting for his life. Papa had his arms around her, and she buried her face in his shoulder, shaking with sobs.

Charlotte's siblings stood beside their grandparents, Lisette and Amelia's tear-streaked faces reflecting her own panic. Mum grabbed her arm and clung tightly to her, murmuring reassurances that seemed to be more for herself than for anyone else. 'He'll be fine, Charlotte. The doctor said we didn't need to worry. It'll stop in a minute. Please, Hugo, listen to what he said.'

Charlotte gripped her mother's hand and watched as Greg worked, now aided by Julien, who had run over as soon as it was obvious that Dad was having a heart attack.

A heart attack. Nausea gripped Charlotte, but she knew she had to stay strong.

Oliver stood close to them, with one arm around Amelia,

his shoulders tense and fists clenched, looking as though he felt utterly powerless. Lisette was beside them, both hands covering her mouth.

As the crowd began to gather, drawn by the commotion, silence descended on the hall. Charlotte stood there, willing time to move faster, praying for flashing lights and sirens—anything that would signal help was on the way for her father. At that moment, her world had narrowed to the desperate struggle for life unfolding before her.

Chapter 17

Maryborough Hospital – three days later

The sterile smell of antiseptic filled the air as Charlotte sat in the dimly lit hospital waiting room. The constant beeping of machines from the ICU echoed in her mind, a haunting reminder of her father's fragile state. It had been days since he was admitted, yet they still had no clear direction, only glimmers of hope that occasionally flickered like candlelight. His condition fluctuated, and the doctors could make no promises.

Her mind was a jumble of worries and regrets, looping endlessly as she struggled to make sense of everything. Just then, Julien appeared in the doorway, his expression haggard. He wasn't a tall man, but now he looked smaller and more vulnerable than Charlotte had ever seen him.

'Charlotte, I need to talk to you,' he said softly, gesturing for her to join him in the hall. She followed him, their footsteps echoing in the sterile corridor.

Once they were away from the others, Julien's composure seemed to crumble. 'I know I should stay,' he began, his voice raw with conflict. 'But I have to follow Emily to Sydney. I can't let her go. You, of all people, know how important it is not to let situations get out of control.'

Charlotte blinked in surprise. 'Have you spoken to her since she left?'

He nodded, the movement heavy with exhaustion. 'Yeah, she sent me a text saying she doesn't ever want to speak to me again. But she did say she hoped Dad was getting better.'

The news hit Charlotte hard. 'What's going on, Julien? Tell me about Rowena.'

Julien ran a shaking hand through his hair, the strands falling back into disarray. 'She's lying. All I know is that Emily doesn't believe me, and I can't believe that she doesn't trust me. I thought we were fine. But something's changed, and I don't understand. I'm worried whether someone else has spoken to her. I have to go and see her, Charlie.'

Charlotte studied her brother's face, seeing the wrinkles etched on his forehead. 'Do you love Emily?' she asked softly. 'Even if she can't trust you?'

'Of course I do. She is my life. I can't believe she left me. She wouldn't even talk to me,' he replied, his voice cracking. 'But I don't know what to do. I don't even know if I can convince her.'

Charlotte pulled him into a hug. They stayed like that for a moment, drawing strength from each other, as the cold hospital light cast long shadows down the hall.

'Whatever happens,' she whispered, 'Greg and I will help you.'

Julien nodded against her shoulder, the tension in his body slowly unravelling.

As they returned to the waiting room, Charlotte was grateful for Greg's reassuring presence nearby. His expression mirrored her anxious thoughts, and when she caught his eye, he approached her.

'We should discuss our trip to France,' he began gently. 'I think we need to postpone it.'

His words tugged at her heart. 'Yes, I thought of that before when I was sitting with Dad. I'll call the school in Lyon and let them know I have to break the contract due to family circumstances,' she replied, her voice shaking slightly.

Greg took her hands in his, squeezing them gently. 'You don't have to face this alone, sweetheart. I'll cancel my flights too. When we go home, I'll do them both.'

Julien's voice broke through their discussion. 'Charlotte, I know this is a big ask,' he began, his eyes dark with concern. 'But seeing you will be here and to allay Dad's worries, would you take over at the store while I'm gone?'

Charlotte felt a lump rise in her throat. She exchanged glances with Greg, who nodded, ready to support her. 'I can, but I don't know anything about it.'

'The staff will help you. They are a great bunch, and they've been fabulous this week. They've all worked extra hours with no complaints while I've been at the hospital.'

Greg put his hand on Julien's shoulder. 'I can help, too, mate—as a friend of the family. I can do the heavy lifting, serve tables, and wash up.'

Overwhelmed, Charlotte reached for Greg as tears spilled down her cheeks.

As they were discussing the details, an alarm went off in Dad's room, and the nurses hurried in.

Mum came out, her face white. 'It's no good. He's having another attack.' Panic surged through the room as chaos erupted again.

Only a few minutes later, the doctor joined them in the corridor, his expression serious. 'We need to take him into surgery,' he said, his voice firm but calm. 'He's stable for now, but we have to act quickly.'

His words sent shockwaves through the family. Charlotte's mother was already in distress, the fear deepening as her eyes brimmed with tears.

Lisette, Amelia, and Charlotte led their mother slowly toward the family room down the hall, trying to shield her from the medical interactions that were taking place as Dad was prepared for surgery. Meanwhile, Julien and Greg remained behind, facing the realities of the store and what lay ahead.

Julien inhaled deeply, trying to maintain composure as he turned to Greg. 'I honestly don't know how I'll manage everything,' he said, his voice barely above a whisper.

Greg stepped closer, his determination solid. 'You focus on your dad and Emily right now. We'll handle the store.'

Epilogue

The General Store

As Charlotte swept the last of the biscuit crumbs into the waste bin, the quiet hum of the General Store enveloped her. The atmosphere felt lighter, almost buoyant. Greg arranged the fresh-baked goods he'd picked up in Maryborough that morning on the counter, his usual easy smile spreading across his face.

'Hey, Charlotte,' he said, glancing over at her. 'Did you hear about the croissants?'

Charlotte rolled her eyes playfully. 'Let me guess, someone else is questioning their authenticity?'

'More than one someone,' he replied with a chuckle. 'A couple of old-timers were discussing how Julien was the croissant king.'

Charlotte laughed, shaking her head. 'Well, we're doing our best here. It's hard to compete with someone like Julien.'

Just then, Amelia breezed into the store, her preschool bag slung over her shoulder. 'You two lovebirds having a moment?' she teased with a raised eyebrow.

'Just discussing pastry politics,' Greg shot back, grinning. 'You know how serious that can get around here.'

'Very serious,' Amelia agreed, leaning against the counter, her expression shifting to one of genuine concern. 'How's Dad doing? Still improving?'

'Yes, Mum called an hour ago,' Charlotte replied, her voice softening. 'Mum's with him as much as she can be. Grandmère and Papa are in Brisbane, too. I think it's helping them all to have each other's company.'

'Good. I hope he knows how many people care about him,' Amelia said, a hint of worry etched in her features.

'He definitely does,' Greg assured her, stepping closer to Charlotte's side. 'And the whole town is rallying behind you guys. Business has been brisk because of it.'

Amelia smiled, but then a playful smirk crossed her face. 'So, when do we get to hear all the romantic details from you two? Have you already picked out your wedding venue?'

Charlotte felt her cheeks heat up. 'Amelia! Oh, please! Not here!'

'I think it's sweet,' Greg interrupted, tightening his arm around Charlotte's waist. 'But I think we'll hold off on wedding plans until we've settled your dad's health concerns.'

'Aw, how practical of you!' Amelia laughed before changing the subject. 'I have to head back to the preschool soon, but let me know if you need extra hands in the store later. I can swing by.'

'Will do,' Charlotte said warmly. 'Thanks for always helping out.'

As Amelia turned to head out, Greg leaned down and whispered to Charlotte, 'Let's take a quick breather in the back. I need a minute away from all this—and I think you do too.'

Charlotte smiled, her heart lightening, and she nodded. They slipped out to the back of the store, leaning against the cool brick wall.

'Thank you once again for helping,' Charlotte murmured, resting her head on Greg's shoulder. The worry of recent events began to lift ever so slightly.

'It's not a chore, Charlotte,' he replied, warmth flooding through him as he squeezed her tighter. 'I'm doing it because I love you—and I'm going to love your family too.'

She looked up at him, her smile radiant as they shared a quick kiss, a promise of their bond growing stronger.

'Ready to head back?' he asked, brushing a strand of hair behind her ear.

'Almost. Just give me a second,' she said, enjoying the moment.

As they walked back into the store, Greg's eyes opened wider when he spotted his parents inside. 'There's Mum and

Dad!' he exclaimed.

Charlotte turned and smiled, knowing Greg hadn't seen them in a couple of weeks. 'They must've come to visit,' she said, returning his enthusiasm.

Greg approached them, his heart full. 'Hey! It's great to see you both!'

'Greg, sweetheart!' his mother said, pulling him into a tight embrace. 'You've been doing so much. We're proud of you.'

'Thanks, Mum,' he said, his voice muffled against her shoulder. When he finally pulled back, he glanced at Charlotte, who was watching the family reunion with affection.

'Greg has really helped, you know,' Charlotte said with a smile. 'With everything going on, we wouldn't have managed without his help.'

'Well, it's a team effort,' Greg insisted. 'And I'm loving it. I might change my mind about that law degree, Dad,' he teased.

'It's your choice, son. It's good to see you, Charlotte. I've heard so much about the wonderful job your brother is doing here.'

Charlotte smiled bashfully. 'We're just a quick fill-in until Dad is back on his feet and Julien comes home.'

'We're really pleased to hear your Dad's recovering well,' Greg's mother said.

Greg escorted his parents to a table by the window, the scent of fresh coffee and baked goods wafting through the air. He settled them comfortably before heading back to the counter to place their order.

'Two coffees and a slice of that chocolate cake with two plates, please!' he said to Charlotte, giving her a playful wink. 'Make sure to give them the good stuff.'

Charlotte laughed as she prepared the order, her heart warm

from the moment with Greg and the reassurance that her father was off the danger list. It was good to see his parents here, too. The only worry was Julien and whether he could convince Emily of the truth.

She paused for a moment, looking out over the main street of Duckinwilla Creek. The sun shone brightly, illuminating the familiar buildings and the gentle flow of life around her.

When Greg returned to her side, he noticed her gaze fixed outside. 'What are you thinking about?' he asked.

She turned to him, happiness almost overwhelming her. 'Just taking it all in, I guess. It feels . . . right being here. Coming home was the right thing to do. Dad's doing better, Mum's settled, and I think I'm here to stay.'

Greg put his arms around her. 'It's amazing how things have turned around. You should be feeling really happy right now.'

Charlotte nodded as a rush of love for this man flooded through her. 'I do. Your support has made all the difference, and everything has fallen into place. The store is thriving, and most importantly, I have you here with me.'

His gaze softened, and she could see the depth of his feelings in his eyes. 'We're going to build something beautiful together.'

She breathed in deeply, feeling light and hopeful. 'Whatever the future holds, I can face it with you beside me.'

'Absolutely,' he replied. He dropped a quick kiss on her lips. 'I can't believe we're here together.'

Greg's parents waved him over from their table. 'Where's our cake, lovebirds?' his mother called, a broad grin on her face.

'Coming, Mum!' Greg said, kissing Charlotte again before he picked up the order.

As he walked away, happiness suffused Charlotte. She was looking forward to her new future, side by side with the man she loved.

Secrets and Surprises

ANNIE SEATON

Duckinwilla Days: Book 2

Heartwarming and compelling tales of love, self-discovery, and second chances in the heart of rural Australia.

Chapter 1

Sydney

The late afternoon sun cast long shadows across Sydney's steel and glass towers, doing nothing to warm the chill that had settled in Julien Johnson's chest. His hands trembled as he stood by the floor-to-ceiling window outside Emily's apartment, waiting for her to emerge. She'd refused to let him inside, reluctantly agreeing to meet him in the bar next door instead. He'd never understood why she'd kept the lease when they moved to Duckinwilla Creek; she sublet it to one of her friends from uni. Now, staring at the urban sprawl below, so different from the open skies of home, he wondered if Emily had known all along their relationship wasn't as solid as he'd believed.

'I'll meet you down there in half an hour,' she said, but he didn't go down without her. As he leaned against the wall, his gaze kept returning to the three cardboard boxes labelled with his name in stark black marker sitting outside the door. Each box felt like another nail in the coffin of their relationship, telling him exactly how their talk was going to go.

Emily was going to put the skids under him.

The thought made his stomach clench. He wiped his sweaty palms against his jeans, determined to fight tooth and nail to keep her. At least she'd agreed to talk; she'd hung up on his calls and ignored his messages after everything had imploded at Charlotte's farewell party the night of Dad's heart attack.

Despite wanting to chase Emily as soon as she left, he'd succumbed to family pressure. He stayed at home for two weeks for two weeks and waited until the specialist advised that Dad's surgery had been successful and he would be coming home in a few days. Julien had no hesitation leaving the store in Charlotte's and Greg's inexperienced hands drove through the night, his mind racing faster than his ute on the quiet highway from Duckinwilla Creek to Sydney. The endless hours of driving had given him too much time to think, to remember, to regret. He hoped he could fix what had broken, but seeing those boxes—the last of their stuff they'd been about to move to their flat above the store—had shrivelled his hopes. When Emily refused to let him in, bile had risen in his throat.

The door opened with a soft click, and she stepped out. Her eyebrows arched when she saw him waiting, but he caught the slight tremor in her hand as she adjusted her handbag strap.

'You might as well take a couple of those boxes down now.' Her voice was ice-cold, but he heard the hurt beneath it. 'It's all your stuff.'

'I'd rather talk to you first.' His voice cracked on the last word.

She shrugged and walked to the lift, stabbing at the down button with more force than necessary. Her back was rigid as she turned away from him, but he noticed how she crossed her arms tightly across her chest as if holding herself together.

The tension in the lift was excruciating as they descended from the third floor. Emily stood beside him, close enough to touch but somehow further away than she'd ever been. The sweet fragrance of her perfume—vanilla and jasmine— transported him back to their flat above the store, where she'd transformed a bland, colourless space into their heaven. Julien remembered coming up after long nights working at the pizza oven in the General Store and how the aroma of Emily's cooking would greet him. He'd find her curled up on their soft couch with a book, looking up with that smile that made his heart skip. The flat felt wrong without her there now, cold and empty as though someone had switched off the sun itself.

'Emily...' he began, but she clutched her bag tighter, angling herself away from him in the confined space. Her knuckles were white against the leather strap.

The lift doors opened with a cheerful, mocking ding that echoed in the tense silence between them.

The bar was quiet this early; the after-work crowd hadn't yet descended from their glass towers. Emily marched past empty tables to the bar itself, claiming a steel stool with decisive movements that showed her anger. When Julien hesitated, eyeing a more private table tucked away in a corner, she cut him off.

'We don't need privacy, Julien.' The fluorescent lights caught the shine in her eyes. 'And if anything upsets me, I'll talk to the barman. This is going to be quick. I don't know why you came all the way to Sydney.'

His heart sank at her tone, so different from the warm voice that used to greet customers at the store. 'What would you like to drink?' he asked.

'I'll get my own.' She turned away, ordering a white wine while he asked for soda water, needing to keep his head clear even though drowning his guilt in something stronger was tempting. The city sounds filtered through the windows—car horns, construction, the rush of life continuing while his world fell apart.

'Emily, sweetheart, please listen—'

'Don't.' Her voice could have frozen Sydney Harbour solid. 'Don't call me sweetheart. Don't pretend this is something it's not.' She took a sharp breath. 'Don't make me remember how things were before you ruined everything.'

'Rowena is lying,' he said, the words tasting like ash in his mouth. Each lie felt like another betrayal, but he couldn't stop. His fingers tapped nervously against his glass. 'I went to school with her. She's always been a user. Why the hell would I look at her when I had you?' His voice cracked. 'She is *not* having my child.'

Emily's green eyes met his, sharp with disappointment but swimming with unshed tears. 'That's what hurts the most, Julien—the lies. You keep lying to my face, even now. I saw you talking to her late one night behind the store. I wasn't supposed to be there, but I forgot my phone and came down.' She gave a bitter laugh. 'Guess that's what they call karma.'

'She is *not* having my child. I'll do anything,' he heard the desperation in his voice and saw his hands shaking as he reached for her. 'I'll give up the store, move back to Sydney—'

'I don't want you in Sydney.' Emily's voice cracked like thin ice. 'I loved Duckinwilla Creek. I loved our life there. The community, the store, everything we were building together.' She brushed away a tear with an angry gesture. 'But I won't build a future on lies.'

The truth pressed against his chest, begging to be spoken. But fear held it back—fear of losing her completely. Each lie was another brick in the wall between them, but he couldn't stop building it, even as he watched it separate them forever.

'Please,' he whispered, his voice rough with emotion. 'Come home with me, Em. Believe me.'

'Why should I?' Emily stood, gathering her bag. Her perfume wafted around him one last time. 'I'm not even disappointed about what happened anymore. I'm more disappointed that you're not man enough to tell me the truth.' She finally looked at him properly, her beautiful green eyes swimming with tears. 'You've broken my heart, Julien. It's going to take me a long time to get over this. Please don't call me or text me again. And take your boxes when you leave.'

He watched her walk away—out of the bar, out of his life. The sound of her heels on the hardwood floor was like nails driving into the coffin of their relationship. The city sounds seemed to mock him through the windows, so different from the peaceful quiet of Duckinwilla Creek. He sat there, head bowed, before reaching for her abandoned wine and downing it in one go.

'Not a good outcome, by the look of things, mate,' the barman said sympathetically, polishing a glass with practised movements. 'Want another drink, mate?'

'Yeah,' Julien replied, guilt and regret settling in his gut like lead. 'Beer. A schooner. Thanks.' The afternoon sun slanted through the windows, reminding him of similar golden light in their flat above the store.

As the after-work crowd began to arrive, filling the bar with the buzz of city life, Julien thought about their time together. He thought about Emily's laugh, the way she'd throw her head back when something really amused her, her eyes alight with love for him. He thought about their flat above the store, how she'd made it feel like home with her little touches: the herbs growing on the kitchen windowsill, the soft throws on the couch, the photos of them together that he couldn't bear to look at now.

But most of all, he thought about truth and lies and how he'd chosen wrongly every time. The beer wouldn't wash away his regrets, but he ordered another anyway. Maybe if he drank enough, he could forget the look in Emily's eyes when she walked away. But he knew he never would; he loved her too much.

The garish city lights began to flicker on outside the bar, so different from the star-filled sky of Duckinwilla Creek, and Julien Johnson sat alone in a Sydney bar, drowning regrets as bitter as the beer in his glass.

Chapter 2

The floorboards of the old farmhouse creaked beneath Amelia Johnson's bare feet as she stumbled from her bedroom early on Saturday morning. Dawn light filtered through the lace curtains—Grandmère's handiwork, yellowed with age but still elegant—casting delicate shadows on the walls. Her head felt stuffed with cotton wool after another restless night; worry about Dad had threaded through her dreams.

She'd stayed up until after midnight working on the farm accounts, knowing Dad would ask about them the moment he got home from the hospital. The numbers had swum before her eyes, but she'd pressed on, just as she always did. Someone had to do it, and it wouldn't be golden boy Julien, currently chasing his heart in Sydney, or Lisette with her perfectly manicured nails and convenient excuses.

The old hallway creaked its familiar song—every board a childhood memory. There, the loose one that had betrayed her sneaking out at sixteen. Here, the dark patch where Guy had spilled Coke and blamed her. Each step was a timeline of the Johnson family history, written in worn timber and chipped paint.

'Really, Amelia?' Mum's voice sliced through the morning quiet before she even reached the kitchen.

Amelia rolled her eyes. *Here we go.*

'It's nearly seven. Lisette's been up since six helping me, and you're just rolling out of bed looking like that?'

Amelia squinted at the kitchen clock through sleep-heavy eyes: 6:50 am. She tugged self-consciously at Julien's old T-shirt, the hem almost touching her knees. Her dark curls—so like Grandmère's in the old photos at *Maison de Rêve*—stood up in wild directions, a stark contrast to Lisette's perfect chignon.

Her sister perched at the kitchen table like a fashion magazine come to life in coordinating pastel workout wear, sipping a kale smoothie. Her pristine lipstick hadn't left a mark on the glass. The morning sun caught the highlights in her expertly styled hair—*naturellement* blonde, as she liked to remind everyone, although Amelia remembered differently.

'Morning, *ma petite soeur*,' Lisette hummed, the French endearment rolling off her tongue with practised precision. Their grandmother would have winced at the affected accent—Grandmère's French was as rich and authentic as her cooking, not this pallid imitation.

'Morning.' Amelia sat and reached for the coffee pot. 'I was up late doing the farm accounts. Oli asked me to update the spreadsheets since they haven't had time.' The "they" encompassed the two of her brothers who worked on the farm and somehow always had more important things to do.

Her mother whisked the coffee pot away before Amelia's fingers could close around it. 'You don't have time for breakfast. Your father's coming home this afternoon, and this place is a disaster.' Ellen's hands trembled slightly as she clutched the pot. Amelia knew she was trying not to let her anxiety show and to cover it with criticism. 'You can help me clean the windows. Go and get changed.'

Amelia sat there for a moment and then pushed herself to her feet. Through the kitchen window, she watched her mother's silhouette move back and forth attacking invisible dirt with the same intensity she'd always applied to raising her children. The morning air carried the sharp scent of Dettol.

Lisette rose from her chair with balletic grace, water bottle in hand. 'I've done my bit. I'm off to my Pilates class.' She paused in the doorway, a picture-perfect smile playing on her lips. 'Have fun, Cinderella.'

The childhood nickname stung more than it should have after all these years. Amelia turned to go change, her bare feet silent on the floorboards that had witnessed so many similar moments. The house smelled of cleaning products and anxiety, every surface reflecting her mother's need to control what she could when so much was beyond her reach.

The kitchen gleamed almost aggressively—copper pots hung in perfect alignment, each countertop stripped of its usual comfortable clutter and polished to a shine that would have impressed even Grandmère, who'd always said a clean house was next to godliness, but a loved house was heaven itself.

'I'll do the bedrooms, Mum,' Amelia called, hurrying through the living room before her mother could object. The space had already been transformed—Dad's old leather armchair positioned precisely to catch the morning light and overlooking the shed where the boys would be working. Fresh flowers—Lisette's artistic touch with Amelia's carefully tended blooms—filled Grandmère's crystal vase on the coffee table.

The farmhouse had grown like a family tree, branching out over three generations since Papa had built it for his bride. The original structure held the kitchen and living room, solid as the foundation of their family. The stairs to the second floor—added when Mum and Dad's family expanded beyond the ground floor's capacity—creaked under Amelia's feet, each step carrying memories.

There's where Guy had fallen and knocked out his front tooth, crying until Amelia gave him her dessert. There's where Julien had hidden her favourite doll during his nasty phase and where Charlotte had found it weeks later, dusty but intact. The upstairs hallway stretched before her, its walls a gallery of family history—mostly the boys' triumphs, she noted with a familiar pang. There she was in the corner, gap-toothed and awkward at seven, half-hidden behind Oliver's football victory.

Amelia worked methodically through the rooms, trying to lose herself in the rhythm of cleaning. The spare bedroom had been prepared for Dad's return with the kind of attention to detail that would have made Grandmère proud—fresh linens crisp as new paper, his favourite books arranged just so, curtains drawn back to welcome the morning light.

By noon, when Lisette finally returned smelling of expensive perfume and virtue, the house sparkled like Grandmère's crystal. Every surface gleamed, and every window caught the light like diamonds. Mum stood in the kitchen, reviewing their work with the critical eye that had always seen Amelia's flaws more clearly than her efforts.

'The bathroom cabinet in the spare room is a mess,' Ellen said, focusing on Amelia while adjusting a dish towel for the third time. The lines around her mouth seemed deeper than ever, her hands betraying a slight tremor. 'And there's dust on the top of the refrigerator.'

'I just cleaned both of those,' Amelia protested, but Ellen had already turned away, fussing with Lisette's flower arrangement.

'Leave it,' Lisette said, her voice carrying that particular tone of martyred patience that made Amelia's teeth ache. 'I'll fix it later.'

Something snapped inside Amelia like a string pulled too tight. The weight of always being the one who was never quite good enough, of watching her brothers sail through life on waves of maternal approval while she paddled in their wake, of

Lisette's perfect daughter act—it all became too heavy to carry.

'I'm going into town,' she announced, grabbing her jacket. The leather was soft with age, a hand-me-down from Charlotte that felt like a hug. 'Now.' Neither her mother nor sister responded, but Mum's look of disapproval spoke volumes in the silence. 'I'll come back and see Dad later.'

The drive into town was like a breath of fresh air. The country road wound through sun-dappled cane fields waving in the stiff early afternoon breeze, past the old Miller place where Tommy Miller had given her that first awkward kiss behind the shed, around the bend where Julien had crashed Dad's truck and somehow emerged without a scratch or consequence—another golden boy miracle.

The family's General Store sat in the heart of town, the warm sandstone walls mellowed by time and weather. Hanging baskets spilled over with a riot of colour—Grandmere's contribution to Julien's store's transformation. Tourist season was in full swing; the street was clogged with rental cars sporting plates from all over Australia, and the footpath teemed with visitors clutching shopping bags and the new tourist guide that Julien had designed.

The original bell above the door jangled as she pushed inside. The air was rich with coffee, and the aroma of freshly baked cinnamon scrolls wrapped around her like Grandmère's embrace. Greg worked the elaborate espresso machine, his movements precise and graceful as he crafted elaborate coffees for a line of waiting customers. He caught her eye and winked, then gestured to indicate he'd have her usual ready in five. For a school teacher, he'd adapted to barista life with impressive speed when Julien had shot off to Sydney chasing Emily.

Charlotte emerged from behind a display of local honey, her

face lighting up at the sight of her sister. The honey jars caught the light, amber and gold. 'Thank God,' she said, pulling Amelia into a quick hug that smelled of coffee and comfort. 'Save me from the locals. Mrs. Henderson just spent twenty minutes explaining why our jam selection isn't authentic enough.'

The store had evolved under Julien's vision when Dad had gone back to the farm. Gone were the dusty shelves of practical farming supplies that had been their father's domain, replaced by artisanal foods, local crafts, and the coffee bar that had become the town's unofficial community centre. But touches of the past remained—the original tin ceiling still gleamed overhead like beaten silver, and the hardwood floors still creaked in exactly the same places they had when Amelia and her siblings played hide and seek between the aisles.

'I had to come to town. Mum's driving me crazy. A cleaning frenzy,' Amelia said, following Charlotte behind the counter. Greg appeared with her coffee—oat milk latte with an extra shot, decorated with a perfect foam heart that eased her emotional turmoil slightly.

'You look like you need this,' he said with the kind of understanding that made it clear why Charlotte had fallen for him, then turned back to the growing line of customers.

Charlotte leaned against the antique cabinet they used for gift wrap storage—another of Grandmère's pieces given new life. 'So, Dad's still coming home today?'

'Yes, this afternoon. We've been cleaning all morning. Apparently, I still can't clean a mirror properly, but Lisette's flower arrangements are worthy of the Louvre.' The bitterness in her voice surprised even her. 'The boys haven't come out of the fields all morning. Not even for smoko.'

'Ah, so Mum's on the warpath.'

'Well and truly. I'm over it.'

'Grandmère always said Mum has impossible standards, but only for certain people.' Charlotte's voice was gentle as spring rain. 'Remember how Grandmère used to sneak you cookies when Mum sent you to your room? She'd say, "The baby of the family should be spoiled, *pas vrai*?" And she handled Mum by equally spoiling all of us grandkids rotten and telling Mum off in rapid-fire French,' Charlotte laughed, the sound warm as the summer sunshine. 'Poor Mum. No wonder she's cranky most of the time.'

'But you've always been Grandmère's favourite, Charlie.'

Charlotte smiled, the expression so similar to Grandmère's that it squeezed Amelia's heart. 'We've always had a special relationship, but Grandmère doesn't have favourites. She just sees what each of us needs.'

'I'm thinking of moving out,' Amelia said.

Charlotte was quiet for a moment, watching Greg manage the morning rush with the same steady patience he brought to everything. 'Maybe it's time you did,' she said finally. 'You've been doing a lot, I've noticed. The boys never help, and Lisette's too precious to get her hands dirty, and Mum . . . well, she's not going to change.'

'I feel guilty even thinking about it. With Dad coming home...'

'They'll figure it out. Or they won't, and maybe that's not your problem anymore.' Charlotte squeezed her arm, her grip warm and sure. 'You know what Grandmère will say.'

'"*Ma petite*, sometimes you have to break their hearts to save your own,"' Amelia quoted.

'Yep, you got it. There's a queue at the counter,' Charlotte said, straightening up. 'I'll go help. Take your coffee in the office if you can't find a table outside.'

Through the store's windows, Amelia watched tourists photographing the building's historic façade, smiling at the blend of old and new that Julien had created. The morning's tension began to ease from her shoulders. Maybe it was time for her to find a path away from family expectations and habits, to find her own way rather than being there for everyone else.

Greg appeared with another coffee; this one was decorated with an intricate leaf pattern that put the store's hanging baskets to shame. 'On the house,' he said. 'You looked like you could use a refill.'

'My hero,' Amelia smiled, and for the first time that day, it felt genuine. She waited until Greg moved back to the espresso machine, and Charlotte gestured to a table where customers were leaving. Amelia walked over and sat, cradling her perfect coffee. Charlotte joined her moments later with her own cup, inhaling the rising steam.

'I need a break,' she sighed, stretching her feet under the table. 'I thought teaching was a hard profession. Now, I have to soak my feet most nights!'

'I wonder how much longer you and Greg will be filling in,' Amelia wondered aloud. 'Have you heard from Julien in the last couple of days?'

Charlotte's face tightened, her usual cheerful expression slipping. 'Yes, I'm a bit worried about him, actually. He really doesn't sound like himself.'

'Has he talked to Emily?'

Charlotte shrugged, absently stirring her coffee until the foam heart dissolved into meaningless swirls. 'I don't know.

He's keeping pretty close-lipped about everything.'

Amelia hesitated, then lowered her voice to match the hushed tone of family secrets. 'Do you think . . . he and Rowena?'

The question hung between them as Charlotte glanced around to make sure no locals were within earshot, although in Duckinwilla Creek, walls had ears and gossip travelled faster than light. The store had been Julien's responsibility since their father stepped back—this temporary arrangement with Charlotte managing things was supposed to be just that: temporary. But Julien's behaviour had been erratic over the past three weeks, and now he was in Sydney.

'It's a pretty big accusation if there's no truth in it,' Charlotte said finally, her voice equally quiet.

'I think Lisette knows something,' Amelia said, watching her sister's reaction carefully. 'Our family dynamics are complicated enough without adding scandal to the mix.'

Charlotte sighed and shrugged her shoulders with her palms upturned—a gesture so like Grandmère's that Amelia hid a smile. 'I'll give him a call later. Maybe he'll actually answer this time.' She paused, then added, 'I just wish he'd talk to one of us properly.'

'What about Emily?'

Charlotte shook her head, her expression troubled. 'I don't want to interfere and put any pressure on her. I mean, none of us know what really happened. And really, it's not our business.'

Greg appeared with another coffee for Amelia. 'Thought you might need another shot before heading back to the farm,' he said with understanding in his dark eyes.

'I'll be buzzing, but your latte art is getting seriously impressive,' Amelia said, admiring the design that seemed too pretty to disturb.

Greg grinned, his eyes crinkling at the corners. 'I even surprise myself sometimes.'

Charlotte looked up at him with such open affection that Amelia felt a familiar ache in her chest.

'You're a man of hidden depths, *mon coeur*,' she teased, the French endearment flowing naturally without Lisette's affected polish.

Greg leaned down and kissed her softly. 'Come and help me at the counter for a while. Julie's about to take a break.'

Charlotte stood and spoke to Amelia before she followed him to the coffee machine. 'Don't rush. Take as long as you like.'

Amelia watched them, joy for her sister mixing with a quiet envy in her chest. They made it look so easy—loving someone and being loved in return—no criticism, no impossible standards, just acceptance and warmth.

She took another sip of her perfect latte, letting the bittersweet feeling wash over her.

Maybe it was time for more than just moving out.

Maybe it was time to start looking for her version of what Charlotte and Greg had found—a love that felt like coming home to yourself.

She dug into her handbag and read the romance novel that she'd added before she left home.

A girl could dream.

Chapter 3

The General Store

Charlotte pressed her forehead against the modern drinks' cabinet, letting the cool glass ease her growing headache as she listened to Julien. The afternoon sun filtered through the front windows, the dust motes dancing as customers moved through the store and making the local honey glow like burnished bronze. The January heat had hit Duckinwilla Creek with a vengeance, and even the store's air conditioning units struggled to keep the temperature bearable. Tourists and local customers drifted in throughout the morning, their complaints about the heat and humidity mingling with hopeful murmurs about the thunderheads building to the east. Charlotte pressed the phone to her ear, glanced across, and a brief smile tilted her lips at Amelia, sitting demurely as she read her novel.

'You're not listening to me, Charlie.' Julien's voice crackled through the phone, thick with something that wasn't just static. 'Emily didn't just leave that night. She looked at me like . . . like I was poison.'

The store's air conditioning unit chose that moment to give up entirely, surrendering to the heat with a loud thump that echoed Charlotte's sigh. She watched a bead of condensation race down the fridge's glass door.

'Then tell me what really happened,' she said, keeping her voice low. The mid-afternoon emptiness of the store felt wrong—in Duckinwilla Creek, walls had ears, and secrets didn't stay secrets for long. 'Tell me the truth because something's not adding up, Jules. Rowena's been—'

The sharp crack of a bottle hitting something hard cut through the line. 'Don't.' Julien's voice had gone dangerously quiet. 'Don't say her name. It makes me see red.'

The store's bell jangled as Mrs Henderson bustled in, her basket overflowing with garden vegetables—the scent of sun-warmed earth and the sweetness of freshly pulled carrots wafted through the store.

'Morning, love!' Mrs Henderson called out, making her way to the counter with what looked like half her garden's produce. 'Got some zucchini that'll make your eyes water. Thought you might want them for the store.'

'Just a tick, Mrs H!' Charlotte called out, then dropped her voice again. 'Jules, you can't hide in Sydney forever—Dad's home. Guy stopped by with him on their way back from the hospital, and Dad's asking questions. He wanted to know where you were and why Greg and I were in the store. Do you want to say hello to him? He's sitting with Amelia near the counter.'

'No. Not yet.'

'When are you coming back?' Charlotte tried to keep curiosity from her voice.

'I can't come back yet.' The words fell like stones. 'Not without Emily.'

Before Charlotte could respond, a commotion at the door drew her attention. Local CWA president Daphne Carmody and secretary Joyce Mason swept in like storm clouds, their footsteps like approaching thunder. Behind them, moving slower but with lips set in a straight line, came Mum, with Lisette hovering in the doorway.

'Got to go,' Charlotte whispered into the phone. 'But this isn't finished. I'll call you later.'

The silence told her Julien had already hung up.

'Hugo. Why didn't you come straight home?' Mum stood with her hands on her hips.

'That's a fine welcome, love.' He reached out and took her hand. 'How did you know I was here?'

'Joyce rang me. She saw you get out of the ute, and she wanted to know if you were going to take the store over again.'

Amelia and Charlotte looked at each other, Amelia's lips twitching

'No, that wouldn't be wise when I'm supposed to be recuperating. Guy stopped to get some milk for the shed,' their father said. 'He had to go to the rural store too. He'll be back in a minute.'

'Amelia could have brought it home. She might as well make herself useful.' When Mum looked away and leaned down to kiss Dad's cheek, Amelia pulled a face at Charlotte.

'Come on, we'll get you home now. You can come in the station wagon with us. Lisette can drive; she's waiting at the door. You should have let me come and pick you up at the hospital.'

'Guy was a good help, and you have enough to do with an invalid coming home.' Dad stood and smiled at Amelia. 'I'll see you at home later, love.'

He stood and moved slowly and carefully between the aisles, each step measured. Charlotte held back tears. Dad's heart attack and the subsequent bypass surgery had aged him a decade in less than a month, turning his hair to silver and deepening the lines around his eyes. He'd lost that awful grey colour and finally had some colour back in his cheeks. Mum hovered nearby, her spine ramrod straight and shoulders tense beneath her crisply-ironed cotton blouse, her lips still pressed into such a thin line they'd almost disappeared. The tiny muscle at the corner of her jaw twitched with barely contained anxiety—a tell-tale sign Charlotte and her siblings had learned to watch for since childhood.

Before Dad reached the door, Daphne Carmody's voice cut through the morning air like a scythe. 'Did you hear about young Rowena?' Her eyes glittered with the peculiar joy of the bearer of bad news. 'Saw her at the medical centre this morning. Looking quite green around the gills, poor dear.'

The temperature in the store seemed to drop ten degrees despite the broken air conditioning. Charlotte saw her mother's hands clench together.

'Some people,' came Lisette's voice from the front door, sharp as broken glass, 'should mind their own business.'

'Lisette.' Their mother's warning came too late.

Amelia stood and moved closer to Charlotte, the sisters unconsciously presenting a united front as Lisette walked to the counter.

'What?' Lisette shook her head; her designer workout clothes were out of place with the groceries and local produce. 'Are we still pretending we don't know what's going on? That Julien hasn't—'

'That's enough, Lisette.' Their father's voice carried authority despite his weakened state. But Charlotte didn't miss how he gripped the counter's edge, his knuckles white with the effort of standing straight.

The door's bell jangled again, this time admitting Greg with young Tommy Fischer, both of them red-faced and panting. 'Sorry to interrupt,' Greg said, his teacher's instinct for tension making him step between Lisette and their father, 'but we've got a situation down at the creek. Fischer's cattle are breaking through—'

'Of course they are,' Lisette cut in. 'Because why should anything in this family go right? First, Charlotte turns up, then Julien ruins everything with Emily, then Dad's heart attack, and now—'

'I said that's enough!' Their father's shout rattled the honey jars on their shelves. In the sudden silence that followed, they all heard his laboured breathing.

'Hugo.' Their mother's voice carried decades of practice at handling family drama. 'Come with me to the car *now.*'

But he waved her off, his face flushed darker. 'No. No more sitting down. No more tiptoeing around this.' He turned to face them all—customers included—one hand still braced against the counter. 'This stops now. The gossip. The secrets. All of it. I'm taking control as of this minute.'

Charlotte held her breath. The sun bored through the side window, turning the store into a greenhouse of trapped heat and rising tension. The air conditioning unit sputtered back to life with a wheeze, stirring the dust motes once again. Outside, a cockatoo screamed a warning to its mates, and somewhere in the distance, a mob of galahs took flight, their wings catching the sun like pink lightning.

'Dad,' she started, but he cut her off.

'I know what's happening with Rowena.' The words fell into the silence like pebbles in a still pond. 'I know what Julien's supposed to have done. And I know why Emily left. Guy filled me in on the way home.'

Mrs Henderson's basket of vegetables hit the floor with a thud, scattering zucchini across the weathered floorboards. No one moved to pick them up.

'Hugo, please,' their mother whispered. 'Your heart—'

'My heart's been breaking watching this family tear itself

apart. We've sorted Charlotte's situation, and I will not let this gossip hurt our family any more. Lisette, go and wait in the car. And apologise to Mrs Carmody on your way out.'

Lisette scuttled to the door and mumbled a soft 'sorry' on her way past the CWA president. She stood at the door and waited.

'Ellen, help me outside, please.' Her father straightened to his full height, and for a moment, Charlotte saw the man he'd been before she'd left for university—the man who'd built the store into what it was today while honouring everything Papa and Grandmère had created, the man whose reputation for fairness matched Papa's in every way. 'No more secrets. No more surprises,' he said as he walked to the door, holding Ellen's hand

Charlotte looked around at her family—at Lisette's perfectly made-up face now showing cracks of genuine emotion, at their mother's barely hidden fear, at their father's determined stance that couldn't entirely hide his trembling hands.

And finally, at Greg, who'd chosen her and become a part of this messy, complicated family despite everything.

And she'd said she'd ring Julien back. Maybe she'd just forget it as Dad had instructed.

Chapter 4

Charlotte's hands shook as she tried to fit the key into the lock at the bottom of the stairs leading to the flat above Duckinwilla Creek General Store. Throughout the week, she and Greg stayed here in the spare room and then spent the weekends at *Maison de Rêve*. She'd been holding it together since her family had left, leaving some curious customers behind. Alone now in the early evening, her composure was cracking.

She paused halfway up the creaky wooden stairs, pressing her fingertips to her temples where a headache had been building since morning. Somewhere in her bag, her phone buzzed again. She ignored it.

The scent of garlic and herbs drifted down the stairwell: Greg had come upstairs while she rang off the till and was cooking because he knew when she needed some TLC. He'd probably heard her dropping things and muttering to herself through the floorboards as she'd packed up. Her shoulders, tight from hours of inventory, relaxed slightly.

When she pushed open the door, he was already holding out her favourite mug, the chipped blue one Julien had salvaged from the store's stockroom during the renovations. He'd remembered it had been her favourite and put it aside. Her brother wasn't all bad; he'd just made some stupid decisions. For someone who ran the store so well, he couldn't do a thing right in his personal life.

Steam curled from the mug as she took it, and she inhaled. 'Chamomile tea. Thank you. You're a darling.'.

'That bad?' he asked quietly.

Charlotte dropped her bag onto the sofa. 'You saw half of it. And yes, Dad lost his cool.'

Greg leaned against their kitchen counter, giving her space even as his eyes stayed steady on her face. 'And the rest? Because I know you too well, there's more.'

'Mum called at morning tea time. She's barely speaking to anyone, but apparently, she can find the energy to tell me I need to "fix things" with Julien.' Charlotte's laugh came out bitter. 'Because clearly, I'm the only one who can convince him that camping outside his ex-girlfriend's house is not a healthy coping mechanism.'

'While also solving the mystery of the missing receipts, stopping Amelia from emptying her bank account on a one-way ticket to Japan, and probably bringing about world peace?' Greg's voice was gentle, but there was an edge there— protectiveness, she knew.

Charlotte opened and closed her fists; a nervous habit she'd developed in the weeks since they'd cancelled their France tickets to stay and help after Dad's heart attack.

Greg crossed to her then, but instead of hugging her, he took her hands, stilling the anxious movement. 'Remember what you told me the day we decided to stay? That some things matter more than Paris in the spring?'

'I remember. I also remember we had actual tickets.' She met his eyes. 'Sometimes I wonder if we made the right choice. If any of the family would do the same for us.'

'They would. They're just—' Greg paused, choosing his words carefully. 'Lost right now. All of them. And they're looking to you because you're calm, logical and settled.'

'And tired,' Charlotte whispered.

'I know.' Greg's thumb traced over her fingers. 'That's why you have me. To look out for you, as I know you would do for me.'

'I just don't know how to stop being the one they all lean on,' she admitted finally. 'I wish Guy and Oliver would step up sometimes.'

'Maybe you don't have to stop. Maybe you just have to learn to lean back occasionally.' Greg pulled her close, and she let herself sag against him, just for a moment. 'And maybe, when things settle, we book new tickets. See if France is still waiting.'

'With our luck, Amelia will probably be living overseas by then,' Charlotte said, but there was a ghost of humour in her voice.

'Then we'll have a tour guide.' Greg pressed a kiss to her forehead. Charlotte felt something loosen in her chest; not all the stress, but enough. Enough to face another day of being there for everyone. Enough to keep trying to guide her family back to solid ground. Enough to believe that someday—soon—France would still be there, waiting.

'I do love you, Greg,' she said softly. 'Even when I'm terrible company.'

'Maybe we could go to France for our honeymoon?' he said against her cheek

Charlotte pulled away and stared at him, one hand over her mouth. 'Um, is that a proposal.'

'Would you rather I got down on my knee.'

'Yes, yes, yes,' Charlotte cried, her voice breaking

'On my knee?' Greg smiled at her

'No silly, that was yes, I'll marry you.'

Greg cupped her face in his hands, his thumbs brushing away the happy tears that had started falling. When his lips met hers, Charlotte tasted salt and sweetness and promise. It was a gentle kiss, tender and lingering, full of all the words they didn't need to say. When they finally pulled apart, Greg rested his forehead against hers, both of them sharing the same happy smile.

Outside, the sun set over Duckinwilla Creek, the sky firing in golden and purple hues, bathing them in a soft light. Charlotte was sure tomorrow would bring new family battles to fight. But right now, with Greg's love, her strength grew.

Chapter 5

Duckinwilla Creek - the next day

The heat was relentless for the third day in a row and pressed against the windows of Lucy Lou's Hair Salon like a thick blanket. The heat of the hair dryers running inside created fog on the glass, turning the main street of Duckinwilla Creek into a shimmering mirage. Inside, the air conditioning hummed a steady balance to the whir of hair dryers, keeping the small salon cool and inviting. Amelia sank into the familiar black leather chair, breathing in the mingled scents of hair products and Lucy's signature lemon candles. Lucy's salon and Jerry's barber shop next door had been fixtures in town since before Amelia was born, the cheerful yellow walls witnessing countless transformations, hearing many secrets and inspiring fresh starts.

Her reflection stared back at her from the mirror—sensible Amelia Johnson, youngest daughter of the town's most talked-about family, wearing the same safe, practical hairstyle she'd had since the first year of high school. The wooden floor creaked beneath the chair as Lucy Lou adjusted its height, her collection of bangles jangling their familiar melody.

'Right then, love.' She draped the cape around Amelia's shoulders with the flourish of someone who understood that a hair appointment was as much for counselling as transformation. 'What're we doing today? The usual trim and natural colour?' Her bright eyes met Amelia's in the mirror, reading something in her expression that made her pause.

Amelia's fingers twisted in her lap beneath the cape. 'Actually, I want something different.' The words came out barely above a whisper, then stronger: 'Something wild.'

Lucy Lou's eyebrows shot up, her red and silver-streaked curls bouncing as she leaned in. 'Wild? You?' She lowered her voice conspiratorially. 'Now, this I have to hear about.'

In the background, the usual suspects—Mabel, Edna, and Doris—sat under their dryers like a Greek chorus, curlers in their hair as per their weekly ritual. Their magazines didn't entirely hide their interest. Amelia caught Mabel's reflection, pretending not to listen, and something inside her snapped.

'I'm just . . . over it, Lucy Lou.' The words felt like a confession. 'So tired of being the sensible one. The reliable one. The daughter who never causes trouble.' She met her own eyes in the mirror, seeing Grandmère's determination there. 'The one who keeps the peace and picks up the pieces and pretends everything's fine.'

The hairdresser began sectioning Amelia's hair; her practised movements were gentle but sure. 'I hear your dad came home from hospital yesterday.' Her fingers worked through a knot with infinite care. 'He's doing well, isn't he?'

'Yes, thank God.' Amelia's throat tightened. 'But that's just one crisis sorted. Everyone in my family's gone mad. Properly mad.' The words tumbled out like water through a broken dam. 'Lisette and Charlotte are at war over the store accounts—as if spreadsheets matter more than being sisters. Julien's off in Sydney making an absolute mess of his life with this Rowena business, breaking Emily's heart in the process. And the boys?' She gave a laugh that wasn't quite steady. 'Guy and Oliver are so buried in the farm; it's like they've forgotten how to have an actual conversation that isn't about cattle or cane or the new mango trees.'

'Sounds like you need more than just a haircut, love.' Lucy Lou reached for her collection of hair dyes, fingers hovering over the bright colours like an artist selecting paints. 'How about we start with some electric blue? Really give the old biddies something to talk about besides your family drama? It'll take a while because I'll have to bleach it first and then dry it so there's no moisture at all, and then I'll put the colours on.'

'Colours?'

'Yes, I think you need a rainbow.'

Amelia caught sight of the trio under the dryers, quickly hiding behind their magazines. 'Why not? 'It's my day off from pre-school, and you know what. I'd rather sit in here all day than be at home.' The recklessness in her voice surprised her. 'They're already talking about us anyway. Did you know Lisette called me Cinderella yesterday? As if I'm the one choosing to stay home and help!' Her voice cracked slightly. 'I'm supposed to love my family, but sometimes . . . sometimes I don't even like them very much.'

'Did you ever think maybe that's normal?' Lucy mixed the bleach with deft rubber-gloved fingers, the pungent smell of chemicals mixing with the lemon candles. 'Loving family doesn't mean you have to love everything they do.'

'But that's just it—I feel guilty even thinking that way.' Amelia watched in the mirror as Lucy began applying the white paste. 'Sometimes I dream about just . . . leaving and going somewhere where nobody knows the Johnsons, where I don't have to be the sensible boring one, where I could just be . . . me. Whoever that is.'

'Where would you go?' Lucy's question held no judgment, just genuine curiosity.

'Melbourne, maybe. Or overseas. I love the assistant work at the preschool, and the director said there's a traineeship coming up soon. I could get my qualifications, and having a pay packet now, I could maybe find a rental in town.'

'Good luck with that,' Lucy Lou said dryly. 'Since your brother's been president of the Chamber of Commerce, there's no rentals available. Everyone wants to live in Duckinwilla Creek now!'

'I could teach English in Japan. I've always wanted to go there. Live in a tiny apartment where no one expects me to cook family dinner or mediate arguments or pretend I don't see what's happening with Julien and Rowena.' She met Lucy's eyes in the mirror. 'Is that awful of me? To want to run away when Dad's just gotten home from hospital?'

'Of course not, darling.' Lucy's voice was gentle but firm. 'Sometimes you need to step away to find yourself. Look at me—I didn't always have red hair and own this salon, you know. I spent three years in Perth doing whatever took my fancy before I came back here. The Creek'll always be here if you want to come back.'

From under the dryers, Mabel's voice carried clearly, 'Did you hear about Julien and that Rowena girl? I heard—'

Before Amelia could hear the latest gossip about her brother, Lucy Lou placed a roll of foil over her head, making her giggle. 'Now sit tight for forty-five minutes, and I'll get the three oldies done,' she said quietly.

'I heard that, Lucy Lou. I'm the same age as you,' Mabel yelled over the noise of the dryer. 'We started school the same day.'

'We'll have none of that today, thank you very much, Miss Mabel, who I *didn't* go to school with. ' Lucy Lou rolled her eyes. 'You've got the wrong person, Mabel. You're getting forgetful.' She winked at Amelia before going over to the dryers, her sharp voice cutting through the gossip like a knife. 'This is a drama-free zone.'

Half an hour later, the three biddies had been permed, primped, and paid their bills.

Lucy Lou chuckled as they walked out. 'I charged them more today. It's about time I put my rates up. Now, come on over to the basin, and we'll get started.' Her eyes were kind as she reached for the orange dye. 'Now, how about we add some sunset red to go with that blue? Really give them something to talk about?'

'Do your worst.' Amelia settled back, feeling the tension lifting from her shoulders. 'At least this drama will be *my* choice.'

As Lucy Lou worked, transforming Amelia's sensible brown hair into a riot of colour, they talked about everything and nothing: Lucy's plans to expand the salon, the secret notebook of travel plans hidden under Amelia's bed, the way the town seemed to be shrinking around her lately.

'You know what the real problem is?' Amelia said as Lucy added the final touches of emerald green. 'Everyone's forgotten how to be happy. It's all business and drama and responsibilities. Even the boys used to be the life of every party, and now they're in bed by nine because they have to check the irrigation system at dawn. When did we all get so . . . old? We're not kids anymore.'

'Sounds like the Johnsons need a good shake-up,' Lucy said, stepping back to admire her work. 'Maybe your new look will start the trend. Sometimes, the smallest rebellions make the biggest waves.'

Amelia stared at her reflection, barely recognising the woman in the mirror with the striking blue, green and red-orange hair. It should have looked ridiculous, but somehow it worked, like a tropical sunset captured in hair, like courage made visible. It reminded her of the paintings in Grandmère's parlour, all bold colours and brave strokes, all bold colours and courageous strokes, like those Cézanne paintings she'd studied in art class at high school.

'Oh, that'll give them something to talk about, all right.' She touched one of the blue streaks gently. 'I'm not sure what Grandmère will say, though.'

'You might be surprised.' Lucy's smile was knowing. 'That grandmother of yours wasn't always the proper lady she is now. Ask her about Paris sometime.'

'Don't tell me Grandmère shares her secrets with you?'

'My clients all know I'm like a confessional. What I hear stays here.'

Amelia giggled. 'You need a sign on the wall that says that.'

As Lucy Lou removed the cape, Amelia stood, feeling much better. Through the window, she could see the main street and all the usual activity.

'Thanks, Lucy.' She reached for her purse, but the words meant more than gratitude for a hair colour. 'For everything.'

'Any time, love.' Lucy winked. 'Now go on out there and show them what a Johnson looks like when she decides to write her own story.'

Stepping out into the heat, Amelia felt the sun on her new hair and smiled. Maybe it was time for all of them to remember how to live a little, to find joy in something besides duty and tradition. And if they couldn't figure it out, well . . . Japan was looking better every day.

Or perhaps, she thought, touching one vivid streak, the real adventure would be staying and being brave enough to change things from within. After all, Grandmère always said the strongest trees bend with the wind but keep their roots deep in home soil.

That thought stayed with her as she walked down the street, aware of the stares and whispers, but for once, not minding them at all.

Chapter 6

Sydney

The lights of the city contrasted with the fading light of the evening; the summer air was heavy with the scent of jasmine from her balcony pots. Emily sat cross-legged on her bed; Julien's letter balanced on her knee. Fifteen stories below, the city thrummed with life—car horns, the wet swoosh of tyres on rain-slicked streets, the constant noise of city living. It was so different from the cicada-song evenings near the General Store, where silence was soothing, and the stars looked close enough to touch.

Her fingers traced the edge of the envelope for the hundredth time, following the familiar loops of Julien's handwriting. She'd read the letter twice already, each word a careful mix of apology and plea, but never entirely stepping into truth. The paper was starting to show wear at the creases, just like her resolve was beginning to fray at the edges.

'Damn you, Julien Johnson,' she whispered, surprised by the crack in her voice. The photo on her nightstand caught her eye— her and Julien at her cousin's wedding, his smile so open then, so unguarded. His arm was draped casually around her shoulders, that easy smile she'd fallen for lighting up his face. They'd been so happy then before the complications of Duckinwilla Creek had slowly choked the trust from their relationship.

Her phone lit up. Another message from him. Her heart jumped—traitor—even as her mind steeled itself against whatever new variation of almost-truth he'd crafted. She swiped it away, but her hand shook. That was the worst part—how her body still responded to him, how her heart still lurched at his name, how some silly part of her wanted to pretend everything was fine.

More apologies, more promises, more carefully constructed sentences that danced around the truth about Rowena. Emily's thumb hovered over the notification before she swiped it away. Even seeing his name on the screen made her heart race, and that scared her more than anything.

The balcony beckoned. Emily stepped out into the jasmine-scented night, gripping the railing as Sydney sparkled below. She missed the Creek's quiet evenings, the way sunset painted the cane fields gold, and how life moved to a gentler rhythm there. But most of all, she missed the Julien she'd first met. Now she wasn't sure where home was anymore. Part of her still longed for the quiet evenings above the General Store, just the two of them, lost in their own world.

But another part of her, the part that had built a successful teaching career and a life in Sydney, knew she couldn't go back. Not without honesty. Not without trust.

'You're stronger than this,' she told herself firmly, gripping the balcony railing.

The memory of their first meeting flooded back—that breezy autumn evening at her friend Sarah's party when Julien's laugh had cut through the crowd with a joy of life she couldn't ignore. He'd been so genuine then, so unguarded. Their first date by the river had been a comedy of errors, with him forgetting the corkscrew for the wine and attempting to open the bottle with his car keys. They'd ended up sharing a warm beer and watching the sunset, and it had been perfect because it was real.

That's what was missing now—reality.

Her phone rang, startling her from her thoughts. It was

Margot, Julien's Grandmère. Emily's stomach clenched.

'Emily, darling,' Margot's warm voice carried across the line. 'I hope I'm not disturbing you.'

'No, not at all,' Emily replied, though her grip tightened on the phone. The lie came quickly. When had she started doing that, too? She knew what was coming.

'I've been thinking about Julien,' Margot began carefully. 'He's not handling this well, *ma cherie*. Maybe if you just talked to him—'

Emily closed her eyes, fighting the urge to give in. 'I can't, Margot. Not yet. Not until he's ready to be honest with me.'

'But surely, what happened before you were properly together—'

'It's not about what happened,' Emily cut in, surprising herself with her firmness. 'It's about the lies. Every time he denies it, every time he looks me in the eye and swears nothing happened with Rowena—that's what I can't handle. I'd forgive him in a heartbeat if he'd just tell me the truth.'

'Silence stretched between them before Margot spoke again. 'Maybe you're just too different. City girl and country boy...'

The words stung, but Emily recognised the attempt to shift blame. Of course, a grandmother would be loyal to her own. 'This isn't about geography, Margot. It's about honesty. And that matters everywhere.'

After ending the call, Emily returned to her desk and pulled out a fresh sheet of paper. Her hand was steady now.

Julien, I've read your letter, and I understand you're sorry for hurting me. But sorry isn't enough this time. I need honesty from you. Not because I want to punish you, but because without truth, there can't be trust. And without trust, there can't be us.

I've forgiven what happened with Rowena. We weren't committed then, and mistakes happen. What I can't forgive is the lying. Every denial, every avoided truth, every carefully constructed story; they're all just more walls between us.

I'm scared, Julien. I'm scared because part of me wants to pretend everything's fine, to come back to the Creek and fall back into our life together. But I'd be betraying myself if I did that. I deserve better than half-truths and careful omissions. We both do.

Until you're ready to be honest – really honest – I need to step back. Not because I don't love you, but because I do. And sometimes loving someone means being strong enough to wait for them to find their way to the truth.

Emily

She sealed the letter quickly before she could change her mind. Tomorrow, she would post it, and then . . . then she would focus on being strong enough to stand by her decision. The hardest part wasn't writing the letter or even sending it; it was knowing that Julien might show up at her door with those eyes that made her want to believe every word he said and have the strength to stand firm.

Emily returned to the balcony, letting the night air cool her flushed cheeks. Below, the city pulsed with life. She thought of Duckinwilla Creek, of the way the stars seemed to hang lower there, of the quiet nights and simple pleasures. She missed it all: the store, the community, the sense of belonging she'd found there. But most of all, she missed the Julien she'd first fallen in love with, the one who hadn't yet learned to hide behind careful words and half-truths.

'Come back to me,' she whispered to the night. 'Not just physically. Come back to being the man who didn't need to lie.'

Until then, she would stay here in her Sydney apartment, with its city views and familiar sounds, rebuilding her life day by day. Because love without trust was like a house built on sand. Emily had worked too hard to let everything she believed in wash away. It was time to look for some casual work at a school; her time in the north was over.

The city lights blurred as tears filled her eyes, but she didn't wipe them away. Sometimes, crying wasn't a sign of weakness—sometimes, it was proof that you were strong enough to feel everything and still stand your ground.

Chapter 7

Late afternoon sun caught the blue and orange streaks in Amelia's newly dyed hair. Charlotte had asked her to drop in to the store on the way home and help out for a couple of hours, and Amelia was happy not to go home. She was restocking the confectionery shelves when Lisette's sharp intake of breath made her turn around.

'Good Lord, what have you done to your head?' Lisette stood in the doorway, her designer sunglasses pushed up into her perfectly styled blonde hair. 'You look like a tropical parrot that had a fight with a paint tin.'

Amelia straightened, squaring her shoulders. 'It's called expressing myself, Lisette. Not that you'd understand anything that doesn't come with a designer label.'

'Expressing yourself?' Lisette's laugh was brittle. 'Bub, you look ridiculous.'

'Don't call me that!' Amelia snapped, slamming a box of chocolate bars onto the shelf. 'I'm not twelve anymore, and you don't get to treat me like I am.'

'Well, you're certainly acting like it. What's next? A tattoo? A belly ring?'

'Maybe! And you know what else?' Amelia turned to face her sister fully. 'I'm thinking of leaving. Getting out of this gossip-soaked town and away from our crazy family.'

Lisette's perfectly shaped eyebrows rose. 'Oh, *la la*? And where exactly are you planning to go, *Bub*?'

'Japan!' The word burst out of Amelia like she'd been holding it in forever. 'I can work in a school there. Live somewhere nobody knows the Johnsons or cares about their drama.'

'Japan?' Lisette's voice dripped with derision. 'You don't even speak Japanese!'

'I can learn! Anything's better than staying here, watching everyone fall apart. Julien's lying to everyone. You and Charlotte are still at each other's throats over the store accounts, and I'm sick of it!'

Their argument was interrupted by the jangle of bell over the door. Rowena stepped inside, hesitating when she saw the two sisters. She looked smaller somehow, less sure of herself than usual.

Lisette's attention snapped to Rowena like a shark scenting blood. 'Well, well. Speaking of family drama.'

Amelia moved to leave, but Lisette grabbed her arm. 'Oh no, stay, *Bub*. You want to run away to Japan? First, let's hear what Rowena has to say about why our family's in such a mess.'

'Lisette, don't—' Rowena started, but Lisette cut her off.

'No more games, Rowena. Tell us why you've been targeting Julien. Is it the Johnson money? The family name?'

Rowena's face crumpled. 'You don't understand. None of you do! You've never had to worry about paying bills or wondering if you'll ever get out of this town!'

'So, you thought you'd use my brother as your ticket out?' Lisette's voice was razor-sharp. 'Force him into a wedding with your lies?'

'No! I love Mason!' Rowena burst out, tears springing to her eyes. 'He's everything to me. But he's a cane worker, and I'm scared. Scared of struggling forever, of never having more than what we've got right now.'

'Who's Mason?' Amelia had watched the scene unfold, her anger fading as she recognised something in Rowena's desperation—the same need to escape that had driven her to

Lucy's salon.

'My boyfriend.'

'So, what's the story with Julien?'

Rowena looked cornered. 'It doesn't matter now.'

'It does, you know. You can't build a future on lies,' Amelia said quietly. 'Trust me, I've watched Julien try.'

Rowena sank onto a nearby chair, her defences crumbling. 'I know. I thought . . . I thought if Julien chose me, all my problems would be solved. I could have forgotten Mason. The Johnsons have everything: money, respect, security. But I've made such a mess of everything.'

'You're not the only one,' Lisette said, her voice softening slightly. 'This whole situation . . . it's hurt everyone. Emily, Mason, Julien. None of them deserved this.'

'I never meant for it to go this far,' Rowena whispered. 'It wasn't a total lie. Julien—'

'We don't need the details,' Lisette said sharply.

Rowena shook her head. 'I just wanted a chance at a better life. But now I might lose Mason forever.'

Amelia touched her newly coloured hair, thinking about choices and consequences. 'Sometimes we hurt the people we love most when we're trying to protect ourselves.'

Lisette shot her a look, something shifting in her expression. 'Is that why you want to run away to Japan? To protect yourself?'

'I want to *find* myself,' Amelia corrected her. 'Away from all this drama and expectations. I love our family, but sometimes love isn't enough.'

Rowena wiped her eyes. 'That's what I thought too. But running away doesn't solve anything. Whether it's being pregnant, dressing in designer clothes, or flying off to Japan—

we're all just trying to escape our fears.'

The three women fell silent. The store was empty. Outside, the resident flock of galahs swooped past, their raucous calls breaking the tension.

'So, what are you going to do?' Lisette finally asked Rowena.

'Tell the truth. All of it. Mason deserves that much.' Rowena stood, squaring her shoulders. 'I need to stop trying to be something I'm not.'

Amelia felt something settle in her chest; not peace exactly, but understanding. 'Maybe we all do.'

Lisette reached out, touching one of the blue streaks in Amelia's hair. 'You know, it's actually starting to grow on me. Very . . . you.'

'Don't get soft on me now,' Amelia said, but she was smiling. 'I'm still thinking about Japan.'

'I know you are, Bub—sorry, Amelia. But maybe make sure you're running towards something, not away from it.'

'You're getting wise in your old age,' Amelia teased.

'Old, I'm not even twenty-one yet!'

The shop bell jangled again as Rowena left, seeming a little more settled.

'Why do you think she came into the store?' Lisette wondered aloud.

'To buy something, I guess. Didn't you see her face when she saw both of us?'

'I did.' Lisette stretched onto her toes.

'You were hard on her, but at least it made her think about her choices.'

'Want to get Friday night fish and chips for dinner and sit by the creek?' Lisette asked suddenly. 'We can talk about this Japan thing properly. No judgment, I promise.'

Amelia hesitated, then nodded. 'Okay. But if you call me Bub one more time, I'm dyeing your hair while you sleep.'

They waited until Charlotte came back in from the storeroom. Her eyes widened as she saw them chatting civilly.

'We're off to Mac's Fish and chip shop for tea. Do you want anything?' Amelia asked.

Charlotte shook her head. 'No, thanks. Greg's cooking tonight.' Her smile was dreamy; she'd been off with the fairies most of the day.

'Where is Greg? Isn't it time to shut up shop?'

'He went to Dunmora to visit his parents this afternoon, and then he was going straight back to *Maison de Rêve*.'

Amelia giggled as they stepped out into the cooling evening air.

'What?'

'Look at the colour of the sky. Same pink as my hair.'

The sun was setting behind the cane fields, painting the sky in shades that almost matched Amelia's hair.

'I can't wait to see Mum's reaction,' Lisette said smugly.

'Don't start. I don't have to eat tea with you,' Amelia snapped.

'Well, you know she's going to go off.'

'I'm eighteen. I can do what I like now.'

'Did you see Charlotte and Greg before he left this morning?' Amelia asked as they walked toward the takeaway store. 'They were practically dancing around each other in the stockroom.'

Lisette's nose wrinkled slightly. 'Oh yes, the great romance of Duckinwilla Creek. It's like watching a Mills and Boon novel come to life.'

'You're just jealous,' Amelia said, grinning at her sister's obvious discomfort.

'Jealous? Of what? The way they finish each other's sentences? The sickeningly sweet looks? The constant hand-holding?'

'The fact that they're happy,' Amelia said softly. 'That they found each other without any drama or complications. I do hope they get engaged soon.'

Lisette was quiet for a moment, her heels clicking on the pavement. 'I did see Greg helping Charlotte with the monthly accounts yesterday. He brought her coffee and sat there for two hours, just . . . being there. Who does that?'

'Someone in love,' Amelia replied.

'At least some things in this family worked out right,' Amelia said, pushing open the door of Mac's café.

They joined the queue at the counter. Lisette studied the menu on the board above them with unnecessary intensity.

'You know,' she said finally, staring at the board. 'I always thought I'd be the first one to find that. The whole happy-ever-after thing.'

'You're always out with someone, though.'

'Yes, but they don't want me,' Lisette protested. 'They're chasing the idea of me. The Johnson name, the family business. No one brings me coffee and just sits with me.'

Amelia reached across the table, squeezing her sister's hand. 'Maybe because you don't let them.'

'Maybe,' Lisette admitted. 'But it's easier this way. Safer. Look at what happened with Julien and Emily.'

'Is that why you're so hard on everyone? Because you're scared of getting hurt?'

Lisette's perfectly made-up face softened. 'Is that why you

want to run away to Japan? Because you're scared of staying?'

'Touché,' Amelia laughed. 'Look at us, the Johnson sisters. One hiding behind her designer clothes and make-up, one hiding behind crazy hair dye, and Charlotte—'

'Charlotte just being Charlotte in love,' Lisette finished. 'Growing up away from us.'

They ordered their takeaway and found a table near the creek where a soft breeze ruffled the water, their conversation flowing easier than it ever had.

'You know,' Lisette said, holding up a chip, 'if you really want to go to Japan, I could help you. Look for some language courses, find out what qualifications you need and how you can get them, whatever you need.'

Amelia looked at her sister in surprise. 'Really? No lecture about family duty?'

'Maybe watching Charlotte and Greg has taught me something. Sometimes, you have to let people find their own way.' Lisette smirked. 'Even if that way involves ridiculous hair.'

'Don't start,' Amelia warned, but she was smiling. 'Tomorrow, we have to deal with this Rowena situation.'

'And Julien, and help Charlotte at the store and make sure Dad really is okay.' Lisette sighed. 'But tonight, maybe we can just be sisters.'

'Sisters with great hair,' Amelia corrected, making Lisette laugh.

'One sister with great hair, one with a tropical disaster on her head,' Lisette teased. 'But yes, just sisters.'

They grinned at each other, the warm evening around them like a cocoon. Outside, Duckinwilla Creek settled into its nightly routine, but for once, neither sister was in a hurry to rejoin it.

Chapter 8

Lisette woke to the sound of Amelia singing in the shower— some pop song massacred with deliberate cheerfulness. She rolled over, burying her face in her pillow to hide her smile. The memory of last night still felt fragile, like a soap bubble that might burst if she looked at it too directly: sitting by the creek with her little sister, really talking for the first time in years.

Her phone buzzed—another message from Charlotte about the store's accounts. Lisette started to type her usual sharp response, then stopped and deleted it. She thought about what Amelia had said about hiding behind designer clothes and cutting remarks. Maybe it was time to try something different.

Coming in early to help with those numbers.

She hit send before she could second-guess herself. The bathroom door opened in a cloud of steam, and Amelia emerged, her blue and orange hair wrapped in one of Mum's best white towels.

'You're going to give Mum a heart attack with that towel,' Lisette said, but without her usual bite. 'The dye will stain it.'

'Already checked. It's colourfast now.' Amelia flopped onto Lisette's bed, damp and warm. 'What are you doing today?'

'Store accounts with Charlotte.' Lisette watched her sister's eyebrows rise. 'What? I can be helpful.'

'I know you can. You just usually choose not to be.'

The words should have stung, but they didn't. Maybe because Amelia said them without judgment, just stating a fact like commenting on the weather or noting the time.

'Well, people can change.' Lisette sat up, reaching for her hairbrush. 'Speaking of which, I did some online research.

There's a language school in Brisbane that offers intensive Japanese courses. Three months, live-in accommodation included.'

Amelia went still. 'You're serious about helping me?'

'Of course, I am.' Lisette focused on brushing her hair, not meeting her sister's eyes. 'But you have to be serious too. No more spur-of-the-moment fixes like—' she waved her brush at Amelia's hair '—this.'

'Hey, I love my hair!'

'And I love that you love it,' Lisette surprised herself by saying. 'But Japan isn't a hair appointment. It's your life.'

Amelia was quiet for a moment, picking at Lisette's duvet cover. 'You know what scares me most? That I'll get there and fail. That everyone will say, 'I told you so,' and I'll have to come crawling back.'

Lisette set down her brush. 'Then don't fail.'

'That simple, huh?'

'No.' Lisette turned to face her sister properly. 'But you've got something now you didn't have before.'

'What's that?'

'Me.' She shrugged at Amelia's startled look. 'And Charlotte. And even Greg, probably, since he's practically family now. We've got your back.'

Amelia's eyes filled with tears. 'When did you get so nice?'

'Don't spread it around. I have a reputation to maintain.' Lisette stood, moving to her closet. 'Now, help me pick something to wear suitable for accounting.'

'Everything you own is suitable for everything,' Amelia groaned, but she got up to look. 'You're like a walking designer catalogue.'

'Yes, well...' Lisette fingered the silk of her favourite

blouse. 'Maybe it's time I learned to be comfortable in something less perfect.'

'Lisette Johnson, was that personal growth I just heard?'

'Shut up and help me choose.'

They settled on a simple sundress—still designer but softer than Lisette's usual armour-like blazers and pencil skirts. As they headed downstairs, Amelia surprised her by linking their arms.

'You know,' Amelia said as they walked into the kitchen. 'I might wait on Japan—just until things settle here. I want to see how this new sister thing works out.'

'Good.' Lisette squeezed her arm. 'Because I'd miss you, you tropical disaster.'

'I'd miss you too, you designer snob.'

Oliver was already at the kitchen table, hunched over his breakfast and scrolling through what was probably a weather app on his phone. He looked up as they entered, though his eyebrows lifted slightly at their linked arms.

Their mother set down her coffee, eyes widening at their easy smiles. 'Well,' she said carefully, 'this is new.'

'Not new,' Lisette corrected, reaching for the coffee pot. Then, unable to resist, she peered over Oliver's shoulder. 'Please tell me you're looking at something more exciting than rainfall predictions.'

'Mango market prices, actually,' Oliver muttered, tilting the phone away from her. 'Some of us have real work to do.'

'Oh yes, because managing the store isn't real work.' Lisette ruffled his hair as she passed, knowing it would annoy him. 'When was the last time you went on a date, dear brother? Or are you married to those cane fields?'

'Leave him alone,' Amelia said, but she was grinning. 'Not

everyone needs to be seen at every social event in a hundred-kilometre radius.'

Oliver shot her a grateful look, then did a double-take at her hair. 'Speaking of being seen, did your head fight with a paint factory?'

'You're about twelve hours too late with that line,' Amelia said, stealing a piece of his toast. 'Lisette already covered the tropical parrot references.'

'At least I got out of bed after dawn to make jokes,' Lisette said, sliding into her chair. 'Unlike some farmers I could mention.'

'I've only been up since four,' Oliver protested. 'Some of us actually work for a living instead of just ordering people around in designer heels.'

'Children,' their mother warned, but there was a slight hint of a smile on her face. A slight hint. It had been a while since their bickering had this much fun to it.

'You know,' Lisette said thoughtfully, stirring her coffee, 'if you let me set you up with Sarah from the bank—'

'No,' Oliver cut her off. 'Absolutely not. The last time you played matchmaker; I ended up stuck at dinner with someone who thought cane was just something you put in wicker furniture.'

'Your standards are impossible,' Lisette sighed dramatically. 'So, she just needs to know the difference between sugar cane and bamboo?'

'And understand agricultural futures, irrigation systems, and sustainable farming practices,' Oliver added seriously.

'Good lord, it's a date, not a job interview,' Lisette groaned.

Later, driving to the store with takeaway coffee balanced carefully beside her, Lisette thought about changes—how they could happen in an instant, like Amelia's hair, or slowly, like the growing peace between sisters. She thought about Charlotte waiting at the store with her quiet determination. About Greg's patient presence and Julien's messy absence. About Rowena's desperate grab for security and her own carefully constructed walls.

Her phone buzzed with a text from Amelia: **Found some online Japanese lessons. Want to help me practise tonight?**

Lisette smiled, typing back: **Only if you help me learn to be less perfect.**

Deal, came the reply. **But I'm not dyeing your hair.**

Thank God for small mercies, Lisette sent back and then added, **Love you, tropical disaster.**

The response was immediate: **Love you too, designer snob.**

Pulling up outside the store, Lisette caught sight of her reflection in the rear-view mirror. It showed the same perfectly styled hair and the same flawless makeup. But something was different. Something in her eyes, maybe. Or something in her heart.

Change, she was learning, didn't always need to be as dramatic as blue and orange hair. Sometimes, it was as simple as letting down a wall, brick by careful brick, until you could finally see what was on the other side.

Chapter 9

The morning rush at *Bean There Coffee* was in full swing, and Emily's fingers ached from tamping coffee grounds. A month ago, she'd been helping run a successful family business in Duckinwilla Creek. Now, she was making five different complicated coffee orders for suited-up bankers who couldn't even be bothered to look up from their phones when they ordered. She'd barely had a spare moment to look at the casual vacancies; the sooner she could get back into teaching the better. She'd kidded herself that working in a coffee shop would be like working with Julien at the General Store.

Boy, had she been wrong.

'Large soy cappuccino, extra hot, no foam!' The order barker, Kelly, called out. 'And hurry up with that banking order; they called twice already!'

Emily bit back a retort. At the General Store, she'd managed inventory, handled accounts, and made decisions that actually mattered. Here, she couldn't even suggest a more efficient way to handle multiple orders without Kelly reminding her she was "just a barista."

The bell above the door chimed, and Emily's heart stopped. She didn't need to look up to know who had just walked in—after months together, she'd know Julien's footsteps anywhere. She ducked behind the massive espresso machine, grateful for once for its bulky presence.

Through the steam and chrome, she caught glimpses of him. He looked terrible: unshaven, with dark circles under his eyes, and his usually neat clothes rumpled. The sight made her chest ache, but she pushed the feeling away, focusing on the banking order. Large flat white, two sugars. Skim latte, extra hot.

Macchiato, no sugar...

'Hey there, coffee girl.'

Emily looked up to find herself face to face with a tall guy in board shorts and a tank top, salt-crusted hair falling over one eye. He leaned against the counter, flashing what he clearly thought was a winning smile.

'Can I help you?' Emily asked, keeping her tone professional.

'Definitely. How about your number for starters?' He grinned wider. 'I'm Micko. I've seen you here before, I always wanted to say hi.'

'No, you haven't. I've just started here and I'm working,' Emily said firmly, turning back to the coffee machine. Fifth order: long black, no sugar.

'Come on, don't be like that. One coffee, that's all I'm asking. When do you get off?'

'She said she's working.'

Emily closed her eyes briefly at the sound of Julien's voice, low and firm. When she opened them, he was standing at the counter, and the difference between him and Micko was stark. Even rumpled and tired, Julien carried himself with the quiet confidence she'd first fallen for.

'Mate, I'm just being friendly,' Micko protested.

'No, you're harassing someone who's trying to do her job.' Julien's voice was quiet but carried an edge Emily recognised from dealing with difficult customers at the store.

Micko looked between them, understanding dawning. 'Oh, right. Should've known a pretty thing like you'd be taken. Whatever.' He pushed off from the counter. 'Your loss, coffee girl!'

The silence that followed felt thick enough to cut. Emily

focused on finishing the banking order, very aware of Julien's presence.

'Long black, please,' he said finally. 'And... Emily? Could we talk? I'm heading back to the Creek today, but I'd like to say goodbye properly.'

Emily's hands shook slightly as she worked the machine. 'Don't think you can soften me up just because you played white knight with surfer boy.'

'That's not what I'm trying to do.'

She risked a glance at him and immediately wished she hadn't. His eyes held the same warmth they always had, and for a moment, she was back in Duckinwilla Creek, planning their future together. She looked away quickly.

'Your coffee will be ready in a minute,' she said, her voice clipped. 'Have a safe trip home.'

'Em, please—'

'Kelly,' Emily called out, already backing toward the staff door. 'I need to check supplies. Can you handle the floor?'

She didn't wait for an answer, pushing through the door into the back room. She stood there in the semi-darkness, surrounded by boxes of coffee beans and paper cups, trying to steady her breathing. Through the door, she heard Kelly's voice: 'Sorry, she's busy with inventory.'

Emily pressed her hands against her eyes, fighting back tears. She'd thought she was stronger than this, thought she could handle seeing him. But one look, one moment of connection, and all her carefully built walls threatened to crumble.

'Get it together,' she whispered to herself. 'He hasn't changed. He's still lying.'

But as she heard the bell chime again, signalling Julien's

departure, she couldn't help but remember the way he'd looked at her, like she was still the most important thing in his world. She stayed in the storeroom until she was sure he'd left, then squared her shoulders and went back out to face another day of coffee orders and condescending customers.

At least making coffee was simpler than untangling her heart.

***

Julien stood outside *Bean There Coffee* for ten more minutes, his untouched coffee growing cold in his hands. The surge of anger he'd felt when that surfer guy started hitting on Emily had shocked him. He'd wanted to do more than just warn the guy off— he'd wanted to grab him by his faded singlet top and throw him out the door. The violence of that impulse scared him.

He dropped the full cup in a nearby bin and ran his hands through his unwashed hair. When had he become this person? Three days of stubble on his chin, rum on his breath from last night, and clothes that looked like he'd slept in them— because he had. His car was littered with takeaway containers and empty beer bottles.

'Come on, Em,' he muttered, watching the door. 'Just give me five minutes.'

Through the window, he could see Kelly efficiently working the coffee machine. No sign of Emily. He knew he was being a stalker; knew he should just get in his ute and start the long drive home. But the thought of leaving Sydney without fixing this made his chest tight.

A customer came out, the bell tinkling. For a moment, he caught the scent of coffee and vanilla – the same scent that used to fill their flat above the store when Emily baked. The memory hit him like a punch to the gut.

Just tell her the truth.

The thought surfaced like it had a hundred times before, but he pushed it away. If he admitted sleeping with Rowena, Emily would never forgive him. Better to keep denying it, go home, give her time to miss him. She loved him—he'd seen it in her eyes just now before she looked away. That had to be enough.

Didn't it?

After twenty minutes, it became clear Emily wasn't coming out. Julien walked the three blocks to where he'd parked his ute, each step feeling heavier than the last. The familiar blue Hilux looked out of place among the sleek city cars. Like him—a country boy pretending he belonged in Sydney. How had he ever thought he wanted to live here and be a chef? He must have had rocks in his head.

He climbed in, the leather seat creaking under him. The dashboard was dusty from his drive down, and Emily's water bottle was on the floor. He should clean the rubbish up, but somehow, he couldn't bring himself to erase that last trace of her.

The engine rumbled to life, and Julien pulled into the morning traffic. As the city buildings rose around him like a glass and steel prison, he thought about the long drive ahead. Two days on the road, just him and his thoughts. Maybe by the time he got home, he'd have figured out how to fix this mess.

You know how to fix it, a voice in his head that sounded suspiciously like Charlotte whispered. *Stop lying.*

'Shut up,' he muttered, turning onto the motorway that would take him north. The morning sun hit his windscreen, nearly blinding him. He fumbled for his sunglasses, finding them under a receipt from the bottle shop.

God, he was a mess. The rage he'd felt at the surfer, the drinking, the lying; it was all spiralling out of control. But the thought of losing Emily forever terrified him more than his own self-destruction.

The city thinned out around him as he headed north. Soon, the skyscrapers would give way to suburbs and then to the endless stretches of highway that would lead him home to Duckinwilla Creek. To the store, to his family, to all the complications he'd been trying to escape in Sydney.

But not to Emily.

He pressed harder on the accelerator as if he could outrun the truth trying to catch up with him. The ute's engine growled in response, eating up the kilometres. His phone buzzed; Charlotte was probably checking on him again. He ignored it.

Two days. Two days of driving through the countryside that would remind him of Emily with every turn. The roadside cafes where they'd stopped on their drive to Duckinwilla Creek that first road trip. The lookout where they'd watched the sunrise. The small towns where she'd insisted on trying every local bakery.

'She'll come back,' he told himself, merging onto the Pacific Motorway. 'Once she realises how much she misses the Creek. Misses me.'

But as Sydney disappeared in his rearview mirror, another thought surfaced, unwanted but persistent: What if she didn't? What if his lies had finally cost him the one person he couldn't bear to lose?

Julien cranked up the radio, trying to drown out his thoughts with country music. But every love song, every heartbreak ballad, just reminded him of what he was running from. And what he was running to.

His phone buzzed through the car speakers. Charlotte's name lit up the display. Julien hit the Bluetooth button on his steering wheel, grateful for the interruption to his depressing thoughts

'Hey, Charlie.'

'Jules? Where are you? Are you okay?'

'On the way back.' He squinted at a road sign as it flashed past. 'Just passed Wyong. And no, not really.'

'What's wrong? What's happened?'

'Nothing. I just thought...' He watched a flock of black cockatoos sweep across the highway. 'I thought if I denied it long enough, it would go away. That Emily would believe me eventually.'

'How's that working out?' Charlotte's tone was pointed but not unkind.

'About as well as you'd expect.' He managed a hollow laugh. 'I'm driving back to the Creek alone, aren't I?'

'Come home,' Charlotte said softly. 'We'll figure it out together. But Julien? No more lies. Promise me.'

He hesitated, watching the highway unspool before him like his own tangled web of deception. 'I'll try, Charlie.'

After they hung up, the highway stretched ahead of him, a ribbon of bitumen leading back to Duckinwilla Creek. Back to the mess he'd made. Back to a home that wouldn't feel like home without Emily in it.

He had two days of driving to figure out his next move. Two days to decide if he was brave enough to tell the truth or if he'd keep building his house of lies until it finally collapsed around him.

The sun climbed higher as he drove north, and somewhere behind him, in a Sydney coffee shop, Emily was probably already forgetting about their brief encounter. Probably laughing with customers, moving on with her life.

Julien pressed the accelerator a little harder as if the extra speed could somehow keep his world from falling apart.

Chapter 10

'You can't hide up here forever.' Charlotte's voice drifted up the narrow staircase to the flat above the store.

Julien stared at the ceiling, counting water stains. 'Not hiding.'

'Really?' Her footsteps creaked on the stairs. 'Because that's exactly what it looks like to everyone in town.'

'Since when do you care what everyone thinks?'

Charlotte appeared in the doorway, hands on hips. The gesture was so similar to their mother's that Julien had to look away. Empty bourbon bottles lined the windowsill where Emily's herb garden used to be. The sight made his stomach turn.

'Since Lucy Lou cornered me at the post office to ask if you were "having some sort of breakdown."' Charlotte crossed to the window, yanking open the dusty curtains. 'Since Dad's blood pressure went up again with the stress. Since you decided that sleeping off hangovers was better than facing what you did.'

Sunlight flooded the small room, highlighting empty takeaway containers and unwashed clothes. Julien squinted against the brightness, his head pounding. He couldn't remember when he'd last eaten anything that hadn't come in a plastic container.

'I didn't decide anything,' he said quietly. 'It just . . . happened.'

'Bullshit.' Charlotte's voice cracked. 'You chose to lie to Emily. You chose to mess around with Rowena. You chose to throw away everything good in your life because you were too scared to admit you were happy here.'

Down below, he could hear Greg working in the store—the familiar rhythm of the cash register, the murmur of conversation with customers. His store, once. His life, once. Now, the counter where Emily had worked by his side was someone else's.

'Grandmère wants everyone at their place tonight,' Charlotte said after a moment. 'And I mean everyone.'

Julien's stomach clenched. 'Everyone?'

'The whole family. Even Lisette's coming back from Brisbane.' Charlotte picked up a dirty mug, grimacing at the mould inside. 'Grandmère's making her *coq au vin*.'

'I can't.'

'You can.' Charlotte's tone left no room for argument. 'And you're going to the preschool to tell Amelia. I'm too busy to run down there while you're wallowing in your misery up here. It's time to man up, Julien.'

He shot up from the couch. 'What? No. Just text her.'

'Everyone else got the summons in person. You need to get out of this flat, and Amelia needs to hear it from family.' Charlotte's eyes softened slightly. 'Besides, those kids from the preschool miss their lolly man.'

The thought of walking through town, facing the whispers and stares, made his chest tight. But Charlotte was right—he couldn't hide forever.

'Fine,' he muttered. 'I'll go.'

'Shower first. You smell like the pub floor.'

The walk to the preschool was like running a gauntlet. Mrs. Thompson clutched her handbag closer when he passed. Old Mr. Peters suddenly found his shoelaces fascinating. Through the newsagent's window, he could see Lucy Lou's head bent close to Jennifer's, both of them watching him pass.

The preschool's bright murals and cheerful gate felt like another world. Through the fence, he could see Amelia in the playground, the newly dyed hair he'd heard about, living up to everything that had been said. She helped a small boy down the slide and looked up at his approach, her smile faltering slightly.

'Jules?' Amelia came to the fence. 'What are you doing here?'

'Dinner at Grandmere's tonight,' he said, his voice rough. 'Grandmere's orders.'

Before Amelia could respond, a small voice piped up: 'Mr. Julien! Did you bring lollies?'

He turned to find Sophie, one of his regular customers, looking up at him hopefully through the fence. Behind her, other children were starting to notice him, faces lighting up with recognition.

'Not today, sweetheart,' he managed.

'When are you coming back to the store?' another child asked. 'Mummy says the new lollies aren't as good as the lolly man's.'

Julien felt something crack in his chest. These kids, their simple acceptance, their uncomplicated joy in sugar and kindness—it was everything he'd walked away from.

'Soon,' he found himself saying. 'Maybe soon.'

Chapter 11

Julien left the preschool, the children's voices fading behind him. He walked slowly, seeing his hometown as a stranger might: the neat shopfronts with their striped awnings, the jacaranda trees dropping purple petals on the footpath, the way everyone seemed to know everyone else's business.

Rowena saw him and froze, her face flushing. 'Julien,' she said, her voice barely above a whisper. 'Can we talk? Please? Just for a minute.'

Through the salon window, Lucy watched, her rainbow-striped apron a stark contrast to her stern expression. Mabel from the newsagent had slowed her pace, probably already planning tomorrow's gossip.

'I don't think that's a good idea, Rowena.' His voice came out harsher than he'd intended. The sight of her made his stomach turn—not with desire anymore but with shame.

'I know I have no right to ask, but—' She wrapped her arms around herself. 'There are things we need to sort out. About everything.'

He pushed past her into Lucy's salon, the bell jingling overhead. The familiar scent of hair dye and coffee hit him— how many times had he ducked in here as a kid, stealing lollies from Lucy's jar while she did his mum's hair?

'Well, if it isn't the talk of the town.' Lucy's voice carried across the empty salon. 'Come to confess your sins?'

'I'm looking for Amelia,' he lied, though they both knew better.

'Your sister's got better things to do than clean up your mess.' Lucy crossed her arms. 'I've known you since you were knee-high to a grasshopper, Julien Johnson. Used to do your mother's hair every Friday, and she'd tell me about her dreams for you all.'

The mention of his mother made him wince. Every Friday, without fail, she'd sit in that chair by the window, planning futures for her children that none of them had quite lived up to.

'Charlotte, the responsible one. Lisette, the ambitious one. Oliver, steady as a rock. And you—you were supposed to be the heart of the family.' Lucy shook her head. 'What happened to that boy, Julien? The one who used to help old Mrs. James carry her groceries even when his friends teased him about it?'

Through the window, he could see his old life playing out without him; Charlotte and Greg at the store, Mrs. Thompson gossiping outside the post office, the school bus dropping off kids who would have once made a beeline for his lolly counter. The town moved on while he stood still, trapped in the mess he'd made.

'I don't know how to fix this,' he admitted.

'Maybe you can't.' Lucy's voice softened. 'Maybe some things aren't meant to be fixed. Maybe they're meant to be learned from.' She pointed her comb at him. 'Look in that mirror, Julien. Really look. Because right now, you're not just losing Emily. You're losing yourself.'

He forced himself to look— really look—at his reflection. Three days of stubble, shadows under his eyes, defeat was written in every line. Behind him in the mirror, Duckinwilla Creek went about its business, the afternoon light turning everything golden. He remembered other afternoons, standing behind the counter of his store, watching this same light paint Emily's hair copper as she laughed at his terrible jokes.

'The truth is,' Lucy said, 'you know Amelia understands Emily better. You need to talk to her because she understands you better. She sees the good in everyone, just like Emily does. And right now, you need someone to remind you that there's still good in you under all these lies.'

As he stepped out of the salon, Lucy's final words followed him: 'The truth might hurt, love, but lies will kill you slowly. Your choice which pain you want to live with.'

He walked slowly along Main Street with no destination in mind. Past the places that held his memories— good and bad. The store where he and Emily had worked side by side, the creek bank where they'd planned their future. The bench where he'd first noticed Rowena looking at him differently and made the choice that would cost him everything.

Rowena's accusation: the catalyst for him spiralling down.

Maybe Lucy was right. Perhaps some things couldn't be fixed. But maybe, just maybe, they could be rebuilt differently but stronger. Starting with dinner at *Grandmere's* and the truth he'd been running from for too long.

Lucy's words echoed in his mind all the way back to the flat. An hour later, showered, shaved, and wearing the only clean shirt he could find in his cupboard he didn't hesitate at the door to Jerry's Barber Shop; he just walked straight in. Jerry looked up, surprise flickering across his weathered face, but said nothing as he gestured to the empty chair.

Julien caught Lucy's approving nod through the salon window as he left half an hour later.

Chapter 12

The gravel crunched under Julien's feet as he walked up the long drive to his grandparents' new home. The French provincial house loomed against the darkening sky. Through the windows, he could see people moving and hear the murmur of voices and clinking of glasses.

Grandmère was waiting on the verandah, her petite figure straight as ever in her navy dress. The look she gave him stopped him at the bottom of the stairs.

'The others are in the kitchen,' she said quietly. 'Come with me.'

She led him around the side of the house to her rose garden. The air was heavy with their scent, mixed with coming rain. They settled on the old bench beneath the climbing Pierre de Ronsard roses, their pale pink blooms nodding in the evening breeze.

'Your grandfather built this bench when we lived at *Maison de Rêve*,' Grandmère said, running her hand along the weathered wood. 'Did you know why?'

Julien shook his head.

'Because I told him I needed a place to think. A place to make the hard decisions.' She turned to face him fully. 'Do you know what the hardest decision is, *mon petit*?'

'Leaving?' His voice was barely a whisper.

'*Non*.' Her voice sharpened. 'The hardest decision is staying. Choosing to face what you've done instead of running away. Choosing to be honest when lies would be easier.' She reached for his hand, her grip surprisingly strong. 'You are not the first person to make mistakes, Julien. But you might be the first in this family to let those mistakes destroy you.'

'I've ruined everything, Grandmère.'

'Perhaps.' She was quiet for a moment. 'Or perhaps you needed to break everything to see what was truly valuable. Tell me, when you were in Sydney, what did you miss most?'

The answer came without thinking. 'Sunday mornings at the store. The kids coming in after school. Emily's laugh when I'd try out new recipes...'

'Ah.' Grandmere's eyes were knowing. 'Not the excitement? Not the big city dreams?'

'No,' he admitted.

'Then perhaps you're not as lost as you think.' She stood, straightening her dress. 'But Julien? No more hiding in that flat. No more drinking instead of feeling. And no more lies— to yourself or anyone else. *C'est compris*?'

'*Oui,* Grandmere.'

'Good.' She cupped his cheek in her hand. 'Now, you will come inside. You will face your family. You will eat my *coq au vin*. And tomorrow, you will start cleaning up the mess you've made— both in that flat and in this town.'

Thunder rumbled in the distance as they walked back to the house. Through the kitchen window, Julien could see his family moving around: Charlotte leaning against Greg, Amelia setting the table, and his parents talking quietly in the corner. The sight made his chest ache with longing.

'They're still your family,' Grandmère said softly. 'Even when you don't deserve them.'

The first drops of rain began to fall as they climbed the stairs. Julien paused at the door, the warmth and light spilling out around him. Maybe Grandmère was right. Maybe staying was the hardest choice—but perhaps it was also the only one that mattered.

Chapter 13

Emily had been staring at her phone for the past hour, watching it light up with Julian's calls, each one sending a fresh wave of anger and disappointment through her chest. Outside, the city hummed with its usual energy, but up here on the fifteenth floor, Emily felt removed from it all, suspended in a moment of decision.

When the phone buzzed again, she finally answered it.

'Emily.' Julian's voice was strong. 'I need to tell you something.'

She closed her eyes, pressing her forehead against the cool glass of her window. 'Let me guess. You finally remembered you slept with Rowena.'

The sharp intake of breath on the other end told her she'd caught him off guard. 'How did you—'

'I always knew.' Emily watched a sparrow hop on her balcony, chasing the toast crumbs from her breakfast. 'But that's not really the point, is it?' She turned away from the window, pacing across her polished floorboards. 'The point is you lied to me when I asked you.''

The silence on the other end stretched out like the dusty roads of Duckinwilla Creek.

'Emily, I—'

'I already knew the truth when we talked, Julian.' Her voice came out steadier than she felt.

Another pause, this one heavy with realisation. 'Why didn't you tell me you knew?'

Emily sank onto her couch, running her fingers through her dark hair. The setting sun caught the rose gold watch Julian had given her for her birthday, making it glint accusingly. 'Because it happened before we were serious. Before you asked me to move to Duckinwilla with you. What happened with Rowena upset me, but we weren't exclusive then.'

'You... forgave me?'

'Yes.' Emily's throat tightened. 'But I can't forgive these lies. Every time you denied it, every time you looked me in the eye and swore nothing happened—that's what I can't get past.'

'I was scared,' Julian's voice cracked. 'When the pregnancy rumour started, I panicked. I thought if you knew about that night with Rowena...'

'You thought I'd leave you?' Emily stood up again, unable to keep still. 'I loved you, Julian. I left Sydney, my job, everything I've built here, to go to Duckinwilla Creek. For you. Because I thought we had something real.'

'We do have something real.' The desperation in his voice made her heart ache. 'Emily, please. I love you. I'll do anything—'

'Love isn't enough without trust.' She moved back to the window, watching the sky turn purple over the harbor. 'You've been lying to me for months. Not just about Rowena, but about everything. Every time you had the chance to come clean, you chose to lie instead.'

'I didn't want to lose you.'

'And how's that working out?' The words came out sharper than she intended, but she couldn't soften them now. 'You know what hurts the most? I would have understood. God, Julian, I grew up in a small town. I know how these things happen. One night at the pub, too many drinks, old history . . . I get it. But you didn't trust me enough to tell me the truth.'

She could picture him there, surrounded by the technicolour sunset of the Creek, the cane fields stretching out beyond the

General Store like a green sea.

'I've made such a mess of everything,' he said finally.

'Yes, you have.' Emily watched a ferry cut across the harbor, its lights bright against the darkening water. 'And I don't know how to fix it.'

'Tell me what to do. Please, Em. I'll do anything.'

She closed her eyes, remembering the way he'd looked at her the first time she visited the Creek, how he'd shown her his favourite spot by the water, the way he'd talked about their future. The memory hurt now, tainted by all the lies that had followed.

'I can't tell you what to do, Julian. That's part of the problem. You need to figure out who you want to be—the man who keeps lying to protect himself, or someone better than that.'

'I want to be better. For you.'

'No.' Emily's voice was firm. 'Not for me. For yourself. Because until you can be honest about who you are and what you've done, nothing between us will ever work.'

The silence that followed was broken only by the distant sound of kookaburras marking the sunset in Duckinwilla Creek.

'I'm so sorry, Emily.'

'I know you are.' She touched the cool glass of her window, remembering the heat of the Creek, the way the air shimmered above the cane fields. 'But sorry isn't enough this time.'

'Are you saying it's over?'

Emily watched her reflection in the darkening window, seeing the strength in her own eyes that had taken so long to find. 'I'm saying I need time. And you need to decide who you really are, Julian Johnson. Because the man I fell in love with wouldn't have kept lying to me, even when the truth got hard.'

She heard him draw in a shaky breath. 'I love you, Em.'

'I love you too.' Her voice softened. 'That's what makes this so hard. But I won't build a life on lies, Julian. Not even for you.'

After she hung up, Emily stood at her window for a long time, watching the city lights come alive below her. Somewhere in the distance, a train whistle echoed, reminding her of the whistle of wind through the cane fields. She thought about Julian, sitting outside the store in Duckinwilla Creek, watching the same stars beginning to appear in the darkening sky.

Love wasn't the problem. It never had been. But trust, once broken, was like the creek itself after a storm—it needed time to settle, to run clear again. Whether their love was strong enough to wait for that clearing, only time would tell.

Chapter 14

The late afternoon sun slanted through the windows of Rowena's flat, the harsh Queensland light making Julien feel exposed, vulnerable. He hadn't wanted to come here – facing Rowena meant facing all his mistakes, all his lies. But Charlotte had been insistent, and when his sister got that tone in her voice, resistance was futile.

'Sit down, Julien,' Charlotte commanded, and he found himself obeying automatically, sinking into the worn armchair. Rowena perched on the edge of her couch, Charlotte and Lisette flanking her like sentries.

'We need to sort this out,' Lisette said, her usual sharp edges softened by concern. 'All of it. No more hiding.'

Julien's chest felt tight. Emily's words from their last conversation echoed in his head: *I love you, but I can't trust you. The memory made him want to curl in on himself.

'I've already lost her,' he said, his voice hollow. 'What's the point?'

'The point,' Lisette snapped, 'is that you're not the only one who's been hiding from the truth. Are you, Rowena?'

Rowena twisted her hands in her lap. 'No,' she whispered. 'I'm not.'

The sound of heavy footsteps in the hallway made them all look up. Mason appeared in the doorway, his presence making the small flat feel even more confined. His face darkened when he saw Julien.

'What's this?' he demanded. 'Some kind of reconciliation?'

'Mason, wait—' Rowena stood, but he was already turning away.

'No need to explain. Guess the rumours were true after all.'

'They weren't,' Julien said quickly, suddenly desperate to clear at least this truth. 'None of them. That's why I'm here.'

What followed was a painful excavation of truth – the drunken night that meant nothing, the rumours Rowena had let spread, the lies Julien had told to protect himself. With each revelation, he felt the weight of his choices pressing down on him.

'I let you believe the baby might be yours,' Rowena admitted, tears streaming. 'Because I was scared of struggling, of never having security. I saw what the Johnsons had, and I... I was weak.'

'While I was working to build our future,' Mason said bitterly. 'Taking management courses, planning our life together.'

The words hit Julien like physical blows. He'd been so caught up in protecting his relationship with Emily, he'd never stopped to think about the damage his lies were doing to others.

'And Emily?' Charlotte's voice was gentle but firm. 'Why didn't you tell her the truth from the start?'

Julien ran a hand through his hair, feeling the familiar shame rise up. 'Because I was terrified,' he admitted. 'Every time I thought about telling her, I imagined her walking away. So I kept lying, thinking if I denied it long enough, it would just... go away.' He laughed bitterly. 'And now she's gone anyway.'

'You're going to give up that easily?' Lisette challenged. 'The brother I grew up with wouldn't have. Remember when you broke Mum's favourite vase? You owned up immediately, even knowing you'd be grounded forever.'

'I was a different person then.'

'No,' Lisette said firmly. 'You're still that person. You've just forgotten how to be brave.'

Her words struck something in him, a chord of truth he couldn't ignore. When had he become someone who hid from the truth? When had he stopped being the man Emily had fallen in love with?

'It's not too late,' Charlotte added softly. 'Emily loves you. She told you that herself.'

'She also said she couldn't trust me.'

'Then prove she can,' Rowena said unexpectedly. 'I'll write down everything, tell her the whole truth about what happened.'

'No,' Julien said, something shifting inside him. 'No more messages or written explanations. I need to face her myself. Tell her everything – not just about that night, but about how scared I've been, how lost.' He stood, suddenly certain. 'I need to fly to Sydney.'

'Now?' Charlotte asked, though she was already smiling.

'Now. Before I lose my nerve.' He turned to Rowena. 'I'm sorry for my part in this mess.'

'Me too,' she whispered. 'Now go fix things with Emily. And Julien? Tell her I'm sorry too.'

As he walked to his ute to head to Brisbane to catch the next flight to Sydney, his sisters followed him out. The late afternoon sun painted everything in shades of gold like the world was offering him one last chance to get things right.

'What if I go there and she still can't forgive me?' he asked, voicing his deepest fear.

'Then at least you'll know you were finally brave enough to try,' Lisette said, kissing his cheek. 'And Jules? Whatever happens, you're still our brother. We've got your back.'

Starting the engine, Julien felt something he hadn't experienced in months— hope. The trip to Sydney stretched ahead of him like a promise. He didn't know if Emily would forgive him, but he knew one thing: he was done hiding from the truth. It was time to be the man she'd fallen in love with again – the man who faced his mistakes head-on, who chose truth over comfort.

As his ute kicked up dust on the familiar road out of town, Julien made a silent promise. To Emily, to himself, to the person he used to be. No more lies, no more hiding. Whatever happened next, he would face it with honesty and courage.

Behind him, Rowena's voice called out Mason's name as she followed him toward the cane farm. Everyone was finally choosing truth over fear. It was time he did the same.

Chapter 15

The Sydney coffee shop was nothing like the store in Duckinwilla Creek. No mismatched mugs, no handwritten specials board, no Lucy Lou popping in for her morning gossip. Everything here was sleek, modern, and efficient.

Emily stared at her perfectly made latte, watching the foam slowly dissolve into the coffee below, just like her dreams of small-town happiness, disappearing one sip at a time.

'Earth to Emily.' Kelly waved a hand in front of her face. 'You're a million miles away.'

'Sorry.' Emily forced a smile. 'Just thinking.'

'About him?' Kelly's voice was gentle. They'd been friends since their first teaching practicum, long before Duckinwilla Creek, before Julien, before everything fell apart.

'About everything.' Emily traced the rim of her cup. 'The job offer came through.'

'The one at Sydney Grammar?' Kelly's eyes widened. 'Em, that's amazing! Head of English Department—it's exactly what you've always wanted.'

Was it? Emily wasn't sure anymore. Once, she'd dreamed of nothing but Sydney's prestigious private schools—polished corridors, faculty meetings and curriculum development. But somewhere between morning coffees at the general store and sunset walks by the creek, those dreams had changed.

'I thought I knew what I wanted,' she said quietly. 'I thought I knew who I was.'

Kelly reached across the table, squeezing her hand. 'You're still you. One man's mistakes don't change that.'

'Don't they?' Emily pulled her hand back, wrapping it around her cooling coffee. 'Because I feel different. Like everything I thought I knew was just... I guess, not really what I wanted.

'How long are you going to hide out here?' Kelly asked finally.

Emily traced a water ring on the table. 'I'm not hiding.'

'Really? Because from where I'm sitting, it looks a lot like hiding.

Outside the café window, Sydney rushed past in a blur of school uniforms and morning traffic. So different from the lazy pace of Duckinwilla Creek, where a five-minute trip to the store could turn into an hour of catching up with neighbours. Julien would always have a fresh muffin waiting when she came on her own from the flat above each morning.

'I have a life here,' Emily said, but the words felt hollow. 'I always did.'

Kelly's expression softened. 'Having a life somewhere isn't the same as belonging there. And Em? You haven't belonged here since you left for Duckinwilla a month after meeting Julien.'

The truth of those words settled in Emily's chest like a stone. Before she could respond, her phone buzzed—another message from Charlotte. She'd been sending updates about the store, about town gossip, about everything except what Emily really wanted to know.

Was Julien okay? Did he still play that silly 'guess the flavour' game with the school kids who came in after classes? She'd caught him once, teaching a shy year seven student how to juggle with wrapped sweets, both of them laughing as the lollies scattered across the floor.

Emily pushed the thoughts away. It didn't matter anymore. She had the job offer. She had her Sydney life back. She had everything she'd thought she wanted before Duckinwilla Creek changed her dreams.

So why did it all feel so wrong? Why did the chime at the door of the coffee shop remind her of the store's door jangle?

Kelly was right. She was hiding. But not from Julien—from the truth about where she really belonged.

Chapter 16

Emily sat at her kitchen counter, staring at the coffee she'd just made but couldn't bring herself to drink. His words from their phone call echoed in her head: 'I love you, Em.'

'I love you too,' she'd told him, and that was the heart of the problem. Love wasn't the issue – it never had been. But trust, once broken, was like the creek itself after a storm – it needed time to settle, to run clear again.

A movement caught her eye. Through her apartment window, she could see a mob of cockatoos swooping past, their raucous calls muffled by the double glazing. They reminded her of mornings at the store, when she'd watch them raid the old fig tree while she watered the herb garden she'd planted along the fence.

Tears spilled down her cheeks as memories flooded back – Julien teaching her to use the ancient cash register, his hands gentle over hers. The way he'd bring her coffee in their flat above the store, always remembering to add just a splash of milk. How he'd laugh at her city ways but defend her fiercely when anyone else did.

Her phone buzzed – another message from Charlotte: *He's different now. Really different. Give him a chance to prove it.*

Before she could respond, a commotion in the street below drew her attention. A familiar ute had pulled up, kicking up dust even on the city street. She stood with her hand on her mouth and rushed to the bathroom, dragging out a face washer and scrubbing t her cheeks, she ran a brush through her tangled hair pulled off her T-shirt and rummaged in her cupboard for a clean one. By the time the three tentative knocks rapped on her door, she had herself tidy but was shaking like a leaf.

She opened the door to find Julien standing there, dark circles under his eyes, and his hair wild like he'd been running his hands through it for hours.

'Hi,' he said softly.

Emily's hand tightened on the doorframe. Her eyes still felt raw from crying, and she knew he could see it despite her attempts to hide it. 'What are you doing here?'

'Being honest. Finally.' His voice cracked on the last word. 'Can I come in?'

She stepped back, letting him enter. The apartment felt smaller with him in it, full of memories she'd been trying to pack away like the boxes still stacked in the corner.

'I slept with Rowena,' he said without preamble, and Emily's breath caught. Not at the words—she'd already known, of course—but at the way he said them. No defensive edge, no careful denials. Just the plain truth, bare and raw.

'When?' she asked.

'That first month, when I came back from Sydney. We'd just started seeing each other, you and me. I hated leaving you, but I couldn't see a future for us. You with your dreams of a head teacher position and me just taking over a small store in a country town.' He ran a hand through his hair. 'But that's not an excuse. It happened. Once. Before I realised—' he broke off, looking at her with desperate eyes.

'Before you realised what?'

'That you were it for me. That what we had was real, not just some city girl passing through my life.' He took a step toward her, then stopped himself. 'But I lied to you when Rowena made her announcement at Charlotte's farewell, and I was too much of a coward to tell you the truth.'

Emily moved to the balcony, needing air. After a moment, he followed her out there. Below, Sydney buzzed with morning traffic, but up here, their world hung suspended.

Julien hesitated, then reached into his pocket. 'Actually, I have something for you.' He pulled out a small, weathered notebook. 'It's every lie I ever told you, written down. And next to each one is the truth. Even the small stuff.'

Emily took the notebook with trembling hands, thumbing through pages of Julien's familiar scrawl. Some entries made her smile despite herself:

Lie: *Told you I loved your city breakfast smoothies*

Truth: *They tasted like lawn clippings, but your face lit up when you made them, so I drank every one.*

Others made her heart ache:

Lie: *Said I was fine when Dad had his heart attack*

Truth: *I was terrified of losing him, of letting everyone down, of not being strong enough*

Lie: *Pretended the store was all I ever wanted*

Truth: *Sometimes, I dream of travelling with you, seeing the world through your eyes before settling back home.*

She looked up at him, really looked at him, seeing not just the man who had lied to her but the one brave enough to bare all his truths.

'You wrote all of this?'

'Started the night you left. I couldn't sleep, and kept thinking about every time I'd chosen the easy lie over the harder truth.' He ran a hand through his hair. 'There's some stuff in there I'm not proud of, Em. But it's all me. The good, the bad, the completely idiotic.'

Emily closed the notebook. 'And Rowena?'

'It's all in there. Every detail of that night, how it happened, why it happened. But more importantly, why I lied about it afterwards.' He took a deep breath. 'I was so scared of losing you that I did exactly that.'

Outside, the morning traffic hummed below them, and somewhere, a kookaburra laughed, the sound incongruous in the city setting like a piece of Duckinwilla Creek had followed them here, reminding Emily of home.

They sat on her balcony chairs, the morning sun warming their faces. Two cups of coffee grew cold between them as they talked, really talked, for the first time in what felt like forever.

'Tell me about everyone,' Emily said, drawing her knees up to her chest. 'I've missed them all so much.'

Julien smiled, and she could see the tension starting to ease from his shoulders. 'Well, you won't believe Amelia's hair—'

'Oh, I heard about that. Blue and orange, right?'

'Like a tropical bird had a fight with a paint tin, Guy says.' He laughed. 'But it suits her, somehow. It makes her look more... herself. She's talking about going to Japan to teach.'

'Japan?' Emily's eyebrows rose. 'How did your mother take that?'

'Surprisingly well, actually. Mum's been different since Dad's heart attack. Softer. Less worried about what people think.' He twisted his coffee cup between his hands. 'She even defended Amelia when old Mrs Wilson made some comment about "proper young ladies" at church.'

Emily tried to imagine the proper Mrs Johnson doing that and couldn't quite manage it. 'And your dad?'

'Getting stronger every day. Makes these terrible jokes about having a "change of heart" about everything.' His voice caught slightly. 'Those first few minutes in the hospital, Em. I've never been so scared. Made me realise what really matters.'

She reached out, touching his hand briefly. 'And the store?'

'Charlotte and Greg have been amazing. They've modernised the inventory system, started a local produce section...' He paused. 'Actually, I'm worried they might leave.'

'Leave? Why?'

'Greg's parents own that big property out past Dunmora, and they're retiring to Elliot Heads. Greg's been talking about maybe taking it over, turning it into something special. Farm-to-table restaurant, maybe a bed and breakfast setup.'

'That sounds perfect for them,' Emily said softly, remembering Charlotte's hidden dreams of something more than the store.

'Yeah, it does.' Julien ran a hand through his hair. 'And that's what scares me. I always thought the store was my future, you know? The Johnson legacy. But watching Greg and Charlotte... they're building something real together. Something honest. I have a feeling that they've made a commitment and are waiting for the right time to tell the family. I sure haven't made it easy for them.'

Finally, she spoke. 'I have conditions. If I come back.'

'Anything.'

'First, no more lies. Not even small ones. If something's wrong, we talk about it.'

He nodded. 'Absolutely.'

'A fresh start,' she corrected. 'Second . . . I want us to build something real. Not just at the store, but in our life together. Something honest and strong, like what Charlotte and Greg have.'

'Deal,' he said softly, and something in his voice made her look up. Before she could move, he pulled her into his arms, holding her like she might disappear if he let go.

'God, I've missed you,' he whispered into her hair. 'Missed your smile, your laugh, even the way you reorganise the store's shelves when you think no one's watching.'

His kiss, when it came, was gentle at first, tentative, as though they were both afraid of breaking this fragile new understanding between them. Then Julien's arms tightened around her waist, and Emily's hands slid into his hair, and suddenly, they were clinging to each other like they'd never let go.

'Was that a yes?' he asked, his voice rough. 'About coming home?'

Emily smiled, feeling truly whole for the first time in months. 'That was a yes to trying. To rebuild trust, to face whatever comes next. Together.'

The smile on Julien's face left no doubt—he loved her. At that moment, Emily knew they had begun to rebuild the trust between them, step by step, together.

Chapter 17

Three months later

The rain fell softly on Mum's roses, each drop catching the glow from the kitchen windows and turning to liquid gold. Oliver stood on the verandah, watching water bead on the purple bougainvillea that had grown quickly up the lattice. The old Queenslander sat proudly on its stilts, weatherboard gleaming pearl-grey in the dim evening light, surrounded by Dad's vegetable garden— a maze of herb beds, and vegetables that somehow thrived together despite conventional wisdom. He'd taken over the gardening as he'd recovered from his heart attack, much to Mum's relief.

Inside the kitchen, warmth and laughter filled the air and spilled though the window. Emily's voice carried through the open windows as she helped Grandmère with the cooking. Dad sat beside Mum at the kitchen table. Grandmère had taken over the farm kitchen for the night.

Emily insisted that Grandmère use the new recipe she'd brought back from Sydney for the chicken sauce. The way she and Julien had found their way back to each other still amazed Oliver; how they'd both needed that time apart to realise what they had together. Now they moved around each other with a new kind of confidence, like dancers who'd finally learned the steps. Emily had taken up a part-time job at the preschool, and Julien was back running the General Store.

Guy was already at the table, absorbed in crop reports on his phone despite Grandmere's pointed looks. Some things never changed.

'Did you hear about Rowena and Mason?' Charlotte asked,

reaching past Julien to steady a pot that teetered near the edge—still the fixer, even now that fewer things needed fixing.

'Moving to Longreach, aren't they?' Emily turned from the stove. 'Mason's got that new position with the mining company.'

'Rowena's excited about it,' Julien added, his hand finding Emily's waist naturally as he reached past her for the bread knife. 'Says she's ready for a new adventure.'

'She'll have one of them when the baby's born,' Mum said.

'*Non, non*,' Grandmère waved them all away from her cooking. 'Too many cooks. Sit, Charlotte, your fiancé is looking lonely.'

'Let them help, Maman,' Dad called from his armchair. 'Soon enough, we'll be missing Charlotte while she's living *la vie Parisienne* with Gregory.'

Oliver watched Charlotte's face soften at the mention of Paris. The tickets sat in an envelope on her fridge; he'd seen them last week when he'd dropped off some excess mangoes from the farm. Two months away, but already her eyes got dreamy whenever France came up.

'It's just a holiday,' Greg said from his spot at the table, but his smile was knowing. Oliver wondered if they'd decided to stay there longer than they were letting on. He pushed away a pang of envy at their certainty, their easy connection. He knew they had plans to settle eventually at Greg's parents' farm.

'A holiday that was too long in coming, but we all appreciated you helping out, didn't we, Hugo? Mum said as she carried a vase of her roses into the dining room. She looked better these days—the shadows under her eyes had faded, and she'd taken up painting again. Right now, there was a smudge of blue paint behind her ear that no one had been game to mention; they still tiptoed around her.

Amelia bounced in from the bathroom, her hair now a more subdued red instead of the shocking pink, blue and orange it had been months ago. 'I still can't believe Rowena's going to be so far away. Who's going to run the book club now?'

'Some of us have actual work to do,' Guy muttered, finally looking up from his phone.

'Unlike Mason, who's clearly just going on holiday,' Emily teased, and everyone laughed at Guy's embarrassed flush.

'Speaking of work,' Lisette had appeared beside Oliver on the verandah, two glasses of wine in hand. She offered him one. 'You missed all the excitement at the store yesterday. Julien brought in Emily's whole class of kindergarteners for a tour.'

Oliver accepted the wine, watching through the window as Julien dramatically re-enacted something for the table, Emily shaking her head but laughing. 'How did that go?'

'Chaos. Complete chaos. But the good kind.' Lisette smiled—actually smiled, without the edge that had been there for the past few years. It looked like she had finally moved on from the drama that had seen her and Charlotte at odds for a long time. 'One little girl asked Emily if she was a princess because she married the man from the lolly shop.'

Oliver choked on his wine. Inside, Julien was now helping Emily serve the *coq au vin*, their movements synchronised like they'd never been apart. It was strange to think how, just months ago, he'd been camped in Sydney, desperate to win her back. Now they looked so . . . settled.

'It's different when you find the right person,' Lisette said quietly as if reading his thoughts. 'Look at them. Look at Charlotte and Greg. Even Rowena and Mason— moving across the state for love and adventure.' She nudged his shoulder. 'You look like you're watching everyone else live while you're stuck in pause.'

'I don't—'

'It's okay.' Her smile was gentle. 'We all get stuck sometimes. Look at me. I nearly ruined everything because I was too proud to admit I was jealous of how easy everyone else made it look.'

Inside, Grandmère was shooing everyone to their seats, the big pot steaming on its trivet. Dad was already at the head of the dining room table, looking tired but happy, his colour better than it had been in months.

'Time to join the circus,' Lisette said. 'Unless you want Grandmère to come fetch us herself.'

Oliver followed her inside, the warmth wrapping around him as it always did. The old dining room looked the same: family photos covering the walls, the ancient sideboard groaning with plates and serving dishes, the chandelier that Papa had restored casting a soft light over everything. But something had shifted in the atmosphere. The tension that had crackled through recent family dinners had eased, replaced by something softer, more forgiving.

'Oliver, *mon petit*,' Grandmère commanded, 'help me with this bread.'

He moved automatically to slice the still-warm baguettes, ending up between Amelia and Lisette, across from Emily and Julien, who were sharing some private joke. Charlotte and Greg sat nearby, heads bent together over what looked like a Paris map, while Guy finally put his phone away as Papa said grace.

'I can't believe you're leaving next week,' Amelia said as they passed dishes around. 'Everyone's having adventures except me.'

'Pre-school isn't adventurous enough for you?' Emily

asked, spooning out vegetables. 'Trust me, thirty five-year-olds is all the adventure anyone needs.'

'Better than Japan,' Mum said, and everyone tactfully ignored Amelia's eye roll.

The conversation flowed easily as they ate; Amelia talked about her upcoming traineeship and her TAFE course, Charlotte and Greg discussed their itinerary, and Emily described her students' reaction to seeing where all the lollies came from. Even Guy emerged from his agricultural reverie to debate the merits of different mango varieties with Dad.

'Mason reckons there's good farming opportunities further north,' Guy mentioned. 'Different crops, obviously, but the principles are the same.'

'You're not thinking of following them to Longreach, are you?' Charlotte asked sharply.

Guy pulled a face. 'Cane doesn't grow at Longreach.'

'Someone's got to stay and look after the family farm,' Oliver found himself saying. 'Besides, who else would sell mangoes at the markets?'

The table went quiet for a moment before erupting in gentle laughter and knowing looks.

'The markets?' Emily leaned forward, interested. 'Where the pretty girl was chatting you up? Amelia mentioned something about her.'

Heat crept up Oliver's neck. 'Nothing happened. She was just asking about the fruit.'

'She was flirting with you,' Amelia insisted. 'And you? You just . . . talked about fruit varieties for ten minutes.'

Outside, the rain fell harder, drumming on the tin roof. The garden would be drinking it in, Mum's roses lifting their heads to the water. Oliver thought about that girl: the way her eyes had crinkled when she smiled, how her fingers had lingered over the fruit selection. Maybe Amelia was right. Maybe he had missed something, too worried about being boring to notice someone might find him interesting. He hadn't even asked her name.

'Oliver will help me with dessert,' Grandmère announced, rising from the table. It wasn't a request.

In the kitchen, she handed him plates while she dished up her famous *crème brûlée*. 'You know what your problem is, *mon cher*?'

'I'm sure you'll tell me.'

'You think too much.' She tapped his forehead with a floury finger. 'Up here, always watching, always waiting. Look at your brother with that phone, your sister with her Japan dreams. Sometimes, the ones who rush around miss what's right in front of them. But you, you see everything except yourself.'

Oliver thought about the girl at the market, about the way she'd written her phone number on the back of her receipt before leaving it carefully on his table. 'I wouldn't know where to start.'

'Did Julien know? Did Greg?' Grandmere's eyes twinkled. 'Love isn't about knowing; it's about trying. About being brave enough to look foolish sometimes.'

Back at the table, the conversation had turned to Emily and Julien's party. 'We should host it at the store,' Lisette was saying. 'Like we did for Charlotte and Greg's engagement.'

'As long as Guy puts his phone away,' Amelia teased. 'I'm just saying if you spent as much time talking to actual women as you do to your spreadsheets...'

'Some of us have a business to run,' Guy protested.

'The farm won't collapse if you look away from your phone for five minutes,' Dad said mildly. 'Trust me, I checked.'

Oliver set down the dessert plates, something heavy settling in his chest. They were right—all of them. About Guy's phone, about his own tendency to overthink, about the way life could pass you by if you let it.

'I'm going to the markets again next weekend,' he said suddenly, surprising himself. 'To sell the last of the mangoes.'

The conversation paused, and he felt everyone trying not to look too interested.

'Really?' Amelia's grin was wide. 'Any particular reason?'

Oliver spooned up some *crème brûlée*, fighting a smile. 'The mangoes won't sell themselves.'

'No,' Emily said softly, exchanging a knowing look with Julien. 'Sometimes, they need a little help.'

The rain drummed on, but inside the dining room at the farm surrounded by the warm chaos of his family, Oliver felt something shift. A decision, maybe. Or just a willingness to step into the dance, as Grandmère had said.

He looked around the table - at Charlotte and Greg planning their adventure, at Amelia practising Japanese on her napkin, at Emily and Julien sharing private smiles, at Lisette relaxed and laughing, at Guy finally setting down his phone to really join them. At Mum and Dad, together and healing, and Grandmère presiding over it all with knowing eyes.

Maybe being quiet didn't mean being stuck. Maybe it just meant he noticed things others missed - like the way the girl's fingers had lingered on the mangoes or how her phone number was still burning a hole in his wallet.

Tomorrow, he decided, he would call. After all, everyone at this table had taken a chance on love at some point. Maybe it was finally his turn.

Wishes and Whispers

ANNIE SEATON

Duckinwilla Days: Book 3

Heartwarming and compelling tales of love, self-discovery, and second chances in the heart of rural Australia.

Duckinwilla Days 1-3

Chapter 1

The early morning sun lit up the colourful shrubs along the driveway as Oliver heaved the last of the suitcases into the back of the minivan. His muscles strained under the weight of what seemed to be Grandmère's entire wardrobe, packed for their month-long trip to France. He'd already unloaded it from Papa's car when they'd arrived from their house, then Grandmère had insisted on checking each suitcase before she announced they were ready to go into the minivan he and Guy had picked up from Bundaberg early that morning for the travellers to take to Brisbane.

'You'd think they were moving there permanently,' Guy muttered beside him, wiping sweat from his brow. At twenty-seven, Guy was the quieter of the two Johnson brothers, content to let the chaos of family life swirl around him while he focused on the farm's spreadsheets and sugar cane yields. 'They've packed enough clothes to last summer and winter.'

'And Mum's packed enough medication to stock a pharmacy, along with Grandmère's clothes. She's packed enough for a royal tour,' Oliver grunted as he agreed.

'Well, I guess it's not every day they take Grandmère back to France,' Guy said. 'At least the cane harvest is finished. Good timing. We can have a bit of a breather while they're all away.'

'You can. It's just in time for mango season,' Oliver added, glancing toward the orchard. 'I'll be flat out. The early varieties should be ready by the time they come home. I noticed some of the Kensington Prides starting to blush.'

'You and your mangoes,' Guy shook his head. 'Sugar pays the bills, brother.'

'Diversification,' Oliver replied with the automatic response he'd been giving for years. 'Plus, people love those mangoes at the markets.'

The screen door banged open as Ellen, their mother, hurried out to the veranda, clutching her passport and a handful of travel documents; she was wearing the same frazzled expression that had become permanent over the past week of preparations.

'Have either of you seen your father's heart tablets? The little blue ones? He swears he packed them, but you know what he's like since he had the heart attack. Can't find anything.'

'Check the kitchen counter, Mum,' Oliver said with a grin at Guy. 'I saw him sorting pills there last night.'

Charlotte appeared behind their mother; she was holding a packet in her right hand. 'Found them, Mum! They were in the bathroom cabinet, exactly where Dad said they were.' She descended the steps with the confidence of someone who'd been mediating family crises her entire life.

'Why so late, anyway, Charlotte? The trip's later than you planned,' Oliver remarked. 'It's already mid-November. You'll just be back for Christmas.'

'I couldn't take time off from the high school to leave earlier. My Year Twelve class needed me leading up to their final exams. And three weeks in France is hardly excessive,' Charlotte replied. 'We'll be home a week before Christmas. Plenty of time to prepare.'

Their mother smiled, a dreamy look crossing her face. 'And for the wedding preparations, too! I can't believe we'll have two weddings to plan next year.'

'Julien and Emily's renewal of vows hardly counts as a full wedding, Mum,' Charlotte said, although she was smiling too.

'Don't tell Julien that! Emily wants the big celebration they didn't have because they got married at the registry office before they came home from Sydney. And then your wedding in May, Charlotte.' Ellen sighed happily. 'So much to look forward to.'

Greg, Charlotte's fiancé of almost a year, came in from the kitchen with an armload of snacks. 'Road trip essentials,' he explained with a wink as he passed Oliver. 'Your mum's worried they'll starve on the three-hour drive to Brisbane.'

'More likely they'll miss the plane because they can't close the door on the minivan,' Oliver said under his breath, causing Greg to chuckle.

The house hummed with the excitement of six people preparing to depart for a long-awaited trip. Grandmère fussed over her travel outfit—a smart navy pantsuit that made her look a decade younger than her seventy years—while Papa pretended to listen to her concerns about plane food. At eighty-two, he'd maintained the ability to tune out selectively, a skill Oliver deeply respected and aspired to master himself one day. With three sisters, he'd been fighting a losing battle since he was in kindergarten.

'*Ooh la la*, to think I will see my cousins tonight after all these years!' Grandmère exclaimed, her hands fluttering excitedly. 'My little village near Lyon, it will have changed so much. When I left as a girl of nineteen to marry your grandfather, I never imagined it would be so long before I returned.'

Papa smiled indulgently. 'Margot, you've told this story every day for the past month.'

'And I will tell it every day until we land in Paris!' she declared, her accent growing stronger with her excitement. 'The family château—well, not really a château, more a large stone house—but the vineyards, the lavender fields. Oliver, you should be coming with us! The French countryside would put hairs on your chest.'

'I think I have enough hair already, Grandmère,' Oliver replied with a grin.

'Oliver!' His father called from the study. 'While you're waiting around, can you please check this itinerary for me again? I'm not sure if we're supposed to transfer in Singapore or Dubai.'

Oliver rolled his eyes as he walked across the living room of the farmhouse to the study, which he and Guy shared with Dad. While they were at school, they had done their homework at the scrubbed timber kitchen table, but when they started working on the farm, Dad had bought them a desk each. It was cramped, but a lot of good planning had taken place in that room over the past few years. He took the crumpled printout from his father's hand. 'Dubai, Dad. It's highlighted right here.' He pointed to the fluorescent yellow streak across the page. 'And Greg has his copy, so it's all under control.' Oliver knew that Dad was nervous about the trip; he'd never been overseas before, but his reluctance to go had been overruled by Grandmère.

'I want my only child to see his heritage, please, Hugo.'

Between Mum—and her desire to see Europe—and Grandmère, Dad had been off to the local post office getting his passport photo taken before he could think twice.

He nodded, running a hand through his thinning grey hair. 'Right, right. Just checking. And you boys have the farm schedule? The irrigation repairs are due next Thursday.'

'We've been over this three times, Dad. Don't stress,' Oliver said patiently. 'Guy's made a spreadsheet. The farm will survive without your supervision for four weeks.'

'Four weeks,' his father repeated, the reality seemingly hitting him for the first time. 'That's a long time to be away from the cane.'

Oliver squeezed his father's shoulder. 'It's only been three years since you handed the running of the General Store to Julien. The cane survived then; it won't even notice you're gone.'

A high-pitched squeal from the kitchen interrupted them, followed by Grandmère's rapid-fire French. Oliver hurried out to find her clutching Papa's arm, both beaming at a tablet held by Amelia.

'Lisette' FaceTimed from Melbourne,' Amelia explained, her hair—currently dyed in vibrant stripes of teal, purple, and pink—catching the morning light as she put the tablet on the dining room table and tilted the screen toward Oliver. 'She wants to wish you all a safe trip.'

Lisette's face filled the screen, her formerly harsh features softened both by the video quality and the gradual mellowing she'd undergone in the past year. Once she and Charlotte had sorted their differences, she'd been much happier. 'You're all looking very smart for economy class travellers,' she teased, her artwork visible in the background. 'Oli, you actually combed your hair for their departure. I'm impressed.'

Oliver ran a self-conscious hand through his dark curls. 'Someone had to look presentable for the neighbours. They'll think we're selling the farm if the whole family leaves at once.'

'Are you sure you can't come join us in France, Lisette?' their mother asked, leaning in front of the tablet screen. 'The invitation from your father's cousins included everyone. And you'd be back in time for Christmas. We could make sure of that.'

Lisette's smile was genuinely regretful. 'The gallery exhibition opens in three weeks, Mum. I can't leave now.' In the year since moving to Melbourne, Lisette had transformed from the sharp-tongued sister to a surprisingly successful art gallery assistant. 'Besides, someone has to check in on the farm boys and make sure they're not living on beer and beef pies.'

'I'll be doing that. I'm taking over the cooking,' Amelia said smugly.

'Heaven help the boys,' Lisette quipped.

'We'll FaceTime you from Paris,' Charlotte promised, squeezing into view. 'You can virtually tour the Louvre with us.'

'Better than nothing,' Lisette agreed before her gaze sharpened on Oliver. 'Though speaking of virtual, Oli, I've been meaning to talk to you about online dating. Amelia mentioned you're still stubbornly single.'

Oliver shot Amelia a filthy look, which she answered with an innocent smile and a flutter of her purple-mascaraed eyelashes. 'Lisette, it's not the time,' he muttered.

'When is the time, then?' Amelia piped up, handing the tablet to Charlotte and crossing her arms. 'You're almost twenty-five, Oli. Your idea of socialising is nodding at the fertiliser delivery guy when he drives out in his truck.'

'I socialise heaps,' he protested weakly.

Guy looked up from his phone for the first time that morning. 'What's happening?'

'Amelia and Lisette are tag-teaming Oli about his love life,' Charlotte explained.

Guy immediately returned to his screen. 'Cane prices are dropping again. Not good.'

'Coward,' Oliver glared at him. 'Where's some brotherly solidarity?'

'He needs to get with it,' Amelia declared, turning to address the family audience. 'It's the twenty-first century! People don't meet in supermarket aisles anymore. They swipe.'

'I don't want to swipe anyone,' Oliver said firmly. 'And

maybe if you spent less time on dating apps and more time on keeping a natural hair colour, you wouldn't have gone through three boyfriends since the Crush Festival.'

Amelia patted her multicoloured hair proudly. 'My parrot hair, as you so lovingly call it, is a conversation starter. And for your information, I've been seeing Myron for three weeks now.'

'Ooh, a record,' Lisette chimed in. 'Play the field, sister. Good to see.' She frowned. 'Strange name, though.'

'Who's Myron?' Ellen asked, momentarily distracted from her travel checklist. 'You haven't mentioned him before.'

'The new barista at the store,' Amelia said. 'Tall, makes amazing latte art.'

Grandmère perked up. 'The one with the tattoos of the little birds? Very handsome. French men appreciate artistic flair, you know. My cousin Antoine had a magnificent moustache that he waxed into points.'

'He draws kingfishers in the foamed milk,' Charlotte confirmed. 'Already a customer favourite. Julien's really happy with him.'

'And Amelia,' Oliver teased.

'We are going to stop by the store on the way out, aren't we?' Ellen frowned. 'To say goodbye to Julien and Emily.'

When no one answered her, she walked away from the table where Amelia had the tablet propped up against the jug of flowers.

'Well, Oli could use some colour himself,' Lisette's voice chimed in from the forgotten video connection. 'Maybe some highlights? You've got that whole brooding farmer look going, but a few golden streaks might soften it.'

Oliver's mouth fell open in horror. 'I am not dyeing my hair.'

'It would bring out your eyes,' Amelia agreed seriously, studying his face. 'And distract from that permanent furrow between your eyebrows.'

'There is no furrow,' Oliver protested, consciously relaxing his forehead.

'There absolutely is,' Lisette countered. 'It's been there since you were twelve and Dad put you in charge of the irrigation schedules.'

'Responsibility etches itself on the face,' Papa contributed sagely from an armchair, clearly enjoying the family entertainment.

'Well,' Lisette sighed dramatically from the tablet, 'at least Mum'll have two weddings next year. Though it won't be yours, Oli, at this rate.'

'Lisette!' their mother scolded, though she looked more amused than upset.

'What? I'm just saying we shouldn't hold our breath. Unless—' Lisette's voice took on a sly tone. 'Has that market girl shown up again? The one with the amazing laugh that Oli wouldn't shut up about last year?'

Oliver's face burned. 'Her name is Sarah, and no, she hasn't.'

'Shame,' Lisette said, not sounding particularly sympathetic. 'Though perhaps we should be thankful. I heard she has a child, and we all know how Oli feels about noise.'

'We're getting off track,' Amelia said, whipping out her phone. 'I've been compiling a list of eligible women in the district for him. There's Melissa Harper, the new preschool teacher at Duckinwilla Primary. She's got that whole wholesome, "I love children".'

'Perfect for a man who scowls at primary school lamington

sellers,' Lisette added.

'I bought a dozen at the last markets,' Oliver defended himself.

'Under duress,' Charlotte reminded him. 'After the little girl cried.'

'She was very persuasive,' Oliver muttered.

'In my village when I was a girl and being courted,' Grandmère interjected excitedly, 'the matchmaker would have paired you with the baker's daughter by now. A good strong woman who can help with the mango harvest!' She clasped her hands together. 'Perhaps I will find you a nice French girl while we are there!'

Amelia continued undeterred. 'Then there's Kaitlyn Webb, who runs that new crystal stall at the weekend markets. Very spiritual, but she makes her own bread and mentioned wanting a vegetable garden.'

The mention of the markets made Oliver's stomach tighten unexpectedly. It had been almost a year since he'd met Sarah at the Dunmora markets during last season's mango harvest. They'd talked for nearly an hour while she admired his fruit and he admired . . . well, everything about her. He'd taken her number, written on a docket that had somehow vanished before he'd made it home. He'd returned to the Dunmora markets the following weekend, but her craft site had been empty. He'd continued visiting those markets for weeks, but she never returned, and he'd eventually given up looking for her there.

'Earth to Oliver,' Amelia was saying, snapping her fingers in front of his face. 'You disappeared there for a second.'

'Forget all that dating stuff; it's time you should get on the road,' he covered quickly, addressing the travellers. 'It's a long drive to Brisbane, and the peak hour traffic could be pretty bad.'

His father glanced at his watch and let out a startled exclamation. 'Oli's right! We need to leave in the next ten minutes or we'll hit peak hour.'

The next few minutes dissolved into a flurry of last-minute checks, bathroom visits, and tearful hugs. Oliver found himself pulled into embrace after embrace, doling out promises to water houseplants and collect mail at Grandmère and Papa's place, and then assuring Dad that he and Guy would keep the farm running smoothly.

'And think about what we said,' Amelia whispered sideways to Oliver after she'd hugged everyone goodbye. 'Life's too short to spend it talking only to sugar cane.'

'We'll have that dating profile set up before they reach France,' Lisette promised from the tablet, which Charlotte was now carrying to the minivan.

'Don't you dare,' Oliver called after them, but his protest was lost in the commotion of final goodbyes.

Guy appeared at his shoulder as they watched the minivan finally pull away, arms waving from every window. 'Thank God. Peace and quiet for a month,' he said with quiet satisfaction.

Oliver nodded, already mentally listing the tasks awaiting them in the fields. 'Peace, quiet, and about two thousand acres of cane, and six hundred mango trees that need our attention.'

'I'll keep you pair in line,' Amelia said. 'What do you want for dinner tonight?'

'Steak?' Guy asked with a hopeful smile. 'And don't forget to leave time for the highlights in Oli's hair.'

Oliver elbowed him hard in the ribs, but couldn't help grinning as they turned back towards the house. The place felt suddenly enormous and empty with just the three of them. But peacefully quiet.

'I'll go and take some steaks out of the freezer in the shed.' Amelia disappeared through the breezeway.

For all Oliver's protests, a small part of him wondered if Amelia might be right. Maybe it was time to 'get with it,' whatever that meant. He was almost twenty-five. But not with highlights. God forbid. He shuddered. And definitely not with swiping on some dating app.

Oliver's thoughts drifted back to the markets, to Sarah's laugh and the way she'd tucked her hair behind her ear while examining a particularly perfect mango. He'd noticed she didn't wear a wedding ring, and when he'd carefully asked about Jett's father, a shadow had passed across her face before she simply said, 'It's just the two of us.' He hadn't pressed further—some stories weren't meant for first meetings between strangers at market stalls.

As he headed to the kitchen to put the kettle on before he and Guy went back out to the fields, he remembered how he'd looked for Sarah every weekend for a month before giving up, assuming she'd moved on or away.

Maybe his sisters were right about one thing—it was time for him to move on, too.

A little voice nagged away at him in a whisper. *But I don't want to.*

But for the time being, he and Guy had a farm to run as well as keeping an eye on Amelia while the oldies were away.

Chapter 2

The first week without the family passed in a blur of work. Oliver threw himself into the cane fields with a focus that even Guy commented on—once, briefly, late on Tuesday night before returning to his spreadsheets. With Dad gone, they'd both taken on extra responsibilities: Guy managing the books and coordinating with the sugar mill, Oliver overseeing the day-to-day operations and the small crew of seasonal workers they'd hired to help with the pre-harvest preparations. He hadn't had time to look at his mangoes all week. The mango harvest was only a couple of weeks away, and he was hoping that there would be no storms before he could get them picked.

Guy was on the back porch that evening, guitar in hand, softly picking out a melody as the sunset painted the cane fields in gold. It was a side of his brother few people saw—the quiet musician who found solace in music after long days of practical farm work.

'Sounds good,' Oliver commented, dropping onto the old sofa chair beside him. 'New song?'

Guy's fingers stilled on the strings. 'Just something I've been working on.' He had a private intensity that contrasted with Oliver's more straightforward approach to life. Where Oliver was practical and present, Guy seemed to live half in his head, observing the world with a thoughtfulness that was often mistaken for detachment.

'The seasonal crew seems solid this year,' Oliver remarked, changing the subject. 'That new worker—Elena?—she really knows her way around irrigation systems.'

Something flickered across Guy's face. 'Elena Santiago. She's worked three harvests on the big Mackay plantations.

Overqualified for what we're paying, to be honest.'

'Then why's she here?'

Guy shrugged, but there was a tension in his shoulders that hadn't been there before. 'Said she wanted to learn about smaller-scale sustainable farming. She's got some interesting ideas about water conservation.'

'Since when do you discuss farming philosophy with the seasonal help?' Oliver asked, surprised.

'Since Dad put me in charge of the books,' Guy replied, putting his guitar against the wall. 'Someone has to think about the farm's future beyond the next harvest.'

Before Oliver could ask what he meant, Guy stood up. 'I should finish those spreadsheets. The mill wants our projections by Friday.'

By Friday evening, Oliver's muscles had reached that state of fatigue where his body seemed to creak with exhaustion. He'd spent the day replacing irrigation lines along the eastern boundary, the sun burning his shirtless back as he dragged sections of pipe through the thick mud. When he finally trudged back to the farmhouse at sunset, his clothes were filthy, his boots caked with rich, dark soil, and his muscles aching.

'Pub tonight? It's Friday,' Guy asked, already dressed in clean jeans and a button-down shirt, his hair still damp from the shower.

Oliver mustered enough energy to shake his head. 'I'm knackered, mate. You go out, though.'

'Suit yourself,' Guy had replied with a shrug. 'There's a new band playing. Might be decent.'

'Tell me all about it tomorrow.' Oliver managed a weary smile. 'I'm going to spend tomorrow in the mangoes.'

Guy grimaced but nodded. 'Fair enough. Don't wait up.'

Now, freshly showered and horizontal on his bed, Oliver stared at the ceiling fan spinning lazily above him. The house was quiet—Guy at the pub, Amelia presumably out with Myron the barista. He'd been too tired to eat a proper dinner, settling instead for a toasted sandwich eaten standing at the kitchen counter. His eyelids had just begun to droop when his bedroom door burst open.

'You're not asleep yet, are you?' Amelia demanded, flicking on the light. 'It's only eight o'clock on a Friday night, for goodness' sake! How old are you, Oli? Anyone would think you were on the downside of fifty. Come on, wake up.'

'Why?' Oliver groaned, throwing an arm over his eyes. 'All right, all right. I'm getting there.'

'Well, hurry up and get there. I have something to show you.' Amelia bounced onto the foot of his bed with an enthusiasm that rocked the mattress.

'Whatever it is, it can wait until morning,' he mumbled. 'I thought you were out anyway.'

'I thought you'd gone to the pub with Guy, but I guess that was a silly thing to hope for. I was in my room doing this.'

'Amelia, I'm stuffed. Go away. I'll look at whatever it is in the morning.'

'No, it absolutely cannot wait until then.' She was practically vibrating with excitement, her laptop balanced on her knees at the foot of his bed. 'Ta-da! Sit up and look at this.'

Oliver squinted at the screen she'd thrust toward him. It took several seconds for his tired brain to process what he was seeing. When it did, he bolted upright, fatigue forgotten.

'What. Have. You. Done?' His eyes widened in disbelief.

Filling the screen was a dating profile. His dating profile, if the name 'Oliver Johnson' and a startlingly flattering photo of him at the Crush Festival in October were anything to go by. He was smiling in the picture—so rare an occurrence that he couldn't even remember who'd taken it—and the sunset lighting made him look almost handsome.

'CountryConnect.com.au,' Amelia announced proudly. 'The premier dating site for rural singles!'

'Delete it,' he said immediately. 'Right now.'

'I will not,' she said, pulling the laptop back protectively. 'You need this, Oli. I'm tired of watching you mope around the farm like some tragic hero in a period drama.'

'I don't mope! And I've never watched a period drama in my life.'

'You absolutely do mope. You've been moping for a year since that market girl ghosted you.'

Oliver felt a flare of irritation. 'Sarah didn't ghost me. I lost *her* number.'

'So you say.' Amelia rolled her eyes. 'And yet somehow you've managed not to meet anyone else in an entire year.'

'I've been busy,' he protested. 'The mangoes and the cane—'

'The mangoes, the cane, the mangoes,' she mimicked. 'Dad has the same excuse, and he and Mum have been married for thirty years! You need a life outside of dirt, sugar cane and mangoes, Oli.'

He reached for the laptop, but she twisted away. 'Show me what ridiculous things you've written about me.'

Amelia relented, angling the screen so he could read it. Oliver's eyes widened as he scanned the profile:

Who am I? I'm Oliver Johnson, twenty-five, Duckinwilla Creek, Queensland.

About Me: Third-generation cane farmer with a secret talent for baking the perfect scone and naming every constellation in the night sky. When I'm not working the land my family has owned for generations, you'll probably find me lost in a good book or taking long walks along the creek with my dog, Ruby. I value honesty, hard work, and people who can appreciate the simple beauty of a Queensland sunset.

Looking For: Someone genuine who understands that the land demands commitment but knows that true partnerships make the work worthwhile. Must love open spaces, starry nights, and the occasional mud on the kitchen floor (I always clean it up eventually). Bonus points if you can spot the Southern Cross faster than I can.

'I don't bake scones,' was all Oliver could manage. He felt as though his eyes were about to pop out of his head. He drew in a big breath. 'And Ruby? What self-respecting cane farmer would have a working dog called Ruby? Honestly, Amelia, that's absolute tripe. Take it down.'

She shook her head. 'Grandmère said you helped her bake scones once when you were twelve. Close enough.'

'And I don't take walks along the creek! When would I have time for that? And I don't have a Ruby. What sort of dog would that be?'

She giggled. 'Oh, I thought a little fluffy wide 'oodle' of some sort might sound enticing.'

Oliver was speechless.

'Details don't matter,' Amelia waved a hand. 'The point is to sell the fantasy, Oli. Truth is overrated. No one wants to date a man whose profile says 'Works seven days a week, collapses into bed by nine, couldn't tell the difference between a good conversation and a fence post.'

'I talk to people!'

'Grunting at the feed store doesn't count.' She scrolled down. 'Look at the rest!'

Oliver scanned the rest of the profile with growing horror. Under "Interests", Amelia had listed hiking, astronomy, classic literature, and—most bewilderingly— "artisanal baking."

'When's the last time you read anything that wasn't a farming manual?' she challenged before he could speak.

'I'm reading that thriller Greg lent me,' he said defensively.

'The one that's been on your bedside table since your birthday?'

He glanced guiltily at the dusty paperback. 'I'm a slow reader.'

'You're a non-reader,' she corrected. 'But women like men who read, so now you read.'

Oliver fell back against his pillows with a groan. 'This is ridiculous. No one's going to believe any of this.'

'Oh, they already do,' Amelia said cheerfully, clicking to another screen. 'You've got three matches!'

'What?' Oliver shot upright again. 'Bloody hell, sis. What have you done?'

'Three women have already expressed interest,' she announced triumphantly. 'And I've replied to all of them.'

'You've been pretending to be me?' His voice rose to a pitch it hadn't hit since puberty.

'Just to get the ball rolling,' she assured him. 'Jessica wants to meet for coffee next week. She seems nice—kindergarten teacher, likes hiking, has a cute Labrador.'

'Oh. My. God.' Oliver buried his face in his hands. 'This is a nightmare. You are a nightmare.'

'No, this is your chance to actually meet someone,' Amelia insisted. 'Look, Oli.' Her voice softened. 'I know you work hard.

I know the farm is important to you. But you can't spend your whole life waiting for some girl from the markets to magically reappear. She's moved away, or she's got a new job, or she's found a man.'

Oliver's shoulders slumped. 'It's not just about Sarah.'

'Then what is it about?'

He sighed, trying to express something he rarely thought about. 'Dating is . . . complicated. Working on the farm with Dad and Guy takes all my time, and most women don't understand that. I've got enough on my plate without adding relationship drama.'

Amelia tapped the screen. 'That's why online dating is perfect. You can be upfront about your lifestyle. These women know you're a farmer—they're specifically looking for someone like you.'

Oliver squinted at her suspiciously. 'Why do you care so much about my love life?'

'Because you're my big brother and I love you,' she said simply. 'And because you're miserable, even if you won't admit it.'

'I'm not—'

'You are,' she interrupted. 'I see how you look when Charlotte and Greg visit, or when Julien and Emily come over. You want what they have, but you're too scared to do anything about it.'

Oliver fell silent, unable to find a convincing denial.

'Just one coffee,' Amelia wheedled. 'With Jessica. Next Friday afternoon at The Bean Counter at Dunmora. I've already set it up. I didn't think you want to go to the General Store. Too much family, and locals to interrupt the "getting to know you bit".'

'You're unbelievable,' he muttered.

'I'm efficient,' she corrected with a grin. 'And if it doesn't work out, there's always Brittany—she's a bookkeeper who likes gardening—or Danielle, who—'

Oliver ran a hand through his damp hair and interrupted. 'Did you ask anyone else about me?'

Amelia's hesitation was brief but noticeable. 'Well—'

'Amelia,' he groaned. 'Who else?'

'I might have mentioned to Kaitlyn at the primary school that my brother was single.'

Oliver stared at her in disbelief. 'Kaitlyn Miller? The one who coaches the under-fives football?'

'That's the one,' Amelia nodded. 'She's pretty, she's sporty, and she's good with kids.'

'And?'

'And what?'

'What did she say?' Oliver demanded, suddenly feeling strangely curious.

Amelia examined her fingernails. 'I won't tell you what she said, though.'

Something in her tone made Oliver sit up straight. 'What did she say?'

'It doesn't matter.'

'Clearly it does, or you wouldn't have brought it up,' he countered. 'What did she say?'

Amelia sighed dramatically. 'She said, and I quote, "If a man has to get his sister to ask her friends to go out with her brother, there's something wrong with the brother".'

Indignation heated his face. 'There's nothing wrong with me!'

'That's what I told her!' Amelia said, patting his knee. 'I

said you were just shy and busy and terrible at talking to women.'

'Not helping,' he muttered.

'But that's exactly my point, Oli,' she continued, her expression growing serious. 'You're a great guy, but you never put yourself out there. You hide behind the farm and your responsibilities. You need to show people—women—who you really are.'

Oliver sighed, recognising the futility of further argument. 'One coffee. That's it. And then you delete this profile.'

'If you absolutely hate it, I'll *consider* deleting it,' Amelia hedged.

'Amelia.' He took a deep breath in an attempt to calm down.

'Fine! If you go on the date and truly hate it, I'll delete the profile,' she conceded. 'But you have to actually try, Oli. No scowling, no checking your watch every five minutes, and absolutely no talking about irrigation systems unless she asks.'

'I don't only talk about irrigation,' he protested weakly.

'Last Christmas dinner, you spent forty-five minutes explaining drip systems to Uncle Bob.'

'He asked!'

'He was being polite! His eyes were glazed over when he went for another beer.' Amelia closed the laptop with a decisive snap. 'Tuesday, four o'clock. Wear that blue shirt Charlotte got you for your birthday—it makes your eyes look less murderous.'

'My eyes don't look murderous,' Oliver grumbled.

'They absolutely do when you're talking to women you don't know,' she said, standing up. 'It's like you're trying to scare them off before they can reject you.'

'That's ridiculous.'

'Is it, though?' Amelia paused at the door. 'Just . . . try, okay? For me. And maybe a little bit for you.'

After she left, Oliver lay back on his bed, staring at the ceiling fan. A date. With a kindergarten teacher. Who thought he was an artisanal baker with a passion for astronomy.

This was going to be a disaster.

He rolled onto his side, catching sight of the moon through his window. Despite himself, he found his thoughts drifting to Sarah again. What would she be doing right now? Had she left the district? Found someone else? He'd looked for her at the markets for weeks after losing her number, but her craft stall site had remained stubbornly empty. He hadn't had the confidence to seek her out.

Coward, that persistent little voice whispered.

Maybe Amelia was right. Maybe it was time to move on. With a deep sigh, Oliver closed his eyes, too exhausted to worry about it anymore. His last thought before sleep claimed him was that he really, really hoped Jessica wouldn't ask him about constellations.

Chapter 3

Oliver wiped his brow with the back of his hand, leaving a smear of dirt across his forehead. The morning had been productive—two irrigation lines fixed, a fence mended where a fallen branch had taken out a section during last week's storm, and a start on clearing the access road to the eastern paddocks. Now, with the midday sun beating down mercilessly, he'd retreated to the shade of the equipment shed for lunch. Guy had gone to Bundaberg for the day to a grower's meeting.

He unscrewed his thermos and took a long drink of lukewarm water before unwrapping the ham and cheese sandwich Amelia had packed. His phone buzzed in his pocket, and he pulled it out with dirt-stained fingers to find a notification from CountryConnections.

'Jessica has sent you a message!'

Oliver groaned. He'd almost managed to forget about Monday's upcoming coffee date, but there it was, a bright, cheerful reminder that at four o'clock on Monday afternoon, he'd be sitting across from a kindergarten teacher who expected him to be an astronomy-loving baker with a penchant for long walks, and with a fluffy dog, to add insult to injury.

Against his better judgement, he opened the app, wincing at the profile photo Amelia had chosen. It really was a good picture of him—caught mid-laugh at last year's Crush Festival, wearing a clean blue shirt (Charlotte's doing) and looking far more approachable than he felt most days.

Jessica's message was short and friendly: 'Looking forward to meeting you at The Bean Counter on Monday! I'll be wearing a yellow dress. See you at 4!'

Oliver grimaced. She sounded nice. Which made what he

was about to do even worse. He typed out a reply, his thumbs hovering over the keys.

'Something's come up on the farm. Need to reschedule.'

His finger hovered over 'Send' for a long moment before he deleted the message with a sigh. Amelia would know he was lying. She'd probably already texted Jessica from his phone anyway, judging by the earlier messages he'd scrolled through with mounting horror. His supposed enthusiasm for Jessica's classroom garden project had been expressed with far more exclamation marks than he'd used in his entire life.

He shoved the phone back in his pocket and took a bite of his sandwich, chewing mechanically as he stared out across the cane fields.

When he'd finished eating, Oliver reluctantly checked his watch. One forty-five. He had the whole weekend to prepare mentally. Amelia had insisted on a Monday date, claiming it would "start his week off right," though Oliver suspected it was just because Jessica wasn't available on the weekend.

'This is ridiculous,' he muttered to himself as he packed away his lunch things.

One coffee. He could survive one coffee, he told himself.

Back at the house, he found Amelia waiting for him, a knowing smile on her face.

'What are you doing home?'

'I only work mornings on Fridays. Haven't you ever noticed?' She held up one hand. 'Don't bother answering. Unless it grows in a cane field or on a tree, you don't notice.'

'That's a bit harsh.'

His sister shrugged and pulled a face. 'Maybe harsh, but true.'

Oliver frowned. Surely, she was exaggerating.

'I've laid out your blue shirt for Monday,' Amelia continued, pointing toward his bedroom. 'And there are clean jeans on the bed. You can't wear what you usually wear.'

'I was going to wear what I've got on,' he said, gesturing to his dirt-streaked work clothes.

Amelia's eyes widened in horror. 'You will not sabotage this date before it even starts, Oliver Johnson. Shower. Blue shirt. Clean jeans. Don't even think about it.'

'I was joking. Where's your sense of humour?'

'You were not.'

'I was. And it's not a date, it's a coffee.'

'It's a date,' she insisted, crossing her arms. 'And you're going to be charming and talk about something other than mango varieties.'

That made him think of Sarah. She'd been fascinated when he'd told her about the different varieties last year at the Dunmora markets. Shame she'd never turned up again after that first time.

'Fine,' Oliver agreed reluctantly. 'I'll be charming and agreeable and wear the blue shirt. But just this once.'

'That's all I ask,' Amelia said with a triumphant smile.

Oliver rolled his eyes but didn't argue.

Forty minutes later, freshly showered and wearing the blue shirt that Charlotte swore brought out his eyes, Oliver trudged out to his ute. He stopped short when he saw it, noticing for the first time in weeks just how filthy it was. A layer of dust coated every surface, and the tray was littered with irrigation parts, rope, and what appeared to be a work boot missing its partner.

Maybe this would work in his favour. One look at his vehicle, and Jessica would realise he wasn't the polished, poetry-reading type his profile suggested. She might even make her excuses and leave early. He could offer to drive her home, and the state of his ute would ensure she never wanted to see him again.

The thought brightened his mood considerably as he climbed behind the wheel and headed toward Bargara Beach.

***

On the other side of Bundaberg in the beachside suburb of Bargara, Sarah Matthews carefully arranged her handcrafted jewellery on a display board and then placed her soaps to one side. The Friday afternoon-evening markets had just opened, and early visitors were beginning to wander between the stalls set up along the foreshore park.

'Mummy, can I put these out?' Four-year-old Jett held up a tray of beaded bracelets, his small face serious with the responsibility.

'Of course, sweetie. Right over here.' Sarah cleared a space on the folding table, watching as her son meticulously arranged the bracelets by colour—a system he'd devised himself and insisted upon at every market.

'Is the mango man coming today?' Jett asked, his eyes scanning the growing crowd.

Sarah's heart gave its now-familiar twinge. 'No, sweetheart. I don't think so.' How long would it take to forget about the man she'd been so attracted to last year? Jett hadn't forgotten him.

Maybe forever, her heart whispered.

'But he might,' Jett insisted with the unwavering optimism of childhood. 'He said I could try the yellow ones next time.'

'The *Nam Doc Mai* variety,' Sarah said automatically, the name forever etched in her memory from Oliver's enthusiastic description. 'And yes, he might come, but the mango season's only just starting. The mangoes probably aren't ready yet.'

Jett nodded sagely, accepting this explanation as he had a dozen times before. 'When they're ready, he'll come.'

Sarah busied herself with adjusting her earring display, using the moment to compose her features. It had been nearly a year—almost to the day—since she'd met Oliver Johnson when he'd set up his mango stall at the market beside her craft stall at Dunmora. One perfect afternoon of conversation had left her smiling for days afterwards, until the realisation set in that he wasn't going to call. He probably didn't want to date someone with a child.

She'd given him her number. He'd written it down carefully on a docket, tucking it into his wallet with a promise to call that weekend. When Sunday night came with no word, she'd made excuses for him—he was busy with the farm, he'd lost the paper, his phone had died. By the following weekend, she'd decided not to go to the country markets; he obviously hadn't intended to call her.

'Stop it,' she whispered under her breath. 'It was one conversation.'

But what a conversation it had been. Oliver had been different from the men she usually met—quieter, more thoughtful, with a passion for his mangoes that had been unexpectedly endearing. He'd spent twenty minutes showing Jett how to tell when different varieties were perfectly ripe, then given him a specially selected fruit "just for being such a good listener." Jett had been enchanted, and if she were honest, so had she.

Perhaps it was because Jett was at an age where he was becoming more aware of other family structures. Lately, he'd been asking more questions about his father—questions that grew increasingly difficult to answer in ways a four-year-old could understand.

'Did my daddy like mangoes too?' he'd asked last week after they'd bought some from the grocery store.

'I think he would have,' Sarah had answered honestly. 'Your daddy liked trying new things.'

It was true. Ryan had been adventurous—a trait that had initially drawn her to him and ultimately taken him away. The motorcycle accident had happened three weeks after their brief summer romance ended, before she'd even known she was pregnant. Sometimes when Jett smiled a certain way, she caught glimpses of Ryan's carefree spirit, a bittersweet reminder of what might have been.

Sarah had long ago made peace with raising Jett alone. Ryan's parents lived interstate and, although they sent birthday cards and the occasional Christmas gift, they'd never been actively involved in Jett's life. She'd built her own support system—friends like Elaine who had become Jett's unofficial grandmother, a small community of other single parents who understood the unique challenges and joys of raising children alone.

Still, watching Oliver interact so naturally with Jett had stirred something unexpected. Not regret, exactly, but a quiet wondering about what it might be like to share the journey of parenting with someone who cared.

'Excuse me, how much for the turquoise necklace?'

Sarah's head snapped up to find a customer examining her display. 'Thirty-five dollars,' she said, pushing thoughts of Oliver aside and pasting on her market-day smile. 'Or three pieces for ninety.'

As the afternoon progressed, the markets filled with families enjoying the balmy spring weather. Sarah kept busy with a steady stream of customers but found her eyes drifting to the entrance whenever a tall, dark-haired man appeared. It was a habit she couldn't seem to break, this hopeful scanning of crowds for a glimpse of Oliver Johnson.

'You're being ridiculous,' she told herself firmly as she made change for a customer. 'He's probably forgotten all about you.'

But Jett hadn't forgotten. Every market day for months, he'd asked about the mango man at Dunmora.

'Can we go back to the Dunmora markets, Mummy?'

'We go to the Bargara Beach markets now, sweetie. They're closer to our home,' Sarah would remind him gently, not wanting to admit that she'd deliberately changed which markets they attended after Oliver never called. It had been too painful to keep setting up her stall at Dunmora, constantly watching for him, wondering if he'd appear with his mangoes and that shy smile that had made her stomach flip.

'Lookin' for someone?'

Sarah turned to find her market neighbour, Elaine, watching her with knowing eyes. The older woman sold homemade jams and had taken Sarah under her wing when she'd first started at the Bargara Beach markets two years ago.

'Just checking the crowd,' Sarah said lightly. 'Good turnout tonight.'

Elaine snorted. 'You've been watching that entrance like a hawk since you set up. That farmer boy from Dunmora never showed up here, then?'

Sarah felt herself flush. 'I'm not looking for anyone.'

'Course not,' Elaine agreed amiably. 'And I'm not seventy-three with arthritis.'

'He's just someone Jett liked,' Sarah insisted. 'He was good with kids.'

'Mmm-hmm.' Elaine began rearranging her jam jars. 'You know, my Tom was good with kids too. That's how I knew he'd make a good husband—fifty-six years we had together.'

Sarah rolled her eyes. 'I talked to the man for an afternoon, Elaine. I'm not planning our wedding.'

'More's the pity,' Elaine replied. 'A girl your age shouldn't be alone.'

'I'm not alone,' Sarah said, gesturing toward Jett, who was carefully counting change for a customer. 'I have excellent company.'

'You know what I mean.'

Sarah did know, but she also knew the reality of dating as a single mother. Most men lost interest the moment they learned about Jett, and the few who didn't usually faded away once they realised her son would always come first. She'd stopped dating entirely after the last disaster—a seemingly nice accountant who'd suggested that boarding school might be 'the best solution for everyone.'

Oliver had been different, though. He'd noticed Jett first, crouching down to her little boy's level to explain how the mango pattern varied with different varieties. He'd answered every one of Jett's rapid-fire questions with the same patience and attention he'd given to adult customers. It was only after Jett had wandered off to look at a nearby toy stall that Oliver had turned that thoughtful gaze on her.

'I figured when he didn't call, it was because of Jett,' Sarah admitted quietly. 'I thought he'd changed his mind about dating a woman with a child.'

A high-pitched squeal jolted Sarah from her memories. 'Mummy! Look, Kimmy's here!'

Sarah turned to see Jett waving frantically at his best friend from preschool, who was approaching with her parents. She smiled and waved, pushing thoughts of Oliver firmly aside. This was her life now—her son, her craft business, her friends. It was a good life, even if sometimes she found herself scanning crowds for a man who'd clearly forgotten her number as easily as he'd taken it.

***

The Bean Counter was busy when Oliver arrived, the lunch crowd still lingering over coffee and cake. He spotted Jessica immediately—her yellow dress bright against the café's muted decor, her blonde hair pulled back in a neat ponytail. She was pretty in a wholesome, approachable way, and she was checking her watch with a slight frown.

Oliver glanced at his own watch. Four-fifteen. Great start.

He made his way to her table, bumping into a chair and nearly upending a water glass in the process. 'Sorry I'm late,' he said as he reached her. 'Farm emergency.'

Jessica looked up with a smile that faltered slightly as she took him in. Was it the mud on his boots that he hadn't managed to completely clean off? Or perhaps the small grease stain on his jeans he'd only noticed in the car?

'Oliver?' she asked, a note of uncertainty in her voice.

'That's me,' he confirmed, sliding awkwardly into the chair opposite her. 'You must be Jessica.'

Her smile returned, though not quite reaching her eyes. 'Yes! It's nice to finally meet you. Your messages were so lovely.'

Oliver made a mental note to kill Amelia slowly. 'Right. Thanks.'

An awkward silence descended. Jessica took a sip of her

water, and Oliver found himself staring blankly at the menu, though he had no appetite whatsoever.

'So,' Jessica said brightly, 'you mentioned you've been experimenting with sourdough lately?'

Oliver blinked. 'Did I?'

'In your message yesterday,' she prompted. 'You said you'd finally mastered the perfect crust.'

'Ah.' Oliver cleared his throat. 'Right. Sourdough. It's . . .crusty.'

Jessica's smile dimmed slightly. 'Are you feeling alright?'

'Fine,' Oliver assured her. 'Just been a long morning on the farm. To be honest, my sister handles most of the baking. I pass the ingredients and I'm . . . um, the taste tester.'

Jessica laughed. 'Well, that's an important job too. I'm hopeless in the kitchen myself—except for cookies. I have to make those with my kindergarteners.'

A waitress appeared, and they ordered—a flat white for him, a chai latte for her.

'You're a kindergarten teacher?' Oliver asked, remembering Amelia's briefing.

Jessica's face lit up. 'Yes! I teach at Elliott Heads. I've just started a garden project with my class—we're growing vegetables and learning about plant life cycles. The children are so excited about it.'

Oliver nodded, genuinely interested. 'What are you growing?'

'Oh, all sorts! Lettuce, carrots, cherry tomatoes—things that grow quickly so the children can see results. We've just harvested our first radishes.'

'You should try sugar snap peas,' Oliver suggested, warming to the topic. 'They're fast-growing, and kids can eat them straight from the vine. My sister Amelia used to grow them when we were kids.'

Jessica beamed. 'That's a wonderful idea! Have you done much gardening with children?'

'Not really,' Oliver admitted. 'Just grew up on a farm.'

'Oh, yes, your profile mentioned you're a cane farmer. That must be fascinating work.'

Oliver relaxed slightly, on familiar ground at last. 'It has its moments. We've just finished the harvest season—the crush, we call it. Now we're preparing for next year's planting and maintaining the ratoon crop.'

Jessica listened attentively, but her attention wandered as he spoke. Farming wasn't her passion, despite the vegetable garden. Their drinks arrived, providing another welcome break in the conversation.

'So,' Jessica said after taking a sip of her chai, 'you mentioned you enjoy astronomy? Have you been to the observatory in Bundaberg?'

Oliver silently added another tally mark to Amelia's death sentence. 'Not recently,' he hedged. 'Been busy with the farm.'

'Oh, they have the most wonderful Friday night viewings at the observatory! They're focusing on the southern constellations tonight.' She paused, looking at him with a hopeful smile. 'Perhaps we could go sometime?'

Oliver shifted uncomfortably. 'I don't really get many nights off, to be honest.'

'I understand,' she said, though disappointment flickered across her face. 'Farming must keep you busy. What about the weekend markets? Your profile mentioned you enjoy them.'

'I do go to the markets,' Oliver said truthfully. 'I sell mangoes there when they're in season.'

'Oh, that sounds lovely! Are they in season now?'

'Just starting,' Oliver said, a plan forming in his mind. 'The early varieties are ripening.'

'Would you be at the Bargara night market tonight, then?' Jessica asked. 'We could walk around, maybe look at the stars afterward?'

'No, not tonight,' Oliver said, seizing the escape route. 'I need to get back to the farm. Lots of work to do before dark.'

'Oh.' Jessica's face fell. 'Some other time, perhaps?'

Oliver stared into his coffee, discomfort mingling with guilt. 'Look, Jessica, you seem really nice—'

'But there's not really a spark,' she finished for him, her smile tightening slightly. 'It's okay, Oliver. I've been on enough first dates to recognise when someone isn't interested.'

Oliver shifted awkwardly. 'I'm sorry.'

'Don't be.' She took another sip of her chai, her eyes studying him over the rim. 'Though I am curious—your messages were so enthusiastic about baking and astronomy, but you don't seem interested in them. Actually, not interested in much at all.'

'That obvious, huh?'

'You have an expressive face,' she said diplomatically. 'So, what parts of your profile are true?'

'I do farm sugar cane,' Oliver offered. 'And I sell mangoes at the markets when they're in season. That's about it.'

Jessica nodded thoughtfully. 'Well, I'm glad we've cleared the air.' She glanced at her watch. 'I should probably get going anyway.'

Relief mingled with a touch of regret as Oliver realised Jessica was actually okay.

'Thanks for meeting me,' she said, gathering her purse. 'My

car's just down the street.' She hesitated, then added with a warm smile, 'For what it's worth, you do seem perfectly nice, even without the sourdough expertise.'

Oliver managed a genuine smile in return. 'Thanks. And I meant what I said about the sugar snap peas. They really are good for kids' gardens.'

'I'll definitely try them,' Jessica promised. 'And if you're ever selling mangoes at the market, I'd love to buy some. We're studying tropical fruits next month.'

'I'll let you know,' Oliver said.

With a final smile, Jessica left, leaving Oliver to pay the bill and contemplate the damage Amelia had done to his reputation. Still, it hadn't been the disaster he'd feared. Jessica had been understanding, even kind, about the whole situation.

As he walked back to his ute, Oliver's thoughts drifted unexpectedly to Sarah. Would she be at the markets this weekend? It was early in the mango season, but some of his early varieties were ready. He could have brought a small selection, set up his usual stall—

'Don't be ridiculous,' he whispered to himself as he climbed into the driver's seat. 'She's probably left the district. Stop dreaming.'

Still, as he drove back toward the farm, Oliver found himself wondering if Sarah's son, Jett, that was his name, still remembered how to tell when a Kensington Pride was perfectly ripe. The boy had been a quick study, his small hands gentle on the fruit as Oliver showed him what to look for.

For the first time since agreeing to this coffee date, Oliver smiled. Maybe a trip to the markets wasn't a bad idea.

Chapter 4

'Can't see you, Grandmère,' Amelia said.

'Is this thing working? Hugo, is the camera on?' Grandmère's voice came through clearly, though the video showed only the ceiling of what appeared to be a French apartment.

'It's on, Margot, they just can't see us because you're holding it wrong,' came Papa's patient reply.

Oliver exchanged amused glances with Guy and Amelia as they sat clustered around the kitchen table, Amelia's laptop open before them. It was Sunday evening, and the promised weekly video call from France had finally connected after three failed attempts.

'Here, let me—' There was a rustling noise, followed by a dizzying spin of images before Grandmère's face appeared, far too close to the camera. Her eyes were magnified comically behind her reading glasses as she peered into the screen.

'Ah! There you are!' she exclaimed triumphantly. 'Can you see me too?'

'We can see your pores now, Grandmère,' Amelia said with a laugh. 'Maybe move back a bit?'

Grandmère shifted, and the camera panned out to reveal her sitting in a sunny apartment, lace curtains billowing in a gentle breeze behind her. Papa sat beside her, looking relaxed in a pale blue linen shirt, his usual serious expression replaced by a contented smile. Their parents stood behind them, Mum's face glowing with excitement and, to Oliver's surprise, Dad wearing a beret.

'Is that a beret?' Guy asked incredulously, leaning forward.

Dad grinned sheepishly and touched the dark blue fabric.

'When in France,' he said with a shrug. 'Your mother says it suits me.'

'You look like an artist, Dad,' Amelia said diplomatically. 'Very . . . European.'

'It was my idea,' Grandmère announced proudly. 'Hugo needs to embrace his heritage!'

'How's France?' Oliver asked, steering the conversation away from his father's unexpected fashion choice. 'Have you seen the vineyards yet?'

'Oh, *mes petits choux*!' Grandmère clasped her hands together, her face radiant. 'We arrived in Lyon yesterday, and tomorrow we go to my village. But already, it is *magnifique*! The food, the people, the buildings—everything is as beautiful as I remembered.'

'Your grandmother hasn't stopped smiling since we landed,' Papa said fondly, patting her hand. 'Even when we got lost trying to find the apartment.'

'We weren't lost,' Grandmère insisted. 'We were exploring.'

'We walked in circles for two hours,' Dad deadpanned, but his eyes twinkled with good humour. 'Carrying luggage.'

'Exercise is good for you, Hugo,' Grandmère said dismissively. 'And we found the most charming little bakery while we were . . . exploring.'

'The bread,' Mum interjected, leaning closer to the camera. 'You wouldn't believe the bread here. And the cheese! I've never tasted anything like it.'

Oliver was taken aback by the change in their usually reserved mother. Ellen Johnson was not given to exclamations or hyperbole, yet here she was, rhapsodising about cheese with shining eyes and flushed cheeks. France clearly agreed with her.

'Where are Charlotte and Greg?' Amelia asked, scanning the background with a frown.

'They've gone to Paris for the weekend,' Ellen explained. 'Charlotte wanted to see the Louvre, and there was a train. So—' She waved her hand vaguely, clearly having embraced the spontaneity of travel.

'Dad let them go off without a detailed itinerary?' Guy murmured to Oliver. 'Who is this man and what has he done with our father?'

Oliver stifled a laugh. Even when they were kids, their father's idea of a day trip to Bargara Beach had always involved military-level planning and multiple backup routes.

'And how are things at the farm?' Dad asked, making a visible effort to sound casual, though they all recognised the strain in his voice. Four days without checking on his crops was probably a personal record.

'Everything's fine, Dad,' Guy said reassuringly. 'The irrigation system on the east field is fixed, and I've scheduled the contractors for the fence repairs next week.'

Dad nodded, clearly fighting the urge to ask for more details. 'And the mangoes, Oli?'

'Coming along,' Oliver reported. 'The early varieties are starting to ripen. I'm thinking of taking some to the Bargara markets.'

'Oh, the markets!' Mum's face lit up further. 'Will you be seeing that lovely girl again? The one with the crafts?'

Oliver felt heat creep up his neck. 'I don't know. Maybe.' He studiously avoided looking at Amelia, who was surely grinning like the Cheshire cat beside him.

'What lovely girl?' Grandmère demanded, leaning closer to the camera again. 'Oliver has a girl?'

'Sarah,' Mum supplied helpfully. 'He met her at the markets last year. She makes jewellery and has the most adorable little boy. I bought some presents from her stall when Oliver was next to her at the Christmas markets. What was his name again, Oli?'

'Jett,' Oliver mumbled, cursing his mother's sudden onset of matchmaking across international borders. 'And I barely know her. We talked once.'

'Why wasn't I told about this?' Grandmère's face filled the screen again. 'Once is enough when it's the right person,' Grandmère declared with the confidence of someone who'd been married for over sixty years.

Amelia snorted beside Oliver, and he frowned.

'Your grandfather proposed to me after one dance,' Grandmère said.

'And then courted you properly for two years before you actually got married,' Papa reminded her with a chuckle.

'Details,' Grandmère dismissed. 'The important thing is, he knew.'

'Speaking of dating,' Amelia interjected gleefully, 'Oliver went on his first online date yesterday!'

Oliver shot her a glare that would have withered the sugar cane, but it was too late. The damage was done.

'Online date?' Mum echoed, her expression a mixture of surprise and delight. 'Who with?'

'A kindergarten teacher named Jessica,' Amelia supplied before Oliver could stop her. 'Very pretty. Blonde. Teaches at Elliot Heads.'

'How did it go?' Dad asked, looking oddly proud. 'Did you take her somewhere nice?'

'I—' Oliver started, but Amelia cut him off again.

'Coffee at The Bean Counter,' she said. 'And it went—'

'Fine,' Oliver interrupted firmly. 'It went fine.'

'Oh, Oliver!' Mum clapped her hands together. 'I'm so pleased you're putting yourself out there.'

'About time,' Grandmère added. 'A man your age should be thinking about settling down.'

'I'm only twenty-five,' Oliver protested weakly.

'Exactly!' Grandmère nodded as if he'd made her point for her. 'When I was twenty-five, I already had your father.'

'Different times, Margot,' Papa said gently.

'The heart doesn't change with time,' Grandmère insisted. 'Now, tell me about this Jessica. Is she French?'

'No,' Oliver said shortly.

'Ah, well, no one is perfect,' Grandmère sighed. 'Will you see her again?'

'No,' Oliver repeated, wishing the floor would open and swallow him whole. 'It wasn't . . . We didn't . . . It just wasn't a match.'

'And that's fine!' Mum said encouragingly. 'The important thing is that you tried. There are plenty more fish in the sea.'

'Or on the internet,' Amelia added with a smirk.

Oliver briefly contemplated sororicide.

'Well, keep trying,' Dad said, in the same tone he used when discussing failed crop experiments. 'You'll find the right fertiliser mix eventually.'

Guy choked on his beer.

'Your father means the right person,' Mum translated hastily. 'Don't you, Hugo?'

'Of course,' Dad agreed. 'Though the principle is the same. Trial and error. Data collection. Eventual success.'

'I think what Dad's trying to say,' Guy said, still coughing slightly, 'is good luck.'

'Exactly,' Dad nodded firmly. 'Good luck with the . . . dating.'

The conversation mercifully moved on to other topics—Grandmère's cousins they would meet the next day, the excellent wine they'd tried at a local restaurant, and Papa's run-in with a particularly persistent street vendor. Oliver found his attention drifting, his thoughts wandering back to the markets and whether Sarah would be there on Friday.

'. . . don't you think, Oliver?' His mother's voice snapped him back to the present.

'Sorry, what?' he asked, blinking.

Ellen's eyes narrowed knowingly. 'I said, if Jessica wasn't the right match, perhaps you should look for this Sarah again.'

'I don't even know if she still lives in Bundaberg,' Oliver said, trying to sound disinterested. 'It's been a year.'

'You won't know until you look,' Mum pointed out reasonably. 'What have you got to lose?'

'His dignity,' Guy muttered under his breath.

Oliver kicked him under the table.

'Well, we should get going,' Dad said, glancing at his watch. 'We're meeting some of your grandmother's cousins for *un déjeuner décontracté*.'

Amelia stifled a laugh, and Oliver grinned at her. Dad's pronunciation was appalling.

'That means lunch,' Mum translated. 'Your father's been confusing the poor locals with his accent everywhere we go.'

'At least you're trying, Dad.' Oliver gave a thumbs-up in front of the screen.

'Call us again next Sunday,' Mum instructed. 'And Oliver, do let us know how the dating goes!'

After a flurry of goodbyes and Grandmère's solemn promise

to find Oliver a nice French girl if all else failed, the call ended, leaving the three siblings sitting in silence.

'That went well,' Amelia said brightly.

'Why the hell did you tell them about my date with Jessica?' Oliver demanded.

'Because you weren't going to,' she replied, unrepentant. 'And they seemed happy about it.'

'Too happy,' Guy agreed. 'Did you see Dad? I thought he was going to start planning a wedding.'

'He compared dating to fertiliser,' Oliver said flatly.

'Which, coming from Dad, is practically poetry,' Amelia pointed out. 'He was trying to be supportive.'

Oliver slumped back in his chair. 'Now they're all going to ask about my dating life every time we FaceTime.'

'Would that be so terrible?' Amelia asked, her tone gentler. 'They care about you, Oli.'

'Besides,' Guy added, standing up and stretching, 'at least it distracts Dad from interrogating us about the farm.' He headed for the door. 'I'm going to check the irrigation timers before bed.'

After he'd gone, Amelia turned to Oliver, her expression unusually serious. 'So, are you going to the markets at Dunmora on Friday?'

Oliver hesitated. 'I don't know. Maybe.'

'To look for Sarah?'

'To sell mangoes,' he insisted, though they both knew it wasn't the whole truth.

Amelia studied him for a moment, then nodded. 'Well, if you need help setting up your stall, let me know. I'm free. Myron is working all weekend.'

'Thanks,' Oliver said, surprised by the offer. 'I might take you up on that.'

Amelia smiled and closed her laptop. 'In the meantime, I've scheduled another date for you on Tuesday, anyway. Her name is Brittany, she's an accountant, and she loves action movies.'

'Amelia!' Oliver groaned.

'Just keeping my options open,' she said with a wink as she left the room.

Oliver sat alone at the kitchen table, contemplating the absurdity of his situation. A sister determined to find him love through the internet, a family cheering from across the world, and him still thinking about a woman he'd met once a year ago.

He'd go to the markets on Friday, he decided. Just to sell mangoes. And if Sarah happened to be there . . . well, he'd cross that bridge when he came to it.

***

'You should try it,' Elaine insisted, pushing another homemade jam scone across the table toward Sarah. 'Changed my life, it did.'

Sarah took the scone despite being already full from the first one. Saying no to Elaine was like trying to stop a tidal wave with a teaspoon—futile and likely to leave you soaked.

'Online dating is not going to change my life,' she said, taking a bite to be polite. 'It's just going to introduce me to a bunch of men who'll disappear the moment they find out I have a four-year-old.'

They were sitting in Elaine's cosy kitchen, the Sunday afternoon sunlight streaming through gingham curtains. Jett was in the garden with Elaine's grandson, Charlie, the two boys engrossed in a complex game involving dinosaurs and what appeared to be world domination.

'Not everyone's like that Richard,' Elaine said dismissively.

'Good riddance to bad rubbish, I say.'

Sarah smiled despite herself. Elaine had never forgiven 'that Richard' for suggesting boarding school for Jett. In Elaine's world, there were few sins greater than not appreciating children.

'Besides,' Elaine continued, pouring more tea, 'my niece met her husband online. Married two years now and expecting their first. And my hairdresser's daughter—'

'Found her soulmate on CountryConnections, I know,' Sarah finished for her. Elaine had been regaling her with online dating success stories for weeks now. 'But I'm not looking for a husband, Elaine. I'm perfectly happy as we are.'

'Course you are,' Elaine agreed readily. 'You and Jett make a lovely little family. But that doesn't mean you can't have more, does it? A partner. Someone to share the load.'

Sarah sighed, running a finger around the rim of her teacup. The truth was, she had considered it. Late at night, after Jett was asleep, when the house was quiet and the worry of being a sole parent pressed heavily in her mind—she'd thought about what it might be like to have someone to talk to, to laugh with, to help make decisions.

'I wouldn't even know where to start,' she admitted. 'What would I put in a profile? "Single mum, makes jewellery, comes with energetic four-year-old who asks a million questions a day"?'

'Sounds perfect to me,' Elaine said with a nod. 'The right man would read that and think he'd hit the jackpot.'

Sarah laughed. 'You're an incurable romantic, Elaine Hargraves.'

'Married fifty-six years? Someone found me appealing.'

They watched the boys through the window for a moment, Jett's dark head bent close to Charlie's fair one as they arranged plastic dinosaurs in formation.

'He asks about him, you know,' Sarah said quietly. 'The mango farmer. Every market day.'

'Ah.' Elaine's expression softened. 'Children remember the oddest things.'

'It's not odd,' Sarah found herself defending Oliver. 'He was kind to Jett. And took an interest in what he was saying. That matters to him.'

Elaine's shrewd eyes studied her face. 'And to his mother, I'd wager.'

Sarah felt her cheeks warm. 'He was nice, that's all.'

'And yet here you are, a year later, still hoping he'll turn up with his mangoes.'

'I'm not—' Sarah began, then sighed. 'Am I that obvious?'

'Only to someone who's known you since you started at the markets when you were pregnant with Jett,' Elaine said gently. 'You scan every crowd, love. Your face falls a little each time he's not there.'

Sarah stared into her tea, embarrassed to be so transparent. 'It's ridiculous. We talked once, Elaine. A few hours.'

'Sometimes that's all it takes,' Elaine said. 'My Tom proposed after our first date.'

'Different times,' Sarah reminded her.

'The heart doesn't change with time,' Elaine countered. 'But chances do pass us by if we don't take them.'

Sarah knew what was coming next.

'Which is why,' Elaine continued, right on cue, 'you should try online dating. If this mango man doesn't show up, at least you'll have other options.'

Sarah ran her finger around the rim of her teacup. 'It's not that simple, Elaine. Most men aren't exactly lining up to date a woman with a child.'

'The right man wouldn't see Jett as an obstacle,' Elaine said firmly.

'That's what I thought about David last year, remember? Three dates in, he suggested Jett might be "happier in a structured environment". Code for "can the kid be somewhere else when I come over.".'

Elaine made a dismissive noise. 'David was a fool. Not all men are like that.'

'And not all men are like Ryan, either,' Sarah said quietly.

Elaine's expression softened at the mention of Jett's father. 'No, dear, they're not. Ryan was a special young man in many ways.'

'He would have been a good dad,' Sarah said, the familiar ache of what-might-have-been rising in her chest. 'If he'd had the chance.'

'I believe he would have,' Elaine agreed. 'But life had other plans.'

Through the window, they watched Jett, now orchestrating an elaborate dinosaur battle with Charlie. His animated gestures and infectious laugh were so reminiscent of Ryan that it sometimes took Sarah's breath away.

'It'll be five years next month,' Sarah said. 'Since the accident. Sometimes I wonder if I'm doing right by Jett, raising him without a father figure.'

'You're doing wonderfully,' Elaine assured her. 'That boy is happy, healthy, and confident. Ryan would be proud of you both.'

Sarah nodded, grateful for the reassurance. 'Jett's been asking more questions lately. Specific ones. What did his daddy's voice sound like? Did he like dinosaurs too? Questions

I sometimes don't have answers for.'

'That's natural at his age,' Elaine said. 'He's making sense of his place in the world.'

'I've been thinking it might be time to visit Ryan's parents again,' Sarah admitted. 'They have videos, photos from when Ryan was young. Things that might help Jett connect with that part of himself.'

'That's a good idea,' Elaine approved. 'And speaking of connections...' She gestured meaningfully toward Sarah's laptop.

Sarah smiled despite herself. 'Back to the dating app, are we?'

'Just saying that moving forward doesn't mean leaving the past behind,' Elaine said wisely. 'It means building on the foundation you already have.'

Put that way, it didn't sound completely unreasonable. And what did she have to lose? If nothing else, it might help her finally stop looking for Oliver in every crowd.

'I'll think about it,' Sarah promised, knowing it would be easier than arguing.

'Put that way, it didn't sound completely unreasonable. And what did she have to lose? If nothing else, it might help her finally stop looking for Oliver in every crowd.

'I'll think about it,' Sarah promised, knowing it would be easier than arguing.

Elaine beamed in triumph. 'That's all I ask. Now, have another scone. You're skin and bones, girl!'

Chapter 5

'You can't wear that.'

Oliver looked down at his faded blue work shirt and relatively clean jeans. 'What's wrong with this?'

Amelia rolled her eyes so dramatically that Oliver worried they might get stuck that way. 'You're going to the cinema, not mending fences. Don't you own any clothes that don't scream "I've been wrestling with agricultural equipment all day"?'

'I like this shirt,' Oliver protested. 'And I have been wrestling with agricultural equipment all day.'

They were standing in Oliver's bedroom, the late afternoon sun slanting through the shutters. Outside, the humidity hung heavy in the air, promising rain later. Oliver had been hoping the weather might provide an excuse to cancel tonight's date, but the downpour had yet to materialise, and Amelia had been monitoring his movements with the vigilance of a prison guard since lunch.

Ten days had passed since the coffee date with Jessica. That hadn't gone well, though at least they'd parted on friendly terms. But Amelia had wasted no time in setting up this second date for Thursday evening, giving him just enough time to recover from the first disaster before launching him into another.

'At least wear the green button-down,' she insisted, rummaging through his wardrobe. 'The one Charlotte got you for Christmas.'

'It's too hot for that.'

'It's too hot for excuses, Oli. Brittany is an accountant—a professional. You can't turn up looking like you've just fallen off a tractor.'

'I haven't fallen off a tractor since I was twelve,' Oliver

muttered, but he took the green shirt she was now brandishing at him like a weapon.

Guy appeared in the doorway, leaning against the frame with a barely concealed smirk. 'Having a fashion crisis, brother?'

'I'm having a sister crisis,' Oliver replied. 'Didn't you have something to fix in the shed?'

'Nope. Everything's running smoothly.' Guy's smirk widened. 'Unlike your love life.'

'It's not a love life,' Oliver protested, shrugging off his work shirt. 'It's a hostage situation.'

Amelia huffed. 'You should be thanking me. Brittany is perfect for you. She's practical, organised, and she loves the outdoors.'

'She's an accountant,' Oliver pointed out, buttoning up the green shirt. 'How much time does she actually spend outdoors?'

'She goes hiking on weekends,' Amelia said. 'At least, that's what her profile claims.'

'That fills me with confidence.'

Guy chuckled. 'Maybe she'll help you organise the farm books. Heaven knows they could use it.'

'There's nothing wrong with my bookkeeping,' Oliver growled, tucking in his shirt and checking his reflection in the mirror. The green did bring out his eyes, though he'd never admit that to Charlotte or Amelia.

'There's nothing wrong with your bookkeeping because I do it all,' Guy corrected. 'Your idea of financial records is a shoebox full of receipts.'

'It's a system.'

'It's a fire hazard.'

'Boys,' Amelia interrupted, 'can we focus? Oli, you need to leave in ten minutes if you're going to make it to Bundaberg by seven. Brittany said she'd meet you in the cinema foyer.'

Oliver nodded, trying to ignore the knot of dread in his stomach. One more date. He could survive one more date. And then maybe Amelia would leave him alone long enough for him to focus on the Bargara market. If the weather held, he'd take his early mangoes and set up his usual stall.

'You look good. She'll love you,' Amelia said, her tone softening as she brushed imaginary lint from his shoulder. 'Just try to relax and be yourself.'

'My self wants to stay home and check the irrigation system before the rain hits,' Oliver said.

'I've got the irrigation covered,' Guy assured him. 'And the rest of the farm. Go watch a movie, eat some overpriced popcorn, talk to a woman who isn't related to you by blood.'

'A novel concept,' Amelia agreed. 'Now go. And remember—'

'No talking about sugar cane prices, irrigation systems, or the latest tractor models,' Oliver recited dutifully. 'I've got it.'

'And no checking your watch every five minutes,' Amelia added.

'And maybe try smiling,' Guy suggested. 'People generally find that less terrifying than your usual expression.'

Oliver scowled at him. 'This is my smiling face.'

'God help us all,' Guy muttered.

Ten minutes later, Oliver was in his ute, driving toward Bundaberg with a sense of impending doom. The sky was darkening with both the setting sun and gathering storm clouds, and the air felt thick with electricity. Perfect weather for a movie, he supposed, if not for the drive home afterwards.

He tried to remember what Amelia had told him about Brittany. Thirty-two, divorced, no children, worked for an accounting firm in Bundaberg. Liked hiking, cooking, and action movies—the last being the only detail that had given Oliver any hope for the evening.

By the time he reached the cinema, the first fat drops of rain were beginning to fall. He parked as close as he could manage and jogged to the entrance, grateful at least for the excuse to keep the date short. 'Sorry, need to get home before the roads flood' seemed like a perfectly reasonable escape strategy.

Brittany was waiting in the lobby, checking her phone with a slight frown. She was attractive in a polished way—sleek brown hair cut in a bob, subtle makeup, wearing a stylish blouse and tailored trousers that made Oliver suddenly conscious of his farm-boy attire despite the green shirt upgrade.

'Brittany?' he approached with what he hoped was a normal, non-terrifying smile.

She looked up, her frown instantly transforming into a bright smile. 'Oliver! Hi!' She tucked her phone into a small leather handbag. 'I was beginning to think I'd been stood up.'

Oliver checked his watch. He was three minutes late. 'Sorry about that. Traffic.'

'No worries,' she said breezily. 'Shall we get tickets? There's a new rom-com showing that's supposed to be amazing. It's got that actor from the TV show about the hospital—you know the one?'

Oliver didn't know the one, but he nodded anyway. 'Actually, I thought maybe that new action film might be good? The one with the explosions?' He gestured vaguely toward a poster featuring a man leaping from a burning building.

Brittany's smile dimmed slightly. 'Oh. I'd heard the plot was a bit—thin.'

'Explosions don't need much plot,' Oliver offered, then

immediately regretted it as Brittany's eyebrows rose.

'I see,' she said, in a tone that suggested she did indeed see, and was not impressed. 'Well, there's a comedy showing too. About a family road trip gone wrong?'

Oliver seized on the compromise. 'Perfect. Comedy works.'

As they got in line for tickets, Oliver's phone buzzed in his pocket. He pulled it out to see a text from Guy.

Eastern irrigation system acting up. Nothing urgent. Enjoy your date.

Oliver frowned, quickly typing back: **Define 'up.**

The reply came seconds later: **Just making noise. I'll check it tomorrow.**

'Everything okay?' Brittany asked as they reached the ticket counter.

'Fine,' Oliver said, tucking his phone away. 'Just farm stuff.'

'Two for *Family Vacation Disaster*, please,' Brittany told the cashier, reaching for her purse.

'I've got it,' Oliver said quickly, handing over his card. One thing his mother had drilled into him was that the person who does the inviting does the paying, and while technically Amelia had done the inviting, he wasn't about to start the evening by letting Brittany pay.

'Thanks,' she said, seeming genuinely pleased. 'Shall we get popcorn?'

Oliver nodded, relieved to have successfully navigated the first hurdle. Maybe this wouldn't be as awkward as the coffee date with Jessica.

The concession line was long, giving them their first real opportunity to talk. Brittany seemed content to lead the conversation, telling him about her job at the accounting firm and a hiking trip she'd taken to Lamington National Park the previous month.

'Do you hike much?' she asked, finally opening a space for him to contribute.

'Not recreationally,' Oliver admitted. 'I do plenty of walking on the farm, but it's usually with a purpose.'

'Like what?'

'Checking irrigation lines, inspecting crops, mending fences—that sort of thing.'

Brittany nodded politely. 'Your profile mentioned you grow sugar cane? That must be interesting.'

Oliver hesitated, remembering Amelia's warning about talking farming. 'It has its moments.'

His phone buzzed again before he could elaborate. Another text from Guy: **Eastern irrigation system definitely making weird noise. Kind of a grinding sound. Still not urgent.**

Oliver frowned. Guy knew irrigation systems. If he said it wasn't urgent, it probably wasn't. But a grinding sound usually meant something needed attention before it became a bigger problem.

'Sorry,' he said, tucking the phone away again as they reached the counter. 'What size popcorn would you like?'

'Medium is fine. With butter, please.'

They collected their popcorn and drinks and found their seats just as the previews were starting. The theatre was about half full, mostly with couples and a few groups of teenagers. Oliver settled in, hoping the film would be at least moderately entertaining.

It wasn't.

Family Vacation Disaster turned out to be an aptly named film, though not in the way the creators had intended. The jokes fell flat, the acting was stiff, and the plot—involving a family getting lost in the woods with a series of increasingly implausible mishaps—made Oliver wonder if the scriptwriter had ever actually been camping.

Beside him, Brittany seemed equally unimpressed, picking at her popcorn without much enthusiasm. Oliver was just considering how to diplomatically suggest they cut their losses and leave when his phone vibrated again.

Eastern irrigation system now making serious noise. Like an angry bull. May need parts from town tomorrow.

Oliver grimaced. The eastern irrigation system controlled water flow to nearly a quarter of their fields. If it failed, they'd lose valuable watering time during a critical growth period. His phone buzzed again:

Don't panic. Not urgent tonight. Elena from the seasonal crew is helping. She's worked on similar systems in Brazil. Seriously, enjoy your date.

Then a third message: **Sorry for all the texts. Will stop now.**

Oliver stared at the message, momentarily distracted from his date disaster. Elena Santiago was the new hire who'd joined their seasonal crew three weeks ago—quiet, efficient, and, according to the supervisor, knowledgeable beyond her pay grade. Guy had mentioned her twice at dinner last week, which was unusual for his brother, who rarely noticed the seasonal workers beyond their productivity metrics.

He typed back quickly: **You called in seasonal help on a Thursday night?**

Guy's response came immediately: She was already at the farm, going over some water conservation proposals with me. Just happened to be here when the system started acting up.

Oliver raised an eyebrow at that. Guy reviewing proposals with a seasonal worker on a Thursday evening? That was certainly new. He slipped the phone back into his pocket, trying to refocus on the movie. On screen, the family's father was now attempting to build a shelter using twigs and what appeared to be the son's hoodie.

'That would collapse immediately,' Oliver muttered.

Brittany leaned closer. 'What?'

'That shelter. The structure's all wrong. You need a proper framework if you're going to use fabric as a cover.'

'Have you built many shelters?' she whispered back, seeming genuinely curious.

'A few,' Oliver admitted. 'When we were kids, Guy and I used to camp out near the creek. Built some pretty impressive structures over the years.'

Brittany smiled, the first genuine one he'd seen from her. 'That sounds nice. I was an only child, so I missed out on that kind of thing.'

For a moment, Oliver felt a connection—a tiny bridge forming across the chasm of awkwardness between them.

Then his phone buzzed again.

And again.

And a third time in quick succession.

'Sorry,' he murmured, pulling it out to check the screen.

Irrigation system now screaming like banshee. May have underestimated issue. Water spraying everywhere. Turned off main valve. Could use a hand when you're free. No rush. Actually, maybe some rush.

'Everything okay?' Brittany asked, obviously noting his expression.

'Farm emergency,' Oliver said apologetically. 'I might need

to step out and make a call.'

'Oh.' Her disappointment was palpable. 'Sure.'

Oliver edged past the other patrons in their row, mumbling apologies as he accidentally stepped on someone's foot, and hurried to the lobby. He called Guy immediately.

'Tell me you didn't flood the eastern field,' he said as soon as Guy answered.

'I didn't flood the eastern field,' Guy replied, then added, 'I may have partially flooded the access road to the eastern field.'

Oliver closed his eyes briefly. 'How bad?'

'Not catastrophic. But the irrigation system housing has a crack, and when we tried to adjust the pressure, it—ah—expressed its displeasure forcefully.'

'I'm coming home.'

'No, don't,' Guy protested. 'I've got it under control now. I shut off the main valve and diverted the water flow. It'll hold until morning.'

'You sure?'

'Positive. Finish your date. I'm sorry I bothered you.'

Oliver glanced back toward the theatre doors. He should go back in. Abandoning Brittany halfway through the movie would be rude, even if the film was terrible. But the thought of sitting through another hour of bad jokes and implausible camping scenarios felt suddenly insurmountable.

'I'll be home in forty minutes,' he decided.

'Oli, don't—'

'It's fine. The date wasn't going great anyway.'

'Did you talk about irrigation systems?' Guy asked, a smile evident in his voice despite the crisis.

'No, I did not,' Oliver said indignantly. 'But the movie is terrible, and we have nothing in common, and now I have an actual legitimate reason to leave early.'

'Amelia's going to kill you.'

'I'll take my chances.'

Oliver ended the call and headed back into the theatre, sliding past the now-irritated row of viewers to reach his seat.

'Everything okay?' Brittany whispered as he sat down.

'Actually, there's a bit of a situation at the farm,' he said quietly. 'Our irrigation system has failed, and there's some flooding. I might need to head back soon.'

Brittany's face fell. 'Oh. That's inconvenient.'

'I'm really sorry,' Oliver said, and he meant it. Brittany seemed nice enough, even if there was no spark between them. 'I can drive you home first, of course.'

'That's all right,' she said, her tone cooler now. 'I drove myself. You should go if you need to.'

'I'll just stay until this scene ends,' Oliver offered, gesturing to the screen where the family was now attempting to fish using the mother's knitting wool. 'No need to rush out this second.'

Brittany nodded, turning her attention back to the movie. The awkwardness between them had returned tenfold, settling around them like a heavy blanket.

By the time the scene ended—with a predictable punchline involving the father falling into the creek—Oliver was itching to leave. He'd be lucky if the rain hadn't turned the access road into a complete mud pit by the time he got home.

'I should go,' he whispered. 'I really am sorry about this.'

'It's fine,' Brittany said, though her expression suggested it was anything but. 'Farming emergencies happen, I guess.'

'I'll get you more popcorn before I go,' Oliver offered, noting her nearly empty container. 'As an apology.'

Before she could protest, he had taken her popcorn bucket

and was edging back down the row, desperate for any excuse to leave the stifling theatre.

In the lobby, he joined the short concession line, checking his phone while he waited. No new texts from Guy, which he hoped meant the situation hadn't deteriorated further.

'Medium popcorn with butter?' The attendant at the counter was young and friendly, with a shaggy haircut and an easy smile.

'Yes, thanks,' Oliver said, handing over his card.

As the attendant prepared the popcorn, Oliver glanced back toward the theatre entrance, mentally calculating how quickly he could deliver the snack and make his escape. When he turned back, he noticed the attendant had added extra butter without being asked.

'On the house,' the young man said with a wink. 'For the pretty lady in the green blouse. I noticed when you guys came in earlier.'

Oliver blinked, taken aback. 'Right. Thanks.'

He took the popcorn and headed back into the theatre, where the dim lighting made navigation challenging. As he reached their row, he could see Brittany's silhouette, but she seemed to be looking at something on her phone rather than the screen. The blue light illuminated her face, and Oliver could swear she was smiling more genuinely than she had all evening.

He edged past the other patrons again, balancing the popcorn carefully, until he reached their seats. As he sat down, Brittany hurriedly tucked her phone away, that same small smile lingering on her lips.

'One popcorn, extra butter apparently,' Oliver said, holding out the container.

'Oh, thank you!' Brittany reached for it just as Oliver's phone buzzed again in his pocket.

The movement of checking his phone while simultaneously passing the popcorn created a perfect storm of clumsiness. The popcorn bucket tilted, and before either of them could react, a cascade of buttery kernels poured directly into Brittany's lap and the bag she was holding there.

'Oh my God!' she gasped, loud enough that several nearby viewers turned to look.

'I'm so sorry!' Oliver whispered frantically, reaching to help but only managing to push more popcorn into the leather bag. 'I didn't mean to—'

'It's fine,' Brittany hissed, though her expression suggested it was very much not fine. 'Just... stop touching it.'

She stood abruptly, clutching her popcorn-filled purse, and shuffled past the other viewers toward the aisle. Oliver followed, acutely aware of the trail of kernels they were leaving and the disapproving murmurs around them.

In the lobby, Brittany was already tipping popcorn out of her purse into a trash can, her movements sharp with irritation.

'I am so sorry,' Oliver said again, hovering uselessly nearby. 'I can help clean—'

'I've got it,' she said curtly. 'You should go deal with your farm emergency.'

'At least let me—'

'Oliver,' Brittany interrupted, looking up with a tight smile, 'it's okay. Really. These things happen. But I think we both know this isn't... working.'

Oliver nodded, relief mingling with guilt. 'I'm sorry about the movie. And the popcorn. And the irrigation system.'

'It's fine,' she repeated, her tone softening slightly. 'We tried. Sometimes that's all you can do.' She paused, then added, 'For what it's worth, I think we would have figured out we're not compatible even without the agricultural emergency.'

'Probably,' Oliver agreed. 'You seem nice, though. And the popcorn guy thinks you're pretty.'

Brittany's eyebrows rose, but a small, genuine smile tugged at her lips. 'The one with the shaggy hair?'

'That's the one. He gave you extra butter.'

She laughed, the sound surprisingly warm after the tension of the last few minutes. 'Good to know.'

'So . . . I'll go, then,' Oliver said, gesturing vaguely toward the exit.

'Good luck with your irrigation system,' Brittany replied, and he couldn't tell if she was being sarcastic or sincere.

Either way, as Oliver stepped out into the now-steady rain, he felt lighter than he had all evening. He'd survived another date. Barely. And now he could focus on what really mattered— fixing the irrigation system and, hopefully, making it to the Bargara market in a couple of weeks.

The drive home was slower than usual, the rain creating sheets of water on the highway that reflected his headlights back at him. By the time he reached the farm, the dirt access road was indeed turning into mud, and he had to concentrate to keep the ute from sliding as he navigated toward the house.

The driveway was crowded with Guy's truck, and beside it, a beat-up blue sedan Oliver didn't recognise. As he splashed his way up the steps, he noticed Guy wasn't alone. A woman sat in the shadows of the porch swing, long dark hair pulled back in a practical braid, hands wrapped around her own steaming mug.

'That was fast,' Guy called as Oliver approached. 'How'd it go?'

'I dumped an entire bucket of popcorn in her lap,' Oliver replied flatly. 'Filled her handbag with melted butter.'

Guy stared at him for a moment, then burst into laughter. 'You didn't.'

'I absolutely did.'

'Smooth operator.'

'Shut up and don't tell Amelia. How's the irrigation system?' Oliver asked, glancing toward the woman who had risen from the swing.

'Stabilised for now,' she said, stepping into the porch light. 'But you'll need to replace the housing and recalibrate the pressure valve. I've seen this issue on the sugar plantations in Brazil.'

'Oliver, this is Elena Santiago,' Guy introduced, a new warmth in his voice that Oliver hadn't heard before. 'She's been helping with the eastern quadrant irrigation.'

'Among other things,' Elena added with a small smile directed at Guy. She was striking rather than conventionally pretty, with intelligent eyes and the sun-weathered complexion of someone who lived outdoors. Something in the way she carried herself spoke of competence and experience beyond her years, which Oliver guessed to be around thirty.

'We appreciate the help,' Oliver said sincerely, shaking her offered hand. 'Especially on a Thursday night.'

'I was already here,' she explained. 'Your brother was showing me some of your sustainability initiatives. My family's farm in Brazil faces similar water conservation challenges.'

'Family farm?' Oliver questioned, glancing at Guy, who seemed unusually interested in the contents of his mug.

'Five generations,' Elena nodded. 'Though I've been travelling, learning different agricultural methods for the past three years. Australia is my final stop before heading home to implement what I've learned.'

'Elena has some innovative ideas for our irrigation system,' Guy said, finally looking up. 'I think Dad would be interested when he gets back.'

Something in Guy's expression—a rare animation, a certain tension around his eyes—caught Oliver's attention. His quiet, spreadsheet-focused brother seemed different in Elena's presence, more engaged, almost vibrant.

'I won't keep you,' Elena said, placing her mug on the small table. 'The rain is letting up, and I should get back to my rental.'

'I'll walk you to your car,' Guy offered immediately.

'No need to get more soaked,' she protested.

'I insist,' Guy said firmly. 'The driveway's treacherous when it's this wet.'

Oliver watched from the porch as Guy escorted Elena to her car, holding an umbrella over her though the rain had indeed slowed to a drizzle. They paused at her door, exchanging words he couldn't hear, but the way Guy leaned in slightly, the way Elena's hand briefly touched his arm—these small gestures spoke volumes.

When Guy returned to the porch, Oliver raised an eyebrow but said nothing.

'What?' Guy challenged, a defensive edge to his voice.

'Nothing,' Oliver replied innocently. 'Just never seen you voluntarily stand in the rain before.'

'She's been helpful with the irrigation planning,' Guy said stiffly. 'Professional courtesy.'

'Of course,' Oliver nodded solemnly. 'Very professional of you to review sustainability initiatives at nine p.m. on a Thursday.'

Guy's expression closed like a shutter. 'Some of us take the farm's future seriously.' He turned toward the door. 'I've got the system diagram laid out on the kitchen table.'

As they headed inside, Oliver cast one last glance at the retreating taillights of Elena's car. His brother had always been the steady one, the predictable one. But tonight, he'd glimpsed something else in Guy—a restlessness that had nothing to do with spreadsheets or irrigation systems.

Chapter 6

Sarah sat cross-legged on her couch, laptop balanced precariously on a throw pillow, the afternoon sun streaming through her living room windows. She'd been staring at the dating profile for twenty minutes, cursor hovering over the bright green 'Activate Profile' button.

'This is ridiculous,' she muttered, pushing a strand of hair behind her ear. 'It's just a dating profile, not a binding contract.'

She'd filled out the questionnaire honestly, chosen photos that weren't too staged or filtered—a candid one from her sister's wedding, another hiking with Jett in a carrier, and one from a night out with Elaine where she was laughing genuinely. The 'About Me' section had taken three drafts, but she'd finally settled on something that felt true without oversharing.

Creating a profile wouldn't mean she had to actually meet anyone, she reasoned. She could just browse, see what was out there. Maybe Elaine was right—maybe it would help her move on from this strange fixation on a man she barely knew.

With a deep breath, she clicked 'Sign Up' and began filling in the fields.

Name: Sarah Matthews Age: 24 Occupation: Jewellery Designer/Market Vendor Location: Bargara, Queensland

She paused at 'About Me,' her cursor blinking in the empty text box. How did one sum up their life in a paragraph? After several false starts, she typed:

Creative single mum with a passion for handcrafted jewellery and beach walks. My four-year-old son and I are a package deal—he's curious, energetic, and the centre of my world. Looking for someone kind, genuine, and patient who enjoys simple pleasures and doesn't mind the occasional dinosaur invasion.

It was honest, at least. No point in hiding Jett—he was non-negotiable. There was no need to say that Jett's father had died in a motorbike accident before she'd even known she was pregnant.

An image of Oliver flashed through her mind—his easy smile, the way he'd looked at her as if really seeing her, how his hands had moved with such care as he'd explained the different mango varieties.

'Stop it,' she scolded herself. 'Three hours of conversation a year ago does not a relationship make.'

She'd replayed their farmers' market meeting so many times it had taken on a mythic quality in her mind. What kind of person fixated on such a brief encounter? She sighed, knowing exactly what Elaine would say: that her subconscious was latching onto the memory of connection because she'd been depriving herself of social interaction outside of motherhood and work.

Maybe Elaine was right. Maybe having someone to share the load would make everything easier. Someone to laugh with after Jett went to bed, someone who might love her son almost as much as she did.

Sarah uploaded a recent photo of herself at the markets, smiling beside her jewellery display, and then sat back, her finger hovering over the 'Create Profile' button.

'Just to look,' she told herself firmly. 'Just to see what's out there.'

With a small surge of something like courage, she clicked the button, then closed her laptop before she could change her mind.

Her phone immediately buzzed. Then again. And a third time in quick succession.

Three notifications from CountryConnections. Three men had already expressed interest in her profile. Her stomach fluttered with a mixture of flattery and discomfort.

She opened the first one and immediately grimaced. The message simply said, 'Ur hot. Dinner?' The profile picture showed a shirtless man flexing in a gym mirror.

The second wasn't much better: 'Single moms are my specialty 😊'

'Gross,' Sarah muttered, nearly ready to deactivate her account immediately.

The third message was more polite, asking about her business and mentioning that he too enjoyed farmers' markets, but something about the professional headshot and carefully curated profile felt staged.

Sarah set her phone down, discouraged but determined. Elaine had warned her there would be plenty of frogs before any princes. This was just part of the process.

'I'll give it a week,' she decided. 'If they're all like this, I'm out.'

Closing her eyes, she tried to imagine a future with someone new, someone who could become important to both her and Jett. But frustratingly, the only face that came to mind was Oliver's, a man she barely knew and would probably never see again.

Outside, the moon cast silver light over her small garden, illuminating the mango tree she'd planted last year after Jett had become enchanted with the fruit. It hadn't yet produced anything, but it was growing steadily, its glossy leaves reaching toward the Queensland sky.

Much like her, Sarah thought—a work in progress, slowly putting down roots, waiting for the right time to bloom.

***

A week later.

'Hand me that wrench, would you?'

Oliver reached out a mud-covered hand without looking up from the mess of broken piping. The irrigation system had chosen a Sunday of all days to fail spectacularly, sending a geyser of water shooting ten feet into the air before Guy had managed to shut off the main valve.

Guy slapped the tool into Oliver's palm. 'You know, most people spend their Saturdays relaxing, maybe seeing friends, going on dates.'

'Most people aren't trying to run a sustainable farm,' Oliver grunted as he tightened a fitting. 'Almost got it.'

The sun beat down on them as they worked, both men covered in a mixture of sweat and soil. The eastern field still needed to be prepped for the late summer planting, the greenhouse required maintenance, and the local newspaper reported farmers' market attendance across the district had dropped slightly in the past few weeks.. The tourists were keeping the numbers up at the Bargara Beach markets, though.

Oliver straightened up, wiping his brow with his forearm, only succeeding in smearing more mud across his face. 'There. That should hold until we can get the replacement parts tomorrow. If we FaceTime with the olds tonight, we won't mention the pump or the irrigation failures to Dad.'

Guy nodded, then checked his phone. 'Amelia messaged: lunch is ready. And she says—and I quote— 'Tell Oliver to wash up properly this time. I'm not having mud all over my dining room chairs again.'

Oliver chuckled. '*Her* dining room chairs. Mum'd love to hear that.'

They reached the porch, where they dutifully removed their

boots and hosed off the worst of the mud. The farmhouse kitchen was warm and fragrant with the smell of homemade bread and vegetable soup. Amelia jumped straight in.

'Look at this one, Oli.'

'This one's special. She makes her own pasta and has the most genuine smile I've seen on that entire app.' Amelia's eyes sparkled with mischief as she handed him the tablet.

Oliver rolled his eyes and reached for the soup ladle.

'She just joined today,' Amelia added casually. 'Seems like the universe is sending you a sign.'

Oliver handed the tablet back. 'The universe is sending me a sign that I need to pick some mangoes before it rains tomorrow.'

'You're impossible,' Amelia sighed, but with affection rather than genuine frustration. 'One of these days, Oliver Johnson, you're going to realise there's more to life than mangoes and irrigation systems.'

'Anyway, you're meeting her for dinner on Wednesday night.' Amelia smirked.

'What!'

The tablet rang, and Amelia shook her head. 'Can't talk now. France is calling.' She answered the call.

'Hi Grandmère.'

Chapter 7

Oliver tugged at his collar for the fifth time in as many minutes, feeling the stiff fabric scratch against his neck. The pale blue dress shirt—his only dress shirt—felt foreign against his skin, accustomed as he was to soft cotton T-shirts and flannel. He'd ironed it himself that afternoon, a task that had taken three attempts and left a suspicious brown mark on the ironing board that Amelia would definitely notice later.

The restaurant, *Maison Azure*, glowed with ambient lighting that somehow made everything look expensive. Crystal glasses caught the light, white tablecloths stretched pristine across each table, and waiters moved quietly between diners. Oliver felt distinctly out of place.

But there was Danielle—his third date—waving from a corner table, looking exactly like her profile picture—sleek dark hair, confident smile, impeccably dressed in what Oliver assumed was the kind of outfit featured in the magazines Lisette always brought home.

'Hello, Oliver. Lovely name, by the way. Very sophisticated. You found the place okay?' Danielle asked as he approached, her smile warm and inviting.

'GPS is a wonderful thing,' Oliver replied, attempting to slide smoothly into his chair but catching the sleeve of his shirt on the back. He recovered with what he hoped was casual grace but suspected he looked more like a clunky fool.

'I hope you don't mind I went ahead and ordered wine,' she said, gesturing to the bottle. 'The Cabernet here is excellent.'

Oliver nodded appreciatively, though his wine knowledge extended about as far as "red" and "white." He accepted a glass, secretly wishing for a cold beer instead.

'You clean up nice,' Danielle said, her eyes appraising him. 'Very different from your profile pictures.'

'Farms and fancy clothes don't mix well,' he admitted. 'This shirt spends most of its life in the back of my closet.'

'Well, it should come out more often.' She smiled, and Oliver briefly felt a flicker of something. Not quite chemistry, but potential.

Maybe.

The waiter arrived with menus, launching into a detailed description of specials that involved reductions and infusions and several ingredients Oliver couldn't pronounce. He nodded as if he understood completely.

'So, tell me more about your farm,' Danielle prompted after they ordered. 'It sounds fascinating.'

This was comfortable territory. Oliver relaxed slightly, describing the seasonal rhythms, the satisfaction of growing his mangoes from seed to harvest, the challenges and rewards. Danielle seemed genuinely interested, asking thoughtful questions about sustainability practices and heirloom varieties.

'It's not just a job,' he concluded. 'It's a way of life.'

'I can tell,' she said. 'Your whole face lights up when you talk about it.'

Their appetisers arrived—an artistic arrangement of something the menu had described as "deconstructed." Oliver surveyed the plate, trying to determine the strategy for eating it. Danielle began confidently, so he followed her lead.

'And what about you?' he asked. 'You mentioned working in urban development?'

Danielle nodded enthusiastically. 'Yes, I help design mixed-use spaces in cities. The goal is creating communities where people can live, work, and play without relying on cars.'

'In Bundaberg?'

'No, I work remotely. Brisbane, Perth, Sydney. I've finished a few projects this year.'

'That's important work,' Oliver said, meaning it. 'We need more walkable communities.'

'Exactly! My dream project would be revitalising a downtown area. Something big, like Chicago or San Francisco.' Her eyes lit up as she continued, 'Actually, I just applied for a position with a firm in Seattle. It would be a huge opportunity.'

'Seattle? That's a long way away,' Oliver said, trying to keep his tone neutral.

'That's the exciting part,' Danielle continued. 'I've always wanted to live in a major metropolitan area. The energy, the culture, the constant innovation.' She leaned forward. 'Don't you ever feel that pull? To experience something completely different?'

Before Oliver could answer, their main courses arrived. His plate featured a carefully arranged piece of fish surrounded by colourful dots of sauce and what appeared to be vegetables cut into perfect cubes. The bright colour of one particular garnish caught his eye—a small pepper. He'd tried growing them a couple of years back, but hadn't seen quite that colour. He stared at it.

'So? Do you?'

He looked up apologetically. 'Sorry, I was looking at the colour of that pepper. Do I what?'

Danielle's expression changed, and held a little bit of exasperation. 'Feel the pull to experience something completely different? The vibrancy of a huge city?'

'Sometimes I think about trying new places,' he said diplomatically, picking up his fork. 'But the farm is pretty rooted, literally and figuratively.'

Danielle nodded, but her enthusiasm had dimmed slightly. 'I suppose we're opposites in that way. I get restless staying in one place too long.'

Oliver speared a bite of fish along with what he assumed was the pretty coloured pepper garnish and popped it into his mouth. The flavours mingled pleasantly for approximately two seconds before the heat hit—a scorching, intense burn that spread across his tongue and down his throat. Not a sweet pepper. Definitely not sweet.

His eyes widened in panic as he reached for his water glass, draining it in one desperate gulp. The heat intensified, bringing tears to his eyes.

'Are you okay?' Danielle asked, concern etching her features.

Oliver nodded frantically, unable to speak, reaching for her water glass too, which she pushed toward him without hesitation. It wasn't enough. The inferno raged on.

With watering eyes and what little dignity he had left rapidly evaporating, he grabbed the water pitcher from the neighbouring empty table and drank directly from it, water dribbling down his chin and onto his only dress shirt.

'Oh my God,' Danielle whispered, half-concerned, half-mortified as nearby diners turned to stare.

'Sorry,' Oliver finally managed to gasp, setting down the now-empty pitcher. 'Not . . . good with . . .spicy food.'

A waiter hurried over with a glass of milk, which Oliver accepted gratefully. The dairy helped calm the fire, but the damage was done. His eyes were red-rimmed, his nose running, and a large water stain spread across the front of his blue shirt.

'Better?' Danielle asked after a moment, her composure

forced.

'Much,' Oliver croaked. 'Sorry about that.'

She offered a smile that didn't quite reach her eyes. 'We all have our weaknesses.'

The remainder of the meal passed with stilted conversation, the easy flow from earlier gone. Oliver tried to recover, asking about her hobbies and family, but there was an undeniable awkwardness that hadn't been there before. The shared glances from nearby tables didn't help.

When the bill came, Oliver insisted on paying, a small compensation for the spectacle he'd created.

Danielle didn't protest.

Outside the restaurant, the night air cool against his face, they faced each other in that peculiar end-of-date moment when intentions are decided.

'This was . . . memorable,' Danielle said with a kind smile.

'One for the record books,' Oliver agreed, attempting a light reply.

'I had a nice time, Oliver. You're a good guy.' The words were genuine but carried a finality that both knew.

'You too—I mean, you're great,' he fumbled. 'I hope Seattle works out. They'd be lucky to have you.'

She nodded, seeming relieved he'd understood. 'I hope you find someone who loves your farm as much as you do.'

Danielle reached up and kissed his cheek, and Oliver watched as she walked to her car, her heels clicking confidently on the pavement.

The drive home was quiet, just the steady hum of his truck's engine and the occasional ping of the cooling radiator. Fields of sugar cane stretched out in the darkness on either side of the road, familiar and comforting. Star-scattered sky above, open land all around. This was his world, and it felt right.

Oliver sighed, turning onto the dirt road that led to the farmhouse. Dating was exhausting. Maybe Amelia was right that he needed to find balance, but these manufactured meetings weren't the answer. He wanted something real, something that felt natural.

As he parked in the shed, he wondered if Sarah ever thought about him, too, or if he'd just been another farmer at another market stand to her.

He went inside, but the house was quiet. Looked like Amelia and Guy were both out. Oliver yawned and headed to bed. They had an early start tomorrow.

As he closed his eyes, he thought about the changes he'd noticed in Guy lately. His brother had always been the steady, reliable one—content with his spreadsheets and working on the farm—but twice this week, Oliver had caught him on the phone, speaking slow Spanish, which he'd apparently been learning from language apps. And yesterday, Elena Santiago had been in their office, bent over irrigation maps with Guy, their heads close together as they discussed water conservation techniques with an intensity that seemed to transcend professional interest.

Oliver smiled to himself. Perhaps both Johnson brothers were experiencing unexpected complications in their carefully ordered lives this summer.

Chapter 8

The mango trees stood in neat rows at the eastern edge of the farm, their leaves glossy in the morning light. Oliver moved deliberately between them, canvas bag slung across his chest, inspecting each fruit closely. The first mangoes of the season were finally ready—their skin blushing from green to a deep amber-red, yielding just slightly to the press of his thumb.

He lifted one to his nose and inhaled the sweet, tropical fragrance. Instantly, an image of Sarah formed in his mind—her pleased expression as she'd tasted a sample slice last year, the way she'd closed her eyes momentarily to savour the sweetness. He remembered how she'd held Jett up to see the colourful display, his eyes wide with curiosity.

'First harvest is looking good,' Guy called from two trees over, interrupting Oliver's thoughts.

'Yeah,' Oliver replied, carefully placing another perfectly ripe mango into his bag. 'Should have a decent selection for Friday's market.'

'Weather report's favourable too,' Guy added. 'Clear skies predicted. Bargara might give you a whole new customer base.'

Oliver nodded, feeling an unexpected flutter of anticipation that had little to do with potential sales. He'd be scanning the market looking for Sarah's stall. The logical part of his brain tried to dismiss the impulse—she might have moved away, might set up at a different market now, might not even remember him. But she had mentioned the beach markets when they'd talked last year.

His hopes lifted.

'You seem distracted,' Guy observed, moving closer with his own half-filled bag. 'Thinking about that disastrous date again?'

Oliver laughed. 'God, no. That memory is safely buried.' The water pitcher incident had quickly become family legend, much to his chagrin.

'So, what then?'

Oliver hesitated, feeling strangely vulnerable. 'Nothing really. I was just wondering if I'll see some of last year's customers over there now that the mangoes are in.'

Guy raised an eyebrow but didn't press further. They worked in companionable silence for another hour, the bags gradually filling with perfectly ripened fruit. The cane was thriving this season—the new irrigation system proving its worth, the expanded greenhouse allowing them to diversify their offerings, the small orchard finally producing at capacity.

As Oliver reached for a particularly fine specimen hanging just overhead, he allowed himself to examine his regret. 'I should have called her,' he murmured to himself, so quietly that Guy, just a few trees away, couldn't hear. 'Before I lost her phone number.'

***

'Mummy, can I mix the blue one now?' Jett asked, perched on his special step stool at the workbench.

Sarah smiled at her son's enthusiasm. 'Not yet, sweetheart. We need to wait for the red batch to set completely.' She gestured toward the rows of soap moulds cooling on the rack. 'Remember what happened last time we rushed?'

Jett's face scrunched in serious consideration. 'They got all swirly together.'

'Exactly. And while swirly can be pretty, these Christmas shop orders need to look just like the samples we showed them.'

Her small workshop, converted from what had once been a

dining room, hummed with quiet productivity. Shelves lined the walls, filled with neatly labelled containers of essential oils, botanical additives, and natural colourants. A large calendar dominated one wall, dates marked in various colours denoting markets, deliveries, and production schedules.

The second Friday in December at Bargara Beach was circled in bold red—the special holiday market that could make or break her entire season. Four local Christmas shops had placed substantial pre-orders, contingent on seeing the final products at the holiday market. It was the opportunity she'd been working towards all year.

Sarah checked her watch. 'Two more hours until we need to pick up your dinosaur backpack from Miss Elaine's.' With Jett now attending daycare one full day a week, she could focus on building inventory without constant interruptions, though she treasured these mother-son production days too.

'Will we go to the farmers' market tomorrow?' Jett asked, carefully arranging dried lavender buds on a piece of wax paper.

'Yes, we need to get vegetables for the week, and maybe some of those strawberries you liked.'

Jett's eyes lit up. 'And mangoes? From the mango man?'

Sarah felt a small jolt at the nickname Jett had given Oliver after their very first meeting. 'The mangoes might not be ready yet, sweetie.'

'But you said summer is mango time. It's summer now.' His logic was impeccable.

'You're right,' Sarah conceded. 'We can certainly check.'

She turned back to her work, measuring oils with precision while her mind wandered. The dating app still sent her daily notifications, profiles of men who had "expressed interest". She'd scrolled through dozens, even exchanged messages with a few, but hadn't accepted any date invitations. Each potential match felt forced, like a jigsaw piece being jammed into the wrong space.

Elaine had gently pushed her to give someone a chance—'You can't find connection if you don't open the door to possibility,' she'd insisted during their last coffee afternoon. Sarah knew her friend was right, but something held her back.

'Maybe the mango man will remember us,' Jett said suddenly, as if reading her thoughts.

Sarah smiled, trying to keep her expression neutral. 'Maybe he will. But remember, farmers' markets are very busy places, and he talks to lots of people.'

'But he called me "the mango expert" and let me pick the best one.' Jett said confidently.

The memory warmed her—Oliver's gentle patience with Jett's many questions, the easy way he'd included her son in their conversation. No talking over his head or exaggerated baby voice like so many adults use with children. Just genuine respect.

'We'll see,' Sarah said, not wanting to build up either of their hopes. 'But either way, we'll get some delicious fruits and vegetables.'

As she poured the melted soap base into another set of moulds, Sarah caught herself smoothing her hair, wondering if she should trim it before Friday. The realisation made her laugh at herself—primping for a chance encounter with a man who probably wouldn't even remember her name.

'What's funny, Mummy?'

'Nothing important,' she replied, helping Jett sprinkle dried roses across the tops of the cooling soap bars. 'Just grown-up silliness.'

Later, after the house had settled into evening quiet, Sarah found herself scrolling mindlessly through her phone. The dating app notification showed twelve new potential matches. She opened it out of habit, then closed it just as quickly.

Instead, she pulled up her calendar, looking at the carefully planned production schedule leading up to the December holiday market. The business was growing—slowly but steadily—and with Jett starting half-day preschool in February, she'd have more consistent work time. Things were falling into place, piece by piece.

She didn't need a relationship to complete the picture. But as she set her alarm for an early production start the next morning, she couldn't help but wonder if Oliver still had her phone number; she'd impulsively scribbled it on the back of a docket. Probably not. Who kept a random phone number?

He'd probably forgotten her.

Besides, he'd never called

Sarah turned off her bedside lamp, dreams of mangoes and market days following her into sleep.

Chapter 9

'You grow the food, but can you cook it?' Tina had asked teasingly when they matched on the app, her profile photo showing her triumphantly holding up a plate of something that looked professionally plated. The question had seemed innocent enough, even charming. A fourth date after the disaster with Danielle hadn't been in Oliver's plans, but Amelia had been relentless—'Come on, Oli. Just one last try before you throw in the towel!'

Now, standing in Tina's immaculate kitchen with its granite countertops and gleaming appliances that looked like they belonged in a cooking show, Oliver was beginning to regret his bravado.

'I'm no chef, but I know my way around basic ingredients,' he'd written back. A statement that, while not technically a lie, was proving to be a significant stretch of the truth.

'These tomatoes are gorgeous,' Tina said, examining the Marmande heirloom tomatoes he'd brought from the farm. Her auburn hair was pulled back in a practical ponytail, and she wore a patterned apron over casual clothes. 'Perfect for the sauce.'

'Thanks,' Oliver replied, relaxing slightly at the familiar topic. 'It's been a good year for them. This variety is particularly sweet.'

'So are you, Oliver.' Tina smiled, her green eyes crinkling at the corners. 'Well, let's get started then. I thought we could make pasta from scratch—nothing too complicated. I do it all the time.'

Oliver nodded with feigned confidence, rolling up his sleeves. He could handle this. After all, how different could cooking be from following the precise measurements for organic fertiliser blends?

'You can measure out the flour while I get the eggs ready,' Tina instructed, pointing to a glass jar on the counter.

Oliver meticulously measured two cups of flour as directed, creating a small mountain on the wooden cutting board. Cooking was just science, he reasoned. Precise measurements, controlled reactions.

'Now make a well in the centre for the eggs,' Tina guided, cracking three eggs into a small bowl.

Following her instructions, Oliver poured the eggs into the crater he'd formed and began mixing with a fork as she demonstrated.

'You seem to know what you're doing after all,' she observed with a smile.

'I'm a quick study,' he replied, not mentioning that this was the furthest he'd ever ventured into cuisine beyond grilling vegetables or boiling pasta from a packet.

As they worked side by side, conversation flowed easily. Tina was a high school biology teacher with a passion for sustainable living, which had prompted her interest in Oliver's profile. She asked thoughtful questions about the farm's operations, sharing her own experiences with a small backyard garden.

'The sauce needs some sugar to balance the acidity,' Tina said as they moved on to the next stage, the pasta dough resting under a towel. 'Can you add about a tablespoon to the tomatoes?'

Oliver surveyed the collection of similar-looking containers on the counter. Grabbing what he assumed was sugar, he measured a heaping tablespoon and added it to the simmering pot.

'So how long have you been teaching?' he asked, stirring the sauce.

'Almost eight years now. I started right after—' Tina paused mid-sentence, her nose wrinkling as she leaned over the pot. 'Wait, did you just add salt to the sauce?'

Oliver froze, spoon in mid-stir. 'I thought it was sugar.'

Tina grabbed the container he'd used and burst into laughter. 'Oh no, that's definitely salt. A lot of salt.'

Oliver's face flushed with embarrassment. 'I'm sorry. I should have asked first.'

She waved off his apology, still chuckling. 'Don't worry about it. We can start over with the sauce. Fortunately, I've got more tomatoes.'

Her easy forgiveness made Oliver relax again. They salvaged what vegetables they could from the over-salted disaster and began a new sauce, this time with Tina clearly pointing out which container held the sugar.

'My turn to confess,' she said as they worked. 'I kill every houseplant I own. My students find it hilarious that their biology teacher can't keep a fern alive.'

Oliver smiled, appreciating her attempt to make him feel better.

When it came time to roll out the pasta dough, they stood shoulder to shoulder at the counter, working together to create thin, even sheets. The kitchen was warm, filled with the aroma of simmering tomatoes and herbs. It felt nice, this shared creation, even with his earlier blunder.

'Now for the garlic bread,' Tina said after they'd hung the pasta strands over a wooden dowel to dry slightly. 'Can you light the oven for me?'

Oliver approached the gas stove, examining the unfamiliar knobs and buttons. Growing up with electric and then cooking on a simple gas camping stove at the farmhouse had left him unprepared for this sophisticated appliance.

'Just turn the knob and press the ignition button,' Tina called over her shoulder as she sliced a baguette.

Oliver did as instructed, turning the knob and pressing what he thought was the ignition. Nothing happened. He tried again, turning the knob further. The faint smell of gas prompted him to keep pressing buttons.

'I don't think it's—' he began, just as he found a box of matches on the counter. 'Ah, maybe these will help.'

In retrospect, the mistake was obvious. The gas had been flowing freely as he struck the match, creating a sudden whoosh of flame that caught the kitchen towel hanging nearby.

'Fire!' Oliver yelped, instinctively grabbing for the burning towel and then dropping it when it singed his fingers.

Tina spun around, eyes widening at the flames now spreading across her counter. With remarkable composure, she grabbed a pot lid and slammed it down on the burning towel, then quickly turned off the gas.

'Are you okay?' she asked, concern evident as she checked his hand.

'Just surprised,' Oliver replied, mortified. The reddening mark on his fingers was nothing compared to the blow to his pride. 'I'm so sorry about your towel. And your counter.'

Tina surveyed the damage—a scorched dish towel, a blackened spot on her otherwise pristine counter, and the lingering smell of burnt cotton in the air. Then, unexpectedly, she began to laugh.

'This is definitely the most memorable cooking date I've ever had,' she managed between fits of giggles. 'Maybe we should order a pizza delivery?'

Relief washed over Oliver as he joined her laughter. 'I think that's safest for both of us. And your kitchen.'

Twenty minutes later, they sat at Tina's dining table with an extra-large supreme pizza between them, glasses of wine in hand, recounting the evening's disasters with the self-deprecating humour of new friends.

'I knew I was in trouble when you called flour "the white powder stuff" while we were making the pasta dough,' Tina teased.

'I should have been honest about my cooking skills,' Oliver admitted. 'Or lack thereof.'

'Where's the fun in that?' she replied, raising her glass in a mock toast. 'To kitchen adventures!'

As the evening wound down, Oliver helped Tina clean up the remains of their cooking. The easy conversation continued, touching on things they had in common. He enjoyed her company, but when he left, the brief hug they shared confirmed what Oliver had known throughout the evening. There was friendship here, genuine and warm, but no spark—no quickening of pulse or lingering glance that suggested something more.

Tina seemed to arrive at the same conclusion. 'This was fun,' she said sincerely. 'We should do it again sometime— maybe with less fire.'

'Definitely,' Oliver agreed, knowing they probably wouldn't. 'Thanks for being so understanding about the cooking disasters.'

'That's what makes a good story,' she replied with a warm smile.

Driving home, Oliver smiled, despite the evening's mishaps. Tina had been great, kind, funny, and intelligent. On paper, a perfect match. Yet something had been missing: the chemistry.

Maybe it didn't exist; maybe that was in Amelia's romance novels.

But then he thought about Charlotte and Greg, and Julien and Emily. You could see the chemistry there, just being with them.

Four dates through the app, each pleasant enough in its own way (barring the hot pepper incident), yet none had sparked anything resembling the easy connection he'd felt in those brief conversations with Sarah.

As he turned into the farm, Oliver made a decision. He was done with the app, done with the awkward first meetings and manufactured scenarios designed to create romance. If a connection happened, it would be unplanned.

Then again, maybe romance simply wasn't for him. He had the farm, his work, and friends who were practically family. It was enough. It had to be.

But as he entered the quiet house—Amelia and Guy must have gone to bed—kicking off his boots and settling into the worn leather armchair by the window, Oliver couldn't help but think of the market tomorrow. Of mangoes carefully arranged in wooden crates. Of the possibility, however slim, of a familiar face at a craft stall.

Chapter 10

In her bedroom at the farmhouse, surrounded by online craft store catalogues and hair dye swatches, Amelia scrolled idly through the CountryConnections app. She'd been spending more time on it lately, not just for Oliver's sake but for her curiosity. The dating scene in rural Queensland was a fascinating social system.

'Let's see who else is out there for Oli,' she muttered, flipping through potential matches. Her brother's reluctance to embrace modern dating was frustrating, but she remained convinced the right woman was out there, just a swipe away.

It had been nearly three weeks since Oliver's disastrous movie date with Brittany, and almost a week since his awkward dinner with Danielle. The cooking debacle with Tina had happened just two nights ago. Despite all these failures, Amelia wasn't ready to give up on her mission to find Oliver someone special.

She paused on a recently activated profile, drawn to a photo of a woman with warm eyes and an engaging smile, standing beside a craft stall at what looked like a farmers' market. Her profile mentioned handcrafted jewellery, being a single mother to a young son, and a love of local produce.

Something about the image tugged at Amelia's memory. She zoomed in on the background of the photo, noticing colourful market stalls. One corner of the frame showed crates of what appeared to be fruit.

'Wait a minute—' Excitement filled her, and her fingers flew over the keys as she quickly opened her phone's gallery, scrolling back through photos from the markets. She'd taken dozens of pictures last year, including several of the family at

Oliver's mango stall.

In the background of a selfie with her friend Megan was the same craft stall from the dating profile. And standing beside it, talking animatedly with Oliver, was the woman from the dating app. She'd never noticed the background of that photo before.

'Oh my God,' Amelia whispered, her eyes widening as connections formed rapidly in her mind. 'It's her. The market girl.'

Oliver had been deflated when she'd seemingly disappeared, checking the Dunmora markets for weeks afterwards.

Amelia studied the profile more carefully. Sarah Matthews, twenty-four, jewellery designer, single mother to a four-year-old son, Bargara resident.

'So, she's been at the Bargara markets, not Dunmora,' Amelia realised, pieces falling into place. Oliver had been looking in the wrong location all this time. Her finger hovered over the "Connect" button, her mind racing with possibilities. This wasn't just another potential date—this was the woman Oliver had been pining over for nearly a year, the one he'd mentioned at family dinners, the one who'd made him smile in a way Amelia hadn't seen before or since.

But simply telling Oliver would be too straightforward, too easily dismissed. He'd find a reason not to reach out, convinced that too much time had passed or that Sarah wouldn't remember him. Or be interested in him.

'This calls for something more creative,' Amelia decided, a plan forming. She'd need a different approach—one that brought them together without either realising until it was too late to back out.

Nodding, she tapped the 'Connect' button, then navigated to Oliver's profile settings. A few quick edits would ensure Sarah wouldn't recognise him immediately—a different display name, some adjusted details. Nothing dishonest, just strategic omissions.

'Sorry, Oli,' she murmured, changing his display name to James Hayes, using their mother's maiden name. 'You can thank me later.'

Next, she composed a thoughtful message to Sarah from "James," mentioning an interest in local crafts and suggesting they might have crossed paths at farmers' markets in the region.

As she sent the message, Amelia felt a flutter of excitement. If her hunch was right, these two people who had been missing each other for months would finally get a second chance. All they needed was a little push—and possibly a reservation at the best restaurant in Bundaberg.

'Operation Market Reunion is officially underway,' she announced to her empty bedroom, already envisioning how she'd coordinate their meeting without either suspecting her involvement until the perfect moment.

***

The early morning sunlight filtered through the kitchen window, casting long shadows across the worn wooden table where Oliver sat nursing his second cup of coffee. A thin layer of soil still caked his fingernails despite his thorough scrubbing—evidence of the pre-dawn hours he'd spent with Guy checking irrigation lines. He looked up as Amelia bounced in, and he scowled.

'What are you so bubbly about? It's not even seven o'clock.'

'Just happy,' she said with a wide grin.

'Why?'

She shrugged and headed for the kettle.

'I want you to delete that app today,' he announced.

Amelia paused mid-step; her hands suspended in the air. 'What? No! You can't give up now.'

Oliver sighed, running a hand through his damp hair. 'I'm done with the digital matchmaking experiment.'

'But you've barely given it a proper chance,' Amelia protested, putting her hands on her hips. 'These things take time.'

'I've given it plenty of time. Time I could have spent on actual farm work.' Oliver stood, carrying his mug to the sink. 'The mango harvest is starting, I've got the Bargara Beach markets next week, and the new greenhouse needs finishing before the first frost.'

'That's months away. It's not even Christmas yet.' Amelia's expression shifted subtly, a flicker of something passing behind her eyes. 'I thought you usually sold at the Dunmora markets? Why the change?'

'Time to try something new,' Oliver replied with a shrug. 'Bargara has more tourists, and Guy thinks we could expand our customer base. Besides, I've searched every corner of the Dunmora markets for a year now. If Sarah's still around, she's selling her crafts somewhere else.'

'What if I told you I found someone perfect?'

Oliver groaned. 'No, no and no. You said that about the last one, and I nearly burnt down her kitchen.'

'Tina wasn't perfect. Nice, yes, but not perfect.' Amelia leaned against the counter, studying her brother. 'This one's different. I can feel it.'

'Your feelings aren't exactly scientific evidence,' Oliver muttered, though there was no real bite to his words. Despite his frustration with the dating process, he could never stay properly cross with his sister for long.

'Just one more,' Amelia pleaded, clasping her hands together dramatically. 'One final date, and if it doesn't work out, I promise I'll never ever mention dating apps or romance again. I'll even help with the greenhouse construction every weekend through autumn.'

Oliver narrowed his eyes. 'Every weekend? Including the rainy ones?'

'Every single one,' she confirmed solemnly.

He considered the offer. Extra help with the greenhouse would be invaluable, especially with the expanding crop schedule Dad had planned when they got back from France. 'Fine. One last date. But that's it, Amelia. I mean it. Last one.'

Her face split into a wide grin, a reaction that immediately triggered Oliver's suspicion.

'Why do you look like that? What have you done?'

Amelia's smile faltered slightly. 'Well... there's something I should probably tell you.'

Oliver crossed his arms, waiting.

'I may have gone in and tweaked a few things on your profile.' She spoke quickly, the words tumbling out. 'And I might have already replied to this woman. And possibly arranged a dinner date. For next Wednesday night.'

The silence that followed was deafening.

'You did what?' Oliver finally managed; his voice was dangerously quiet.

'I was trying to help!' Amelia protested. 'Your profile was too... farmy. All soil health this, and sustainable agriculture that. I added some depth, mentioned your love of reading, how you volunteer at the community garden, your hidden talent for—'

'You pretended to be me again?' Oliver interrupted, genuine anger flaring. 'That's crossing a line, Amelia. What if I meet this woman and she expects someone completely different?'

'I didn't make anything up,' she insisted. 'Everything I added is true. I just . . . highlighted your more redeemable qualities.'

Oliver shook his head in disbelief. 'And you arranged another date without even asking me?'

'You would have said no.'

'Exactly! Because it's my life, not yours to manage!'

Amelia had the grace to look contrite, shoulders slumping slightly. 'I know. I'm sorry. I got carried away. But, Oliver, her profile—you should see it. She's smart and funny and runs her own business. She loves farmers' markets and cooking with fresh ingredients.'

'I've heard all that before.' Oliver's eyebrows shot up.

'What difference does that make?' Amelia challenged. 'Are you suddenly too good for women who like things you don't?'

'That's not fair and you know it,' Oliver replied, his tone softening slightly.

'It's just a date, not a marriage proposal,' Amelia pointed out. 'And from her messages, she seems very independent. The kind of woman who doesn't need saving but might enjoy some company.'

Oliver sighed deeply, the fight draining out of him. Part of him wanted to remain angry—Amelia had seriously overstepped the mark again—but another part recognised the genuine affection behind her meddling. She worried about him out here on the farm, working endless hours with only the occasional social interaction at markets or with the family.

'Where and when?' he asked tersely.

Amelia's face brightened. 'Next Wednesday night at eight. I've booked a table at Tides.'

'Tides?' Oliver repeated incredulously. 'That seafood place in Bundaberg? That's almost an hour's drive! And it's super expensive.'

'It's the best restaurant in the region,' Amelia defended. 'I wanted you to make a good impression.'

'With my credit card, I assume?'

'Of course not. It's my treat.' She paused, a mischievous glint returning to her eye. 'You might even have to stay the night.'

Oliver's glare could have withered cane stalks. 'Don't push it, sis. This is the last time. The mango season is starting, and I'll be too busy for this crap. Because that's what it is. It's not natural, and I'm over it.'

'Just give it a chance,' Amelia urged, more seriously. 'A proper chance. Wear something nice again, be open to possibility, and see what happens.'

Oliver nodded curtly, already turning to leave the kitchen. 'I need to check the eastern orchard. Tell Guy I'll meet him at the tool shed in twenty.'

As he strode across the yard, boots crunching on gravel, Oliver's irritation gradually subsided, replaced by a familiar resignation. One more date. One last obligation to fulfil before he could close this chapter and refocus entirely on the farm.

And the following week, he'd be selling at his first market of the season at Bargara. Regardless of how this final blind date went, he would be at his stall early, arranging golden-red fruit in wooden crates, scanning the crowd for a familiar face that had nothing to do with algorithms or dating profiles.

***

Sarah sat cross-legged on her sofa, a mug of herbal tea balanced on the armrest, Jett's quiet snores drifting from his room. The house was peaceful in these late evening hours, the only sound the occasional ping from her laptop.

Another notification from the dating app.

She'd been about to delete her profile entirely when the message had arrived—different somehow from the others, more thoughtful, less formulaic. Something about the description of farm life, of finding beauty in simple moments, had caught her attention.

After weeks of disappointing interactions, she'd nearly written it off as another dead end. But the follow-up message had been unexpected, mentioning a reservation at Tides, a restaurant she'd always wanted to try but could never justify as a single-income household with a growing four-year-old.

'Last chance,' Sarah murmured to herself, taking a sip of cooling tea. 'One final attempt before I'm officially done with this whole experiment.'

She opened the app one more time, studying the profile picture—not particularly revealing, just a man standing in what appeared to be an orchard, his face hidden by a wide-brimmed hat. The description mentioned sustainable farming, a love of literature, and volunteer work at community gardens.

Something about it tugged at her memory, though she couldn't place exactly why. Perhaps just the mention of farming brought Oliver to mind, as so many things seemed to these days.

Sarah closed the laptop decisively. Next Wednesday night, she would go on this date. She would be open to the possibility, as Elaine was always encouraging her to be. And if nothing came of it, she could delete the app with the satisfaction of knowing she'd truly given it a fair chance.

Her phone buzzed with a text from Elaine, offering to watch Jett on Wednesday evening. Sarah smiled at her friend's uncanny timing—or perhaps not so uncanny, given Elaine's persistent encouragement of Sarah's dating efforts.

Thank you. I have a date. Last one! Pick him up at seven?

Elaine's response came immediately: Perfect! Wear that blue wrap dress. And HAVE FUN!

Sarah shook her head, amused by her friend's enthusiasm. The blue dress was perhaps a bit much for a first date, but after months of practical mum clothes and work attire spattered with soap materials, the thought of dressing up held appeal.

As she readied herself for bed, Sarah's mind drifted to the farmers' market scheduled at the beach for the following weekend. Jett had been asking all week if the mangoes would be there and if the mango man" would remember them.

'Don't get your hopes up, sweet boy,' she whispered to herself, echoing the gentle caution she'd offered her son. Advice she would do well to follow herself, for more reasons than one.

Chapter 11

Oliver adjusted his collar one last time before stepping through the glass doors of Tides. The restaurant was everything Amelia had described—elegant without being pretentious, with floor-to-ceiling windows overlooking the marina. Soft jazz played in the background as servers glided between tables with quiet efficiency.

'Reservation for John—I mean, Hayes,' he quickly corrected as he spoke to the hostess, glancing around at the other diners, wondering which stranger would be his final dating app attempt.

'Yes, sir. Your guest has already arrived. Right this way.'

Oliver followed, mentally rehearsing his introduction. Best to be straightforward about Amelia's interference, he decided. Start with honesty and—

He stopped abruptly, nearly colliding with the hostess when she paused at a corner table. The woman seated there looked up from her menu, and the recognition was instantaneous.

'Sarah?' The name escaped his lips before he could process what was happening.

Her eyes widened, lips parting in surprise. 'Oliver? Oliver Johnson?'

The hostess, misreading their stunned expressions for pleasant surprise, smiled. 'Enjoy your evening,' she said before discreetly retreating.

For a long moment, neither spoke. Oliver stood frozen beside the table, unable to reconcile the Sarah from the Dunmora farmers' market with the woman before him in a blue wrap dress, her hair falling in loose waves around her shoulders.

'I don't understand,' Sarah finally managed, her voice

barely above a whisper. 'You're . . . James Hayes? From the app?'

'No.' He shook his head, finally regaining enough composure to slide into the chair opposite her. 'I'm Oliver Johnson from the farm. And you're Sarah. From the Dunmora markets last year.'

'Yes,' she confirmed, still looking dazed. 'This is—'

'Unexpected,' Oliver finished. What was Amelia up to? A different name? Or was another date about to turn up here? One for him, and a James for her. Suddenly, he felt possessive.

Their eyes met, and something about the sheer improbability of the situation struck them both at once. A laugh bubbled up from Sarah's throat, tentative at first, then growing. Oliver couldn't help but join in, the tension that had been building in his shoulders for the past twenty-four hours dissolving into genuine amusement.

'I've been selling at the Bargara Beach markets for months now,' Sarah explained once their laughter subsided. 'I switched after... well, after I thought you weren't interested.'

'I looked for you at Dunmora for weeks,' Oliver admitted. 'I never thought to check Bargara.'

'I'm guessing you didn't know either?' Sarah asked, drawing curious glances from nearby tables.

'Not a clue,' Oliver confirmed, shaking his head. 'My sister Amelia set this up. She . . . well, she apparently hijacked my profile and arranged this date without telling me who you were and changing my name so you wouldn't know who I was.'

'That explains it,' Sarah said, her initial shock giving way to curiosity. 'The messages seemed a bit different in style from your profile.'

'Which I also didn't write,' Oliver admitted, running a hand through his hair. 'Amelia thought my original was too "farmy," whatever that means.'

Sarah smiled, the familiar warmth in her expression bringing Oliver back to their conversations over mangoes and soap. 'And here I was, convinced I was meeting a complete stranger for my last attempt at online dating. But you know what? I love your sister already.'

The waiter approached with water and wine menus, giving them a moment to collect their thoughts. After placing their drink orders, an awkward silence settled between them—filled with unasked questions.

'So,' they both began simultaneously, then laughed again, some of the awkwardness dissipating.

'Ladies first,' Oliver offered.

Sarah took a deep breath. 'I've been wondering . . . why didn't you ever call me?' The question had been circling in her mind for a year, and seeing him sitting across from her now, it simply tumbled out.

Oliver's expression turned rueful. 'I meant to. I really did.' He hesitated before continuing. 'I kept your number in my wallet for days, taking it out almost every night, telling myself I'd call the next day when I wasn't so tired from harvest.'

He met her eyes directly, honesty evident in his gaze. 'Then one day I went to pay for something and realised it wasn't there anymore. I tore apart my truck, my house, everywhere I could think of. Never found it. By then, so much time had passed, I figured you'd think I was strange for suddenly calling out of the blue if I did find it.'

'I would have been happy to hear from you,' Sarah said quietly, surprised by her own candour. 'Even out of the blue.'

The waiter returned with their drinks, taking their dinner

orders before leaving them to their conversation once more.

'Can I ask you something?' Oliver ventured once they were alone again.

Sarah nodded.

'Your son—Jett, right? I've been remembering bits and pieces from our market conversations. How is he?'

Sarah's expression softened at the mention of Jett, but Oliver noticed a hint of wariness too. 'He's wonderful. Growing too fast, talking constantly, obsessed with anything that grows.' She paused, studying Oliver's face. 'You remember him?'

'Of course,' Oliver replied, genuinely surprised by the question. 'The mango expert. Small guy, big questions.' He smiled at the memory. 'He's hard to forget.'

'Most men I've met seem to view single motherhood as a drawback,' Sarah admitted. 'Something to be tolerated rather than embraced.'

'Those men are idiots,' Oliver stated flatly, then looked slightly abashed at his own bluntness. 'I mean—children are part of who you are. That's not a negative.'

Sarah felt something tight in her chest begin to loosen. 'You knew he was my son? I wondered if you might have thought he was my little brother or something.'

Oliver looked genuinely surprised. 'No, it was pretty clear he was yours from the way you interacted.'

A comfortable silence settled between them before Sarah spoke again, her voice quieter. 'His father died before Jett was born. A motorcycle accident.' She rarely shared this detail so early, but something about Oliver's straightforward acceptance of Jett made her want to be equally open. 'We weren't together when it happened—it was a summer thing that had ended a few weeks before. I didn't even know I was pregnant then.'

Oliver's expression held simple compassion without the awkward pity she often encountered. 'That must have been incredibly difficult.'

'It was,' Sarah acknowledged. 'But also strangely . . . clarifying. Nothing focuses your priorities like becoming a single parent unexpectedly.'

'Is that when you started your business?' Oliver asked.

Sarah nodded, grateful for his perceptiveness. 'I needed something flexible, something I could build while being home with Jett. Something that was mine.'

'You've done an amazing job,' Oliver said, his admiration evident. 'With both your business and Jett.'

'Thank you,' Sarah replied, feeling unexpectedly emotional at the simple acknowledgment. 'Ryan—Jett's father—he was adventurous, always seeking the next thrill. I see that in Jett sometimes, that fearlessness.'

'And the curiosity,' Oliver added with a smile. 'The way he examines everything so carefully before making up his mind.'

'That he gets from me,' Sarah laughed softly. 'Poor kid got my overthinking tendencies.'

'I wouldn't call it overthinking,' Oliver corrected gently. 'More like... thoroughness. It's a good quality.'

As their conversation shifted to other topics, Sarah felt a quiet sense of relief. Sharing Jett's origin story often created awkwardness, but Oliver had received it as simply another part of who they were—not a complication or a burden, but their history, honoured with the respect it deserved.

As they shared dessert—a mango sorbet that both agreed wasn't as good as fresh mangoes from Oliver's farm—Sarah realised how different this felt from her other dating attempts. There was no forced conversation, no mental calculation of compatibility factors. Just the easy rapport they'd discovered a year ago, now given room to breathe and expand.

When the bill arrived, they both reached for it simultaneously.

'Please, let me,' Oliver insisted. 'Technically, my sister invited you, so it's only fair.'

'Next time, then,' Sarah replied, then realised the implication of her words. 'I mean—if there is a—'

'I'd like that,' Oliver said simply, saving her from her stammering. 'Very much.'

Outside, the night air was cool and clear, stars visible despite the marina lights. Oliver walked beside Sarah toward the parking lot, close enough that their hands occasionally brushed, sending small currents of awareness between them.

'Where are you parked?' he asked as they reached the first row of cars.

'Just over there,' Sarah pointed to a modest sedan a few spaces away. 'You?'

'Back corner,' Oliver nodded toward the far end of the lot. 'I'll walk you to your car.'

They moved slowly, neither seemingly eager for the evening to end. When they reached Sarah's car, she turned to face him, illuminated by the soft glow of a nearby lamppost.

'This was unexpected,' she said softly. 'But I'm glad it happened.'

'Remind me to thank Amelia,' Oliver replied, his voice equally soft. 'Though I'll never hear the end of it.'

Sarah laughed quietly, her eyes meeting his. The moment stretched between them, full of unspoken possibilities.

Oliver moved first, one hand gently cupping her cheek as he leaned down. Sarah rose slightly on her toes to meet him halfway, their lips coming together in a kiss that was gentle at first, then deepening as her arms wound around his neck.

When they finally broke apart, both slightly breathless, Oliver rested his forehead against hers for a moment.

'I'll see you at the market Saturday next week?' he asked.

'We'll be there,' Sarah confirmed. 'Jett's been talking about mangoes all week.'

'I'll save the best ones for him,' Oliver promised, reluctantly stepping back as Sarah unlocked her car door.

'Goodnight, Oliver.'

'Goodnight, Sarah.'

He watched her drive away, remaining in the parking lot long after her taillights had disappeared. The night felt full of possibility in a way he hadn't experienced in years—perhaps ever.

The drive home passed in a blur, his mind replaying moments from the evening: Sarah's laugh, the way she listened so intently when he spoke of the farm, the softness of her lips against his. For once, the farm wasn't the last thing he thought about before falling asleep.

The market day couldn't come soon enough, but with over a week to wait, Oliver knew he'd need to find the patience that farming had taught him. Good things, like the perfect mangoes, couldn't be rushed.

Chapter 12

Oliver arrived at the farmers' market before dawn, the eastern sky just beginning to lighten from black to deep purple. The familiar routine of setting up his stall—unfolding tables, arranging crates, positioning the hand-painted "Johnson Family Farm" sign—normally centred him, but today his movements were rushed and distracted.

He'd selected the mangoes with extra care, culling through the morning's harvest for the most perfect specimens—unblemished, fragrant, with that perfect give when gently pressed. The premium fruit always went to market, but today he'd brought truly exceptional pieces, arranging them in wooden crates lined with green tissue paper that made the golden-red skin glow.

'Someone's in a good mood,' Guy remarked, helping unload the last of the produce from the truck. 'You're whistling.'

'Am I?' Oliver hadn't noticed.

'Yep. Same tune for the past twenty minutes.' Guy studied his friend's face. 'I take it the date wasn't as disastrous as predicted?'

Oliver arranged a display of heirloom tomatoes, trying and failing to suppress a smile. 'It was . . . unexpected.'

'Unexpected good or unexpected bad?'

'Good. Definitely good,' Oliver admitted. 'Turns out I already knew her.'

Guy's eyebrows shot up. 'No kidding? Who—' He stopped mid-question as realisation dawned. 'Wait. Not the market woman? The one with the kid who loves mangoes?'

Oliver nodded, pleased he wouldn't have to explain the whole story.

'Well, I'll be damned,' Guy laughed, clapping Oliver on the shoulder. 'Amelia will be insufferable when she finds out her meddling actually worked.'

'She doesn't know yet,' Oliver said. 'And I'd appreciate keeping it that way until after market hours. I need time to process everything without her twenty questions.'

'Your secret's safe with me,' Guy promised. 'But I want details later.'

As Guy headed back to the truck for another crate, Oliver's attention was caught by movement at the empty stall space beside his. The market organisers had been setting up a stall next to his, something about adjusting the layout for better customer flow. He hadn't paid much attention when they'd assigned him his spot earlier.

Now, a familiar figure was unfolding a portable table. Oliver froze, his hands still holding a mango mid-arrangement.

Sarah.

She hadn't noticed him yet, her back turned as she carefully laid out a folding display rack. Her hair was pulled back in a practical ponytail, and she wore a simple sundress with a denim jacket against the early morning chill.

'Need a hand with that?' Oliver found himself saying before his brain had fully caught up.

Sarah turned, the display rack wobbling precariously in her hands. Her eyes widened in surprise, then lit up with recognition and pleasure.

'Oliver?' The rack tilted dangerously, and he stepped forward quickly to steady it. 'What are you—' Her gaze shifted to his stall, understanding dawning. 'You're my neighbour!'

'Looks that way,' he replied, unable to keep the smile from his face. 'The market gods have a sense of humour.'

'Or the universe is trying to tell us something,' Sarah said with a small laugh. The warmth in her eyes made his heart do that strange flip it seemed to manage only in her presence.

'Where's Jett?' Oliver asked, helping her set the display rack down securely.

'With Elaine at the jam stall. She's giving him breakfast—I had to set up early, and he was still half-asleep.' Sarah glanced at Oliver's meticulously arranged mangoes. 'Those look amazing.'

'More picking yesterday,' he said, following her gaze. 'Picked the best ones for today.'

A significant look passed between them, acknowledgment of their unexpected dinner date hanging in the air.

'Mummy!' A small voice called out excitedly. They turned to see Jett running toward them, dodging between early market-goers with Elaine following at a more sedate pace. The boy skidded to a stop, his eyes growing wide as he registered Oliver standing beside his mother.

'The mango man!' he exclaimed, his whole face lighting up. 'Mummy, the mango man is right next to us!'

'I see that,' Sarah replied, smiling at her son's enthusiasm. 'What a nice surprise.'

'Hello, mango expert,' Oliver said, crouching down to meet Jett at eye level. 'Want to see this year's crop?'

Jett nodded vigorously, practically vibrating with excitement.

'Perfect timing,' Elaine said as she reached them, her knowing eyes darting between Sarah and Oliver. 'I was just bringing this little man back to help set up, but I see you've found some . . . assistance.' The emphasis she placed on the word made Sarah's cheeks colour slightly.

'Elaine, this is Oliver Johnson,' Sarah introduced. 'Oliver, this is Elaine, my market mentor and Jett's honorary grandmother.'

'The famous mango farmer,' Elaine said, giving Oliver an appraising once-over that made him feel like he was being evaluated for far more than his fruit-growing abilities. 'Sarah's mentioned you.'

'Has she?' Oliver couldn't help glancing at Sarah, who was suddenly very interested in arranging her soap display.

'Mummy said your mangoes are the best in Queensland,' Jett supplied helpfully, earning a stifled laugh from Elaine and an even deeper blush from Sarah.

'Did she now?' Oliver felt an absurd burst of pride.

'I may have said something along those lines,' Sarah admitted.

'Well, I'll leave you young people to your setup,' Elaine announced. 'My jams won't arrange themselves. Sarah, dear, we'll catch up later.' The significant look she gave Sarah spoke volumes.

As the market officially opened at seven, the usual early birds began trickling in. Having neighbouring stalls created a unique dynamic—Oliver and Sarah could chat between customers, share observations, and watch each other's spaces during brief breaks. Jett alternated between helping his mother arrange her soaps and sitting at a small folding table beside Oliver's stall, drawing pictures and occasionally assisting as Oliver's "official mango selection consultant".

By nine o'clock, the market was in full swing. During a rare quiet moment, Oliver leaned against the side of his stall, watching as Sarah wrapped a purchase for a customer.

'This is nice,' he said when the customer had left. 'Being

neighbours.'

'It is,' she agreed, adjusting her display. 'Though a bit distracting.'

'Am I distracting you?' Oliver asked with a grin.

'You know you are,' Sarah replied, a smile playing at the corners of her mouth. 'I've nearly given the wrong change twice.'

'I'll try to be less . . . whatever it is,' he promised, not sounding particularly sincere.

Sarah laughed. 'Please don't.'

During a lull in customers, both of them watched as Jett concentrated on his drawing, tongue poking out slightly in focus.

'I really did lose your number,' Oliver said suddenly, picking up their conversation from their dinner date. 'I must have pulled out a note and not noticed it came out with too. But—'

'But what?' Sarah prompted gently when he didn't continue.

Oliver met her eyes. 'I wasn't sure if you'd want me to call anyway. We'd only met that time. I thought maybe I'd imagined something that wasn't really there.'

Sarah nodded, understanding. 'I wondered if you'd found out I was a single mum and decided it wasn't worth the complication.' She glanced at Jett, lowering her voice. 'It's happened before. Men seem interested until they realise Jett is part of the package.'

'That wasn't it at all,' Oliver assured her. 'Honestly, I thought you were probably just being nice to the guy who sold you mangoes.'

Sarah laughed softly. 'I'm nice to lots of people who sell me things. I don't give them all my number.'

The admission hung between them, simple but significant.

'Look, Mummy! I drew the farm!' Jett interrupted, holding

up his drawing proudly. What appeared to be trees, a house, and several stick figures covered the page in vibrant crayon colours.

'It's beautiful, sweetie,' Sarah praised, accepting the artwork. 'Who are all these people?'

'That's me,' Jett pointed to a small figure. 'And that's you. And that's the mango man.'

Oliver peered at the drawing, touched by his inclusion in the boy's imagination. 'You've even got the orchard rows right. Very accurate.'

Jett beamed at the praise. 'Can I see the real farm sometime?'

The question caught both adults off guard. Sarah looked momentarily flustered, unsure how to respond to her son's directness.

'I think that would be great,' Oliver said carefully, holding Sarah's gaze. 'If your mummy thinks it's a good idea.'

'We'll see,' Sarah told Jett, stroking his hair. 'The farm is very busy, especially during harvest.'

'Actually,' Oliver said, an idea forming, 'we're having a small harvest festival next month. Nothing fancy, just some families from Duckinwilla Creek coming to pick their own fruit, hayrides for the kids, that sort of thing. You both would be welcome.'

Sarah considered this, clearly appreciating the casual nature of the invitation. 'That sounds nice. We'll have to check our calendar.'

Oliver nodded, understanding her caution. Their connection was wonderful but still new. In the light of day, with Jett present, the reality of their situation required more careful navigation. Sarah wasn't just thinking about her own heart but her son's as well.

The day passed quickly, with both of them steadily selling their wares. When Jett grew restless in the afternoon, Oliver showed him how to arrange the mangoes by colour gradient, a task the little boy took to with serious dedication. Sarah watched them together, her expression soft.

As the market began to wind down, Sarah looked over at Oliver. 'This has been one of my best market days in months.'

'The soap business booming?' Oliver asked.

'That too,' she said with a smile. 'But I meant having you next to us. It's been nice.'

'I'll have to thank the market organiser for the placement,' Oliver said. 'Though I'm not sure my total focus was on selling mangoes today.'

'Mine wasn't entirely on soap either,' Sarah admitted.

As they began packing up their respective stalls, Oliver selected a small crate of his finest mangoes. 'For the mango expert and his mum,' he said, placing it on Sarah's folded table.

'We can't take all those,' Sarah protested.

'Course you can,' Oliver insisted. 'They're perfect right now—be a shame to let them sit.'

'Will I see you again soon?' Oliver asked, not quite ready for them to leave.

Sarah smiled, the warmth reaching her eyes. 'We come to the market most Saturdays. And there's that harvest festival to consider.'

'I could call you,' Oliver suggested. 'If I had your number. Again.'

'You could,' Sarah agreed, reaching into her bag for a business card. This time, she wrote her number directly on the front. 'And maybe take care when you open your wallet.'

Oliver laughed, tucking the card carefully into his shirt

pocket, patting it twice for good measure. 'I've learned my lesson.'

As they said their goodbyes, Jett surprised Oliver with a quick hug around his legs before darting back to his mother's side. The simple gesture affected Oliver more deeply than he could have anticipated.

He watched them weave through the market toward the parking area, Jett turning back once to wave enthusiastically. Something significant had shifted in his life today. The caution was still there—both of them careful not to rush forward too quickly—but beneath it lay a foundation of understanding that felt solid. Real.

For the first time, Oliver found himself thinking beyond the next harvest, the next season. Thinking of a sweet woman and her child.

And it didn't feel frightening at all.

##

The following Tuesday afternoon, Oliver invited Sarah and Jett to the farm. While Sarah helped Amelia organise kitchen supplies for the upcoming harvest festival, Oliver took Jett out to the chicken coop. The warm Queensland sun filtered through the gum trees, casting dappled shadows across the gravel path as they made their way toward the weathered structure.

'Do you know how to check for eggs?' Oliver asked, holding the wooden gate open for the boy.

'I do.' Jett nodded solemnly, his four-year-old face serious with concentration. 'You have to be gentle. And you look under the hens very carefully.'

Oliver smiled, handing Jett the small collection basket he'd found in the shed. 'That's right. And you have to stay away from Mr. Cranky Pants.'

'Mr Cranky Pants,' Jett giggled, eyeing the large red rooster who watched them suspiciously from his perch. 'He doesn't like visitors.'

'Good memory,' Oliver praised as they stepped into the coop, the familiar scent of hay and feed greeting them. The hens clucked softly, already accustomed to Jett's careful approach after his few visits.

'Did you know my real dad?' Jett asked suddenly as they collected eggs together, the question catching Oliver off guard with its directness.

Oliver carefully placed another egg in the basket before answering. 'No, I didn't have the chance to meet him.'

Jett nodded, accepting this. 'He died before I was borned. On a motorbike.'

'Your mum told me,' Oliver said gently. 'I'm sorry that happened.'

Jett seemed to be working through something, his small face scrunched in concentration. 'Mom says he would have loved me a whole lot.'

'I'm sure that's absolutely true,' Oliver affirmed.

'But he's not here,' Jett continued matter-of-factly. 'So he can't take me fishing or build forts or teach me to ride a bike.'

Oliver wasn't sure where this conversation was heading, but he knelt down to Jett's level, giving the boy his full attention. 'No, he can't do those things. That's really tough.'

Jett locked eyes with Oliver. 'Mummy says you have a boat. A small one for the creek.'

'I do,' Oliver confirmed. 'For fishing sometimes.'

'Could I go with you to the creek? Sometime?' Jett asked. The hope in his little face tugged at Oliver's emotions. 'Just to try it? I've never been fishing.'

'I think that sounds like a plan. If Mum says yes.'

'She will,' Jett said with surprising confidence. 'She says you're good at explaining things. Like the mangoes.' He paused, then added with devastating simplicity: 'I think my real dad would be okay with you teaching me stuff. Since he can't.'

Oliver swallowed against the unexpected tightness in his throat. 'That's a very kind thought, Jett. Thank you.'

Jett nodded, seemingly satisfied with the exchange, and returned to the serious business of egg collection.

Later, when Oliver mentioned the conversation to Sarah, her eyes filled with tears.

'He's never said anything like that before,' she whispered. 'About another man teaching him things his father would have.'

'Kids surprise you,' Oliver said. 'Just when you think you understand them.'

Sarah smiled through her tears. 'Ryan would have liked you, I think. You're different to him, but you have that knack for finding joy in simple things.'

It was the best compliment she could have given him—not that he could replace Jett's father, but what he and Sarah shared.

Chapter 13

The Johnson farmhouse, which had known a month of relative quiet, erupted into chaos once more as the minivan pulled into the driveway, kicking up dust in the late afternoon sun. Oliver, Guy, and Amelia stood on the porch, watching as doors flew open and their travel-weary family spilled out amidst exclamations, stretching limbs, and an explosion of luggage.

'Home at last!' Ellen called, her face lighting up despite obvious exhaustion. 'The French countryside was magnificent, but nothing beats the sight of home.'

Grandmère emerged next, somehow looking as put-together as if she'd just stepped out for afternoon tea rather than endured a twenty-four-hour journey. 'Oh, *mes chéris!* The farm is still standing! Guy, Oliver—you haven't burned anything down!'

'Disappointed, Grandmère?' Oliver teased, stepping forward to help with bags.

'Never, *mon petit.* Though perhaps a small kitchen fire would have been dramatic.' She patted his cheek affectionately before turning to embrace Amelia. 'Your hair! It is now blue and silver! Like the night sky!'

Amelia preened, touching her freshly dyed locks. 'Changed it last week. Thought you'd appreciate something new to come home to.'

Hugo Johnson descended from the driver's seat, looking simultaneously relieved and invigorated. 'The irrigation system held up?' he asked Guy, bypassing any conventional greeting.

'Not a single issue,' Guy confirmed with the hint of a smile. 'The new setup in the eastern field is performing thirty percent better than projected.'

'And the mangoes?' Hugo turned to Oliver.

'Harvest went perfectly. We've been selling out at the markets every weekend.'

Hugo nodded, satisfied. 'Good. Good.' Then, in an uncharacteristic move, he pulled both sons into a brief, firm hug. 'Missed you boys.'

Charlotte and Greg were the last to emerge, laden with carry-on bags and souvenirs. 'We need reinforcements!' Charlotte called. 'Papa fell asleep in the back seat, and he's sound asleep and snoring.'

'Let him rest,' Ellen advised. 'He hardly slept on the plane. We'll get home to their place when we unload our luggage.'

As they unpacked the van, the house filled with voices calling out questions, observations, and demands.

'Where's the gift we got for Lisette? The little painting?' 'Did anyone feed my sourdough starter while we were gone?' 'Is there any food in this house? I'm starving!' 'Someone put the kettle on!' 'My legs feel like they've been folded in half for days.'

After the initial flurry subsided and Greg had left to drive Grandmère and Papa to their place, the family gathered in the kitchen where Amelia had prepared dinner. A roast chicken with vegetables sat at the centre of the table, alongside fresh bread from the bakery in town and one of Oliver's prized mangoes, cut into perfect slices.

'You three have managed well,' Ellen observed, helping herself to a glass of wine that Hugo had poured. 'The house isn't even a disaster.'

'Oli's developed some domestic skills,' Amelia said with a mischievous gleam in her eye. 'He's been cooking. And cleaning. Almost like he was trying to impress someone.'

Oliver shot her a warning glance that went completely

ignored.

'Impress someone?' Charlotte perked up, her travel fatigue momentarily forgotten. 'Who?'

'No one,' Oliver replied too quickly. 'I just got tired of living in Amelia's mess.'

'My mess?' Amelia laughed. 'That's rich coming from Mr. Leaves-Mud-Covered-Boots-in-the-Hallway.'

'Actually,' Guy interjected, his quiet voice somehow cutting through the banter, 'he has been on his best behaviour lately. Even ironed a shirt last week.'

The kitchen fell silent as all eyes turned to Oliver.

'You ironed?' Ellen whispered, as if witnessing a miracle. 'A girlfriend!'

'It's not—' Oliver began, but Amelia interrupted.

'Her name is Sarah,' she announced triumphantly. 'The market girl from last year. She's back in his life, and he's been disgustingly happy about it.'

A collective gasp rippled through the room, followed immediately by a barrage of questions.

'The one with the laugh?' Charlotte asked.

'The one with the jewellery?' Lisette's voice chimed in from the tablet that had been propped up on the counter to include her in the homecoming.

'How did this happen?' Hugo demanded, looking bewildered.

Oliver sighed, knowing resistance was futile. 'It's a long story.'

'We have time,' Ellen insisted, settling more comfortably into her chair.

Reluctantly, Oliver recounted the tale—how Amelia had hijacked his dating profile, arranged a dinner with an unknown woman who turned out to be Sarah, and how they'd reconnected after nearly a year apart.

'So, you've been seeing each other?' Charlotte pressed when he finished. 'How many dates?'

'We've been spending time together,' Oliver said carefully. 'Markets on Saturdays. She brought Jett to the farm for a visit, too.'

'Jett?' Hugo questioned.

'Her son,' Oliver explained. 'He's four. Smart kid. Loves mangoes.'

'Well, that speaks to his good taste,' Guy murmured.

'And you like him? The boy?' Ellen asked, her expression softening.

Oliver nodded. 'He's great. Full of questions. Wants to know how everything works.'

'Just like you at that age,' Hugo observed quietly, his expression thoughtful.

'When do we get to meet them?' Ellen leaned forward eagerly.

Oliver hesitated. 'I hadn't really thought about—'

'Nonsense,' Ellen interrupted. 'Of course they must come to dinner. How about this weekend?'

'Mum, they're not—we're not—' Oliver fumbled for words. 'It's still new. I don't want to overwhelm them.'

'We won't overwhelm them,' Amelia said with a grin.

'Together, we are exhausting,' Oliver corrected, shaking his head 'And numerous. And loud. And Grandmère would want to be here too when she hears.' He frowned at Amelia. 'As I am sure she will soon, if not already?'

Amelia grinned back at him. 'Probably.'

'All the more reason for a proper introduction,' Charlotte

argued. 'Better to know what she's getting into sooner rather than later.'

Oliver looked to Guy for support, but his brother merely shrugged. 'They have a point. Might as well rip off the Band-Aid.'

'Friday,' Ellen decided, already planning. 'I'll make my special roast. Charlotte, you make that lovely dessert—the one with the berries. Grandmère can share her stories about the lavender fields? She makes soap, you said? She'd appreciate that.'

Oliver watched helplessly as his family organised what was beginning to sound like an elaborate welcome ceremony rather than a simple dinner.

'I'll need to ask her first,' he reminded them. 'She might already have plans.'

Hugo smiled. 'A chance to meet the Johnson family? Who would refuse?'

***

'Your entire family?' Sarah's voice held a note of panic even through the phone connection. 'All at once?'

Oliver paced the length of the porch, phone pressed to his ear as the sunset painted long shadows across the yard. 'I tried to postpone, but they're . . . insistent.'

'That's a diplomatic way of putting it,' Sarah replied with a nervous laugh. 'I'm not sure, Oliver. It seems like a big step.'

'It is,' he agreed. 'And if you're not comfortable with it, I'll tell them you're busy. I'm good at disappointing my family. Years of practice.'

That earned a genuine laugh. 'I'm sure that's not true.' She paused. 'Would Jett be welcome? I don't always have a sitter available.'

'Of course,' Oliver said quickly. 'They specifically included him in the invitation. My sister Amelia is already planning activities to keep him entertained.'

Another pause. 'What should I bring?'

Oliver felt a surge of hope. 'Just yourselves. Mum insists on handling everything else.'

'I can't show up empty-handed to meet your family for the first time,' Sarah protested.

'You won't be empty-handed. You'll be wrangling a four-year-old.'

'Fair point,' she conceded. 'What time?'

They worked out the details, and when Oliver hung up, he found Amelia leaning against the doorframe, arms crossed and a smug expression on her face.

'She said yes?' his sister asked, though it wasn't really a question.

'She said yes,' Oliver confirmed. 'But if anyone mentions wedding bells or French countryside honeymoons, I'm disowning the lot of you.'

Amelia mimed zipping her lips. 'We'll be on our absolute best behaviour.'

'Somehow, that's even more terrifying.'

##

Friday evening arrived with perfect early summer weather, the kind that made the farm look like a scene from a postcard—golden light spilling across green cane fields, the mango trees casting long shadows, the farmhouse glowing with welcome.

Oliver had spent the afternoon in a flurry of last-minute tidying up that earned knowing smirks from Guy and outright teasing from Amelia. By six o'clock, he'd changed his shirt twice and was contemplating a third when the sound of tyres on gravel announced Sarah's arrival.

He stepped onto the porch just as her car pulled up beside his truck. Jett was out first, bursting from the vehicle with the boundless energy of childhood.

'Are there cows too? I saw the chickens last time,' he called up to Oliver, who was descending the steps. 'Mom said there might be cows.'

'No cows, I'm afraid,' Oliver replied, unable to suppress a smile at Jett's enthusiasm. 'But we have some new kittens in the shed.'

Sarah emerged more slowly, smoothing down a simple floral dress. She looked beautiful but unmistakably nervous.

'I brought this,' she said, holding up a small basket. 'Some of my lavender soap and honey-oatmeal bath bombs. I know you said not to bring anything, but—'

'It's perfect,' Oliver assured her, briefly squeezing her hand. 'Mum and Grandmère will love it. Ready?'

Before Sarah could answer, the screen door banged open, and Ellen Johnson appeared, wiping her hands on her apron.

'You must be Sarah!' she exclaimed warmly. 'And this handsome young man must be Jett! We've heard so much about you both.'

Oliver couldn't get over the change in Mum since they'd been overseas. She glowed with happiness.

'You have?' Sarah glanced questioningly at Oliver.

'Apparently, I talk about you,' he admitted quietly. 'A lot.'

What followed was a whirlwind of introductions as the Johnson family materialised seemingly from all corners of the house. Charlotte and Greg arrived moments later with the promised berry dessert. Grandmère swept in from the living room, immediately taking Sarah's face between her hands and declaring her '*magnifique*' before launching into rapid-fire questions about soap-making techniques.

'Is it true you use real lavender? From the garden? In France, my cousin Mathilde grows the most beautiful lavender fields. The scent! *Incroyable*!'

Amelia knelt down to Jett's level, introducing herself as "the sister with the cool hair", which earned her an instant fan.

'It's blue!' Jett observed, wide-eyed.

'And silver,' Amelia confirmed. 'Like a superhero, right?'

Jett nodded solemnly. 'Or a robot princess.'

'I like the way you think, kid,' Amelia laughed. 'Want to see the kittens while the grown-ups talk about boring stuff?'

After a confirming nod from Sarah, Jett eagerly took Amelia's offered hand and disappeared toward the back door.

'He'll be completely safe with her,' Oliver assured Sarah, noting her momentary hesitation. 'Amelia's surprisingly good with kids. She just never grew up herself.'

'I heard that!' Amelia called over her shoulder.

Guy stepped forward with a friendly nod, while Hugo Johnson remained standing slightly apart, his expression difficult to read. Oliver had expected his father's immediate enthusiasm—Hugo normally loved meeting new people connected to the farm—but tonight he seemed unusually reserved, his gaze lingering thoughtfully on Jett, who was now excitedly telling Amelia about a dinosaur he'd brought along.

Dinner itself was a boisterous affair, Ellen's roast declared a triumph, the table conversation flowing from French adventures to farm updates. Sarah answered questions about her soap business with growing confidence, but Oliver noticed his father's unusual quietness. He contributed occasionally but seemed to be observing more than participating. He began to worry that his heart was playing up again.

When Sarah excused herself to help Jett with a second serving, Hugo leaned toward Oliver.

'She seems lovely,' he said in a low voice, 'but have you really thought this through, son?'

Surprise jolted through Oliver. 'What do you mean?'

Hugo glanced toward Jett, then back to Oliver. 'Taking on a readymade family is different from starting fresh. The boy's young, impressionable. If things don't work out between you and Sarah—'

'Dad,' Oliver interrupted, keeping his voice even, 'I care about both of them. A lot.'

'I don't doubt that,' Hugo replied. 'But farming life isn't easy on relationships, even without the added complexity of a child.' He paused. 'I just want you to be sure. For everyone's sake.'

Before Oliver could respond, Sarah returned with Jett, and the conversation shifted to lighter topics. But Oliver remained aware of his father's subtle scrutiny throughout the meal, the careful way he observed Sarah and Jett's interactions.

After dessert, while Charlotte and Amelia cleared the table and Grandmère regaled Jett with tales of all the different types of cats they saw in France, Oliver found his father on the back porch, gazing out at the moonlit orchard.

'You don't approve,' Oliver said, joining him at the railing.

Hugo turned, surprised. 'That's not it.'

'Then what is it, Dad? You've barely said two words to Sarah all night. I'm sure she's noticed.'

Hugo sighed, running a hand through his thinning hair. 'When your mother and I started out, it was just the two of us against the world. Hard enough figuring things out together without adding—' he gestured vaguely.

'A child,' Oliver finished. 'You can say it.'

'It's not that I don't like them,' Hugo clarified. 'But farming is an all-in proposition, Oliver. The hours, the stress, the uncertainty—it's why so many farming marriages fail. Add a young boy who's already lost one father figure—'

Oliver understood then. His father wasn't being judgemental—he was worried. For all of them.

'Did you know,' Oliver said carefully, 'that Jett asked me yesterday if we could plant a special mango tree just for him? So, he could watch it grow every time he visits?'

Hugo's eyebrows raised. 'Did he now?'

'He's already thinking long-term, Dad. He sees a future here.' Oliver paused. 'And so do I.'

Hugo studied his son's face, then nodded slowly. 'You know your own mind. Always have.'

Inside, they could hear Jett's delighted laughter mixing with Grandmère's theatrical storytelling. Hugo's expression softened at the sound.

'He's a good boy,' he admitted. 'Reminds me a bit of you at that age. Full of questions.'

'He is,' Oliver agreed. 'And Sarah's done that all on her own. Imagine what she could do with a partner.'

Hugo gave his son a sidelong glance. 'Is that what you want to be? Her partner?'

'I'm figuring that out,' Oliver replied honestly. 'But I know I want the chance to try.'

Hugo clasped Oliver's shoulder, his grip firm. 'Then you have my support. Whatever you need.'

When they returned inside, Hugo approached Sarah, who was helping Jett build something with napkins and dessert spoons.

'Sarah,' he said, his voice warmer than it had been all evening, 'Oliver tells me you're interested in growing your own herbs. I've been experimenting in the kitchen garden. Perhaps you and Jett might like to see them before you head home? If you have time, that is.'

Sarah's surprise quickly turned to genuine pleasure. 'We'd love that, Mr. Johnson.'

'Hugo, please,' he corrected. 'And afterwards, maybe Jett would like to help me pick out a spot for a special mango tree. One that would be just his to watch over.'

Jett's eyes widened with delight. 'Really? My very own tree?'

'Every member of this family has one,' Hugo explained seriously. 'It's tradition.'

Oliver felt a rush of gratitude toward his father—not for merely accepting Sarah and Jett, but for recognising what they might mean to his future.

Later, as Hugo showed Jett the different herbs with a patience Oliver rarely witnessed in his practical father, Sarah moved to stand beside Oliver.

'Your dad wasn't so sure about us at first,' she observed quietly.

'How could you tell?'

'I raised a child on my own,' Sarah replied with a small smile. 'You develop a sixth sense about these things.'

'He's coming around,' Oliver assured her.

Sarah nodded, watching Hugo lift Jett onto his shoulders to better see the huge mango tree across the garden fence. 'That's Oli's tree,' he said.

'Oli?' Jett giggled. 'That's not his name.'

Family wasn't just given, Oliver realised. Sometimes it was carefully, thoughtfully built—one mango tree at a time.

'We should probably head home,' Sarah said eventually, noticing Jett's valiant but failing battle against sleep. 'It's well past his bedtime.'

'Of course,' Ellen agreed, though she looked reluctant to see them leave. 'But you must come back soon. Perhaps for Sunday lunch next week? We'll be more rested by then, less jet-lagged.'

'That's very kind,' Sarah began diplomatically.

'Let's not overwhelm them, Mum,' Oliver interjected, recognising Sarah's polite hesitation. 'They might need some recovery time from the Johnson experience.'

Ellen looked ready to protest, but Hugo placed a gentle hand on her arm. 'Oli's right, love. Let them breathe.'

The goodbyes were warm and slightly chaotic, with Ellen insisting on packing leftovers for them to take home and Grandmère extracting a promise from Sarah to share her lavender soap recipe "for comparison" with her cousin Mathilde's methods.

'I'll walk you to your car,' Oliver said, taking the container of leftovers from his mother before she could add yet another item to the already substantial care package.

The night air had cooled, and stars were brilliantly visible in the clear country sky. Jett, despite his tiredness, looked up in wonder.

'So many stars,' he whispered.

'More than you can count,' Oliver agreed, opening the car door so Sarah could settle Jett into his booster seat.

Once Jett was buckled in, already half-asleep, Oliver and Sarah stood beside the car, momentarily alone.

'I'm sorry if that was overwhelming,' Oliver said quietly.

'Don't apologise,' Sarah replied, her face softened by the dim glow of the porch light. 'They're wonderful. Exactly as you described them—loud, opinionated, but wonderful.'

'They liked you,' Oliver said. 'Both of you.'

'The feeling's mutual.' Sarah glanced back at the house. 'It's nice to see where you come from, who shaped you.'

Oliver nodded, feeling oddly vulnerable. There was something intimate about introducing Sarah to his family, to the farm that had been his whole world for so long.

'I was thinking,' he began, suddenly nervous. 'Would you like to go out sometime? Just the two of us?'

Sarah raised an eyebrow. 'Are you asking me on a proper date, Oliver Johnson?'

'I believe I am,' he confirmed, a smile tugging at his lips. 'Though it seems backwards, doesn't it? Meeting the family before our first non-blind date.'

'We've never done things in the conventional order,' Sarah reminded him. 'Why start now?'

Oliver laughed softly. 'True enough.'

'I'd love to,' she said. 'Elaine has been offering to babysit for weeks. She's frighteningly invested in our relationship.'

'She and Amelia should never meet,' Oliver said with mock horror. 'The combined force of their meddling would be unstoppable.'

Sarah's laugh was cut short as Oliver leaned down to kiss her, his hand gently cupping her cheek. Unlike their previous kisses, this one held the promise of something deeper, something taking root.

'Goodnight, Sarah,' he whispered when they finally parted.

'Goodnight, mango man,' she replied with a teasing smile.

Oliver stood in the driveway long after her taillights had

disappeared down the dark country road, the farmhouse behind him alive with the sounds of his family, the orchard around him silent and steadfast. For the first time in years, the farm felt not just like his responsibility, but like a home he might someday share.

Epilogue

The early morning light filtered through the kitchen windows as Oliver checked his market crates one final time. The mangoes gleamed like jewels against their tissue paper nests—perfect, unblemished, each one selected with meticulous care. Market days had taken on new significance these past months, transformed from routine commerce to something he now looked forward to.

Amelia padded into the kitchen in her pyjamas, hair tousled and currently a subdued lavender—tame by her standards. She made directly for the coffee pot, pouring herself a generous mug before hopping onto the counter, legs dangling.

'You're up early,' Oliver observed, securing the last crate. 'Thought you'd be sleeping in after your late night.'

Amelia shrugged, blowing steam from her mug. 'Couldn't sleep.'

Something in her tone made Oliver pause. He studied his sister's face, noting the slight puffiness around her eyes. 'Everything all right?'

'Myron and I broke up,' she announced without preamble, taking a long sip of coffee.

'I'm sorry,' Oliver said, genuinely surprised. Unlike Amelia's usual brief entanglements, her relationship with the artistic barista had lasted more than three months—a record by her standards. 'What happened?'

'Nothing dramatic. We just want different things.' She attempted a casual tone that didn't quite succeed. 'He's moving to Brisbane next month. Wants to work in some fancy café where they charge fifteen dollars for avocado toast.'

Oliver leaned against the counter beside her. 'And you

didn't want to go?'

'The farm's home,' Amelia said simply. 'I know I joke about leaving, about all the places I'll see, but . . .' She gestured vaguely toward the window where the early sun was painting the cane fields gold. 'It gets under your skin, doesn't it?'

Oliver nodded, understanding perfectly. 'It does.'

They sat in companionable silence for a moment, the only sounds the distant crow of a rooster and the gentle ticking of the kitchen clock.

'Maybe I need to put you on a dating app,' Oliver finally joked, nudging her shoulder gently. 'Return the favour.'

Amelia snorted into her coffee. 'Oh, what a brilliant idea. 'Farmer's sister seeks local man with flexible definition of normal hair colour, must tolerate excessive enthusiasm and strong opinions.''

'Could work,' Oliver grinned. 'You never know where you might find someone perfect for you.'

'Says the man who literally found his perfect match through an app that his sister hijacked,' Amelia retorted, but she was smiling now.

'Technically, I found her at the markets first,' Oliver corrected. 'The app was just a roundabout way back.'

'Semantics,' Amelia waved dismissively. 'The point is, you're disgustingly happy now.' She hopped down from the counter and rinsed her mug. 'Speaking of which, how's the farm weekend market idea coming along? Sarah seemed interested when I mentioned it last week.'

'We're discussing it,' Oliver said carefully. 'It's a big undertaking.'

'But brilliant,' Amelia insisted. 'Having craft vendors right here at the farm every other weekend would bring in a whole new customer base. Sarah's soaps, those honey people from Bargara, maybe even that woodworker with the cutting boards.' Her enthusiasm was returning, eyes brightening with each idea. 'We could start small, just a few stalls. See how it goes.'

Oliver smiled, recognising the familiar signs of an Amelia project gathering momentum. Perhaps it was exactly what she needed right now. 'I'll talk to Dad about it. And Guy.'

'Already did,' she admitted. 'They're on board. Dad thinks it's "innovative marketing" and Guy says the numbers look promising.'

'Of course you did,' Oliver laughed, shaking his head as he picked up the first crate. 'Let me get through today's market first, all right? One thing at a time.'

As he loaded the truck, Oliver found himself considering Amelia's idea more seriously. Having Sarah's craft stall here at the farm regularly would mean more time together, bridging their separate worlds in a way that felt right somehow. Worth considering, at least.

***

Three months later

'Higher, Uncle Oli! I can't reach it!' Jett called from beneath the mango tree, his small arms stretched toward a particularly fine specimen just beyond his grasp.

Oliver smiled at the boy's casual use of "uncle"—a title that had been given by Jett a few weeks ago and stuck, feeling more natural with each use. He reached up, easily plucking the mango and placing it in Jett's waiting hands.

'Careful with that one,' he instructed. 'It's perfect for the special display.'

Jett examined the fruit with expert concentration before gently placing it in his basket alongside others he'd collected.

Five years old now, he'd become an authoritative judge of mango quality, much to the amusement of the weekend market customers who now regularly visited the farm.

Amelia's farm market idea had exceeded even her optimistic projections. What had started as a small gathering of five local vendors had quickly grown to fifteen regular stallholders, attracting visitors from as far as Bundaberg and Maryborough. The Johnson farm had transformed from a quiet agricultural operation to a bustling community hub every other weekend, with Sarah's craft stall as one of the central attractions.

'Mummy!' Jett called, spotting Sarah approaching through the orchard rows. 'Look how many I found!'

Sarah smiled, her hair pulled back in a loose braid, cheeks flushed from the summer heat. 'That's quite a haul. Are you leaving any for the customers?'

'Only the ordinary ones,' Jett assured her solemnly. 'I'm getting the special ones.'

'Of course you are,' Sarah laughed, meeting Oliver's gaze with shared amusement. 'Amelia's looking for you. Something about the parking arrangements for tomorrow's market.'

'I'll find her in a minute,' Oliver replied, watching as Jett darted ahead, carefully balancing his precious basket of mangoes. When the boy was safely out of earshot, Oliver reached for Sarah's hand, gently tugging her closer. 'How's the soap tent coming along?'

'All set,' she confirmed. 'The holiday collection is ready to launch. Elaine's helping with the display tomorrow.'

'You've been busy.'

'Says the man who's been up since dawn tending to his precious mangoes,' she teased.

Oliver smiled, taking in the sight of her—the woman who

had transformed his life in ways he was still discovering. The past three months had unfolded with a natural rhythm that felt both surprising and inevitable. Sarah and Jett had become fixtures at the farm, first as weekend visitors, then staying for dinners, and gradually occupying more space in his heart than he'd known was available.

'Thank you,' he said suddenly, surprising himself with the intensity of feeling behind the simple words.

'For what?' Sarah asked, her expression softening.

'For showing me that love was worth the awkward journey,' Oliver replied, thinking of dating app disasters, misplaced phone numbers, and the winding path that had eventually led them back to each other. 'For taking a chance on a farmer who couldn't even handle a hot pepper without causing a scene.'

Sarah laughed, the sound still as captivating as the first time he'd heard it across a crowded market. 'That pepper story gets more dramatic with each telling.'

'It was traumatic,' Oliver insisted with mock seriousness. 'I nearly died of embarrassment.'

'Well, I'm glad you survived,' Sarah replied, standing on tiptoes to kiss him briefly. 'Jett and I have grown rather attached to you.'

The casual acknowledgment of their connection sent warmth spreading through Oliver's chest. He'd never been one for grand gestures or poetic declarations, preferring to let actions speak instead. But some moments, he was learning, called for a bit of both.

'Wait here,' he said, releasing her hand and moving toward a specific tree nearby. With practiced movements, he selected a perfect mango, its skin blushing golden-red in the afternoon sun.

In the distance, they could hear Jett chattering excitedly to

Amelia about his mango selections, the farm bustling with pre-market preparations. But for this moment, standing amidst the orchard rows where their story had begun, there was only the two of them—connected by that peculiar magic of finding your way back to where you were always meant to be.

'Mum! Uncle Oli!' Jett's voice broke the spell as he came running back. 'Grandmère says to come quick! She's making crepes with the mangoes!'

Oliver laughed, catching Sarah's eye with a shared look of affectionate resignation. 'We'd better not keep Grandmère waiting. She gets, shall we say, creative when she's impatient.'

As they walked hand in hand toward the farmhouse, following Jett's excited lead, contentment settled over Oliver. The journey had been unexpected, occasionally awkward, and entirely worth every step.

Later that evening, after Jett had devoured two of Grandmère's crepes and charmed the entire Johnson family with his enthusiastic questions about the farm, Sarah found him sitting alone on the porch steps, small hands wrapped around a mango, his expression unusually serious.

'Hey, sweetie,' Sarah said, settling beside him on the step. 'Everything okay?'

Jett nodded, but continued studying the mango with intense concentration.

'It's been quite a day,' Sarah offered, gently brushing his hair from his forehead. 'Lots of new people to meet.'

'Mm-hmm.' Jett rolled the mango between his palms, a habit he'd picked up from Oliver. 'Uncle Oli's family is big.'

Sarah's heart warmed at his casual use of 'Uncle Oli,' a name he'd adopted without prompting a few weeks ago. 'They are big. And a little loud sometimes. Does that bother you?'

Jett shook his head. 'I like them. Grandmère tells funny stories, and Amelia said I could help her collect the eggs tomorrow.' He paused, his small face scrunching in thought. 'Mom, does Uncle Oli live here all the time?'

'Yes, this is his home. He lives here with his family, just like we live in our house.'

Jett seemed to contemplate this information carefully. 'And we live in our house.'

'That's right.'

'But you like Uncle Oli a lot.' It wasn't a question, but a statement of fact, delivered with the directness only children can manage.

Sarah felt her cheeks warm. 'Yes, I do like him. Very much.'

Jett nodded solemnly, as if confirming a suspicion. 'I saw you kissing him by the mango trees. Like people do on TV.'

Sarah bit back a smile. 'You did, huh?'

'Uh-huh.' Jett looked up at her finally, his eyes serious. 'Does that mean he's gonna be your boyfriend now?'

Sarah weighed her words carefully. 'Would that be okay with you if he was?'

Jett returned his attention to the mango, turning it over in his hands. 'I guess. He knows a lot about mangoes and chickens and stuff.' He paused, his voice growing quieter. 'But what about our house? What about my room with the dinosaur wallpaper?'

The question revealed the real concern hiding beneath his casual inquiries, and Sarah wrapped an arm around his shoulders. 'Oh, sweetheart. Nothing's going to happen to our house or your dinosaur room. Uncle Oli and I are just getting to know each other better.'

'But Damon at daycare said when his mum got a boyfriend, they moved to a new house, and he had to share a room with a new brother he didn't even like.' Jett's voice wavered slightly. 'And he couldn't take his special bookshelf because it didn't fit.'

Sarah pulled him closer. 'Every family is different, Jett. Whatever happens between me and Oliver, I promise we won't make any big changes without talking to you first. Your happiness matters very much to me.'

From the doorway, Oliver watched the quiet exchange, careful to remain unnoticed. He'd come looking for them when Sarah had been gone longer than expected, only to halt at the sound of his name.

'But do you love him?' Jett was asking, his voice small but determined. 'Like in the stories?'

Sarah's reply was gentle. 'It's still early days, sweetie. Love takes time to grow, just like the mangoes on Uncle Oli's trees.'

Jett considered this, then offered his next question with disarming innocence. 'Does he make you happy? Your eyes get all crinkly when he's around. Like when you eat chocolate cake.'

Sarah laughed softly. 'Yes, he does make me happy.'

'That's good then,' Jett decided, apparently satisfied with her answer. 'Because you should be happy, Mum. But I still don't want a new brother.'

'Noted,' Sarah said solemnly, though her lips twitched with amusement. 'No new brothers on the horizon.'

Oliver stepped back silently, giving them a moment longer before he deliberately made his footsteps audible as he approached. 'There you two are. Grandmère's asking if Jett wants to help her make hot chocolate. Apparently, it's a 'secret French recipe.''

Jett perked up immediately. 'With marshmallows?'

'Knowing Grandmère, probably with some fancy French chocolate she smuggled in her suitcase.'

Jett looked to his mother for permission, suddenly vibrating with renewed energy.

'Go ahead,' Sarah smiled. 'Just don't drink too much or you'll be bouncing off the walls all night.'

As Jett raced inside, Oliver settled onto the step beside Sarah. 'Everything okay? You two looked deep in conversation.'

Sarah leaned against his shoulder with a sigh. 'Just navigating the complex emotional terrain of being a single parent who's dating.'

'Ah,' Oliver nodded. 'The boyfriend talk?'

'Complete with concerns about moving houses and acquiring unwanted siblings.' She glanced up at him. 'For the record, I assured him his dinosaur room was safe.'

Oliver chuckled, but there was a tenderness in his eyes as he looked at her. 'Kids notice everything, don't they?'

'Especially the things we think we're being subtle about.' She touched his hand lightly. 'He said I should be with you because you make my eyes crinkly like when I eat chocolate cake.'

'High praise indeed,' Oliver said, taking her hand in his. 'I'll do my best to keep those eyes crinkling.'

'He'll need time,' Sarah said quietly. 'To adjust to sharing me. To understand that this doesn't change how much I love him.'

'We have all the time in the world,' Oliver assured her. 'No rush, no pressure. We'll figure it out together, the three of us.'

Jett's excited voice drifted out to them as he recounted something to Grandmère, followed by her delightful laughter.

'You're good with him,' Sarah said softly. 'Most men I've dated couldn't see past the "single mother" label to the actual child behind it. He was just an obstacle, or worse, an afterthought.'

'Those men were idiots,' Oliver stated simply. 'Jett's not just part of the package, Sarah. He's amazing in his own right. Smart, curious, enthusiastic about mangoes—what's not to love?'

Sarah smiled, leaning into him as the evening air cooled around them. 'You Johnson men have a way with words when it counts.'

'Only when it matters,' Oliver replied, dropping a kiss on the top of her head. 'Only when it matters.'

THE END

Don't forget to look for Duckinwilla Days:4-6 available now in print and eBook

Annie Seaton

Also by Annie Seaton

Daughters of the Darling
From Across the Sea
Over the River
By the Billabong
Beneath Still Waters
Under Darling Skies

A Bec Whitfield Mystery
Bowen River
Shadows on the Shore
Storm Season

The Happy Outback Hotel (2026)
Outback Strangers
Outback Secrets
Outback Dreams
Outback Hearts
Outback Spirit
Outback Promise
Outback Horizon
Outback Silence
Outback Whispers
Outback Flame

Duckinwilla Days
Coming Home
Secrets and Surprises
Wishes and Whispers
Chasing Dreams
New Beginnings
All Together Now
Home to the Outback
Lucy
Angie
Jemima
Isabella

Duckinwilla Days 1-3

Porter Sisters Series
Kakadu Sunset
Daintree
Diamond Sky
Hidden Valley
Larapinta
Kakadu Dawn

Others
Whitsunday Dawn
Undara
Osprey Reef
East of Alice
One Summer in Tuscany
Four Seasons Short and Sweet
Follow the Sun
Ten Days in Paradise
Deadly Secrets
Adventures in Time
Silver Valley Witch
The Emerald Necklace
A Clever Christmas
Christmas with the Boss
Her Christmas Star
The Emerald Necklace

The Augathella Girls Series
Outback Roads
Outback Sky
Outback Escape
Outback Wind
Outback Dawn
Outback Moonlight
Outback Dust
Outback Hope
Boxed Sets
Augathella Girls 1-4
Augathella Girls 5-8

Augathella Short and Sweet Series
An Augathella Surprise
An Augathella Baby

Annie Seaton

An Augathella Spring
An Augathella Christmas
An Augathella Wedding
An Augathella Easter
An Augathella Masquerade Ball

Boxed Sets
Augathella Short and Sweet 1-3
Augathella Short and Sweet 1-4

Sunshine Coast Series
Waiting for Ana
The Trouble with Jack
Healing His Heart
Sunshine Coast Boxed Set

The Richards Brothers Series
The Trouble with Paradise
Marry in Haste
Outback Sunrise
Richards Brothers Boxed Set

Bondi Beach Love Series
Beach House
Beach Music
Beach Walk
Beach Dreams
The House on the Hill Boxed Set

Second Chance Bay Series
Her Outback Playboy
Her Outback Protector
Her Outback Haven
Her Outback Paradise
The McDougalls of Second Chance Bay Boxed Set

Love Across Time Series
Come Back to Me
Follow Me
Finding Home
The Threads that Bind

Duckinwilla Days 1-3

Love Across Time 1-4 Boxed Set

Bindarra Creek
Worth the Wait
Full Circle
Secrets of River Cottage
A Clever Christmas
A Place to Belong
Hearts in Harmony

Annie Seaton

Annie lives in Australia, on the beautiful north coast of New South Wales. She sits in her writing chair and looks out over the tranquil Pacific Ocean.

She writes contemporary romance and loves telling stories that always have a happily ever after. She lives with her very own hero of many years, and they share their home with Barney, the rag doll puss, who hides when the four grandchildren come to visit.

Stay up to date with her latest releases at her website: http://www.annieseaton.net

If you would like to stay up to date with Annie's releases, subscribe to her newsletter here: http://www.annieseaton.net

Duckinwilla Days 1-3